Run To Glory!

Run To Glory!

by

William Sears

Library of Congress Cataloging in Publication Data

Sears, William.
    Run to glory!

    I. Title.
PS3569.E195R86   1989   813'.54   89-3297
ISBN 0-87961-194-4 Cloth
ISBN 0-87961-195-2 Paper

Books for a better world

Naturegraph Publishers, Inc.
3543 Indian Creek Road
Happy Camp, California 96039
U.S.A.

For Ron and Lois

Illustrated by award-winning artist,
Shirley Gitchell Johnson.

"He's a wizard! Everybody knows that."

1.

"Don't let the baby horse die, Grandfather."

"No one can help the poor little devil now."

"You can, Grandfather. I know you can."

"Too late, Son."

"Please Grandfather. If anybody can save the little horse, you can. Everybody says you're a wizard with sick animals."

The old man didn't answer. He knelt beside the tiny wrinkled body. Gently he ran his fingers over the trembling foal.

"There's still a chance, isn't there, Grandfather?"

"Slim. Mighty slim."

"But a chance!"

I could tell by the way Grandfather shook his head that there was no chance at all.

Not any.

I wish you could have seen that pitiful baby horse the first time we laid eyes on it. It was too weak to lift its tiny head. A puny, shriveled-up little thing that didn't seem to have a friend in the whole world. It had a woebegone lost expression on its sad face. When those big eyes looked up at you, you wanted to cry just watching it.

I've been around horses long enough to know that all new baby horses are skimpy looking things, but this one was the limit. You could have put a Shetland pony inside all that extra loose skin. The little horse was all knee bones, ribs, and eyes. Baleful looking eyes. Saucer-big and lonesome as the end of summer.

I wanted to scoop the little horse up in my arms, but I was afraid I'd break it. The foal must have known how I felt because it opened its big eyes again and looked at me, imploring.

It had coal black lashes longer than a girl's. It stared with eyes as dark and glistening as two huge ripe olives. It seemed to be saying: "Please help me! I don't feel good!"

I stroked the soft velvet nose and said, "Don't you worry. Everything's going to be all right now that my grandfather's here. He's a real miracle-worker with horses. Everybody in the whole county knows that."

I must have spoken the words out loud because Grandfather grunted and said, "None of that. I can't help the little fellow now. Too late."

"You have to, Grandfather. Somebody's *got* to help him." I patted the foal's head comfortingly, hugged him, and whispered in his ear, "Everything will be all right. You just don't know my grandfather. He's a real wizard of a horse doctor. You'll see."

"This is real life, son, not the movies."

2.

Even I knew that everything wasn't going to be all right. Ever again. Not for that sick little horse. Just born and already dying. It wasn't fair.

If you want to know the truth, deep down inside, I didn't want to get involved with this small horse at all. Sure, I felt sorry for him. I wished I could help him. I cried because I couldn't. But I'd already had more than my share of suffering and sorrow with pets.

They worm their way into your heart until they're like a member of your own family, but no matter how much fun and happiness they bring you at first, the day is certain to come when something terrible will happen to them, and you'll wish you were dead.

Grandfather says I'm pet-prone and will always be having heartaches over some lame duck. Well, maybe I am and maybe I will. I don't care. It's not my fault. I love animals. When they get in trouble, it makes me feel funny in the pit of my stomach, and I have to try to help them. Wouldn't you?

I hadn't known this little chestnut foal more than ten minutes and already I felt like I was losing a close friend. I took it out on Grandfather.

"You promised me this horse was going to win the County Fair Stakes someday."

"That was before we knew he had an incurable blood disease."

"That only makes it more of a challenge, Grandfather. That's what you always tell me. Anybody can do the impossible, you said, but it takes real star-stuff to pull off a miracle. Now is the time for you to do that, Grandfather. A miracle, just like in the movies."

"This is real life, son, not the movies. This little foal is finished."

"Then why did you buy him?"

"Greed," Grandfather said. "I'm sorry, lad, but we're far too late to help this sick little beggar."

I was sorry, too.

Sorry we'd ever heard about the little horse. Grandfather had bought it sight unseen because its mother, Mignonette, was a world-famous trotting mare from a long line of champions. And the lines of its sire went all the way back to Greyhound II, who held several world speed records. Grandfather explained it all to me, but what good is a potential champion trotter if it can't even live long enough to get up on its feet?

Maybe I *was* pet-prone, but Grandfather was race horse prone. It was one of his biggest weaknesses. After all, my grandfather was supposed to be the slickest horse trader in our whole state. Everybody said that. He was a horse trader's horse trader. Nobody ever got the best of Grandfather.

Until now.

For the first time in his entire horse trading life, my grandfather had been outsmarted. And by his bitterest enemy, Mayor Sam Raffodil. And it was all his own fault.

Grandfather had swallowed the hook like an immature child on the clumsiest bait in the world. It was a dumb, blind and reckless thing to do. Grandfather said all these things about himself, *I* didn't.

Grandfather was so eager to own just one first-class champion trotting horse before he died, that he'd allowed himself to be hoodwinked like a country bumpkin. "I deserve everything that's coming to me," he admitted.

Mr. Raffodil relished his triumph with glee. At long last, after many futile and unsuccessful attempts to outwit my grandfather in a horse trade, Mayor Sam Raffodil had finally accomplished exactly what he had publicly announced unto the whole town from the courthouse steps that he would do to Grandfather. Sooner or later.

Mr. Raffodil had finally done it. "I've hung your hide out on the fence to dry, old man," Mayor Raffodil gloated, "and I'm loving every minute of it!"

Every word was true. Mr. Raffodil had finally shot my grandfather down in flames. He had humiliated him publicly, exactly as he had promised, and it was a bitter pill for Grandfather to swallow.*

---

* I know that's a trite old expression, but what Grandfather himself said that Mr. Raffodil had really done to him, is too vulgar to use here.

The First Furlong!

"The unvarnished and unshellacked truth."

3.

I don't want you to think my grandfather was anybody's fool, so I'd better fill you in on how this seemingly impossible tragedy happened. After all, grandfather was the most famous horse trader in all of Green Valley. In fact, he was the scourge of the entire county. Maybe even the state.

Grandfather could out-trade, out-trot, out-pace, and out-fox anybody in our part of the county when it had anything to do with horses. He could out-think them, too. If David Harum had ever tangled with my grandfather, he'd have had to send for the calvary.

Most surprising of all, Grandfather's horse trading never actually involved anything dishonest. During his deals, he was always straight as a string. Except maybe for being just a little bit "slippery" on non-essentials, to which horse traders are entitled. Grandfather said that, I didn't.

"Doesn't slippery mean lying a little?" I questioned him suspiciously.

"Never!"

"What does it mean then?"

"Just what it says: Slippery."

"But not crooked?"

"Never!"

"Cross your heart and hope to die from a sudden bolt of lightning right here by the barn where you're standing with that metal shovel on that manure pile, that you've never once been dishonest in horse trading?"

"All that," he said confidently, crossing his heart.

Grandfather went on to educate me in his philosophy of proper horse trading fundamentals. "Truth," he said, "is the foundation of all good horse trading. If somebody happens to think you mean something entirely different than what you actually *do* mean when you explain it to them so carefully, and in plain simple King's English, that's not your fault. I mean, if you tell the plain unvarnished truth about a stallion, colt, mare or filly, that," he said, "is horse trading."

"Don't you ever varnish the truth a bit, Grandfather?"

He was shocked. At least his eyes looked shocked.

"Never! I might shellac it a trifle here and there, as a necessary undercoat. But with integrity. And no varnish!"

I shook my head. "I can't seem to get hold of what you're saying."

"That," he said, "is what is meant by *slippery.*"

4.

"He's a sweet-talking, silver-haired snake," is the way the mayor of our town, Mr. Sam Raffodil Senior, described my grandfather.

Of course, everybody in Green Valley knew that Mr. Raffodil hated my grandfather. They were worse enemies than the Hatfields and the McCoys. Much worse.

For years, Mr. Raffodil had been threatening to skin my grandfather alive, and hang his hide out to dry on the fence by the finish line of the County Fair Stakes. But up until this tragic episode of the little sick horse, the "skinning" had all been on Grandfather's side.

Actually, a deadly feud sprang up between Mr. Raffodil and my grandfather on the very day Mr. Raffodil stepped off the Northern Pacific Express train from Duluth.

Mr. Raffodil walked down Main Street with the leading local real estate agent of our town, Mr. August Clevenger.

The truth is, Mr. Raffodil *strutted* down the Main Street of our town on that first day. He was showing off in front of everybody. I'm not saying this because I'm on Grandfather's side. Mr. Raffodil strutted, pompously. I mean it.

Mr. Raffodil kept pointing to the various buildings and businesses he intended to buy whether the people wanted to sell them or not. Sort of a "she loves me, she loves me not" in real estate.

"I'll take that one," he instructed Mr. Clevenger. "Also those two. Skip that one. I want the livery stable immediately. Money is no object. See to it, Clevenger!"*

Mr. Raffodil was tired of being a small frog in a big pond like Duluth. That's what he told Mr. Clevenger. The time had come, Mr. Raffodil said, to be a big frog in a small pond.

Unhappily, Mr. Raffodil had chosen our town, Green Valley.

"A really *big* frog, I mean," Mr. Raffodil insisted. "Make your deals big and fast. Overpay. Talk loud. Pound on the table with your fist. It puts the fear of God into them."

Mr. Raffodil was talking too loud right now. Too loud and far too boisterously. Mr. Raffodil wanted people to overhear him. Everybody in our small town square was listening. No one was too pleased.

The more they learned about Mr. Raffodil from his own words, the less pleased they were.

---

* In a short time, whenever anybody in our town wanted somebody else to do something for them; children, grownups and old-timers, they would snap their fingers and say: "See to it, Clevenger!"

"Tiny bubbles in the water."

5.

Mr. Raffodil spotted my grandfather's team of matched dapple greys standing by the city watering trough. Grandfather was sitting in the buggy chatting with his good Sioux Indian friend, Mr. I.J. Little Fork.

Raffodil walked over to Grandfather's horses, lifted the soft skin of their noses, looked at their teeth, then turned to his agent.

"I want this team of matched greys, too, Clevenger," he said. "I'll need something smart to get around in. Offer the cripple any reasonable amount if he throws in the buggy. See to it, Clevenger."

Grandfather was still walking with two crutches at the time. He'd been kicked by a stallion who didn't care to be castrated. Even by a veterinarian physician as renowned and skilled as my grandfather. Mr. Raffodil could see the two crutches leaning against the buggy seat. Unfortunately, he couldn't see my grandfather's eyes.

"See to it, Clevenger," Mr. Raffodil repeated. "Immediately."

Mr. Raffodil walked away.

Grandfather was only temporarily crippled, and it was his legs, not his head that was injured. So when Mr. Raffodil started to walk away after his insult, Grandfather tickled the greys, Shadrach and Meshach, under the tail with the buggy whip.

Shadrach accidentally caught Mr. Raffodil in the small of the back with his nose and pushed hard. He deposited Mr. Raffodil, head first, into the watering trough.

"I say," Grandfather called out apologetically, "I *am* sorry about that, stranger." Grandfather climbed down from the buggy and hobbled over to the watering trough on his crutches.

Mr. Raffodil rose up in the water. He was soaking wet. Saturated. Dripping a deluge from the brim of his hat, Mr. Raffodil flushed red with a cascade of inner rage that nearly turned the water into steam. No one was *ever* permitted to treat Mr. Samuel Raffodil Senior in such a highhanded and cavalier fashion.

"You did that deliberately, old man," Mr. Raffodil fumed. "If you weren't on those crutches, I'd throw you into the watering trough myself."

Grandfather whipped his crutches out from underneath his arm. "Don't let that stop you," Grandfather said, smiling frostily.

Grandfather handed his crutches to Mr. Little Fork, but unfortunately, in swinging them around, he accidentally whacked Mr. Raffodil on the shoulder with the heavy end of the crutches, and toppled him backwards into the water a second time.

All you could see was Mr. Raffodil's hat floating on top of the water. Mr. Raffodil was totally submerged. You could tell where he was by the tiny bubbles floating to the surface.

Grandfather turned to the real estate agent.

"He may drown in there if he insists on going under that way. Better pull him out quick."

Grandfather pointed his crutch at Mr. Raffodil who had popped up suddenly, slipped, and sunk out of sight once again.

"See to it, Clevenger," Grandfather barked. "Immediately!"

"I'll make that cripple pay."

6.

Quite a large crowd had gathered around the watering trough by this time. The laughter had a very unsettling effect on Mr. Raffodil when he surfaced. This was not the sort of introduction to the town of Green Valley which he had planned for himself.

Grandfather took his time climbing back up into the buggy. Chief Little Fork handed him his crutches. Mr. Raffodil was standing up in the center of the circular watering trough still shedding a Niagara. He was in such a rage that his face looked like a dripping blue gargoyle.*

Mr. Raffodil scooped up his hat and clamped it back on his head. Unfortunately, it was full of water and came down on all sides like a shower. Mr. Raffodil shook his fist angrily at Grandfather as he crawled out of the circular pool. He sat on the stone edge and began squeezing the water out of his clothes.

"I want that cripple's name, Clevenger!" Mr. Raffodil shouted, angrily. "I'll make him pay for this. This town isn't big enough for the two of us!"

It sounded exactly like an old Western movie showdown on Main Street. Grandfather called out cheerfully to Mr. Raffodil as he turned the team of matched greys around. "You keep the watering trough, and I'll keep the town."

---

* An exaggeration, but very close to the truth, the inward truth.

Grandfather clucked his teeth. "Giddap Shadrack, Meshach!"

Everybody agreed that Grandfather shouldn't have poked Mr. Raffodil in the chest with the rubber end of his crutch as he drove by. It knocked Mr. Raffodil off the stone edge. He waved his hands wildly before toppling over backwards into the watering trough, sinking out of sight a third time.

"He's beginning to look like part of the fountain," Grandfather observed, snapping the reins across Shadrack's rump and hurrying the team and the Abednego buggy toward home.

Grandfather was too far away to hear Mr. Raffodil swear eternal vengeance as he spit out a mouthful of water containing a small fish.

He shouted at the crippled old gentleman that he would pay him back in full for the indignity and humiliation he, Samuel Raffodil Senior, had been forced to suffer. In public yet!

"If it takes me the rest of my life!"

Actually, the watering trough encounter was one of the better things that happened between Mr. Raffodil and my grandfather during the next few years.

The worse things were yet to come.

"Watch my smoke."

7.

I realize that all of this makes Mr. Sam Raffodil Senior sound like a very mean, prejudiced and unkind man. But what's the use of lying? If you had lived in our town of Green Valley as long as I had, sooner or later you'd find out the truth for yourself.

To be honest, when you first met Mr. Raffodil you didn't like him at all. But if you were patient and took the time to really get to know him, you *hated* him.

If you were fool enough to go into the Raffodil's yard on "trick or treat" night, you'd most likely get a blast of rock salt in the seat of your britches from Mr. Raffodil's scatter gun. Accompanied by his delighted laughter. As far as I know, Mr. Raffodil was the first person to put soap and chili peppers in the children's Halloween chocolates.

And I'm only telling you about the good side of Mr. Raffodil.

We could never prove that Mr. Raffodil set out the poison that killed our puppy, Patches, but Mr. Raffodil was always chasing him out of their backyard with stones, and threatening to do him bodily damage if the dog didn't stay home.

He didn't stay home, of course. Puppies often don't. Sure it was Patches fault, too, I admit. He liked eating the dog biscuits the Raffodil's left out for their own dog Wolf. Patches liked Wolf, too.

But when Mr. Raffodil asked me, the morning after Patches

died, "How's your darling little dog today, William?", I said, "He's dead. And you know it."

"What a shame!"

"It will be a shame, when I tell the town marshall about it!"

"You do that," he said laughing. But Grandfather warned me, "No use, the whole city hall's in his pocket."

A few months later, when I was still quite young, my mother and I were shopping in Raffodil's Dry Goods Store. Mr. Raffodil caught me peeking inside his outside jacket pocket. He grabbed my hand roughly.

"What are you doing in there you little sneak thief?!"

"I wasn't stealing. I was just investigating."

"A likely story!"

"My grandfather said you have the city hall in your pocket, and I was trying to see what it looked like." If everybody in the store hadn't laughed, I think Mr. Raffodil would have had me arrested. That's how much he hated my grandfather and anybody associated with him. Even small relatives.

I know this is supposed to be a love story about a boy, his grandfather, and a horse, but unless you have this important background, you won't be able to appreciate the full tragedy of what happened in our town about the sick little horse.

Grandfather had it all his way for such a long time with Mr. Raffodil. He out-foxed the Raffodils time after time. That's what fooled everybody. People just couldn't understand why Mr. Raffodil, knowing that Grandfather was trying to get the best of him, would keep on buying horses from Grandfather. But he did.

The reason was simple. Each time Mr. Raffodil was more convinced than ever that this particular time he, Sam Raffodil Senior, was at last out-smarting the Old Master.

Only "old master" is *not* what Mr. Raffodil called Grandfather. Although it nearly rhymed with what he really called him.

Grandfather said that, I didn't.

Every time Mr. Raffodil was taken in by one of Grandfather's special deals and got the worst of it, the townspeople loved it. Mr. Raffodil, of course, hated it. He swore eternal vengeance each time that Grandfather out-witted him. He vowed each time that never again would Grandfather hoodwink him on a piece of horseflesh. He just wouldn't bite.

But everytime Mr. Raffodil said that, Grandfather rose to new heights to meet the challenge. Somehow, he found a new way to sell Mr. Raffodil another horse. Not crooked, just "slippery."

"The Raffodil-Grandfather contest is the longest running show in our part of the country," Grandfather's friends boasted. "We can't wait for the next dramatic episode." The loud and raucous laughter of the townspeople never failed to reach the ears of an enraged and humiliated Samuel Raffodil Senior.

"It's all Sam's fault," Grandfather declared. "He shouldn't announce publicly to the whole town that I'll never be able to sell him another horse. It arouses my ingenuity. I just can't refuse that kind of a challenge."

"How long can you keep on doing this Grandfather?" I asked.

"That," he said with a cackle, "is what I'm trying to find out. I've hooked a live one." Grandfather was so pleased with himself that he gave me a grizzly bear hug which was all right, but also a whisker rub on my cheek.

"I *hate* that!" I told him.

Grandfather scooped me up at the knees with one arm, held me aloft, and danced me around the barn, whirling like a ballet dancer until his crutch fell out from under his other arm. Gracefully he set me down on the oats box and joined me there. "That," he told me, "was a little barnyard ballet. A dance of victory. Because I have already found a wonderful new horse to sell to Sam Raffodil."

"He'll never buy it. He said so."

"There's always more than one way to skin a possum."

"You usually say to skin a skunk, Grandfather."

"I know," Grandfather grinned wickedly. "But as long as I'm having such a marvelous winning streak with Sam Raffodil, I'm very humble and generous."

"In a pig's eye!" I replied. "It won't work this time. You've sold Mr. Raffodil your last horse."

Grandfather gave me ball for ball.

"In a pig's eye," he said.

"*Really!*"

"Just watch my smoke."

"Another horse?"

"A pipperoo!"

"You're going to sell it to Mr. Raffodil?"

I couldn't believe it.

"This, I'll have to see."

"This horse will bring you nothing but grief, Sam."

8.

A beautiful black stallion named Ebony started Mr. Raffodil on his final downward skid. According to our post mistress, Gladys Tidings, it was one of the few unfortunate mistakes which Grandfather made. It led Mr. Raffodil white-faced with fury, to seek undying revenge both in this world and in the next. And it didn't matter whether his vengeance was fair or not. Even if it took all of his money in every bank he owned throughout the entire state. He detested the very ground on which my grandfather limped. And planned to crush him like a cockroach on the sidewalk. Naturally, he announced it publicly.

When Grandfather, for the second time, offered to call off the feud and become friends again, Mr. Raffodil went into one of his worst spasms.

"Again?" he shouted, *"Again!* We never *were* friends. We never shall be! I detested you from the first moment I laid eyes on you."

"I remember," Grandfather nodded. "Through the water."

That was the spark that ignited the flame which burst into fire. The town marshall, Carl Anderson, had to pry them apart again, even while the spectators were shouting and taking sides.

Right in front of the post office.

Our post mistress, Gladys Tidings, held a lot of power in our town. She worked the night shift at the telephone company as well as the day shift at the post office, so there was hardly anything she didn't know about everybody in Green Valley. Between the mail—especially the post cards—and the phone company listening-post, all vital information passed through her hands.

Everybody called her "Glad" Tidings although most of the stuff she peddled was punk. Still, when Gladys Tidings announced that Mr. Raffodil had sworn to avenge himself on Grandfather, or die trying, people accepted it as gospel truth. Usually Glad Tidings was right, unless the mail was too hard to steam open.

Her pronouncement was made even before Grandfather sold the big black stallion Ebony to Mr. Raffodil.

He didn't *sell* it exactly. Mr. Raffodil practically took it away from Grandfather by force. At least that's what it seemed like to an innocent bystander. But that was what Grandfather called using "the old shellac."

Ebony was the most beautiful horse my grandfather had ever owned. The most beautiful that any of us had ever seen. Grandfather bought Ebony the day he went to Hill City to take care of some sick cows.

When Grandfather was told about some of Ebony's grave shortcomings and special trouble-talents, he knew it was destiny. Grandfather took one more look at the big black and said, "That is Sam Raffodil's new horse."

The afternoon Grandfather led Ebony into our barn, I took my first look, and said:

"Wow!"

Grandfather grinned.

"You're absolutely right," he said.

"Is this the horse that you plan to—"

"He is."

"I want him myself," I shouted. "I'll pay it off out of my

allowance for the next one hundred years!"

"I figure that's how Sam Raffodil will feel."

Ebony was satin black. Sunlight shimmered off his rippling muscles. Ladies "oohed" and "aahed!" at Ebony whenever he did his high-stepping, high-school horse prance up Main Street.

Grandfather, of course, insisted that the ladies were "oohing!" and "aahing!" at him, not the horse, but we both knew better. Grandfather wasn't even in the ball game with that black horse, Ebony.

Mr. Raffodil couldn't help himself any more than I could, from the first moment he set eyes on Ebony from his second floor bank window, he was a goner. Mr. Raffodil had to buy that magnificent black horse.

Mr. Raffodil went right out of his mind the morning Grandfather drove Ebony past the Raffodil Bank. Actually, Grandfather had to go around the block several times before Mr. Raffodil happened accidentally to be at his window looking out.

"We've made contact with our victim," Grandfather chuckled.

Mr. Raffodil, peeking out of the side of a windowshade, knew he was looking at the perfect animal to match his newly-elected lofty station as mayor of Green Valley. He would never tell Grandfather that. He hated that old man, and was green with envy about Ebony belonging to my grandfather.

"Mr. Raffodil," my grandfather told me, "is caught on the horns of a horrible dilemma. He wants this black horse so desperately, he can taste it. On the other hand, he has vowed publicly never to buy another horse from your innocent, harmless old grandfather."

"You're not all that innocent or harmless, Grandfather." We both knew it, but Grandfather told me not to worry, we'd sell the horse anyway.

"To Mr. Raffodil?"

"Bingo!"

"Never!"

"His Honor, the mayor, is already in the bag."

"How come?"

"Sam Raffodil Senior is infected with a bad case of the 'gotta-haves'! We shall play upon his weaknesses and short-comings like Johann Sebastian Bach seated at the keyboard of the Weimar Chapel organ."

"What does all that mean?" I asked.

Grandfather was unable to restrain his laughter. He punched me in the ribs and said, "It means that Sam Raffodil is going into the watering trough again."

"I like it," I told Grandfather, "and hope it's true, but I don't think you can fool Mr. Raffodil this time."

"Trust your sly old grandfather," my sly old grandfather said.

"I was provocated."

9.

Grandfather explained, "I will tell Mr. Raffodil that the horse is not mine. That I am merely taking care of it for a friend in Fergus Falls."

"But that's lying!" I said. "I thought you told me..."

"Not lying," he explained. *"That* is the old shellac. I've actually given this horse to a friend of mine in Fergus Falls. I am telling the absolute horse trading truth."

"Really?"

"Really."

"What friend?"

Grandfather began to chuckle. "I've only given the horse to him temporarily, of course."

I looked at him suspiciously. "That old shellac is awfully close to lying though, isn't it?"

Grandfather waved the palm of his hand from side to side at the wrist to show me that it *was* close, but still legitimate.

"Slippery," he said, "not crooked."

"To *me* that sounds crooked. And it won't work."

It worked. Mr. Sam Raffodil Senior, mayor of Green Valley, always insisted on owning the very best of everything there was to be owned, even if he had to take it away from somebody else by foreclosing on a mortage or calling in a loan.

Grandfather leaked the news to Mr. Raffodil that Ebony wasn't really his horse. When Mr. Raffodil heard that, he insisted on buying Ebony at once. He telephoned Fergus Falls trying to locate the real owner. Unsuccessfully.

Mr. Raffodil finally had to come to Grandfather.

Grandfather did his best to sweet-talk Mr. Raffodil out of the deal. At least anyone who overheard their conversation would have thought so, and testified to it.

"The horse is not for sale, Sam," Grandfather said. "My friend in Fergus Falls wants to hang onto him. You can see why. He's such a beautiful animal. He's a personal pet, Sam. My friend just wants me to break Ebony of some very bad habits."

"*Everything* is for sale."

"Everything except this horse, Sam."

"Let's telephone your friend in Fergus Falls."

Grandfather shook his head and started to drive off, but Mr. Raffodil caught Ebony by the bridle and hung on.

"Not so fast."

"Besides," Grandfather explained, "this horse is very treacherous. His looks are deceiving, Sam. He's like a sleeping volcano. All green and lovely on the slopes, but molten lava boiling up inside."

"Hogwash!"

"That's why my friend sent the horse to me, Sam. To try and cure him of these evil habits."

"Baloney!"

"Trust me on this one, Sam."

"I wouldn't trust you if you brought the Angel Gabriel as a witness."

"You forget all about this horse, Sam. He'll bring you nothing but grief."

But Mr. Raffodil had heard that the mayor of Hill City wanted to buy Ebony (a story a slippery fellow had leaked), and he couldn't bear the thought of a rival owning Ebony and outdoing him.

Besides, Mr. Raffodil was convinced that Grandfather was only making up excuses so he could jack up the price. Mr. Raffodil was determined—no other mayor was going to outbid him for this beautiful black horse.

"Money is no object," he said.

"You haven't heard the price yet, Sam."

"I don't care *what* he costs. I'll double the price if necessary."

Grandfather objected. "You don't want this horse, Sam. He'll bring you nothing but grief. I'm telling you for your own good."

"That," I whispered to myself in the buggy, "is the old shellac."

I must have said it out loud because Grandfather dug a sharp elbow into my ribs to quiet me down.

10.

"I want him!" Mr. Raffodil insisted.

Grandfather turned to Mrs. Raffodil who had come out of the bank to see what was happening.

Immediately, she only had eyes for Ebony.

Grandfather appealed to her, "Can't you talk some sense into your husband Minnie?"

But Mrs. Raffodil always backed her husband, especially against my grandfather. Sam Raffodil only loathed my grandfather, Minnie Raffodil abominated him.

"Why should she abominate me?" Grandfather often asked me. "Me, a sweet, innocent old man."

"You're not all that sweet and innocent Grandfather," I repeated. "Like Mr. Raffodil says, sometimes you're a sly, cunning, silver-haired snake."

"Isn't *snake* a little strong?"

"Okey. An eel, then. A slippery eel."

"That," Grandfather said, "I can live with."

"Buy the horse, Sam," Minnie Raffodil said abruptly, and walked back into the bank.

Grandfather sighed.

"It's on your own head, Sam. I tried my best to warn you about this horse. All these people are eyewitnesses. Better let the mayor of Hill City..."

"He's mine!"

"So be it," Grandfather said, bowing his head in sorrow, and taking the money.

Grandfather parted with Ebony much against his will. Or so it appeared to an innocent bystander who was not versed in the deceitful ways of shellac and varnish which horse traders in general use.

It was a cash money transaction right on the spot. Grandfather calculated what the mayor of Hill City ought to pay for Ebony if he had the chance and doubled it. Since the deal was transacted right in front of Mr. Raffodil's bank, money was no problem. Mr. Raffodil went in and returned with the cash. Grandfather was so delighted with the disaster he knew was coming, that he threw in the buggy to boot.

"I've outfoxed you this time, old man," Mr. Raffodil leered. Sam Raffodil proudly led Ebony and the buggy across the street into his livery stable.

Suddenly Grandfather turned a bright, happy, pixie face to the crowd which had gathered. He waved to them:

"You're all eyewitnesses!"

"How big is this victory over the Raffodils going to be, Grandfather?" I asked him as we walked home.

"We won't know for sure," he said, "until tomorrow night at the band concert."

"What terrible thing is going to happen at the band concert tomorrow night, Grandfather?"

But Grandfather wouldn't tell me, and went off into gales of laughter, and wound up singing "Wait 'till the sun shines, Nellie."

That was always an ominous sign of something big afoot for Grandfather. I knew I wasn't going to miss the band concert tomorrow night.

No, not for a million dollars!

Ebony bowls over the mayor, the crowd—and especially Her Honoress, Minnie Raffodil.

11.

The mayor always officially opened the new summer session of band concerts. This summer, the mayor was Sam Raffodil Senior who with his wife Minnie drove proudly down the middle of Main Street seated in their shiny newly-painted buggy, as black and shiny as their marvelous horse, Ebony. The buggy was trimmed with bright gold wheels.

Sam and Minnie Raffodil were sitting like royalty in the golden leather seats, bowing to friends, as they made their way through town behind the high-stepping gait of that wonderful black stallion.

It was indeed a handsome sight to behold!

Everyone bowed back, nodded to His Honor and Mrs. Honor, and called out their approval. Some even applauded the lovely sight which the four of them made: Sam, Minnie, Ebony and the buggy.

Mr. Raffodil ate it up.

He kept tipping his hat to those who didn't owe him any money.

Grandfather had neglected to tell Mr. Raffodil (or me) that Ebony, among his many good points, did have one very grave weakness. A deathly fear of loud noises and automobile horns.

Whenever a car honked or a band played their trombones and trumpets extra loud, and especially when the people cheered, Ebony would sit right down on his hindquarters, wherever he was, harness and all. Especially when the automobile horns bellowed. Nothing could make Ebony budge. Except my grandfather who was very clever and had learned to put in earplugs so Ebony couldn't hear the loud crowd noises and car horns.

Not tonight, however.

Naturally this could lead to trouble at a band concert where the people sitting in their cars always became impatient for the concert to begin, and started tooting and hooting and honking their horns and shouting for action.

Since Mr. Raffodil was a very prominent and important town official, he didn't appreciate being embarrassed, or humiliated, anywhere. Particularly not in the middle of Main Street in front of the bandstand surrounded by a large crowd of his fellow citizens, during the first chorus of "She's Only a Bird in a Gilded Cage."

It really upset him.

Upset is exactly the right word for it.

Rudely. And literally.

When the horns started bleating, and honking for the concert to begin, and it did, with loud cymbals, trombones, trumpets and French horns, Ebony promptly sat down.

The first "sit-down" strike ever seen in our town.

The buggy tipped forward at a dangerous angle, and Mrs. Minnie Raffodil flew forward and bounced off Ebony's rump, toppling into the arms of District Attorney Haskell Jorgenson.

It was quite a sight. Mrs. Raffodil's head was down and her feet were up. She looked like a teapot under a tea-cozy made of ruffled petticoats, with two purple-covered legs for handles.

The laughter was very rewarding. There wasn't anyone in the entire brass section who blew the right notes on the final chorus of "She's Only a Bird...." Mr. Emmett Mulberry missed his kettledrum entirely and his mallet hit the glockenspiel player on the thumb. That started a small fight within the band, adding to the excitement.

Mr. Raffodil didn't find any of this amusing. He had been

thrown clear himself, and was trying to find his wife underneath all those petticoats. He was quite put out with Minnie when she wouldn't surface. He fumbled around clumsily trying to find her hand or her head.

"For God's sake, Minnie, I know you're in there! So come on up!"

No one could budge Ebony no matter how hard they heaved and pulled. They finally had to send for Grandfather who by a piece of good luck, happened to be close by in the front row sitting beside me with Ebony's ear plugs in his pocket. Grandfather tried his best to get Ebony up on his feet, but he certainly took his good-natured time.

While all this was going on, Grandfather kept reminding Mr. Raffodil that he had warned him about this treacherous black horse.

"Sitting down when he hears loud noises and automobile horns is one of the bad habits I was supposed to break him of, Sam. I warned you about that."

Out of the goodness of his heart, Grandfather was willing to buy the troublemaker back on the spot at a reduction of fifty percent. If Mr. Raffodil threw in the buggy. I thought Mr. Raffodil was going to throw the buggy at Grandfather. But, he finally did agree, if only someone would help him rescue Minnie.

"I warned you that this horse would cause you grief, Sam," Grandfather kept repeating, loud enough for everyone to hear. "But you insisted on buying him. So did Minnie. In front of eye-witnesses, on Main Street. You can't blame me, Sam."

"Get that horse out of my sight!" Raffodil shouted. "Out! Out! Both of you! Out!" He included me. "All of you. Out!"

"Lovely petticoats, Minnie," Grandfather said, complimenting Mrs. Raffodil on her colorful underskirts when she finally did surface. "Especially with the purple stockings; even with the runs."

Mrs. Raffodil drew back her parasol and tried to lambaste my grandfather over the head with it, but it opened up suddenly and pulled Mrs. Raffodil over backwards into District Attorney Jorgenson's lap once again. This left her speechless except for a few dirty words.

Grandfather got Ebony to his feet twice, but the automobiles honked him back down into a sitting position. No matter how often Grandfather told the Raffodils that he wasn't to blame, and that he had repeatedly urged them not to buy this treacherous beast, Minnie Raffodil knew instinctively that Grandfather was entirely to blame for all her troubles and humiliation. She didn't know exactly how Grandfather had managed it, but she just knew in her heart that he was guilty. Absolutely.

Minnie tried to jerk her parasol free from District Attorney Jorgenson's jacket, taking a sleeve with it. She kept screaming at her husband:

"Kill him! Kill him!"

Meaning Grandfather of course.

12.

I helped Grandfather drive Ebony all the way back to the barn. The auto horns started honking again, louder than ever. Now that the crowd knew why Ebony sat down, they were trying to incite a repeat performance. The band joined in with a loud rendition of "The Wabash Blues" with lots of brass, trumpets and trombones. The crowd was hoping that Ebony would do his famous sit-down trick again, and dump Grandfather and me out onto the street as well.

Grandfather, however, had been too smart for them. He had already put the soft rubber plugs in both of Ebony's ears.

Nothing could have been more beautiful than the sight of Ebony's high-stepping prance as he drew the beautiful painted buggy behind him like it weighed nothing, downfeathers from a duck's neck. Ebony paid no attention to the violent horn-tooting that was trying to make him "sit down" again. He continued his glorious "high school horse" prancing and dancing until all their trouble-making turned into thundering applause.

"Honk! Toot! Blah! Ahoooaah! Beep!" the horns hollered. "Over there! Over there! The Yanks are Coming!" blared the band. The crowd yelled and shouted. Grandfather kept doffing his cap in time to the tooting of the auto horns and the rhythm of the music. He touched Ebony on the tail with his whip, and the big black beauty went high-stepping twice around the bandstand, and then was off down Main Street in a cloud of smoke.

"What a marvelous old man!" someone cried.

Mrs. Minnie Raffodil swung at them angrily with her parasol, but only the thin struts were left. Besides, she missed by a mile.

It was great fun!

Everyday was an exciting day when you spent time with Grandfather. You never knew from one moment to the next what was going to happen, or which way the ball would bounce. You could walk into his barn perfectly innocent and say, "What's up for today, Grandfather?" and he would tell you, "Today we are going to make local history."

You usually did.

As soon as we left the crowd behind at the band concert, Grandfather gave Ebony his head. The big black raced for home, with me hanging on for dear life, and Grandfather egging Ebony on with a touch of the whip.

I knew Grandfather was making believe that he was in the homestretch at the fairgrounds as he kept yelling at Ebony: "Go! Go! Go!"

I was glad to get into the barnyard alive. But as soon as we were inside the barn, violence broke loose on all sides.

Grandfather began to yell and shout and laugh himself sick. He threw his crutches through the only good, unbroken window. He embraced me, and gave me a fierce grizzly bear hug. He scooped me up, whirled me around, and threw me into the piled up hay in the corner of Beauty's stall. Grandfather doubled up his fists and pounded them against the wooden walls of Prince's stall who tried to stomp on him as Grandfather kept yelling.

"Beautiful! Beautiful!"

"Ebony?"

"No!" he gasped. "Sam and Minnie Raffodil!"

That's when I knew that Grandfather had done it all on purpose. He didn't stop pounding on the wooden walls until he had slivers in both hands. Grandfather laughed until he had tears in his eyes. He poked me in the ribs quite joyfully.

"Cut that out!" I yelled. "That hurt!"

When I crawled up out of the oats bin, Grandfather admitted that he did have some personal shortcomings.

"You could have fooled me!" I yelled.

"Perhaps," Grandfather said, "this time, *snake-in-the-grass* is not too strong."

Then he went off into another outburst of self-appreciation.

"I'll tell you one thing," I warned him, "You'll never sell Mr. Raffodil another horse."

"Don't say that."

"I mean it. You're through."

"Want to bet?"

I hesitated. "Not against you, Grandfather."

He was still chuckling, laughing, and enjoying himself thoroughly. I limped out the barn door and went home to bed with my bruises.

"Peterson's! Anderson's! Gunderson's! Ours!"

13.

Grandfather and I found out the next day that he would not have to worry about selling another horse to Mr. Raffodil. Mr. Raffodil had bought himself a horse from someone else, and all on his own. It caused a buzz of excitement in our town of Green Valley.

When we learned that the horse had come from Goshen, New York, where they held the great Hambletonian Race for Champions, we were shocked ourselves.

Mr. Raffodil not only bought a wonderful trotting mare, but he had already sent her back to Goshen to be bred to another world-champion. One of the country's most famous sires, Mr. Raffodil was determined to clean Grandfather's clock on the race track, where it would hurt him the most. Especially his pride. Mr. Raffodil stopped all other work except "grinding up Grandfather."

The trotting mare came back in foal. Everybody in our town knew everything about her. Her name was Mignonette. Her pedigree went all the way back to the very best there is in harness racing. Grandfather was secretly drooling over the soon-to-be-born foal.

From his livery stable, Mr. Raffodil issued frequent bulletins on the approaching birth, almost every hour. You'd have thought the mare was the Queen Mother and the coming baby horse was the Crown Prince.

"He may be," Grandfather muttered.

"Maybe she'll be a girl prince."

"Whatever," Grandfather said. "We'll not have anything to compare to her in this town. Ever again. This is a once in a lifetime."

When Pete Devlin offered to work at half-price, Mr. Raffodil put him to work. Mr. Raffodil said he'd forgiven Pete for the part he'd played in helping Grandfather sell the Raffodils the "backup saddle pony." Pete kept Grandfather posted on the approaching birth.

Pete Devlin still owed Grandfather for an appendicitis operation for his wife, a hayrack, three cows, a bicycle for his son, and other miscellaneous gifts he'd generously given to Pete over a ten year period, expecting no return. Pete's family seemed to be sick a lot whenever Pete ran out of money.

Grandfather told Pete he'd cancel all these past debts and throw in two hundred dollars in cash if Pete could figure out a way he could buy the foal for Grandfather.

A few days later, Pete assured Grandfather that it was in the bag. He'd already approached Mr. Raffodil on behalf of an out-of-town buyer, and Mr. Raffodil had promised him a decision that very day. Pete told Grandfather to stick close to the phone and wait for his call.

Pete Devlin was known around our town as "Corky" Devlin. Not because he had the buoyant quality of a cork and could stay on top of stormy water, but because of the corkscrew nature of his business deals and his personal familiarity with bottle corks. Grandfather knew that Pete was about as reliable as the winter weather.

That alone should have touted Grandfather off the foal. Still as Grandfather himself told me later, "Greed is a terrible thing." It can be all consuming. Especially if a potential champion trotting horse is involved. One with lines that go back to Mignonette and Greyhound II—no matter how remote.

Grandfather and I sat playing cribbage for hours. Every time our party phone rang, I followed the rings excitedly. Our telephone number was four longs. I kept hollering out whose number it was with each long ring, the way all our neighbors did:

"Peterson's!"

"Anderson's!"

"Gunderson's!"

"Ours!"

Grandfather wearied of it after a while because it never got beyond Gunderson's. He told me to shut up and deal the cards.

Finally, the phone ring *was* ours!

"C'mon down," Pete Devlin told Grandfather. "You've bought yourself a foal."

14.

The look on Mr. Raffodil's face was nothing compared to the look on my grandfather's face when he found out that Mr. Raffodil was expecting him. Mrs. Raffodil was there, too. And all their friends. It was a command performance.

They had all been invited for dinner for just one thing: To be eyewitnesses to Mr. Raffodil's triumph over Grandfather in a horse trade. They had all been invited to watch Mayor Sam Raffodil nail Grandfather's hide to the wall at long last.

"Come for your foal, old man?" Raffodil laughed.

"So you knew about my deal with Pete Devlin?"

"Knew!" Mr. Raffodil gloated, "Pete and I arranged it!"

"There's no fun in *your* deals, Sam," Grandfather said.

"Not for you maybe."

Mr. Raffodil jerked a thumb toward the nearest horse stall.

"Get your foal off my property. I don't want it dying on my premises!"

Frank Hartman, who had come down to bid on the little foal himself, was very upset by Mr. Raffodil's callousness. Mr. Hartman, like Grandfather, loved horses. He had been Grandfather's chief rival every year in the county fair races. One year Grandfather won, the next year Mr. Hartman. They almost took turns it seemed.

Mr. Hartman was now only interested in what could be done to help the little foal. He came over to where Grandfather was bending down over the tiny wrinkled horse.

"Don't give this scoundrel a cent," he told Grandfather. "He's swindled you pure and simple."

"I know. It's the foal I'm worried about. The poor little devil is dying."

Mr. Raffodil stuck a leering face in between them, still gloating over Grandfather. "Of course he's dying, fool! Do you think I'd let you near him if he weren't?"

Mr. Hartman and Grandfather's Sioux Indian friend, Mr. Little Fork, both objected at the same time. Both were very angry.

"Don't give him a nickel," they advised Grandfather. "Not a cent. Take him to court. Tell the whole county exactly what this animal abuser has done."

Grandfather was taking out his wallet. "I never go back on a deal." Grandfather counted out fifteen hundred dollars for Mr. Raffodil, then took out another two hundred. He walked over to where Pete Devlin was hiding behind some stacked hay in the next stall. Grandfather handed the money to him.

"Thanks, Pete," Grandfather said. "For everything. Here's your two hundred dollars."

Pete Devlin looked miserable.

"Raffodil made me do it," Pete whined. "I didn't have a choice. My wife's very sick."

"It's not your wife who's sick, Pete," Grandfather told him. "I hereby cancel all your debts, but don't ever let me see your face around my barn again."

Minnie Raffodil was delighted at the turn of events. She shrilled at Grandfather.

"I don't think this foal is going to sit down at any band concert. Or go forward when I say 'Whoa!' "

"Can't you give them a little something to boot, Grandfather?" I asked. "Like a whack across the shins with your cane?"

Mr. Raffodil didn't care anything at all about Mignonette and her little foal. He had finally beaten my grandfather in a horse trade. That was all that mattered to him.

"You," he sneered at Grandfather, rubbing it in, "have bought yourself a dead horse."

"Not yet," Grandfather replied confidently. "This sick little fellow may live to haunt you yet, Sam."

Mr. Raffodil offers to sweeten the pot.

15.

Mr. Raffodil scoffed. "Take my word for it. The foal has the same rare blood sickness as the mare. They're both dying. And even a famous country horse doctor like you with all your fancy cures is not going to discover any secret poultice, or miracle remedy that can save this little horse."

Mr. Little Fork picked up the pitchfork again and said something quite threatening in the Sioux language. I could tell it was about something unpleasant he wished to do to Mr. Raffodil's insides.

Grandfather put his arm around my shoulder when he saw I was crying. We walked over to where the tiny horse lay on the fresh straw Mr. Little Fork had arranged for him.

"Please don't let the little horse die, Grandfather."

"You said that, son," Grandfather whispered quietly, "But there's nothing I can do now. Not a blessed thing."

"Sure you can Grandfather. I *know* you can. Everybody says you're a wizard with sick animals."

"Too late."

"Please, Grandfather, won't you at least try?"

Grandfather didn't answer. He knelt down once more beside the tiny wrinkled body. Gently he ran his fingers over the trembling, feverish foal.

"There's still a chance, isn't there, Grandfather?"

"Slim. Mighty slim."

"But at least a chance."

Mr. Raffodil came over to the stall. He overheard my last

words, and ridiculed them.

"There's not the slightest chance in this world," he laughed. "I've had the finest veterinarian doctors from both Minneapolis and Duluth. Not some has-been hick vet. These veterinary doctors were the best experts from the university, with all their laboratory equipment." Mr. Raffodil leaned scornfully against the door of the stall. "Do you think I'd let you get your hands on even a half-dead foal, if there was one chance in a million it might survive?"

Grandfather stroked the little foal's head. He looked up at Mr. Raffodil with a big smile, "This puny little horse may live to make a fool of you some day, Sam."

"That foal is totally incurable," Mr. Raffodil snapped. "Make up your mind to it. I paid through the nose to be sure."

Grandfather stood up. "The trouble with you, Sam, is that you never really enjoy horse trading. There's too much mean-ness in your deals."

"Don't mealy-mouth me, old man. I'm loving every minute of this deal. And I'll enjoy it much more when it comes out in the local paper how Sam Raffodil sold the great local race horse expert a dead foal."

Grandfather smiled. "I doubt if a horse-loving editor like Seth Lewis will print the story the way you'd like to read it, Sam."

"He'll print it the way I tell him to print it. I bought the paper yesterday. Lock, stock, and barrel. *Whatever* I need in this town to make your life miserable, old man, I'll buy. And I'll keep on buying until it becomes unbearable for you to live here. I'll keep it up until I've got everything I need to run you out of this part of the country. Forever. Just like I promised I'd do. I'll do it if it's the last thing I ever do, and if it takes the last cent I have!"

"It probably will," Grandfather said cheerfully as he bent down and patted the little horse on the head again. "I'm afraid you've out-smarted yourself this time, Sam. I'll probably raise this little foal to be a record-breaking trotter."

Raffodil snorted. Minnie Raffodil shrieked happily. "Seeing that wicked old man fondling a dying horse feels so good, Sam!"

she crowed. "It tastes so sweet!"

"No miracle trick from your bag of country doctoring is ever going to make that foal run," Sam laughed.

"He'll run," Grandfather said confidently. "Count on it!"

"Never!"

"You tell him, Sam!" Minnie cried gleefully.

Sam did just that. He said to Grandfather: "Just to show you there are no hard feelings over this horse trade, I'll throw in the mother, too. Mignonette is already famous in harness circles and she's yours. Free. For breeding purposes."

Mr. Little Fork, Grandfather's Indian friend, came over from the next stall. "Too late for that," he said to Grandfather. "The mare is dead."

"Oh, pity," Mr. Raffodil said, smiling his mortage foreclosing smile that never reached his eyes. "Just when I was about to throw in something to boot. To sweeten the pot."

"A whole teepee full of famous, secret Indian cures."

16.

Grandfather picked up the little chestnut foal and tenderly carried it out to the wagon. He laid it down gently on the blankets and hay Chief Little Fork had prepared. The foal opened up two of the biggest, saddest eyes you'd ever want to look at. I started crying again. I couldn't help myself. I bent down and picked up a good sized rock to heave at Mr. Raffodil. Grandfather shook his head.

"None of that," he said. He ruffled my hair affectionately. "It's all right, son." Grandfather turned and spoke softly to the foal. "We're taking you home, little fellow, where you can be among friends."

You could tell the little horse liked my grandfather, and that it was sorry to be in such terrible condition for a champion race horse. How would you feel if your mother had died in the barn of someone who didn't love either of you?

Grandfather was a good loser, I'll give him that. He never let on to Sam or Minnie Raffodil that he'd been outwitted. He seemed thoroughly pleased by the deal he had made.

"This little foal will be a real challenge, Sam," he said.

That infuriated them both. They wanted to see Grandfather acting outraged and beaten. They wanted him to grovel a little, with at least his spirit broken. Grandfather just smiled through it all. Even when I was crying because I knew the truth, Grandfather acted as though he had just completed the greatest horse trade of his entire life.

Grandfather turned the buckboard around and called out cheerfully to the Raffodils before leaving.

"This little weakling may grow up to be a world-beater someday, Sam. Someday, somewhere, on some race track, you'll be looking at the back of my orange-black-and-white racing silks. I hope it will be at the finish line of the County Fair Stakes."

Mr. Raffodil laughed scornfully.

"I'm trembling all over," he yelled back. "You're not only a patsy, old man, you're a damned fool. How I've longed to see this day!"

Mr. Raffodil divided the fifteen hundred dollars with his wife Minnie so that Grandfather could see the transaction. He wanted all his friends and neighbors, and all the guests he had invited to dinner, to see Grandfather's humiliation with their own eyes, too. So they would know that he, Sam Raffodil Senior, had come out on top. But most of the people had gone back silently into the house when they heard that Mignonette had died. Saddened, they had lost all interest.

"Well done, Sam," Minnie Raffodil said proudly.

"Who's got the last laugh now, horse doctor?" her husband taunted Grandfather. "You're welcome to take the mare home for fertilizer."

Grandfather was livid. I could feel him tremble on the seat beside me. He didn't care a whoop about the fifteen hundred dollars, but I knew he would never forgive Mr. Raffodil for the heartless way he'd treated both Mignonette and her sick little foal.

If Grandfather hadn't been so violently angry inside, I'm sure he never would have lost his head and boasted so openly. He even fooled me. Grandfather slowed the buckboard in front of Sam and Minnie Raffodil long enough for a few choice closing remarks.

"I have some horse doctoring tricks up my sleeve, that they never heard about in Minneapolis or Duluth, Sam. Or even at the university veterinary department you bragged about so loudly. Chief Little Fork here has a whole teepee full of secret

Indian cures that go all the way back to Pocahontas. So put this in your pipe and inhale it. I'm telling you right now to your face that the little dying foal in the back of this buckboard will trot someday, Sam. Maybe even in the County Fair Stakes. And when that day comes, he'll make you eat his dust, and you'll both laugh out the other side of your mouths."

"I'm laughing already!" Raffodil jeered. "On both sides!"

He was, too. So was Mrs. Raffodil. Their insulting laughter followed us as we drove out of the yard and started for home.

We could still hear it even way out on Elm Street.

The Wizard of Odds.

17.

"Will he?" I asked Grandfather. "Will he *really*?"

"Will he what?"

"Trot someday in the County Fair Stakes."

Grandfather sighed. "Most likely the foal will die before we get home."

I fought back the tears. Even though the little horse and I were still practically strangers, it already seemed like I was losing a close friend. I turned to Mr. Little Fork who was in the back with the foal.

"What about those secret Indian cures Grandfather says you know about? Can't we try one of them?"

"Your grandfather was using poetic license to cover his wrath."

"You mean there aren't any magic Indian remedies? Not even one? Out of a whole teepee full?"

"Not that *I* know," Mr. Little Fork said. "The only horse doctoring I've learned came from your grandfather. But I'll phone the reservation when I get home, just in case."

It wasn't much to hope for.

I turned to Grandfather.

"How can a human person be so mean and cruel as Mr. Raffodil?"

"Don't misjudge Sam," Grandfather told me. "He did all he could for both animals medically, be sure of that. Not out of a sense of love or affection for them the way we would, but because Sam had a big investment tied up in Mignonette and her little foal. Winning the County Fair Stakes with his own horse, and beating me to the finish line in any race, is the biggest thing in Sam's life right now. He's obsessed with it. Everything revolves around that. When Sam learned the horses were going to die in spite of everything he tried to prevent it— and be sure he tried—Sam couldn't resist the chance to try and get the best of me out of the deal. Fair or foul."

"I hate him!"

"No, son, you don't hate Sam, you hate what he does."

"It's the same thing! I hate what he did to Mignonette, and what he's doing to this little horse. Most of all, I hate *him!*"

"I have to accept some of the blame myself," Grandfather said. "I was so all fired eager to own a real first-class champion trotter, I was willing to pay any price. Ambition stole away my good sense. Now I'm paying for it. Sam was right, you know. Even when Pete Devlin told me the little foal was sick, it didn't worry me, I figured I could cure anything they threw at me. I was a foolish, silly, vain old man. Make no mistake about that. I admit it."

Grandfather hugged me and said, "Why don't you jump over into the back end and comfort that little fellow the rest of the way home."

No one said anything for a long time. All three of us were lost in our thoughts. I slipped over the back of the seat and sat down on the hay beside the little horse. Mr. Little Fork changed places with me and went up in front with Grandfather. I put the foal's head in my lap and began to stroke him gently.

"Grandfather was only joking," I told him. "You're not really going to die on the way home. He's the very best miracle horse doctor in all of Green Valley County. Maybe in the whole state. He can cure anything they throw at him."

Grandfather grunted and shouted at the horses. "Giddup, Beauty! Prince!" He called over his shoulder to me, "None of that."

I hugged the little horse and said, "Don't you pay any

attention to what he says. He's a real wizard! Especially when the odds are against him. You'll see. The tougher the case, the better my grandfather is."

Grandfather drowned me out, shouting, "Beauty! Prince! Giddup!"

"Nobody who's loved as much as you are little horse, dares to die. Otherwise, how can we kick Mr. Raffodil in the shins, and show him. You hear me, little horse?"

He blinked when a teardrop hit him smack in the eye.

The Second Furlong!

"Simmer down."

18.

The foal was still alive when we carried it into the barn. Mr. Little Fork made a nest of hay and straw in one corner of an empty stall. The little horse took up hardly any room at all. Grandfather fussed over it for nearly an hour.

"What'll we call it?" I asked him.

"No use giving a name to something that won't last 'till morning," Grandfather said.

"Everybody needs a name," I objected. "Even if it's only for a few hours. It's like baptizing somebody before they die away. It's only decent. Otherwise no one knows who they are, or who it was that died. If people in the next world say: 'Who is that? Coming into this world?' They won't know. That would be terrible."

Grandfather stroked the soft chestnut head.

"This poor little devil is in agony right now. He's suffering something fierce. Anything will seem better to him than what he's had so far in this world."

Mr. Little Fork said, "Even so, the boy makes sense. That little horse should have a name."

"What do you suggest?" Grandfather asked.

Mr. Little Fork said, "Call it 'Redskin.' He's the right color for it. And he's got a tough spirit. More important, the Raffodils would hate it."

I had an inspiration. Since Mr. Little Fork was helping us take care of the foal, and had already suggested an Indian name, I offered what I thought was an even better suggestion. I was still trying to find a way to get even with Mrs. Raffodil for the terrible things she said, and I couldn't help dreaming of that wonderful impossible day when this little red foal would breeze past Mr. Raffodil's champion horse in the homestretch and win the big County Fair Stakes. Like Grandfather said.*

I reminded Grandfather and Mr. Little Fork how the Raffodils had both laughed as we drove off, so I said: "Why don't we call the foal 'Minnie-Ha-Ha' after Mrs. Raffodil; then, when she laughs on the other side of her face, we can have a real horse-laugh on them both while they watch the sick little horse come roaring down the track toward the finish line."

Grandfather looked up. "Obviously you haven't examined our little friend very carefully. He's going to be a colt, not a filly."

"All right," I said, "let's call him 'Hiawatha' then."

Grandfather looked over at Mr. Little Fork, who nodded. "It's better than 'Redskin'," he said.

Grandfather agreed.

"Hiawatha it is."

The chestnut foal closed his big eyes and laid his head down in my lap. I think he was very happy to be called something.

The little red horse was still alive the next morning. I was down at the barn before the sun was up. I was petting his neck and combing his mane with my fingertips when Mr. Little Fork walked into the barn.

He had news for Grandfather.

"I've learned that many, many years ago, we had a severe blood sickness among the horses on the reservation. A disease very much like this little fellow seems to have."

"So?"

Grandfather eyed Mr. Little Fork quizzically.

---

* He says he never said that, but he "implied" that. And since he's death on my telling "lies," he couldn't wriggle out of it.

"Many of them died."

"That's encouraging."

"But quite a few, surprisingly, survived."

I looked up hopefully. "Was it a secret old Indian formula handed down from your tribal ancestors?"

"No," Mr. Little Fork said, "it was an accident. We discovered that those who went into the river and were covered with leeches who sucked their blood became very thin and bony, but over half of them lived through it. The others who didn't go into the water all died."

The horse doctor in Grandfather became alert.

'I remember reading something similar in one of the old medical journals about an epidemic in Australia years ago. It was in one of the old *Standard Bred* magazines. Maybe I can find it." Grandfather turned to Mr. Little Fork. "What was the reason given for the cure of some of the horses on the reservation?"

Mr. Little Fork shrugged his shoulders. "I wish I could remember, or say it *was* a secret old tribal remedy handed down for generations. The truth is, nobody seemed to know why. I questioned everybody I could. They couldn't even remember. We didn't have experts to give us any fancy names in those days. Some horses lived, some died. That's about the size of it. But apparently it had something to do with the leeches sucking out all that poisoned blood."

Mr. Little Fork certainly didn't talk like an honest-to-goodness tribal Sioux Indian. He said "many years ago" instead of "many moons ago." He admitted that he didn't know beans about secret Indian folklore medicine for anybody, especially horses. I think they spoiled Mr. Little Fork when he went down to the University of Minnesota.

It made you lose confidence in him. Still, you couldn't help liking him. His face had more lines in it than an old window-shade. They were mostly smiling lines. Mr. Little Fork not only had a kind outside face, but he was a kind person inside too.

Those people are hard to find nowadays. Most of the people

you meet are outside kind but inside mean, like Mr. Raffodil.
Especially when they find out that when you ask for help, what
you really want is something that's going to be a darned
nuisance, or a bother for them to do. Something troublesome.
Maybe they still smile at you when they say, "I'll think about it,"
but their eyes are cold and their lips are tight, and you know
they're not going to think about it at all, or do a blessed thing to
help you. In any way. They don't ever intend to help or even
want to. Already, as you turn to leave, they're forgetting all about
you and going back to their own business.

Things everywhere these days are not as friendly as they
used to be. Or as safe. It used to be that if you had trouble along
the roadway, or asked anybody if they could stop and lend a
hand, they were happy to be a good neighbor. Nowadays, they
speed on by you as if they didn't even see you were in trouble.
Everyone seems to be afraid of other people like they were each
living by themselves on their own separate islands. If they do
stop beside your car these days, they steal your buggy wheels
while you've gone for help.

Grandfather said all of this stuff, I didn't. He warned me that
the world was going to get a lot worse, too.

"You and I," he said, "will have to compensate these days by
being extra nice to people, and lend a hand wherever we can.
The worse the world gets, the better we have to become."

"If you say so Grandfather, but I'd sure like to knock a
couple of heads. I've already started a list, and Sam Raffodil
Senior and Sam Raffodil Junior are at the top. Their names are
lined in red with plenty of exclamation marks!"

To which Grandfather said, "Simmer down."

"Man the leeches!"

19.

Mr. Little Fork was Grandfather's kind of person. Tough, but nice. Nothing was too much trouble for Mr. Little Fork to do if it made you feel better. I don't think that Mr. Little Fork thought it was better to give than to receive, I just think he never thought of receiving at all. He was a happy giver, and a lot of fun to be with. It made you want to give him something in return. It even made you want to become a red Sioux Indian.

I could see that Grandfather was still very interested in what Mr. Little Fork said about the strange horse remedy and the leeches.

"It's over three hundred miles to your reservation," Grandfather said. "This little fellow could never make the trip."

Mr. Little Fork nodded. "I'm not even certain the leeches are still there after all this time. And who knows, maybe it wasn't even the leeches that did the trick."

"As I recall my folklore medicine and those old-time veterinary journals," Grandfather said, "there may be something to it. But we have to face it, the reservation's too far away to be of any help to us now."

I turned to Grandfather. "Is a leech anything like a bloodsucker?"

"They both make their living the same way," Grandfather said.

"If it's leeches you want," I told him, "I know where there are zillions of them. Bloodsuckers by the bucket!"

"Where?"

"Just a few miles from here. Below the Mississippi River bridge near the old sawmill. Right near old Joe Anderson's farm. You know, that place called 'The Frenchman's Nose,' where us kids aren't supposed to go near on account of the drownings."

I said it all in one breath, I was so eager to help Hiawatha.

I told Grandfather and Mr. Little Fork how I had waded in the river there once and had come out covered with bloodsuckers. It took several minutes to pick the clinging pieces of slimy dark red-grey pulp off my body. Yuckkk!

A bunch of us had gone swimming "no clothes, nonies." The thought of all those bloodsuckers still made my stomach sick. Every one of us kids was covered with bloodsuckers. I told Grandfather that just remembering it now was nauseating.

Grandfather got up from the oats box.

"Well," he said shaking his head wonderingly, "we've got nothing to lose. It may be about as scientific as rubbing a broken leg with a dead toad by a tree stump in the moonlight, but everything else has been tried. Besides, who knows?"

Mr. Little Fork gathered Hiawatha up gently in his arms while Grandfather hitched up the dapple-greys, Meshach and Shadrach, to the Abednego buggy.

I jumped in and hollered:

"Man the leeches!"

"God bless these bloodsuckers, every one!
If they're here!"

20.

Grandfather lifted the little chestnut foal from the wagon and waded out into the shallow water of the old Mississippi River swimming hole. He lowered Hiawatha gently into the stream, a little at a time.

Hiawatha quivered once or twice, rolled his frightened eyes up at Grandfather, then at me, and finally he appealed to Mr. Little Fork for help. His eyes looked wild and terrified. They were white and bloodshot red.

"Water's fairly warm here," Grandfather said, "but it may still be too cold for the little fellow with his fever and all. This may be totally the wrong thing to do, in his condition. If only I could have remembered more from that old Australian horse journal."

"What other choice do we have?" Mr. Little Fork asked.

Grandfather nodded.

"Still, it goes against all the horse-doctoring I know. The shock may kill him. Or at least give him double pneumonia!"

Mr. Little Fork said something in Sioux.

Grandfather said, "What does that mean?"

"What has he got to lose?"

"Right. A man about to be hanged by the neck, doesn't worry about a pain in his foot."

Mr. Little Fork grunted.

"Our real worry is that there won't be any leeches here at all."

I was disappointed when he said that. To me, this was the time for Mr. Little Fork to demonstrate his profound Indian wisdom about the mating habits of leeches, and where they spent the summer along the riverbed. The best Mr. Little Fork could come up with was a pitiful, "Maybe we'll get lucky."

I was standing barelegged up to my knees in the water. I began praying out loud.

"Let there be lots of bloodsuckers here, dear Lord, and I'll straighten out my life as soon as I can. And I take back what I said before about wishing that every bloodsucker in the whole world was dead as a doornail. I never knew they were good for anything until now. God bless these bloodsuckers, every one! If they're here!"

Slowly I pulled one leg out of the water. It was covered with leeches! Zillions of leeches!

Grandfather smiled. "Good," he said.

"Can they get through his hair, Grandfather?"

"Have faith."

We waited for quite a few minutes.

When I saw little Hiawatha's head sticking out of the water like that, I said, "It's the same as baptizing him, isn't it, Grandfather?"

Grandfather just grunted. He was busy with horse-doctoring things. I scooped up a handful of water and let it fall down over Hiawatha's face. His right ear wriggled and twitched when the drops hit him.*

"I baptize you," I said, "with the good Indian name of Hiawatha, in the name of the Father, and the Son, and the Holy Ghost."

Mr. Little Fork said, "Amen!"

---

* For a pictorial view of this dramatic moment see the cover of this book.

Grandfather carried Hiawatha back to the wagon. He was covered with horrible bloodsuckers and was trembling violently. They had burrowed down into his skin. His eyes looked terrified and wild. You could see that Hiawatha didn't like having those bloodsuckers on him at all, any more than I had, and he kept trying to shake them off by making his skin jump and twitch in spasms, and by whipping his chestnut tail. I knew just how Hiawatha felt. Bloodsuckers are fierce. I could see Hiawatha's heart beating in his throat.

Grandfather wrapped the little foal in blankets and sat with him in the back of the buckboard and held him in his arms. "It's all right," he kept saying over and over. "It's all right."

Mr. Little Fork drove and I sat up in front with him. I could hear Mr. Little Fork making strange musical sounds. I leaned forward to listen.

"Is that a horse-healing old Indian chant?" I asked him, hopefully.

Mr. Little Fork shook his head.

"Is it an Indian prayer you used to recite as a boy at dawn outside your teepee, gazing at the rising sun?"

Mr. Little Fork shook his head. "As a boy, I lived in a tenement apartment house in Minneapolis."

"What is the music then?" I asked, disgusted.

Mr. Little Fork raised his voice and sang loud enough for me to hear the words:

"I've got the blues, the Wabash blues."

"Great!" I told him. "Just great."

I guess the good old days of Geronimo, Chief Joseph, Sitting Bull, and Pretty Redwing were out the window. Modern red Indians are becoming just like anybody else.

Isn't it a pity?

21.

Hiawatha didn't die that day. Or that night either. We picked off the last of the leeches and bloodsuckers. They were fat and full of his sick blood, and stubborn. They clung onto Hiawatha for dear life.

Hiawatha didn't look like he was cured to me. He looked sicker than ever. His eyes were filmed over, glazed and dull. He dropped his head onto the straw with a thud. He looked so pitiful and exhausted that I cried out.

"He's dead!"

Grandfather chuckled, then patted my shoulder.

"Sleeping, I think. That's a good sign. Very good."

The next morning, Hiawatha was even worse. Grandfather, on the other hand, was still more confident. He began smiling to himself.

He said to Mr. Little Fork and me, "Did you gentlemen ever consider what a perfect retribution it would be, if these leeches did cure Hiawatha? Retribution for Sam Raffodil, I mean?"

"It's too deep for me, Grandfather, but I'm certainly willing..." I shut right up because Mr. Little Fork put it more simply.

"Explain."

"You'll love it," Grandfather assured us. "It's right out of the good book."

"The Bible?"

"No," Grandfather said, "the dictionary."

Grandfather picked up the *Webster's Dictionary* which he'd

brought down from the house, and read out loud to us.

"Bloodsucker. A person who preys on another." Grandfather looked up, smiling. "Except that kind of leech sucks out all the *good* blood. Our little fellows suck out the poisons. Doctors have used leeches to bleed people down through the centuries. So it's not too surprising we hit on this old Indian home cure."

"Holy harpoons!" I said. "If anybody had ever told me those icky bloodsuckers were the good guys, I'd have belted them."

"Do not speak ill of leeches ever again."

Mr. Little Fork let loose with a long flow of Sioux Indian words.

"Are you talking to Manitou, the Great Spirit, thanking Him for His kind help?" I asked, hopefully.

"No," Mr. Little Fork said.

"What then?"

"I was saying that if anybody had ever told me those icky bloodsuckers were good for anything, I would have belted them."

We all laughed at that. Even though I knew Mr. Little Fork hadn't really said that. We were all feeling so darn good about Hiawatha staying alive this long that we just didn't care. We laughed at everything. Even things that wouldn't be funny on a normal day.

"I'm very encouraged," Grandfather said, a few days later. I still couldn't see anything encouraging about the way Hiawatha looked, except that he wasn't dead. Grandfather doctored the chestnut foal with all the medicine he knew. Even with some he made up on the spot. He admitted that nothing seemed to help much.

"Still," Grandfather said, "I have this good feeling."

Grandfather said they would drum him out of the veterinarian society and revoke his license if they ever saw the shortcuts and unorthodox things he was doing to try and save Hiawatha's life.

"It's not in the medical books at all," he said.

"Can the books save him?" Mr. Little Fork asked.

"I don't think so."

"But *you* can, Grandfather," I said. "I know you can! You're better than the books."

"None of that."

Grandfather packed Hiawatha with hot water bottles and blankets when he went into a chill, and sponged his head and body with cool water when the fever raged. Grandfather even gave Hiawatha an alcohol rub and I helped. I had to go to Potter & Casey's Store to get more alcohol, but as a reward I was allowed to sponge Hiawatha off. I think he liked it.

I slept in the barn with Hiawatha two nights before my father found out that the lump under the sheets on my bed was only pillows and my winter coat. He ordered me to stay home and sleep in my own bed. He must have seen my heart-stricken face.

"Except for tonight, of course," he said, as he gave me an understanding hug.

I was off like a shot for Grandfather's barn.

"Do you know the nesting-place of the eagle?"

22.

Mr. Little Fork was a Sioux Indian. You know that.

But he was a lot more too. He was Chief I.J. Little Fork, but he gave up being Chief. However you do that. I often called him *Chief,* and *Chief Little Fork,* but he said he preferred to be called plain Mr. Little Fork.

I've already told you, I lost interest in him as a decent red-blooded, red Indian long ago. Even more so when I found out his initials I.J. stood for *Isaiah* and *Jeremiah.*

"What's the world coming to?" I asked Grandfather.

"Ask Mr. Little Fork," he suggested.

That was easy to do these days because Mr. Little Fork came over regularly to work in the barn with Grandfather to pay off what he still considered to be a debt.

"I had my money's worth the night of the big party at the reservation," Grandfather told him. "Let's cancel the debt once and for all."

"No," Mr. Little Fork insisted. "It's an honest debt, and I have to pay."

There wasn't much to do at Grandfather's barn, except talk, so Grandfather said that if Mr. Little Fork insisted on paying, he could work the debt off at the rate of two dollars an hour talking, or four dollars an hour doing miscellaneous chores. Mr. Little Fork agreed immediately.

Mr. Little Fork was very stoic and silent with most people, but when he was around Grandfather, he became almost as windy as Grandfather himself, so I figured he'd be free and clear of his debt in no time.

When I first met Mr. Little Fork, I remembered that my Grandfather had said that he was a genuine full-blooded Sioux Indian. It was one of the happiest days of my life.

I was the only boy in our town who could go on and on, naming almost every Indian tribe in North America, including the San Blas, Zuni, Hopi, Navajo, Chiricahua, Apache and the Mescalero, and on and on. I loved all the Indians like those in Eric Somerly's song: the Chickasaw, Choctaw, Saginaw, Arapahoe, Blackfeet, Iroquois, Mohawk, Cherokee, Ojibwa, Chippewa. You name the state, and I could tell you the names of all the Indian tribes there.

This book is too small to hold them all, so if I've left out your tribe, don't get sore at me. Take it out on Sam Raffodil Senior and Junior, they're the unwelcome ones who are taking up so much extra space in this book that I can't dwell on the decent things like the Cree, the Crow, the Papago, the Poorman's, the Oneida, the Algonquin, the Seminole, the Ogalla Sioux, the Nez Perce, the Dakota, the Pueblo, the Tlinkit, and the Shoshone. For starters.

To me, all these Indian tribes and people were among the noble race of red men. I never met an Indian I didn't like. Except John Winter Wolf who always beat me wrist-wrestling. But he was only *part* Indian, and part Irish, like me. But much stronger. He used to say he loved being Indian but hated being Irish.

When I first met Mr. Little Fork, I was thrilled. A real, honest-to-goodness Sioux Indian. I expected him to speak in short terse phrases full of woodsy wisdom. Mostly he said, "Your grandfather is a remarkable man."

I knew that already, so Mr. Little Fork was a great disappointment to me. I figured if there wasn't going to be any folklore, I might as well join Mr. Little Fork and volunteer to work around the barn for a little of that two-dollars-an-hour talking money myself. But Grandfather turned me down cold.

"Are you a relative of Chief Sitting Bull?" he asked me.

"No, sir."

"Have you shot wild buffalo on the great plains?"

"No, sir."

"Can you trap, hunt, or trail the smallest animal through the great black forest, the desert, the mountains and the valleys?"

"No, sir."

"Do you know the nesting place of the eagle?"

"No, sir."

"You're not worth the money."

Grandfather did let me work with Mr. Little Fork in taking care of Hiawatha to make sure he didn't die or anything. As it turned out, Mr. Little Fork taught me some very useful things, and told me many wonderful legends about the American Indians. He had a lot of pretty good stuff in him after all, if you dug deep enough and prodded him.

Grandfather gave me the job because I told him what a wonderful thing he had done for Mr. and Mrs. Little Fork in helping them against Mr. Raffodil.

"After all," Grandfather pointed out, "who was it that put us onto that good thing, winter hay? It was Mr. Little Fork. He's really not in debt to us at all. We made money on his wisdom but he has a deep sense of pride. That's why we worked out his 'talking' deal."

"I'm proud of you, Grandfather," I told him. "I'd like to do good things for my fellowman like you do."

Many people hinted that my Grandfather was not nearly as kindly and charitable as he appeared to be on the surface. They claimed that a lot of Grandfather's kindly acts and good deeds were not done because of a sweet nature at all, but only to get the best of Mr. Sam Raffodil Senior.

Grandfather was amused when he heard such comments. He even admitted that often times our neighbors were right.

"If I can give a helping hand to one of God's creatures, and root Sam Raffodil in the tail at the same time," he said, "that's my kind of sweet charity."

"Doesn't God frown on that?" I asked him.

"Not at all."

"Really?"

"You have my word."

"But didn't you gouge Mr. Raffodil a little on the winter hay prices? Just like he gouges other people?"

"I didn't *gouge*," Grandfather protested, peeved. "I just let a little hot air out of Sam Raffodil's miserly balloon. Your angelic grandfather didn't keep any of the profits for himself, did he?"

"No."

"Well, then?"

"It just doesn't seem all that angelic to me," I pointed out. "You're sure God doesn't frown on it?"

"He loves it."

"How do you know?"

"I asked Him. He said 'Go after that big shark Raffodil, and stick it in his gizzard.' "

"*God* said that?"

"Well, maybe not in those words, exactly. It was more of a feeling that came over me when I thought about Sam Raffodil Senior and what he'd done to the Little Forks of this world."

"Now that," I told him, "I can understand. Stick it to him good!"

"Thank you. No applause, please."

What a grandfather!

23.

The truth is, Grandfather actually did do a lot of kind and charitable things for people long before Sam Raffodil Senior ever came to our town. In fact, Grandfather himself reminded me of this. When it came to modesty and shyness, Grandfather took a backseat to no one. He said that.

"If you don't toot your own horn, no one else will," Grandfather explained. "But toot it softly, gently, sweetly, and pianissimo as your Grandfather does."

"That's just bragging," I told him, cutting through the candied apple.

It wasn't *my* fault that he became upset. Grandfather had taught me to see right through all humbug.

"You're doing your grandfather an injustice on this one," he objected. "I'm just protecting my friends. So they won't get caught up in Sam Raffodil's terrible net. Take from the rich and give to the poor. That's my motto."

"You *stole* that motto!"

"I know it. I'm trying to do just like the Lord Jesus. Take from the rich and give to the poor."

"That wasn't the Lord Jesus," I told him, "that was Robin Hood."

"Same thing," Grandfather bragged. "It makes Sam Raffodil either a Pharisee or the Sheriff of Nottingham. Take your choice."

Grandfather chuckled merrily and jabbed me in the ribs with the handle of the hayfork, doubling me up into the empty oats box. Grandfather was a scream, all right. He knew the difference between Jesus and Robin Hood. He just thought *I* didn't.

Sometimes when Grandfather was very pleased with himself, he was a little hard to take. And, like I said, if you weren't fast on your feet, between the oats box and the backseat of the buggy, you could wind up black and blue with assorted bruises.

One morning I was lying down beside Hiawatha in the soft hay, feeding him from a bottle. He reached over and bit me on the arm. Real gently. It was like saying, "Thanks."

Hiawatha let go and whinnied. Grandfather came over and looked down at us.

"That," he said, "is the best sign yet."

The next afternoon, Mr. Little Fork, Grandfather and I were saddle-soaping the racing harnesses, and talking about the County Fair Stakes, when we heard a funny rattling and scraping sound in Hiawatha's stall. When we went to peek in, the little chestnut foal was standing up all by himself!

Well, maybe it would be more accurate to say that he was *leaning* up. Hiawatha had propped himself against the wall of the stall.

He whinnied happily when all three of us congratulated him.

Grandfather gave me a grizzly bear hug and a whisker rub, and all three of us began to laugh out loud. Grandfather even did a few dance steps without his cane.

"I believe," he said, "that we're finally out of the woods."

He patted Hiawatha on the withers and almost knocked him down. I hugged Hiawatha round the neck and held him up. Mr. Little Fork just smiled.

"Is he going to be a champion trotter, Grandfather?" I asked.

"Can't tell yet," he said. "To soon. He may never get back to normal. As a champion trotter that is. After what he's been through."

"He's got to!" I said.

"We've saved his life. That's miracle enough."

"No, it isn't!" I insisted. "It's not *nearly* enough! Hiawatha has to become a real champion trotter. He has to make Mr. Raffodil laugh out of the other side of his mouth. He has to run that wicked old man right into the Mississippi River. You promised!"

"It's still going to be a long hard pull for the little fellow just to survive," Grandfather reminded me. "Remember, only a small handful out of hundreds of *healthy* foals ever become champion trotters. Even when they get all the breaks, good health, the right food, the right training, with everything in their favor from the very beginning, most of them never make it to the starting line. Turning this sick, skinny little fellow into a champion trotting horse is now more up to him than to us. The chances are one in a million."

I looked at Mr. Little Fork. "You said he had a fierce spirit."

"He *has.* Or he wouldn't be here now."

"Well, then?"

"It's a long shot," Grandfather said. "No use getting our hopes up too high."

"But he *will* make it, won't he?"

Hiawatha whinnied very loud—just before he fell down flat on the floor. Grandfather laughed. So did I. And so did Mr. Little Fork.

"Apparently *he* thinks so," Grandfather said, "and that's good enough for me."

Grandfather leaned down and began to stroke Hiawatha's soft red nose.

"Yes, sir," Grandfather said, "I've got a sneaking hunch that this little chestnut horse is going to run Sam Raffodil Senior all the way to the shores of the Gichee Gumee."

"Really?"

Grandfather agreed. "Really," he said. "Right smack dab into the shining big sea waters, or his name is not Hiawatha."

"Really Grandfather?"

"Really!"

Hiawatha whinnied, and got up on his feet again. It was like taking a bow. I stood there and laughed and cried. Even my pet goose, GOG, got into the act. He hollered, "Honk!"

"You can say that again," Grandfather laughed, and the goose did. Even twice.

"Honk! Honk!"

Grandfather gave me another grizzly bear hug. Mr. Little Fork offered Hiawatha a carrot.

"It appears," Grandfather said, "that we have got ourselves a trotting horse. Look out, Sam Raffodil!"

I shouted out, "Hooray!"

The Third Furlong!

"Show-off time!"

24.

If this were a motion picture instead of a story in a book, you'd see a skinny little chestnut foal whose skin was still too big for his body frolicking in a farmyard meadow, running beneath the apple blossoms, kicking up his heels, and pulling mouthfuls of clover from a nearby loaded hayrack, while Grandfather and I watched through the open barn door.

The apple blossoms would turn to autumn leaves, and the gold and red oak, and the deeper red maple tree leaves would float whirling to the ground. Perhaps one perfect maple leaf would fall on the end of Hiawatha's nose startling the little horse into tossing his mane, pawing at the turf, and kicking his hind heels high into the air before racing around the farmyard fence lickety-split like the wind, just as though he were entered in the big County Stakes Race and knew exactly what was expected of him.

The autumn leaves would dissolve into big soft white snow-flakes until the whole countryside looked like a Christmas card. The snow would turn into rain, the apple trees would have new blossoms once again, showing how fast the time was passing.

The little chestnut horse transformed into a two-year old colt right before our very eyes. Mignonette's sick little foal now appeared sturdy and strong, and gamboled and raced along the farmyard fence faster and faster with each passing week.

In a far off hidden corner of the meadow, you would see Sam Raffodil Senior and Sam Raffodil Junior hiding behind the hazelnut bushes, watching Hiawatha carefully, taking photographs over the white picket fence and shaking their heads, not at all pleased with what they were seeing. With worried frowns they would climb into their fancy buggy and drive off, Mr. Raffodil cuffing Sam Junior alongside the head on general principles.

Before you knew it, Hiawatha was a frisky young three-year-old horse, pulling the light single buggy down Main Street on a Saturday afternoon to pick up the mail. Grandfather stopped at my house to pick me up on the way.

"It's show-off time," he said.

Mr. Raffodil, who had sold my Grandfather the sick little colt, thinking it would die almost immediately, was watching out of his office window over the bank, chewing viciously on his big black cigar.

All of this happened exactly the way I'm telling you, but it took a long, long time. I nearly died waiting. But one day, there at last, was a wonderful racehorse named Hiawatha. He was galloping around our barnyard and kicking up dirt with his happy flying feet. Every time Mr. Raffodil saw Hiawatha, it made him nervous, and gave him an upset stomach, so naturally Grandfather took Hiawatha downtown a lot more often than was necessary. He liked to see Mr. Raffodil suffer.

Everybody had expected Hiawatha to die, not only Mr. Raffodil. That was to have been the best part of Mr. Raffodil's revenge. Instead, here was Hiawatha looking dangerously like a first-class trotting horse. Every time Hiawatha went high-stepping along Main Street in front of the bank, which was quite often, sooner or later Mr. Raffodil would look out of the bank window, and Grandfather would wave. Sometimes Hiawatha would whinny. It was almost like he was saying, "Take that!"

Mr. Raffodil angrily threw down his cigar on those occasions; once he jerked down his windowshade. Fortunately, the whole shade came down bodily, and Mr. Raffodil could still see what he now called "that damned red horse!"

"I'll kill myself if he can run fast!" he said.

When I heard that Mr. Raffodil had said that, I wanted to send him my stopwatch with Hiawatha's four furlong time on it, and a loaded pistol. Grandfather said I'd have to stop being so bloodthirsty. How fast Hiawatha could run was our business. Nobody else's.

What upset Mr. Raffodil most of all was the fact that he hadn't outwitted Grandfather after all. He hadn't bested him in a horse trade in any way. Grandfather had come out on top again. Hiawatha was the greatest victory of all, and everyone knew it. The whole town was talking about it behind Mr. Raffodil's back. They loved Grandfather for being the champ again. It was a bitter pill for Mr. Raffodil to swallow. In fact, he choked on it the very first time Grandfather drove Hiawatha downtown.

When the townspeople saw what had been that sick and dying little foal now highstepping down Main Street in the show-off trot Grandfather had put him into, they all stopped whatever they were doing, came out into the street, set down their parcels, and applauded wildly. Both Grandfather and Hiawatha ate it up. Especially when Grandfather saw Mr. Raffodil glaring out the window of his office, his big black cigar up against his nose, smoking.

Everybody applauded except those who were behind in their mortgage payments or at the Raffodil Grocery Store. They banged on the benches and the sides of buildings secretly with their fists or feet so Mr. Raffodil couldn't see them clapping. It was a triumph for Hiawatha and his driver, Grandfather.

Finally, I said, "Let's go home now. We've already driven around the block twice."

"One more time," Grandfather chuckled, punching me in the biceps. "This is all part of the Lord's revenge on Sam Raffodil."

He couldn't sell me that.

"It looks a lot more like its part of *your* revenge."

Grandfather dredged up one of his most innocent looks. "I,"

he said, "am only the instrument of justice."

"Hog wash!" I said in pig Latin, to take some of the sting out of it. I slid quickly over to the far end of the buggy seat when Grandfather reached for my kneecap.

"I'm not so sure God is as good a friend of yours as you keep saying," I told him.

Grandfather grinned, and punched me in the ribs with his elbow. "Oh, no? Who is it driving this marvelous red horse around the block? Is it Sam Raffodil the animal abuser, or is it your lovable, wise old grandfather?"

There was considerable quiet appreciative laughter among the citizens of Green Valley everytime Hiawatha came strutting uptown. People would come out of their stores, their shops and hotel rooms just in case something exciting developed. They smiled big smiles, and if Mr. Raffodil wasn't in sight, they applauded noisily as Hiawatha and Grandfather trotted by.

But what they liked best was when Grandfather and Mr. Raffodil would start hollering at each other when they met accidentally in front of the bank, the post office, or the city hall, even though Grandfather would sometimes have to drive around the livery stable several times to make that accidental meeting happen.

"I've got all the time in the world," Grandfather would tell me, when I complained about it.

I reminded him, "The doctor says your wunky heart could go any minute, according to Grandmother." I snapped my fingers. "You could go just like that, she said."

"Not since I discovered this wonderful new medicine, this 'Sink Sam Raffodil Senior Elixir,'" he said, taking a swig out of a bottle of tonic water.

"That's got nothing to do with God at all," I objected. I tried to punch Grandfather on his biceps. I missed, and wound up in his lap, where he did some unpleasant things to my kneecaps and rump.

"I hate being pinched!" I yelled at him.

"Horse training is not all trophies, military bands and screaming grandstands. Right?"

"Right."

"Or showing off in front of pretty girls. Right?"

"Right."

"Or..."

"I KNOW all that, Grandfather."

"Do you?"

25.

A week later Grandfather was called over to Hill City. An emergency. They needed his advice about two very sick horses. They were worried it might be the beginning of some kind of an equine epidemic. I wanted to go with him, but Grandfather said no, not this time. He said I should stay home and take care of the chores.

"That's what partners are for. To share the work."

Grandfather told me confidentially that he was also going to look at a local Hill City trotting horse, a grey that had won a lot of local races, and had built quite a reputation for himself.

"We have to have something quite special to enter into the County Fair Stakes this year," he reminded me.

"What about Dakar or Tropical?"

"Too slow to run against this so-called wonder horse that I hear Sam Raffodil is thinking of bringing in from New York."

"Hiawatha's fast enough," I reminded him for the fiftieth time. "If you'd only give him a chance."

Icy eyeballs.

Sigh. Patience.

"Hiawatha will get his chance," Grandfather assured me, "but not until *I* say he's ready. He hasn't the stamina to stay the distance yet."

"You can't fault a person for trying."

"You not only can fault them, you can fire them if you're the boss. Remember that."

Before he left, Grandfather became more gentle. He tousled my hair, and gave me my final racing stable instructions. "You behave yourself while I'm gone, hear? No funny stuff. Don't hitch up Hiawatha unless I'm here with you. Not under any circumstances. Understand?"

"You know me, Grandfather."

"I *do*. That's why I'm giving you these exact, specific, careful instructions." Grandfather tapped me on the collarbone with the end of his pointing finger. He never missed hitting the target, my clavicle bone. "That chestnut colt stays in the barn until I get home. Clear?"

"Clear!"

"He stays there all day Friday and all day Saturday. Agreed?"

"Agreed."

"I'll be back Saturday night. And don't forget the chores. Remember that. Not *some* of them, all of them. Training racehorses is not all trophies, military bands and screaming grandstands. Right?"

"Right."

"Or showing off before pretty girls. Right?"

"Right."

Grandfather was quite nastily covering all of the bases, one at a time. "It also means manure shoveling, cleaning out the stalls, forking down the hay into the mangers, and doing all the - - - -."

"I *know* all that! I'm a horse trainer, too, remember!"

"Good. Then I'll say goodbye."

This, of course, was still another rotten side of my grandfather. He was usually quite a decent person. Most grownups are that way. But sometimes, they carry things too far. All a parent or grandparent has to do is *tell* you what they want, and have faith you'll do it. There's no need to keep harping about it in such detail. And when they want you to give up some habit they don't like, and maybe even *you* don't like, but are hanging onto because the cure they offer is worse than the habit—all that stuff—they should say what they want. Outright. No sly hints. Say it right out. Don't pussyfoot. Let 'em just throw their cold water on the fire. No need to stomp on it over and over and over, and kick the ashes around. Just because a fellow may have forgotten to do some little unimportant thing a time or two in the past. Or maybe three times. Possibly four. Why harp on it?

Once I told Grandfather how I felt about all of this.

"You should have a little more faith in your grandson, Grandfather," I said. "After all, I'm a relative."

"I *do*," he said. "I do have faith. I also have a lot of hope. And heaven knows how much charity and forgiveness."

This is sarcasm, and part of the smart-aleck grandfather type of talk that I dislike. Even though there may be more than a kernal of truth in what he said.

I had some pretty smart sarcastic rejoinders of my own, but I swallowed them. I was glad I did, the way things turned out.

Crisis Sunday!

The terrible thing that was about to happen in our town on a peaceful Sunday was not Grandfather's fault, in any way. It was all mine. Hook, line, and sinker. Every part of the dreadful disaster that came to be known as *Crisis Sunday*.

If I'd known then what I know now, I would have taken the next bus out of town to the Minnesota Northwoods, and would have hidden forever in some far off lumber camp.

It all began at midnight, two nights later.

The Methodist Church clock on the corner across the street went "Boom! Boom! Boom!"

I was sitting up in bed eating a triple-decker peanut butter sandwich, part white, rye, and part whole wheat. Suddenly I was taken with a strange seizure; it was like a brilliant flash. It seemed to explode inside my head.

I realized that I had already *kept* my promise to Grandfather. Every word of it. I *hadn't* taken Hiawatha out of the barn to exercise him all day Friday and all day Saturday, exactly as Grandfather had instructed. I had been a faithful and trust-worthy partner. I was filled to the brim with race horse owner integrity.

That didn't mean I had to give up being creative.

Right?

Grandfather hadn't said a word about what I should do on Sunday if he were accidentally detained. Had he? Not in any actual words, I mean. Of course he had planned to return

Saturday night and did not expect to be held up by a horse with critical heaves.

If Grandfather had returned Saturday night like he promised he might have issued further orders for me.

But he *didn't* return.

Did he?

No, he did not.

Shouldn't I look upon this as special guidance that came to me out of the night? A well-deserved gift to a part-owner in a famous trotting horse. A horse whose whole career might be saved by this sudden, unexpected special guidance.

Wasn't this a perfect chance to demonstrate that a certain racehorse was ready to run in the County Fair Stakes? No matter what Grandfather thought? And bury the Raffodils in the shining big sea waters? Up to their Gitchie Gumies?

You tell me!!

Every horse trainer knows that horses can go stale if they miss their regular workouts. I was so eager to have Hiawatha race in this year's County Fair Stakes against the Raffodils that I didn't want Hiawatha to interrupt this training for a minute. Just in case there was the faintest, most remote, outside chance he might be ready to run to glory. Somebody had to show Grandfather that Hiawatha *was* ready. And *did* have all the stamina he needed.

Who else was there to prove it?

Except me?

I was certain that Grandfather was wrong about Hiawatha. That big red horse certainly looked ready to me. It would be tragic if Hiawatha *was* ready, and we didn't race him. On the other hand, it would only be poetic justice if we entered him in the County Fair Stakes, and he beat Mr. Raffodil's horse forty ways from Sunday and shamed them instead of himself.

Of course, what I *really* wanted, was not poetic justice, but "blood all over everything" justice. That's why I did the bad thing I did. I admit it now. I was bad.

It touched off some of the nastiest trouble that ever happened on Main Street in our town. Especially on such a quiet peaceful Sunday morning when everybody was going home from church.

But, it *was* exciting!

"Whoa! Whoa! You darned horse!"

27.

I hitched Hiawatha up to the bright new golden racing sulky Grandfather had especially ordered from Chicago. It was a beauty. It looked like it was going thirty miles an hour when it was standing still with no horse in it.

I had never put the harness on Hiawatha by myself before, but I had watched Grandfather very carefully. Memorizing. Just in case such an emergency as this might turn up unexpectedly.

Hiawatha was much bigger outside the barn than he was inside. And a *lot* bigger than he was when Grandfather was there with me. Hiawatha stomped around the sulky in a frenzy. He acted as though he didn't know any more about hitching up a horse than I did.

Hiawatha bucked.

Violently.

He went up on his hind legs and towered over me, swaying from side to side. He backed up too far. Finally he side-swiped me with his rear end, and knocked me galley-west.

I bounced off the empty hayrack. I saw stars for a moment.

Eventually I quieted Hiawatha down by taking him back into the barn to his own stall. I gave him some oats, and went up to the house to have some milk and a peanut butter sandwich to think it over.

If Hiawatha wasn't any more ready to race than he was to be hitched up to the sulky, maybe Grandfather was right, and this wasn't Hiawatha's year.

I felt much braver with food in me. Grandfather said you have to let the horse know who was boss. So far, it was Hiawatha. But I planned to change that. When would I ever have another chance like this to fulfill my great adventure?

I slowly backed Hiawatha between the traces, and, with aching arms and a bruised body, hooked the harness into what seemed to be the proper places.

If my pet goose, GOG, hadn't been sitting on top of Hiawatha's back, I wouldn't have been able to control him at all. GOG was frolicking around, running up and down Hiawatha's back eager for action.

"Honk!" he hollered, sitting up between Hiawatha's ears.

Sometimes I think that the only one Hiawatha really had any respect for was that weird goose. Once GOG had laid a goose-egg in a corner of Hiawatha's stall, and the chestnut ate his hay from way over on the other side, so he wouldn't spill any on the gosling. He was also very careful where he stepped. Hiawatha didn't bite the little gosling even once after it was hatched and started walking around.

It was a darn nuisance for me trying to fork large bunches of Hiawatha's hay down without burying the fuzzy little thing in the manger.

People think it's some sort of a miracle in the Bible where the lion lies down with the lamb, but I think that's pretty mild alongside of a love affair between a horse and a goose. Sometimes I almost felt jealous. Grandfather says many racing stables have pets for the horses, just to keep them calm.

"A pet is no novelty," he said. "Not even a honking goose who runs up and down the horse's back, and even sits on top of his head between his ears. Although," Grandfather admitted, "it is a little weird."

Fortunately, I had practiced quite a few loud "Whoas!" in the barn before leading Hiawatha outside to hitch him up on that *Crisis Sunday* morning.

Anybody at all familiar with horses could see that Hiawatha was badly in need of a workout. He was far too frisky. He kicked the planks in his stall and whinnied loudly, terrifying the nesting gosling until GOG honked at him and protected the baby with her wings. I was sure Grandfather would be grateful for my foresight as a trainer and partner in getting a good "workout" inside our big red horse.

Hiawatha had always been very gentle inside the barn, and in the sulky, when Grandfather handled him. I hardly recognized him when he backed me through Grandmother's prize roses, across the cornfield up into the chicken-run, doing bad things to the fence and setting free all the chickens, who went squawking noisily down the middle of the road.

"Whoa! Whoa!" I kept shouting. "Whoa! Hiawatha! Whoa! Whoa, you darned horse!"

But he didn't.

"Don't tickle a horse under the tail with a racing whip!"

28.

It was a good thing for me that Uncle Clifford and Grandmother had gone off to church in Uncle Cliff's Model-T Ford, or both of them would have been out of the house on a dead run, hollering nasty things at me, and putting me out of the horse training business.

I had timed it well.

I eventually coaxed Hiawatha to a stop just inside the pigpen gate which he had knocked open. Fortunately, only half the pigs escaped, not all of them, like the chickens. They were much noisier, however, and squealed up a storm.

I got out of the sulky and led Hiawatha out onto the street. I patted his neck the way Grandfather did, called him a "fine fellow," like Grandfather did, then crawled up into the sulky for the umpteenth time. Like Grandfather didn't.

We started down Maple Street toward the Soo Depot moving just as nice as you please at a lazy comfortable walk. I drove Hiawatha very cautiously that first block.

Holy Harpoons! Did you ever sit in a racing sulky behind a big trotting horse?

There's nothing like it in all the world! I mean *nothing!* President of the United States is ashes!

Ever since I'd been five years old I'd never wanted to grow up to be a cowboy, or an Indian, or even a railroad engineer. All I'd ever wanted and dreamed about in the whole wide world, was being a harness racing driver like my Grandfather.

Now, in the middle of Maple Street, I'd reached my lifelong ambition. I was a race driver! And still in grade school!

"Let Sam Raffodil play *that* on his piano!" I told myself happily on that wonderful blue-skyed sleepy Sunday morning in Green Valley.

I did learn a surprising thing. You practically sit up inside the horse's rump when you're driving a racing sulky. With the horse's wobbling back-end staring at you like that, it's almost embarrassing, until you get used to it. Especially when he lifts his tail to get rid of his wind. He perfumes you every time when he gets rid of his hay. You cringe back, trying to get out of the target area, until you realize that those harness drivers are smart and know just how far back to sit. At first I kept looking the other way. After we ran into a ditch, I cut that out fast.

Unfortunately, Grandfather hadn't shown me how to braid Hiawatha's tail and tie it up with ribbons, so I kept getting unexpected nasty stinging lashes of horsehair across the face. These are not at all helpful to a beginning harness race driver.

"You're not supposed to whip me, you idiot!" I hollered at Hiawatha. "I whip you!"

I knew Hiawatha wasn't hitting me on purpose with his tail, and there *were* a lot of flies, but like I said before, Grandfather said you had to let the horse know who was boss. It had worked before, so this time I decided to tickle Hiawatha just once underneath his tail with the end of the racing whip to set him straight. Again I called him a "fine fellow" and "splendid horse."

Hiawatha must have thought I was lying, because the moment that whip tickled him under the tail, we had our first really exciting moment of that Sabbath Sunday morning.

I also learned right then and there about tickling horses under the tail with the end of a racing whip.

"Maple Street! Elm Street! Washington! Hickory! Home!"

29.

Well, sir, we had some fun for a few blocks.

I also learned a lot of other new things about driving a horse in a harness race. Hiawatha's tail never bothered me a bit after that. It stuck straight out behind him with me sitting under it like an umbrella.

There wasn't a blessed thing in this world I could do about it but hang on to the reins and holler: "Whoa! Whoa!"

That chestnut colt kept trotting up a cyclone. We went around our block four times without stopping. We took the corners on the dead run: Maple Street! Elm Street! Washington! Hickory!; Maple Street, Elm Street, Washington, Hickory! We flew around those blocks! And around two more times. Maple Stree, Elm Street, Washington, Hickory! Wow!

It was just like being in a regular horse race. Except I had the track all to myself. Not counting the time Hiawatha zipped around Mr. Buffington's loaded hayrack with Mr. Buffington on top. I didn't like the way the hayload slowly tipped over, and fell into the ditch. But I did like the way Mr. Buffington kept running up the falling bales like a dancer in the movies.

Apparently Mr. Buffington didn't like it, however. He kept screaming at us. Words a young boy shouldn't be hearing. Fortunately I couldn't hear much. Hiawatha was going so fast, Mr. Buffington sounded like a voice fading away as it falls down into a deep rocky canyon.

I pulled on the reins to try and stop Hiawatha, but lost one rein in the process. The big red horse went around in a sweeping circle at the intersection. I pulled violently on the other rein, and Hiawatha made a "U" turn and a bigger circle the other way.

I recovered the rein with the end of the whip, but accidentally brushed Hiawatha in an unpleasant place, and we were off again! Around the block in the opposite direction. No one was in command as Hiawatha went racing off.

Hickory! Washington! Elm! Maple!

Wow!!

By the way he picked up speed, I knew Hiawatha was heading for home.

My pet goose GOG kept flying after us running down the middle of the street, "honking!" for all he was worth. He flapped his wings and tried to fly up into the sulky beside me. No luck. He was a casualty. He finally took to the air in desperation. GOG made a big swoop and landed on top of Hiawatha's back.

I saw our neighbor Mrs. Casey throw open her bedroom window for a better look. She already had her telephone in her hand. She was shaking her head, and pointing her shaming finger at me.

"Shame on you!" she yelled. "Shame! Shame! With your grandfather away in Hill City! And your grandmother in church! In the house of God!"

"Swallow it!" I yelled back at her in the midst of my personal danger. "You old gooseberry gossip!"

Grandfather taught me that one. Besides I couldn't hear Mrs. Casey too well, what with GOG's "Honks!" and Hiawatha's "Whinnies!" and my "Whoas!"

But I did hear her yell as I went past her open window:

"I'm going to tell your grandfather!"

I knew that.

"And the town marshall!"

"Stuff it!" I yelled, hanging on for dear life, and having no time for Mrs. Casey.

"You can't keep this a secret, you wicked boy!" she shouted

after my rapidly retreating back.

You could never keep a secret of any kind in our town with Mrs. Casey and her telephone. Except the time she had acute laryngitis. There's no time to tell you about that. Pity.

Her threatening "Wait 'till your grandfather gets home!" was totally wasted on me. At that precise moment, Hiawatha suddenly swerved and raced into our own barnyard. He ran right up into Uncle Cliff's garage and stopped with his nose to the wall. He stopped so abruptly I went right out the front of the sulky and rolled up to the middle of Hiawatha's back. I fell in disgrace onto the stack of old used one quart oil cans. It made a wonderful racket as they rolled everywhere leaving oil traces along my entire body.

My first horse training workout was over.

"Who's that handsome young race driver, so brilliantly controlling that fierce-looking huge red stallion?"

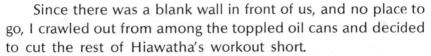

Since there was a blank wall in front of us, and no place to go, I crawled out from among the toppled oil cans and decided to cut the rest of Hiawatha's workout short.

I backed Hiawatha out of the garage by the bridle and backed him into Grandmother's vegetables. I turned the sulky, and led Hiawatha round the barn several times to cool him off. Then I unhitched him and put him back in his stall.

My heart was still pounding a mile a minute. I was scared stiff. But I'll tell you this, it was the kind of *scared-stiffness* you'd give your right arm all the way up to your shoulder, to enjoy every Sunday morning the rest of your whole darned life.

I even thought of writing a popular song called "Maple Street! Elm Street! Washington! Hickory! Home!" Maybe my Indian Uncle Walter and his Mississippi Jazz Bandits would write an arrangement of it for me.

No wonder Grandfather loved driving in harness races. His stock went up right through the ceiling as far as I was concerned, and poked a hole in the sky. I knew that I had never lived until the moment I had crawled up into that sulky and said, "Giddup!"

In fact, it was so exhilarating, and so bloody marvelous, that after I got over being sick to my stomach and throwing up twice behind the barn, I decided to try it out just one more time.

Both Hiawatha and I were temporarily pretty exhausted, so he was much more cooperative this time. Besides, I now knew how to hook him up to the holes in the harness myself.

I had been born again!

Hiawatha had worked off some of his extra steam, I guess. He really *was* a "fine fellow" this time and I told him so. Hiawatha was as docile as a baby in a buggy. With me sitting proudly in the sulky, Hiawatha and I walked slowly and elegantly all the way down Main Street to Potter and Casey's Store at the other end of town where the Northern Pacific Railroad tracks cross Main Street.

This time my pet goose, GOG, sat cockily up in the sulky beside me. I think GOG thought he was driving. The three of us waited patiently at the foot of Main Street until the ten o'clock Mass let out at St. James.

I knew that in about ten minutes Angela Raffodil would be walking down the street toward "Snob Town" where the Raffodil's lived. Once Angela saw me driving a real live race-horse in a brilliant red racing sulky, perhaps she'd have a different opinion about who was a small fry, too short, and too young for a date. Maybe Angela would realize that as a horse owner, trainer and driver, I was plenty old and mature enough for anyone.

Angela was Sam Raffodil's sister. That, of course, was already two strikes against her, but wow! Was she something! On her own, I mean.

I may have said that before. It was always hard for me to believe that both Sam and Angela had come out of the same bin. Angela was a real pea-cutter! A looker! Everybody said so, and this was my chance to twist her around my little finger.

The clock in the town hall tower boomed out the final stroke of eleven. Ten o'clock mass was out!

Slowly, I started Hiawatha walking up Main Street. His deep red chestnut coat glistened in the morning sun like the Indian head copper pennies I shined up for my coin collection.

The clop-clop-clop of his metal shoes on the hard packed gravel street had already attracted considerable attention among the early church leavers.

As soon as I saw Angela coming down the walk with her mother, Minnie-Ha! Ha!, I began to talk to Hiawatha with my hands, using the reins professionally the way my Grandfather had taught me. I was a different man entirely. A professional who had gained years of experience during my brief Maple Street! Elm Street! Washington! Hickory! Home! workout.

Hiawatha pricked up his ears, laid them back nervously, and went into a nice easy trot. I talked to him a little more and Hiawatha lengthened his stride. Pretty soon he was trotting along magnificently.

All eyes were on me. They were really on Hiawatha, but *some* of them were on me. No doubt people were saying, "Who's that handsome young race driver so brilliantly controlling that fierce-looking, huge red stallion?"

Of course, Hiawatha was only a young colt and not really a stallion, but boy, oh boy, was he *strutting* his stuff!

I knew that if Sam Raffodil Senior ever got a good look at Hiawatha, and the way his fantastic stride was eating up the ground on that Sunday morning, he'd have had a very queasy stomach approaching ulcers. He would begin hating himself all over again for ever selling Hiawatha to Grandfather even though he was dying at the time.

Mr. Raffodil had given that horse-doctoring old wizard the chance to save the little foal's life. Soon he'd be paying for it. Through the nose. Grandfather said that.

Since Mr. Raffodil never went to church unless Minnie Ha! Ha! made him, or somebody in the family died or got married, the chances of Mr. Raffodil seeing Hiawatha on this particular Sunday morning were slim.

But his beautiful daughter, Angela Raffodil, spotted me and pointed at me excitedly. Angela nudged her mother with her handbag. I couldn't hear what she was saying, but I knew it must be complimentary. Hiawatha and I were a sight to behold! Angela even waved encouragingly to me until her mother scolded her!

I had another bit of overflow luck, too. Margie Kelly and Sam Raffodil Junior were riding down Main Street side by side on their bicycles. Naturally, I ignored Margie's childish comment as she flew by. Margie almost fell off her bike when she recognized me. She whirled around, rode back, and shouted at me.

"William Sears! Will *you* ever catch it when your grandfather gets back from Hill City! You're not supposed to hitch up that chestnut colt by yourself. You know it!"

Fortunately her strident and unpleasant voice faded off into the distance as Hiawatha and I trotted on to our destiny.

The doomed vehicle.

31.

Gently I urged Hiawatha into his full trot. It was a magnificent sight to behold. Hiawatha's metal shoes made a very satisfying Boom! Boom! Boom! Boom! sound as they hit the dirt on Main Street. Hiawatha arched his neck, snorting loud and dramatically with every single high-stepping prance. Every now and then my goose, GOG, would holler out: "Honk! Honk!"

All three of us loved the attention we were getting. All three of us were naturally shy and retiring, but this was real admiration the crowd was giving us, real button-popping appreciation. They stopped and stared at us as though we were "some pumpkins!"

I think the eleven o'clock Mass was even better, although Jimmy Middleman plumped for the twelve o'clock.

I don't think Hiawatha would have bolted if Sam Raffodil Junior hadn't persecuted us during all three Mass performances. Several times he deliberately skimmed as close as he could to Hiawatha with his bicycle. When Sam passed right beside Hiawatha's ear, Sam jangled the bell on his handlebars as loudly as he could. He also screamed bloody murder.

In ten drama-packed seconds, I learned from firsthand experience what Grandfather said it took most apprentice harness racing drivers *years* to pick up. I also learned what Grandfather meant when he said you couldn't trust some young race horses who were still green, hard to manage, and unreliable. Especially when some horrible person tries to frighten them to death when they've already had a hard day.

And that's not *all* I learned.

Hiawatha shied toward the curb, broke his stride, and rose up on his hind legs. He went so high up into the air that even though I was still sitting in the sulky seat, I almost had my shoulders pinned down flat on Main Street.

Hiawatha's eyes were rolling. He jerked his head back and forth in fear. Snorted and rose up again on his hind legs. We went up and down violently three times with Hiawatha's front legs going in a circle like he was riding a bicycle himself.

GOG was "honking" frantically, walking up and down on me, balancing himself, first on my stomach, then on my head, as the sulky rose and fell.

Sam Raffodil Junior was laughing his head off. He kept jangling his bike bell as loudly as he could, waving his arms in Hiawatha's face and yelling "Run! Run! Run!"

Margie Kelly was trying to stop him.

Mr. Marty Barnes, the town butcher, was afraid Hiawatha was going to crash into the buggy where his wife and their three children were sitting. Mr. Barnes jumped out into the street and shook his whip in Hiawatha's face. He lashed him once across the neck leaving a mark. The surprise pain and attack drove Hiawatha crazy.

Hiawatha jumped for safety toward the middle of the street. I nearly snapped my neck off. It was like being shot out of the pouch of a sling shot. I barely hung on. I had the reins wrapped around my wrist the way Grandfather showed me, and which I had forgotten during our first workout when I lost the reins. Otherwise I might have rolled backwards all the way down to the Northern Pacific Depot.

I could hear Sam Raffodil's raucous "Hee Haw!" over the jangling of his bicycle bell. Margie Kelly kept shouting, "Be *careful,* William! Stop that Sam!" Hiawatha finally took Sam Raffodil Junior's advice and began to run. I mean *RUN!*

In a flash, I couldn't hear anything. Only the wind in my ears. Hiawatha was racing down Main Street for all he was worth. We were flying toward the main intersection at Church Street and Main in the heart of downtown Green Valley. We were roaring along like the Twin Cities Express.

Two brand new motor cars were innocently heading for each other, toward that same Main Street intersection. I was roaring toward them from an entirely different direction.

All three of us were timed by fate to arrive at the center of that intersection at exactly the same time.

I began to wish that I had gone to church myself, or had stayed in bed, or had never heard of a red race horse named Hiawatha.

As I saw the two cars and the bright red racing sulky coming into the biggest and most popular intersection in our town, I prepared for the worst. I gritted my teeth and hung on. I groaned:

"Too late!"

GOG decided to fly overhead rather than stay on board such a doomed vehicle.

"Ahooouuuaah! Ahooouuuaah!"

Quite obviously it was going to be a head-on three vehicle crash. Two brand-new motor cars, one horse, and one brand-new race driver who wished he were back home with the easy stuff:

Maple Street, Elm Street, Washington, Hickory! Home!

I had to do something quick. But what? Hollering at the cars at the top of my voice, "Clear the road!" hadn't worked at all.

The two cars were speeding blissfully along toward the intersection quite unaware of each other, and both totally unaware of a world champion trotting horse making his first big run down the center of Main Street.

Hiawatha and I were on a collision course with two very important persons in our town.

It was destiny that we all arrived at the exact same time. There were eye-witnesses on all four corners. I wasn't one of them.

I had my eyes closed and I was yelling a mixture of "Whoa! Hiawatha!" and "Hail Mary full of grace," and I knew I couldn't count much on either.

Hiawatha finally roared into view of the two drivers. It startled them. The drivers of the two vehicles applied their brakes violently and swerved. Unfortunately, they swerved toward, rather than away from each other!

The cars were both shiny new tin-lizzy Fords. One was being driven by Mayor Sam Raffodil Senior; the other one was being steered happily by its proud new owner, Mr. Carl Anderson, the town marshall, who had saved up for seven years to buy the car. He had told everybody that all week long.

Both of their automobile horns were blaring out warnings at me:

"Aaahhhooouuuah! Aaahhhooouuuah!"

That's when my goose GOG deserted me and flew up overhead for safety.

I tried to slow Hiawatha down by tugging gently backwards on the reins. I forgot that Grandfather had warned me to be very careful about doing that to Hiawatha. It meant *speed up,* not *slow down.* Hiawatha felt the gentle pull, and took off as though Grandfather had hollered "Go!" at the top of the homestretch.

Hiawatha streaked for the opening between the two Model-T cars. I was sure he would never make it. One of the cars blared out its claxon horn again:

"AAAHHOOOOUUUAH!"

In a flash, Hiawatha whipped the sulky forward toward that rapidly closing bit of daylight, and Zing! he popped us through like a watermelon seed shooting out of your fingers. I'm telling you, Hiawatha zipped himself, me, and the sulky, all three, right through that tiny narrow gap without hitting anything! Without a scratch or a sound except for a slight "tick" on the very back of the sulky seat from a front fender.

GOG was honking his head off from up above trying to tell Hiawatha what to do.

"Honk!" he hollered his dire warning to the red horse.

The automobile horns honked in reply. That's what saved my day. When the horns continued to blare out:

"Aaaahhhooouuuah!" Hiawatha took off as though he had a twelve o'clock luncheon date in Duluth. The two cars, at full speed, trying to avoid Hiawatha, swerved headlong toward each other with brakes squealing louder than the drivers. They smashed head-on, plowing into each other with a crunching, sideswiping door-crumbling crash!! The sound confirmed the nickname "Tin Lizzies."

Everyone was upset by the noise. Elmo Peterson said the mayor and Marshall Anderson put on a lot better show than the twelve o'clock Mass, but, of course, he is a Lutheran.

Mr. Raffodil, going east, had turned left; and Marshall Anderson, going west, had also turned left. I didn't find out until later that Mr. Raffodil Senior lost two fenders, and that Marshall Anderson went sliding out over the open turned-down windshield of his sports roadster. He slid forward out along the hood and down onto the street, and then slid on for quite a distance.

Both Mr. Raffodil and Marshall Anderson had been trying out their new Ford cars for the first time. They had just arrived that week from the factory in Detroit.

Fortunately, neither Mr. Raffodil nor Mr. Anderson was seriously hurt, other than their feelings, and small things which their lawyers for purposes of litigation and lawsuits described as superficial bruises, contusions, and supreme indignity.

They were both blistering mad however, about having to scrape up the loose parts of their new automobiles off Main Street. And the marshall did skin himself a little sliding down onto the road and beyond, doing nasty things to the knees of his new Sunday going-to-church suit.

And you know who they blamed.

"Over the river and through the woods
with Grandfather's horse I go!"

33.

By that time, Hiawatha was striding along in his best racing form, going like the wind toward the foot of Main Street. If this had been the county fair, I'm sure we would have won the big stakes race hands down, no matter what horse Mr. Raffodil brought in from New York. GOG had circled the sulky twice, but finally zoomed down and landed on my head.

The only further bad luck we had was caused by two more automobiles. The first car saw us coming and blew its horn: "Aaaahhhooouuuah!" Hiawatha went three wide, missed the ditch, and wheeled on lickety-split. Every time Hiawatha heard that "Aaaahhhooouuuah," he threw himself into a higher gear and went even faster.

He breezed past the Dow Lumber Company, Tong Lee's Chinese Laundry, the Oakleaf Dairy, the Soo Line railroad tracks, and skimmed alongside the swampy marsh lands that led toward the old Mississippi River bridge.

The second car turned out of the freight yards in front of us, its horn hollering out a warning: "Aaaahhhooouuuah!" Aaaahhhooouuuah!"

The horn sent Hiawatha blazing up over the old Mississippi River bridge. The loose boards rattled a tattoo: bang! bang! bang!, and the whizzing sulky wheels went "whoosh! whoosh! whoosh! whoosh! between the side struts of the narrow bridge. Both GOG and I were still hanging on for dear life.

In no time, Hiawatha was down the north bridge ramp and

out into the countryside. He must have been on his second or third wind by then. My hands were raw red from hanging onto the reins. My shoulders were numb, and GOG's feathers were much the worse for the wind, too.

GOG hadn't been able to keep his balance as the sulky careened around some of the corners, so I had to grab him by one leg with my free hand, and drive with the other. The goose didn't add to the Sunday morning quiet. He flapped his wings and screeched out, "Honk! Honk! Honk!" Some of the worst "honks" I ever heard. He was really bedraggled. If I hadn't been so busy I'd have laughed at him, he looked so awful. I learned what it meant to have ruffled feathers.

People peeked out of their parlor curtains. Doors and windows popped open. There was a lot of disapproving teeth clucking and "Shame on you!" head shaking, as Hiawatha, GOG and I shattered the serene Green Valley Sunday Sabbath right down the middle.

To me it will always be:

"Suicide Sunday!"

Hiawatha never broke stride once on that fantastic run. Not even when the "Aaaahhhooouuuah!" horns kept bellowing, or when people waved their hats at him, and bravely ran out into the street to try and flag down the runaway, and save that young boy and his goose. They thought Hiawatha was out of control and that I was in grave danger!

I was. We both were. All three of us. Hiawatha, GOG and myself were all scared to death, but having the time of our lives.

Hiawatha zoomed between the people, dipping down into a ditch and up the other side to avoid children, zipping around vehicles and buggies, scattering the Sunday-going-home-from-church crowd like ducks fleeing in terror from a mad fox.

It began to look as though Hiawatha was going to run all the way to Hill City to complain to Grandfather about the way I was treating him. The more trouble Hiawatha encountered while escaping from town, the faster he ran. The farther Hiawatha trotted, the stronger he became. Faster and faster.

It was downright bloody marvelous! I wasn't in grave danger. I was in heaven! I was so excited, I yelled out loud with happiness. I knew that nothing was going to stop that big red horse until he had run himself out.

If this horse wasn't ready for *this* year's County Fair Stakes, I wasn't a judge of horse flesh. He would make mincemeat out of all the Raffodil's, including their fancy imported horse.

"Wait until I tell Grandfather!" I hollered to Hiawatha when he finally did slow down. I jumped off the sulky and threw myself around his neck and rubbed his soft velvet nose which I now knew would be way out in front at the finish line of the big County Stakes race.

"Hot diggety dog, you wonderful horse," I cried.

I danced a little jig on the country road.

To my sudden horror, I realized I could never tell Grandfather the truth. Not unless I wanted to be skinned alive myself before the big race came. Grandfather could be prickly mean and bodily-threatening cruel if there was the faintest hint of horse abuse.

Here I was with the perfect certain answer to all our problems, but I couldn't breathe a word because I'd disobeyed Grandfather. I had taken Hiawatha out on my own. Now, I would have to swallow all my good news, and remain totally silent about what I knew. I couldn't tell Grandfather that he had the fastest-running long-distance horse our small country valley had ever seen.

I practiced ways I could break the joyous news to him:

"A funny thing happened to me, Grandfather, when I was racing over the old Mississippi River bridge."

Then I could hear those loose planks go Bang! Bang! Bang! Bang!, and Hiawatha's *legs* go with them!

If I knew what was good for me, I'd keep my mouth shut.

Hundreds of eyewitnesses for my grandfather!

34.

I was back in the sulky, and Hiawatha was going along home at a leisurely recovery-room lazy trot. I was cooling him off after his miraculous Sunday morning run. That's when I noticed that we were way out at the old Joe Anderson farm, about three miles outside of town.

GOG had given up trying to ride atop my head or sit beside me on the buggy seat. He flew up to his favorite and safer perch on Hiawatha's back. GOG was still sore about my hanging onto his leg and pulling him back to safety several times. GOG didn't understand about rescue work, only pain and discomfort. He beak-bit me several times on the hand trying to get away.

Old Joe Anderson was standing by his front gate watching us approach. Old Joe never went to church on Sundays. His wife went. Old Joe said that since he didn't believe in God he wasn't going to be a hypocrite like some people he could mention who didn't believe in God either and only went to church because it was good for business. Old Joe Anderson talked that way, without punctuation.

"You trying to kill that horse?" he hollered at me. "I saw the speed at which you were driving him."

"No, sir," I protested. "The shoe was on the other foot. I've been trying to get this horse to slow down and stop running since Main Street."

Old Joe Anderson didn't believe me.

"You telling me that Hiawatha horse ran like that all the way out here from downtown?!"

"No. In town he was slower, but when he hit the Mississippi River bridge, those bang, bang planks set him off. Zoom!"

"That's a lie!" Old Joe scoffed. "Impossible!"

"Maybe so, but Hiawatha did it just the same!"

I turned Hiawatha around, jumped off the sulky, and began to walk him slowly back toward town, the final step in cooling him off properly. Grandfather said it had to be done gradually and thoroughly. I knew that was important. Warm up slowly, "scoring" a few times around the track well before the race, then cool off your animal gradually after. As assistant trainer I had to know those things.

Old Joe Anderson was at me again.

"Your Grandfather ought to have more sense than to let a snot-nosed kid like you run a good horse to death."

He bellowed it at me rather than just saying it quietly.

"My grandfather's in Hill City," I told him. "My driving Hiawatha like this was all sort of an accident."

"I suppose the horse hitched himself up by accident?"

"Actually," I replied evasively, "it was a peculiar circumstance the way Hiawatha got hitched up."

Old Joe Anderson not only didn't believe in God, he didn't believe in peculiar hitching-up circumstances, either.

"You young mealy-mouthed kids are all alike," he snarled. "You not only steal me blind in my watermelon patch, but you lie about how far and how fast a horse can run. What's the younger generation coming to?"

"I don't know," I told him, honestly.

"Well, *I* do!" he barked. "Get off my property."

"This property," I told him, "is a public road. It happens to belong to the County of—"

"Get off it!"

"Yes, *sir!*"

I jumped up into the sulky and Hiawatha whisked me out of firing range, then I jumped off again to continue the necessary cooling-off period. The three of us, actually two of us, walked toward home. GOG waddled over to the center of my seat on the sulky like he was driving. Old Joe Anderson yelled sarcastically down the road at us.

"The goose is a better driver than you are, kid! Probably knows more about horses, too."

I ignored him, other than saying some very bad things under my breath. Old Joe kept shouting at us but I tried not to listen. I did hear a few "grandfathers" and "telephones" and "you'll be sorrys"—things like that. All of which I had heard many times before. I put my fingers in my ears so I wouldn't hear any more.

I was exhausted, but I was also exhilarated. I didn't want any more trouble. Nor anything to interfere with the pleasure of our thrilling Sunday morning workout. Besides, all three of us had more than enough workout for one day. At that, Hiawatha looked better than I did. My hands were all swollen up from hanging onto the leather reins; my tail was really dragging.

I walked Hiawatha slowly around my Grandfather's barn, going via Maple Street, Elm Street, Washington, Hickory, then home.

It took forever! *Walking.*

Needed: A ton of hatching and plotting.

I finally unhitched Hiawatha and led him into the barn. I threw a blanket over him after he walked into his stall. Hiawatha went right off to sleep standing up.

When I came out of the barn, Mrs. Casey was sitting by her window, holding her binoculars in one hand, and the telephone in the other. She obviously was still spreading the news all over town. I heard Mrs. Casey say into the phone, rather disappointedly, "They're all home alive anyway." She yelled across at me, "So you're back. After half killing that horse!"

Mrs. Casey returned to the telephone. As I headed up to the house, she shouted after me, "Everybody knows what you've done while your grandfather was away."

"Thanks to you!"

"And he'll know every last detail as soon as he gets home."

I knew he would if Mrs. Casey had anything to do with it. Chances were she'd already been on the party line with the post mistress, "Glad Tidings." Another carrier.

Not of mail or disease, but gossip.

While lying in bed exhausted, with every bone in my body crying out in agony, especially my arms and shoulders, I realized I'd have to think up a remarkably good story to explain to Grandfather why I'd given Hiawatha the Sunday workout. It would have to be a logical story that didn't conflict too much in basic fundamentals with what he'd probably hear by morning from several hundred eyewitnesses. With sordid details added by Gladys Tidings at the post office. They called her "Glad" Tidings, though most of the stuff she repeated was sad.*

I wasn't worried. Grandfather refused to talk to Mrs. Casey, ever. Grandfather had told Mrs. Casey to her face that she was a blabbering—whatever rhymes with ditch—and should go soak her head in a rain barrel. So, I was safe there.

I telephoned Raffodil's house that night on the chance that Angela might answer. Wow! Was she something! I wanted to get Angela's own eyewitness reaction to my wild sulky ride down the middle of Main Street. I figured some personal good should come from such a courageous and dangerous ride. To offset the bad which I knew would soon be on the way. Sam Raffodil Junior answered the phone, so I made believe I was Chinese and hung up.

When I called Margie Kelly, a poor second choice as an eyewitness to anything, she hung up. After yelling herself hoarse and not letting me get a word in. "You could have killed yourself!" she shouted. "And don't ask me to go to the county fair with you. My parents say you're altogether too irresponsible. Don't ever dare speak to me again as long as you live. Ever! Not in public nor in private. You hear me? *You* are icky!"

So much for fame.

Margie Kelly had been telling me for years not to dare speak to her again, ever, as long as I lived, either in public or in private, so I didn't go into a decline over it. Besides, Margie Kelly's parents thought everybody was irresponsible, except Baptists, and Margie's older brother Arthur who really *was* irresponsible, not to mention impossible. But that's another story. And far too depressing to repeat here, the way I was feeling right then.

Okey?

---

* Did I say that before? Good! It bears repeating.

I had a ton of "hatching and plotting" to do all on my own before my grandfather came back from Hill City. I sat on the oats box until it was dark, and couldn't come up with a blessed thing. Except to throw myself on the mercy of the court which I knew meant hanging by the neck until you were dead.

Hiawatha and GOG whinned and honked sympathetically in the barn, but their stuff wasn't any good either.

All's well that ends.

I waited all week for Grandfather to say something about my now notorious Sunday Sabbath workout.

But he didn't.

That worried me. I did notice how carefully Grandfather went over Hiawatha the morning after he came home from Hill City. Carefully, inch by inch, from head to all four hooves. Making ominous Grandfather noises throughout.

Still, he never said a single word to me.

"Can I help you with that, Grandfather?" I asked.

He gave me the old icy eyeballs, stabbing me with a few icicles, but remained silent. I didn't like the feel of the atmosphere in the barn at all. In fact, for the entire first week after his trip to Hill City, the stable, the stalls, even the oats box had a wind-chill-factor of a bitter winter frost.

I was certain Grandfather knew every last detail concerning my famous Sunday sulky ride. Both truth and lies. Everyone else in our town knew exactly what had happened, why shouldn't Grandfather?

Some people claimed that the famous Sunday automobile crash on Main Street could be heard all the way down to the sawmill. Everybody was talking about it. You can't expect over three thousand people in a small town to keep their mouths shut. I'd never had any luck with even one person. Margie Kelly for instance.

I asked my friend Jimmy Middleman, who said he had heard

on the way home from church exactly what the people were saying about me personally.

"Is it good or bad?" I asked him anxiously.

"Mixed reviews."

I knew that our nosey neighbor, Mrs. Casey, had been spreading the worst side of the story, long before Hiawatha had reached the arches of the Mississippi River bridge. Grandfather once remarked that if we ever had a newspaper strike, all we had to do was to supply Mrs. Casey with a few extra phones,and we'd have quicker and better coverage than the *Duluth Herald* and the *Minneapolis Star Journal* combined.

I became certain that Grandfather knew all about my wild ride when I saw Mr. Raffodil's lawyer going in and out of Grandfather's house several times in one day. And once even the town marshall. Grandfather didn't look very pleased about either visit. I knew it must be about the car crash since they came with their attorneys. Mr. Raffodil came with three.

Grandfather always said he wouldn't cross the street to see a lawyer unless they were going to hang him—the lawyer, not Grandfather. Grandfather also said that every time he went into a law office those attorneys "whereased" and "wheretofored" him out of a few more hard earned horse trading dollars. Of course, of late he'd been dealing mostly with Mr. Raffodil's sharp city lawyers. Whenever they were needed, they came into town on the Midnight Express from Duluth.

If you're an attorney or lawyer yourself, don't take offense. Grandfather always tried to be fair. "A good honest attorney," he said, "who doesn't talk like a museum parchment is the salt of the earth. It's a pity there aren't any in this town."

Grandfather always says that it's hard to get good craftsmanship any more in almost every profession. People don't care, and don't turn out the first-class work you used to get in the past from carpenters, plumbers, doctors—almost anybody. Integrity is leaking away its life in almost every phase of living. Grandfather is always harping about the old days.

"The old days may have been outclassed by the present,"

he admitted, "but the workmanship was better then and people were proud of it."

I have to be careful about saying, "Grandfather *always* says" because he's death on that. Grandfather says the people who always say always are double losers. When you're talking to your wife, a friend, or even an enemy, the temptation is to unjustly accuse them, saying: "You *always* do this or that." They don't really.

Nobody "always" says anything. According to Grandfather, that phrase breaks up marriages, ends love affairs and is responsible for cooled-off friendships everywhere. Even your family can say it often enough to burn your biscuit. Whenever you say "always" it weakens your case. It isn't true, and you haven't been fair.

Does this mean anything to you? Me, neither. I was just trying to keep from thinking about how that Hiawatha horse had gobbled up the ground crossing the Mississippi River, and how I could tell Grandfather.

I was bursting to share with Grandfather the entire wonderful story about Hiawatha running like the wind for over two miles. I wanted to assure him that Hiawatha was the fastest race horse in all the world. That he *could* win the big county fair race. He *could!* Hands down! Hiawatha *didn't* have to wait another year. Hiawatha was ready right now! And I was the hairpin who *knew* it. I wanted to tell Grandfather that the longer the race, the better. Hiawatha could run all day. I mean *all day!* I'd have to admit that I learned all that by accident and under circumstances unfavorable to my reputation as a reliable grandson and horse trainer; but that I'd paid for it already. Through the nose.

My poor body, shoulders and hands still hadn't recovered after a full week. But I didn't care. All I cared about was finding a way to tell that icy-cold old man that he had a hot horse. But I couldn't breathe a word of it. It had to come from him. I'd waited so long, it was killing me.

The tension between Grandfather and myself began to ease off as my aching bones recovered. One day, Grandfather finally chuckled. He even roughed up my hair in a friendly way. Earlier in the week when he had roughed it up he pulled a few hairs loose, and once when he swung the pitchfork handle around he caught me across the rump and accidentally butted me into the wall of Hiawatha's stall. Another time he patted me jovially on the back and knocked me into the oats bin. I was pretty sure it had something to do with my Sabbath Sunday sulky ride.

But now at least we were friends again. Sort of, anyway. Or would be when Grandfather started talking to me again.

Grandfather never mentioned a single word about my famous workout. I think he knew I'd learned a pretty good lesson from it all by myself without a sermon from him. Also I was already a little black and blue from his many kindnesses to me during that first week.

The Town Marshall pried them apart.

37.

Mr. Raffodil sued Grandfather for the damages to his car. The town marshall, Carl Anderson, sued Mr. Raffodil for being on the wrong side of the street. Mr. Raffodil claimed that Hiawatha drove him over there on purpose. Mr. Raffodil held Grandfather directly responsible for almost everything that happened to him. He was only too pleased to add the criminal actions of his grandson. Me. Who was a minor.

Grandfather managed to keep me out of the court case somehow. The best part was when Mr. Raffodil had to pay all the damages himself. His lawsuit backfired. It cost Mr. Raffodil more money than the price he had charged Grandfather for Hiawatha in the first place.

The judge was on my side. He said it was *not*, in his opinion, reckless driving to guide a running horse between two treacherous, speeding gas-propelled modern automobiles without touching either one. Of course, automobiles were not the most popular thing in our town just then. Especially with Judge Becker, who raised horses.

Besides, according to Judge Becker, everybody in their right mind knew that such a passing fad as the automobile would never replace the horse. Such mechanical contraptions were, in fact, a menace on our public streets. End of quote from Judge Becker.

Mr. Raffodil was particularly upset because it had been Hiawatha who personally had caused him to pay out all of that money in damages. The red horse was beginning to get under

Mr. Raffodil's skin, not to mention inside his wallet where the pain was much more aggravating. Hiawatha was already getting even with Mr. Raffodil and he hadn't even run in a race yet.

"This is only the beginning, Sam," Grandfather told Mr. Raffodil, sticking it in and twisting it on the courthouse steps. "Someday that chestnut horse is going to cost you your shirt where it will really hurt. In the big race, the County Fair Stakes."

"The day you enter that red horse in a race against me, old man," Mr. Raffodil vowed, "will be a day you'll regret as long as you live. And it'll be a race you'll never win. Never! I promise you that!"

Grandfather offered Mr. Raffodil a wonderful healing remedy for his black and blue bruises from the car crash.

"Leeches, Sam," Grandfather said. "Use leeches. A secret Indian remedy. Bloodsuckers, Sam, like yourself."

The town marshall had to pry them apart again.

The judge did have one serious recommendation for Grandfather before the court broke up.

"You'd be a lot better off," Judge Becker suggested, "if you'd put the harness on your grandson, and turn the chestnut colt loose."

Grandfather's face told me he agreed completely with the judge.

"It's lonesome in the barn when no one talks to anybody."

38.

"Are you still mad at me, Grandfather?"

Silence.

Grandfather had never asked me about Hiawatha's miracle Sunday run that had astonished all of Green Valley. People were still gossiping about my wild Sunday Sabbath ride down Main Street.

Since the deputy sheriff's visit, and two more later, Grandfather had remained outwardly friendly, but inwardly arctic. His comments were still on the distant, chilly side. I could tell he wasn't thawed out yet as long as he kept saying:

"Hiawatha, will you tell this close friend of yours to get some more clover down into these mangers?"

I made believe Hiawatha had told me, and pitched the hay down.

"Thank the boy, if you will, Hiawatha."

"I can hear you, Grandfather. I don't need any horse to tell me what to do."

But, Grandfather was no longer Alaska, he was becoming Canada and sometimes even as far south as our own state, Minnesota. Of course, it didn't help any when we went shopping together downtown in the buggy to have people look at me, then quickly turn their heads away, and giggle. Then whisper to each other with even louder giggles, pointing at me with their heads.

"Morning, ladies," Grandfather would say cheerfully. "I think you know my grandson."

They fled like a gaggle of geese hardly able to suppress their laughter. Grandfather accidentally poked me on the toe of my tennis shoe with his cane, forcefully enough to get my attention. The toe had become quite tender during the past week. Grandfather pointed his cane at the still retreating backs of the giggling young ladies.

"You," he said, "seem to be the cynosure of all eyes."

"If that means what I *think* it does, it's a lie!"

"Your grandmother keeps getting anonymous phone calls asking to speak to the *Mighty Sabbath-Breaker.* She keeps asking me who that could be. Any ideas?"

"It beats me," I told him.

"It could come to that," he said, missing my tennis shoe this time.

I tried to break the ice on the way home.

"Are you still mad at me, Grandfather?"

"No," he said, wearily, "I'm not angry. Just disappointed."

"Not nearly as disappointed as I am myself," I told him.

"I'm glad you learned a lesson."

"Did you see the perfect star in the left front hoof of Hiawatha?" I asked. "That's where he kicked the sprocket of Sam Raffodil's bicycle on that Sunday morning when Sam teased him and tried to get him to bolt."

"I saw it."

"I'm sorry Hiawatha didn't kick Sam in the seat of the pants instead."

"That wasn't the kind of disappointment I meant."

"I know. You were disappointed in *me.* But I'm glad you're speaking to me again. It's lonesome in the barn when no one talks to anybody."

"I couldn't trust myself to speak the first week or so."

Then Grandfather chuckled very nicely, and I knew that everything was all right again, or fairly all right. Especially when we sat down on the oats box together.

"Why didn't you buy the trotter in Hill City?" I asked him.

"Too much money, and too slow. It's beginning to look as though we'll just have to take our licking this year. We can't win it with Tropical or Dakar. We need a horse at least four seconds faster. No one around these parts knows where I can find such a horse."

"I know where, Grandfather. But he's at least ten seconds faster."

Grandfather eyed me suspiciously. "You do?"

"And how!"

"And where might this world-beater trotting horse be hiding?"

I jumped off the oats box and ran to Hiawatha and swatted him on the rump. He danced away.

"Right here!" I shouted. "It's Hiawatha!"

GOG honked and Hiawatha whinnied. He danced another step or two, showing he agreed with GOG. I hurried back to the oats box.

"Honestly, Grandfather, I think Hiawatha's ready to run a wonderful race."

Grandfather shook his head. "Not this year."

"Yes, this year!"

"Later perhaps."

"Not later, *now!*"

Grandfather was patient. He shook his head. "It's a big mistake to try and bring young horses along too fast. Even if they can outrun the wind in emergencies. That can fool you. I told you that."

"Yeah, but Hiawatha—"

"I've always been against racing two year olds, son. You know that. Even in short sprints. Sometimes even three year olds like Hiawatha. Especially when they've had a history of poor health and spindly legs. It's not fair to the horse, son. Hiawatha will get his chance later. I promise you."

"Hiawatha's legs are tough as hickory," I told Grandfather, remembering the pounding his legs had taken on the hard dirt road and across the long wooden Mississippi River bridge.

"He may have hidden weaknesses that won't show up until we work him hard."

"He's *been* worked hard! Real hard," I objected.

Grandfather waved me aside. "Besides," he added, "Sam Raffodil is bringing in the finest trotting horse money can buy. A proven champion. Sam is determined to take the county fair driving championship away from us this year."

"He'll never do that! Not if you give Hiawatha a chance."

"He might. I hear tell he's sent all the way to Goshen, New York again, and has purchased the winner of last year's biggest stakes race, the Hambletonian."

"Is that bad?"

"It's not good. They tell me the horse has blood lines that go all the way back to that grand champion, Uhlan."

"That *is* bad!"

"It about sews up the big race for Sam Raffodil."

"Isn't that illegal? Bringing in a horse not raised in this state?"

"It *was* illegal, up to this year."

"So?"

"Sam Raffodil's working on it. He has enough influence to get the rules changed."

"That's crooked."

"Isn't it though. But Sam has the pull."

"You mean he has the money."

"It doesn't hurt."

"Can't we hatch and plot?"

"We can try, son."

"I wish you'd let me tell you about Hiawatha."

Grandfather shook his head, and gave me a grizzly bear hug and a fierce whisker-rub. I was so sad (and mad), that I forgot to say:

"I *hate* that!"

The Fourth Furlong!

"Boom! Boom! Boom! Boom!

39.

A few days later I finally screwed up the courage to tell Grandfather all about Hiawatha's wild ride over the Mississippi River bridge. I didn't care what it cost me. I had to tell him. I wanted him to know that he was wrong about Hiawatha's legs. They were tough. And he *had* been worked hard. By *me.* Accidentally, of course, but I was sure Hiawatha had no hidden weaknesses. Not one. He was a winner!

Even if Grandfather fired me as assistant trainer, I made him listen. Grandfather put down the harness he was working on and told me to go ahead and get it out of my system.

"It was fantastic!" I glowed. "Whoooosh! Hiawatha kept going faster and faster. The farther he ran the faster he went. He was much better when he got over the Mississippi River bridge than he was when he was racing in between the cars down Main Street."

Grandfather winced at the thought. His friendly hand on my knee grew sort of clutchy and claw-like.

"And when Hiawatha hit that old Mississippi River bridge," I exclaimed, "Boom! Boom! Boom! Boom! He kept firing off those old planks until it sounded like cannon fire aimed at Sam Raffodil's head."

Grandfather showed his anxiety. I could see he didn't like the picture of Hiawatha racing over such a leg-breaking course. But he *was* interested in how far and how fast Hiawatha had run.

I could tell Grandfather was pleased about Hiawatha's speed and stamina, but miffed with me for endangering his precious horseflesh by letting Hiawatha run away.

"I didn't run away with Hiawatha," I protested. "Hiawatha ran away with me."

"I suppose Hiawatha escaped from his stall and hitched himself up to the sulky all by himself, too?"

Grandfather's eyeballs were icy. I hurried on to explain.

"If I hadn't done it, you'd never know how marvelous Hiawatha is right now, and ready to run."

"It's good to have the expert opinion of a veteran professional race horse trainer," Grandfather said, giving me a frosty wintry look. "There's nothing to beat experience and good judgement in those things. Maybe we should call in Saphead Phillips for a second opinion."

I got sore.

"Okey! So it was only my first ride. I'm telling you that Hiawatha horse *flew* over the ground like a Halloween witch on a broomstick! He was absolutely fantastic! No matter *what* I say about how good Hiawatha was, he was much better than that. So sue me!"

I walked out of the barn and didn't come back until it was time for evening chores. As soon as I walked in, I could tell that Grandfather had been pleased by my news about Hiawatha, even if he had been miffed with me for taking such terrible chances with his precious horse.

Grandfather was right, of course. But *I* wasn't the one who took the chances, it was Hiawatha. I didn't have a thing to do about it after that first "Ahooouuuaah" horn. I was an innocent victim of circumstances.

But try and tell Grandfather that. He would come up with that same smart-aleck comment, "I suppose Hiawatha hitched himself up and threw you into the sulky." Stuff like that. But Grandfather was keenly interested in how far and how fast Hiawatha had run on that Sunday morning.

"Tell me again," he said. "Slowly, and with more details."

He raised one eyebrow up like a teepee. I seized my chance.

"Yes, *sir!* Hiawatha must have run three miles lickety-split."

"Old Joe Anderson's farm is only two-and-a-half miles from town," he corrected.

"Okey! Two and a *half* miles. It only seemed like five furlongs! That red horse *flew.* Cross my heart and hope to die!" Suddenly I felt queer. I looked at Grandfather suspiciously. "How did you know Hiawatha ran all the way out to Old Joe Anderson's farm?"

"I have friends out that way."

"Spies, you mean!"

Grandfather chuckled. "Old Joe himself told me, but his story was confirmed by several eyewitnesses along the way peeking out their curtains, standing on their porches, and reporting to each other!"

"And to you! I hate that Mrs. Casey and her friend old 'Glad Tidings!' "

"They were only the least of some several hundred eyewitnesses."

"There's no privacy any more."

"Not if you race a magnificent horse down Main Street when church lets out after three separate Masses, and scramble a few automobiles, and wake up the entire countryside screaming 'whoas!' mingled with wild goose 'honks!' and 'aaahooouuh!' automobile horns. It's pretty hard to keep all that a secret." Grandfather tousled my hair, chuckling and hooking his little finger in a snarl and pulling. Hard.

I changed the subject. "Hiawatha was magnificent though, wasn't he?"

"We'll see."

"He was! And, Grandfather, isn't it strange that 'aoooh-hoouuah!' automobile horns make Ebony sit down, but make Hiawatha run like the wind?"

Grandfather gave me a big whisker-rub and cackled merrily. "You knew, of course, that Hiawatha's dame, Mignonette, was by Moon Shadows out of Gold Bullion."

"No, I didn't."

"She was."

"Is that good?"

"Gold Bullion was probably the greatest distance trotter ever bred."

"Not any more, he isn't," I argued. "He now has a great-great-grandson that can give him a mile head start and knock him for a loop. I mean a really *great* great-grandson. The very greatest! And he's standing right over there in that stall eating clover, and is just waiting to be entered in this year's County Fair Stakes. So he can win it. Everybody stand up and take your hats off!"

I stood up myself and gave Hiawatha a military salute.

"Try to hold it down a little," Grandfather suggested. "I'm beginning to detect the slight odor of hyperbole and prejudice."

"Just you wait until you see Hiawatha run over a piece of ground. He'll knock your eyes out. He could run all the way to Hill City and be back before dinner with the mail."

Grandfather cocked another teepee-tent eyebrow at me and made them go up and down alternately. He's the only person I know who can do that. Grandfather did that whenever he felt I was "embroidering" the truth. I could never make my own eyes do that even though I practiced by the hour in front of a mirror.

I shrugged.

"Perhaps there *is* a mite of exaggeration in there," I admitted. "But just a mite."

That was one of Grandfather's favorite expressions when I caught him slicing the baloney too thick himself. But at least we were full friends again. The crackling electric storm atmosphere inside the barn that might explode any minute was over. Things were back to normal.

"Two and a half miles, you say."

Grandfather began to chuckle to himself again. As he curried down Hiawatha, he began to hum:

"Back Home in Indiana."

"Look out, Sam Raffodil!" I whispered to myself.

"Thunderbolt!"

40.

The next morning Grandfather rose at dawn and took Hiawatha down to the fairgrounds for a secret workout all by himself.

I ran down to the barn just in time to see the sulky and Grandfather's back moving off into the morning mist. I started to run after them, but Grandfather hollered at me.

"Get after the chores! This little workout is strictly between this red horse and me."

They were back shortly after the sun came up. Grandfather looked as though he had swallowed Sam Raffodil Senior whole. His smile went around both sides of his face, and up into his ear holes. He was humming happily to himself, "This little piggy had roast beef."

"How was Hiawatha?" I asked, helping him unhitch.

"There is a time," he said, "in the affairs of men which if taken at the flood leads on to fortune."

"For gosh sakes, what does that mean?"

"Shakespeare said that. And how right he was."

Grandfather cackled to himself while he was unhitching Hiawatha. He harnessed up the team of dapple greys, Shadrach and Meshach to the Abednego buggy and motioned for me to crawl up beside him.

"I've just been informed that Sam Raffodil's grand champion trotter from Goshen, New York, is about to arrive at the Northern Pacific freight yards on the nine-fifteen 'flyer' from Minneapolis."

"Mrs. Casey?"

"Glad Tidings."

Grandfather helped me up into the buggy.

"Let's go down to the depot," he said, "and take a look at this new wonder horse. He is arriving in his own private express car."

Grandfather was still chuckling to himself.

"What's so funny?" I asked.

Grandfather whisked the palm of his hand across the front of my eyes. "Whoosh!" he said.

"Hiawatha?"

He nodded.

"Just like I said?"

"Just like."

"I said whoosh! first, remember."

"You'll get full credit."

"That's great!"

"It's against the fifth commandment," Grandfather said, "but we'll do it anyway."

"Come again?"

"Thou shalt not steal."

"Steal what?"

"The County Fair Stakes."

Grandfather laughed out loud and tickled Shadrach and Meshach under the tail with the whip in his left hand, and grabbed for my kneecap with his right. While I was off balance, the horses leaped into action, and I wound up in the back seat of the buggy again.

There was a big crowd at the station. Half of them were the regular train meeters, but the other half were there out of curiosity. They came to see Sam Raffodil Senior's new black wonder horse.

Everyone knew exactly why Mr. Raffodil had bought it. It was another attempt to hang Grandfather's horse racing hide out on the fence to dry. There had been several advance stories in our local newspaper about how outstanding the new arrival was, an established national champion trotting horse. There were pictures, too, of course.

Mr. Raffodil now owned the local newspaper, so the photos made the front page.

Most of the people in our town of Green Valley had never seen a national champion trotting horse before. Including me. When they led the big black horse down the ramp from the express car, everybody "oohed" and "aahed." Including me. The horse was named Thunderbolt, and the name suited him.

He was big and black and beautiful. His coat was so glossy you could almost see yourself in it. Thunderbolt appeared to have racing muscles he hadn't ever used yet. Grandfather and I were going to need a lot of powerful prayers when we raced against this trotter. Anybody could see that. I had to keep thinking hard about how fast Hiawatha had run on our Sabbath-Sunday ride. I leaned over and told Grandfather how I felt.

"Don't waste your sympathy," Grandfather replied. "Hiawatha has some pretty fine blood lines himself."

"But Hiawatha was sick for a whole year. That's what you said yourself, Grandfather."

"One of those rare times I was wrong."

"But look at that Thunderbolt! He doesn't look as though he'd ever been sick a day in his life. He's big. *Real* big."

"So was Goliath."

Sam Raffodil Junior didn't miss his opportunity to come up and gloat. "How do you like them apples?" he asked, pointing at Thunderbolt. Sam threw out his chest as he told me, Margie Kelly and every other kid within thirty feet, how great a horse Thunderbolt really was. Sam recited Thunderbolt's lifetime record. I had to admit it was impressive.

"If true," I said.

"It's true all right," Sam bragged. "Thunderbolt is a national champion, and my old man owns him. He's not some local leech plug that races cars on Main Street."

"We'll see about that," I argued, but my heart wasn't in it. That big black horse had "disaster for Hiawatha" written all over him.

"He's in perfect shape," Sam boasted, "Not sickly like some horses I know."

Margie Kelly nodded. She was staring at Thunderbolt like she was in a trance. Her eyes were two ripe bing cherries.

"He's beautiful!"

He was, too.

The townspeople took one look at Thunderbolt, and they all figured that Grandfather was down the drain. Frank Hartman and his horse Wildfire didn't have a ghost of a chance, either. Mr. Hartman admitted it to Grandfather as they both studied the confirmations of the new horse.

"You'd better settle for second right now," Hartman told Grandfather.

"Really?" Grandfather said with a grin. "You think poor old Thunderbolt here can only come in third?"

"You know what I mean."

Grandfather didn't seem worried at all. Even when Mr. Raffodil announced that Thunderbolt would work out the next morning. A mile. "And he'll do it in two-two flat," Mr. Raffodil promised. "Breezing. Everybody's welcome to come watch the winner of next year's County Fair Stakes. Eight o'clock sharp."

Grandfather chuckled. "Sorry about that Sam, but they'll all be too late to watch the winner. I'm working Hiawatha out at six."

"You're whistling in the dark, old man," Mr. Raffodil snapped.

He was right. No horse had ever run a two-two flat mile on our half-mile county fair track. Not even within four seconds. Two-six was about it, and usually won easily. In fact, it was still the track record. Sometimes two-eight or two-ten would win the Stakes. All the horses were Grandfather's.

"You'd better take your chestnut nursling out into the

country again," Mayor Raffodil advised Grandfather, while winking at the crowd, "and turn him over to those healing leeches."

Everybody laughed. They all knew how Grandfather and Mr. Little Fork had cured Hiawatha.

"It's the bloodsuckers who live in town that I'm worried about, Sam," Grandfather replied.

That got even a bigger laugh.

Mr. Raffodil bit on his cold cigar until it stood straight up alongside his nose again.

"Besides," Grandfather added, "they tell me Hiawatha outran your new black tin-lizzie Ford car. Wait 'till you see what he does to your new four-legged black horse."

Grandfather pulled me up into the buggy, tickled Meshach and Shadrach with the end of the buggy whip, and hollered "Giddy up!" and drove away from the freight yards looking like he didn't have a care in the world. He was whistling to himself:

"Giddy-Up Napoleon, It Looks Like Rain."

No one paid too much attention to us. They were still oogling that huge black horse and all those muscles rippling under that shiny black coat glistening in the sun. I felt a little queasy every time I looked at Thunderbolt. I decided to pray for Hiawatha every morning and every night. I figured he'd need my prayers in spite of the "Whoosh!"

"We'll have to outfox him."

41.

Maybe Grandfather wasn't worried about Thunderbolt, but I was. I noticed that Grandfather drove all the way back to the barn in silence. He was feeding Hiawatha his oats and rubbing the chestnut colt lovingly on the nose when he finally spoke.

"What did you think of the big black horse?"

"Wowie!"

"Me, too," Grandfather said. "He's not going to be a sitting duck."

"That's your meat, Grandfather," I told him. "You always say you like to go up against the big ones."

Sometimes Grandfather could get a little peeved when I reminded him of certain things he said. Especially at times like this when the things he said were things he wished he hadn't said.

A faraway look came into Grandfather's eyes, and he grinned mischievously.

"All the way to Anderson's farm before he stopped running, you say?"

"All the way. Easy. Like taking candy from a baby."

I thought this would comfort him. It didn't.

"It won't be that easy this time."

"It won't be hard, either," I argued. "You did try out Hiawatha yourself this morning at the fairgrounds in a secret workout, didn't you?"

"We took a few laps."

"Well?"

"Well what?"

"How did Hiawatha do? Did he go 'whooosh!' or not?"

Grandfather didn't answer me. But he *did* seem less worried. At least he was singing, "There'll be pie in the sky when we die."

I knew Grandfather was up to something, and that his idea, whatever it might be, was working because he kept smiling and chuckling to himself all weekend. Sometimes he would even talk to himself and say, "Is that so?" And then he would answer himself and say, "That is so."

"Are you talking to me, Grandfather?" I asked him, knowing he wasn't.

Grandfather's eyes were far away in Duluth or somewhere, he never even heard me. Once, when he was putting oats in Hiawatha's bin, he chuckled right out loud and said, "I'll be a son of a blue-eyed, ring-tailed, spavin-backed tree toad!"

He never said things like that unless the roof was about to fall in. I hoped it would fall right on top of Sam Raffodil's head.

When Grandfather came out of his trance, I said, "Are you going to run Hiawatha in the County Fair Stakes after all, Grandfather?"

"If we can't out-trot Sam's big black horse," he said, "we'll have to out-fox him."

"How will we do that?"

"I'll have to meditate, son," he said, walking over to the oats box with a harness to mend. He sat down and motioned for me to join him. That was always a good sign.

"Hatch and plot," he explained. "That is the order of the day. Hatch and plot."

I could tell that Grandfather was onto a good thing. He said he couldn't tell me another word about it until he had cooked it a little longer.

"But you won't be ashamed of it, I can promise you that," Grandfather said, reaching for my kneecap. I fled to safety and peeked out at him from underneath Hiawatha's stomach.

The way Grandfather was laughing to himself I wouldn't

want to be in Sam Raffodil Senior's shoes for all the money in the world.

Grandfather kept chuckling all through dinner. It was very disturbing. I didn't suffer too much though because the telephone rang. It was Father. He told me to come home and eat where I lived unless my grandfather had taken out adoption papers.

"Is that an order?" I asked.

"Shall we go round again?" Father asked.

"I'm on my way."

The Whitewash Brush.

42.

Grandfather gave me permission to paint the star on Hiawatha's hoof with crimson colored enamel, the star where Sam Raffodil Junior's bicycle sprocket had struck him.

"It's a memento of my first day as a famous racing driver," I told Grandfather.

He nodded. "Suicide Sunday!"

Quickly I said, "Maybe we should change Hiawatha's name to Shooting Star."

"Not until we run the Raffodils into the shining big sea waters," Grandfather said. "We've got to keep our promise."

"Why do you suppose God turns out a bad person like Mr. Raffodil?" I asked him.

"Nobody's all bad," Grandfather told me. "That's only for the motion pictures. The villain wears a black hat, kicks the dog, and drinks whiskey. The hero wears a white hat, pets the dog, and orders sasparilla or milk. In ten seconds everybody in the movie house knows who to like and who to hate, who to cheer for and who to boo."

Grandfather explained in more detail.

"In real life son, it takes longer. People can improve or they can slip backwards; or keep doing a little of each every day."

"Maybe," I said, "but Mr. Raffodil's got a very black hat, I'll tell you that."

"Well, of course, I was only using a figure of speech," Grandfather explained. "We all try to make ourselves look better than we really are. There isn't a manjack in all of Green Valley, or in the whole State of Minnesota for that matter, who doesn't use a whitewash brush on himself."

"Even *you,* grandfather?" I said, shocked.

"I buy it by the hundred pound sack," he said. "We're all of us the same. Like a basket of apples. We keep the shiny red ones on top for everyone to see, but we try to cover up the spotted bad ones underneath."

"Aren't there *any* nice people?"

"They're all nice, son, as long as they're trying to dig down into their own basket to root out the bad apples."

"Sam Raffodil Junior needs a whole new basket," I told Grandfather.

"The Raffodils are all right," Grandfather replied. "They both probably have a lot of good stuff in them down deep, if you'd care to sink a shaft."

That was a belly laugh for Grandfather.

"You usually say, 'If you care to blast!' Grandfather!"

"It's best not to hate *any* of your fellow human beings, son. Of course, if the good Lord pressed us unduly, we'd both know right where to look for our candidates, but that's because we're prejudiced. We've both got to try to rise above this Raffodil prejudice. Anybody can love the people they get along with. The real test is to get along with the people you don't like."

"If you're talking about Sam Raffodil Junior," I told him, "I'm not even going to try. A little good-natured hatred never hurt anybody."

"Except ourselves, son."

Grandfather had several favorite songs. When he was really happy and contented, he sang "Pie in the Sky." When his "hatch and plot" things were beginning to develop the way he liked, he usually sang or hummed "Wait 'till the Sun Shines, Nellie." But when he was very pleased with himself, and the volcano was about to blow, he always sang "Back Home Again in Indiana."

That's how I knew a really fine crisis was building up. I could feel the earth tremours and visualize the lava bubbling up and rumbling down the outside of the crater. I liked those times the best.

Margie Kelly and I were sitting on the wooden fence by the garden discussing why she wouldn't go to both the county fair and the big summer picnic with me even if I were the last person left alive on the earth.

Grandfather came walking up from the barn. He wasn't even using his cane to walk with. He was limping along briskly from side to side and stabbing the air with his cane as though it was a deadly rapier. He was whistling "Back Home in Indiana!"

When Grandfather came up beside me, he reached up suddenly and poked me in the chest with the rubber end of his cane and knocked me off my perch. I fell backwards into Grandmother's sweet peas. Annoyed, I crawled back up on the fence again beside Margie.

"Better get home and get a good night's rest," Grandfather told me. "Tomorrow at sunrise, we're doing a mile time trial with Hiawatha." He laughed as though he had some wonderful secret knowledge. "If old Sam Raffodil knew what I had up my sleeve, he'd pitch and toss on his bed all night long. He's in for a mighty big shock about our big red horse, I'll tell you that!"

Grandfather laughed uproariously, winked at both of us, and whispered:

"Top secret!"

He stabbed me with the rubber end of his cane and pushed me off the fence a second time down onto the sweet pea patch. Grandfather went humming happily up the garden path stabbing at imaginary swordsmen with his cane. He was good at it. A rickety, arthritic but robust seventy-five year old, D'Artagnon. Grandfather said that, I didn't. He also said, as he attacked the evening air with his cane:

"Take that! And that! And that!"

Stab. Stab. Stab!

Margie Kelly's eyes were headlights on bright. She was always astonished at the things Grandfather said and did.

"He's marvelous!" she said.

"You can have him."

"Does he really need that cane?" Margie asked.

"Only for child abuse," I replied.

I was very upset with Grandfather for revealing his secret workout plans for Hiawatha in front of Margie Kelly. I could see disaster looming ahead.

Two Snakes in the Grass.

Two Snakes in the Grass.

Obviously, Grandfather had never paid any attention to what I had told him in confidence about Margie Kelly. Margie was a nice girl, very pretty, very smart, but a deadly "carrier" of other people's secrets.

Margie was a juvenile Mrs. "Glad" Tidings. The poor kid couldn't help herself. She simply told everybody everything she knew and loved doing it. There was a certain evil innocence about it.

It was like opening a faucet.

I was sure Sam Raffodil Junior *and* Senior would soon know all about Hiawatha's mile workout tomorrow morning.

As soon as Grandfather left us, Margie Kelly became antsy. She couldn't wait to get away from me. She was burning up to get to a telephone so she could share the exciting news with Sam Raffodil Junior.

Margie began to fidget nervously. "I've got to go home to dinner," she said.

"You just *had* dinner."

"I forgot my dessert," Margie cried over her shoulder as she fled eagerly and rapidly up the path and disappeared between houses.

"There," I said to myself, "goes the old ball game!"

I went inside to tell Grandfather what a grave mistake he'd made.

"You've certainly done it this time," I said, peeved.

"I know," he agreed. "How long do you think it will take Little Miss Loose-Lips to put the secret news on the grapevine?"

"She's probably on the phone right now."

"Good."

"I warned you that Margie Kelly was punk at keeping secrets."

Grandfather nodded. "I know. A regular blabbermouth I think you said."

"Really!" I whistled. "You *knew* what she'd do?"

Grandfather grinned wickedly. "If she's the tattletail you've led me to believe, she gets a bonus as big as her mouth."

You had to admire the old rascal. He'd told Margie Kelly his secret on purpose so she'd blabber to the Raffodils.

I went home feeling much better about things myself. I was surprised when I found myself walking down the middle of Maple Street, kicking pebbles, and scoring sensational goals against the Chicago Blackhawks from every impossible angle. Suddenly, I realized I was whistling "Back Home in Indiana."

I was up before dawn. The roosters hadn't even crowed a single "crow!" by the time I reached the barn. Grandfather already had Hiawatha hitched up to the sulky. That red horse looked wonderful. He wasn't black like Thunderbolt, but his red chestnut coat was every bit as glossy and shinny as the New York horse's coat.

We fooled around doing the last odds and ends of the chores, then set out for the fairgrounds.

Even the glorious morning sunrise couldn't make the fairgrounds exciting at this time of the year. It was empty and sad-looking. It was hard to believe that in a few weeks time this same drab old place would become alive with banners, balloons, hot-dog stands, the noise of the merry-go-round, the Ferris wheel, and all the exciting action of the county fair.

I could hardly wait for the fair to begin. But right now on the misty morning of Hiawatha's secret workout, the fairgrounds were as dead as last year's Christmas tree.

Grandfather walked Hiawatha slowly around the track once and slowed up at the turn leading into the homestretch. The tall grass behind the inside rail moved suspiciously. It was stirring far more than the light breeze could account for. I studied it carefully.

Being a boy who can see a grey squirrel in an oak tree at a hundred feet, or a chipmunk in a dark hole, I had no trouble at all in spotting a human being hiding in the grass. It was double vision, really. I could see four eyes and two heads and I wouldn't have given you a nickel for either one of them wholesale. It was Sam Raffodil Junior and Sam Raffodil Senior.

I leaned over to Grandfather and whispered softly. "Hey! What do you think I just saw?"

Grandfather hollered out, "Whoa! Whoa! Hiawatha! Easy, boy! Steady!"

Hiawatha wasn't acting up at all. He was walking slowly and sedately, but Grandfather kept shouting as if Hiawatha were a frightened runaway. The more I tried to talk to Grandfather and tell him about what I'd seen in the grass, the louder he shouted at poor Hiawatha. Grandfather wheeled the sulky around and started back down the stretch. "Whoa now! Whoa, Hiawatha! No nonsense."

As far as I could see, Hiawatha was behaving perfectly. It was my grandfather who needed a bridle-bit and a tight rein. Grandfather slowed the big chestnut in front of the grandstand, then spoke to me out of the corner of his mouth.

"I saw the snake-in-the-grass," he said. "Remind me to give your little girlfriend Margie Kelly the well-earned blabbermouth bonus. It's a triumph to get Sam Raffodil out of bed this early."

"She's not my girlfriend," I objected. "And it's not just Sam Raffodil Senior. It's *two* snakes-in-the-grass, both with binoculars. Both Sam Raffodils are hiding in there."

"I know," Grandfather said, quite happily.

"We don't want them spying on us."

"Yes, we do," he said, "That's all part of our secret 'hatch and plot'! "

Grandfather warmed Hiawatha up thoroughly before letting him out. After scoring two or three times, Grandfather was ready to see what the chestnut colt could do. He drove Hiawatha toward the top of the stretch again, not far from where the two snakes were in the grass.

Grandfather dropped me off the back of the sulky almost in front of them so they had to hide deeper in the grass, hugging the ground. He handed me one of his stopwatches. Grandfather was talking a lot louder than necessary.

"I want you to stay up here and watch how Hiawatha takes the corner coming into the homestretch," he told me. "He has a tendency to go wide. We can lose a lot of ground that way unless we correct him. When I reach the starting line I'll holler 'Go!' You start your stopwatch and clock the mile. I'll give you another shout when I pass the finish line. Then stop your watch. Understand? We'll know exactly how fast this chestnut horse can run a mile."

"All right, Grandfather."

I kept staring at the spot where the Raffodils were hiding so they wouldn't dare stand up for a better view. I was pretty sure they were about to start their stopwatches with mine. Knowing Sam Raffodil Junior, I was sure he'd have his own stopwatch. Probably seventeen jewels in a leather case with his initials printed on it in gold. Both the watch and the case.

All right! So I'm a sorehead. Anyway I decided to climb up on the fence so they wouldn't be able to stand up and get too good a look.

Grandfather took Hiawatha around the track once more at an easy pace. Then he swung Hiawatha around and started down the homestretch for the regulation running start. When Grandfather reached the finish line of the mile, I heard him holler "Go!" and I started my stopwatch.

Hiawatha hugged the rail like a toy train on a track, trotting smoothly and powerfully. Grandfather held him tightly in hand. You could tell that Hiawatha was fighting to be turned loose. He went by me like a shot on this first circle of the half mile track. It was going to be a very fast four furlongs.

"Holy Mackerel!" I hollered as I looked at my stopwatch. Grandfather was still holding Hiawatha in check, but when they reached the middle of the backstretch the second time, Grandfather gradually let the chestnut colt out. Hiawatha responded beautifully. He was full of run. When Hiawatha came around the turn where the Raffodils were hiding, he was really kicking up the dirt. Grandfather never laid a whip to him once. When Hiawatha crossed the finish line, Grandfather let out another yell, and I stopped the watch.

When I looked down at my watch, I nearly fell off the fence. Two minutes and three seconds! The best time Hiawatha had ever made before on a mile trial was two minutes and eight seconds. We both thought that was fantastic at his early stage of training.

Thunderbolt, the champion, was a two-two trotter, but could probably do better. Even so, Hiawatha had almost equalled Thunderbolt's best time for a mile!

Grandfather went all the way around again and slowed down to a walk as he came up beside me. I ran over to meet him, shouting at the top of my voice.

"Two-three! Two-three! He's a world-beater, Grandfather! He ran the mile in two-three. Even Thunderbolt at his best can't do much better than that. Just wait 'till Hiawatha's had more training, and a few more workouts, he may break the two minute mile!"

Grandfather was delighted. "Good!" he said. "Good!"

"Good? That's perfect! Hiawatha is ready for that old Thunderbolt right now!"

Grandfather hesitated. "Well," he said, "I don't know, son. He ran the first seven furlongs in what must have been record time, but he was slowing up very badly at the end of the mile. He couldn't have gone another furlong. Hiawatha is an out-and-out sprinter. No doubt about it. What we need is a shorter race. Hiawatha tends to slow up something fierce as he reaches the mile post."

I objected violently. "But, Grandfather, don't you remember. I told you how Hiawatha—"

Grandfather squeezed my biceps painfully. Until I cried out.

"He slows up something fierce I tell you!" Grandfather barked at me, drowning me out. "He'd be better at seven furlongs. Much better. No doubt about it. Maybe we can get the stewards to change to seven furlongs this year. Even at a mile, we've still got a good chance. Yes, sir, we'll enter him in the big race against Thunderbolt. But this Hiawatha horse is a pure sprinter, and if we have to go much further than seven furlongs, we're in for real trouble."

I jumped up onto the back of the sulky and the three of us started toward home. I was pretty annoyed with Grandfather. So were my biceps. I was still yelling at him.

"Let go of my arm! You're killing me."

"No, I'm just trying to shut you up."

"But, Grandfather have you forgotten that when Hiawatha went over the old Mississippi River bridge he was still racing up a storm, and that was a lot longer than a mile."

Grandfather clamped one hand over my mouth and drove with the other, singing "Wait 'till the Sun Shines, Nellie" at the top of his voice, until we swung off the track and were out of range of the Raffodil's ears.

"Let's not give Plotter-Sam any idea that Hiawatha can run all day," Grandfather cautioned me.

"All right," I snapped, "but if Hiawatha can run that fast for a mile, why did you let Mr. Raffodil find out about it? Why didn't you surprise him on race day?"

"I plan to," Grandfather grinned. "Besides, Hiawatha can't run that fast."

I showed him the stopwatch. "But he *did!* Look at that! The proof is right here on the stopwatch. Look for yourself. Two minutes and three seconds! *Flat.*"

Grandfather laughed and laughed, and I got madder and madder. I jumped off the back of the sulky and headed for the stable.

"Cool off your own horse!" I said, peeved.

Grandfather grabbed me up in his arms and gave me a big grizzly bear hug. He made my cheek raw with a whisker rub, and accidentally stuck one end of his long white moustache up my nose and made me sneeze. Grandfather was still laughing.

"I can just see Sam Raffodil's face when he gets a look at his stopwatch. He'll panic."

Grandfather was so tickled and happy about everything that I began to laugh, too. I couldn't help myself. And I didn't even know why.

"I didn't think Hiawatha had it in him to run a two-three mile yet," I said. "After being so sick, and having so few workouts and so little training."

"He didn't," Grandfather said. "It was much slower."

"But I clocked it myself in two-three."

"You just *thought* you did."

"I don't understand."

"And neither does our friend Sam Raffodil," Grandfather explained. "That's why I asked you to stay up on the turn, so they couldn't stand up and see what was happening. I started that mystery mile run about a half furlong beyond the starting line, and when we came into the stretch the last time and my stopwatch reached two-three, that's when I yelled out for you to stop your watch. The truth is I hadn't crossed the finish line yet, but I wanted Sam Raffodil to get that fast two-three time for a mile on his stopwatch so we could give him something to worry about."

Now *I* was worried.

Ruffling up my hair, Grandfather said, "After this blazing workout you might be wise if you bought into this famous race horse stable before it's priced out of sight."

"I thought I *was* a part owner!"

"Just honorary. Now I'm talking cash money and real ownership."

"How about the chores I do?"

"This is over and above. We've got ourselves a real champion here," Grandfather chuckled, "Make no mistake about that. It might be worth a whole dollar of your cash money to get in on the ground floor."

"Okey, I'm in," I told him. "I'll raise the money somehow. But if Hiawatha can't really run a mile that fast, how can he be so good as a sprinter? And what good will it do to let Mr. Raffodil *think* he can run that fast, if he can't?"

Grandfather chuckled again. "You have no faith."

"Maybe not, but I can read a stopwatch. Thunderbolt will beat Hiawatha by at least five seconds."

"Will he?"

"Well, gee whiz, it seems to me—"

"Trust your wise old grandfather," my wise old grandfather said.

"I hate it when you say that!"

"Put on your gas mask."

46.

Grandfather wrote a letter to the County Board of Racing Stewards that very night. Mr. Raffodil was chief steward and was assisted by Mr. Fletcher Potter and Mr. Gerard Stevens, both of whom were in his pocket. They were all nice people except Mr. Raffodil and Mr. Potter.

Grandfather's letter proposed the friendly suggestion that the final heat of the County Fair Stakes this year should be shortened to seven furlongs instead of the regular mile.

"It will be a better distance for the locally trained horses," Grandfather's letter explained, "and will give them a better chance against an acknowledged famous outside champion."

"Would you really rather have seven furlongs than the regular mile?" I asked Grandfather while we were having dinner.

"I have something quite different in mind," Grandfather answered, smugly. "Quite spectacularly different."

"Then why suggest a seven furlong sprint?"

"Sam Raffodil won't be able to sleep trying to figure out that very thing, and it won't hurt Sam to be miserable for a few nights."

The board bluntly refused to accept Grandfather's suggestion. Whatever Grandfather suggested Sam Raffodil was against on principle. Whatever Mr. Raffodil was against, Mr. Fletcher Potter echoed immediately. Mr. Gerard Stevens was eventually bullied into the same opinion, or at best the same decision.

When Grandfather received the letter of refusal, he chuckled right out loud, and went down to the barn singing "Wait 'till the Sun Shines, Nellie." He even gave Hiawatha an extra half measure of oats; and wrestled me to two falls out of three by sitting on top of me. Followed by a double-decker strawberry ice cream cone at Sweetman's.

The next Saturday afternoon, all three horses were working out at the track: Thunderbolt, Wildfire and Hiawatha. When Grandfather brought Hiawatha out onto the track, he was covered with hay dust, mud, dirt and was uncurried. He looked terrible. Grandfather drove Hiawatha about as poorly as a man could. He engineered it so Hiawatha broke stride time after time, lugged out coming down the stretch, and in every way possible was a total disappointment to the crowd. There were even some boos. I knew Grandfather was doing it deliberately.

"You're not fooling anybody with those old tricks," I told Grandfather. "You made Dakar look seedy last year, remember, so you could catch Mr. Hartman by surprise and beat him, but you can't fool Mr. Hartman or Mr. Raffodil or anyone else two years in a row with the same old hokum. They're on to you."

Grandfather was delighted.

"I know that," he said, happily. "But Frank Hartman and Sam Raffodil *know* that I know that they know that. Right now, they're both thinking a mile a minute. They're trying to find the skunk I've got hidden in the woodpile."

"Are you that skunk, Grandfather?" I asked.

"Put on your gas mask," he said. "I'm about to lift my tail!"

47.

A few days later, both Grandfather and Mr. Frank Hartman received urgent telephone calls from the county fair racing stewards, Mr. Sam Raffodil Senior, Mr. Fletcher Potter, and Mr. Gerard Stevens. Both Grandfather and Mr. Hartman were ordered to appear at once at the racing stewards' office.

Actually, the call was from Mayor Raffodil because Mr. Potter and Mr. Stevens heard about the meeting at the same time Grandfather and Mr. Hartman did.

When Grandfather and Mr. Hartman walked into the steward's office, which was really Mr. Raffodil's office over the bank, all three of the stewards welcomed them in an overly friendly way. They oiled their way into the discussion with back-slapping, cigars, and unimportant talk about the crops and the weather.

Grandfather knew immediately that there was trouble ahead. Especially when he saw the track medical examiner there with his big black bag. Grandfather and the doctor had gone round together year after year. Honors to Grandfather. The doctor usually gave in when Grandfather passed the medical exam with flying colors.

One year, at election time, Grandfather had cast his ballot for mayor by naming his sorrel horse Dakar as his write-in choice. Dakar was very popular, he had won two straight heats and the final championship at the county fair that same year. If Sam Raffodil hadn't been the opposing candidate, Grandfather admitted that he might not have voted for a horse. But he said that circumstances being what they were, he felt people had a right to choose between a horse and a horse's... never mind what he said. The point is it added fuel to the Grandfather-Raffodil feud. Especially when stories appeared in the gossip columns of the Duluth and Minneapolis papers, reporting that Dakar had actually won one precinct.

I sometimes suspected that Grandfather no longer needed even that one cane, but that it had become such a useful part of him, he refused to give it up. He could work magic with it. Grandfather could poke you, trip you, and shove you around the barn with the rubber end of that cane like it was another leg. And in emergencies, he could hook you around your ankle, or catch your biceps and pull you close, nose to nose. Grandfather could hold you in captivity as a prisoner so you couldn't escape to the old swimming hole until he was good and ready, and had had his full say.

Grandfather had been kicked so hard, and "jarred" by wild animals so badly he'd been given up for dead several times, but he refused to give in. Everybody thought Grandfather was a goner, except Grandfather. Once when the doctor told Grandfather he was going to die for sure, and asked Grandfather if there was anything he could do for him, Grandfather said, "Yes. You can get the hell out of my bedroom and let me get some sleep."

People thought it was pretty miraculous the way Grandfather always seemed to bounce back. He clung to life with a fierce and joyous tenacity. He said it wasn't because he was afraid to die, but because he just hadn't used up all his living-credit yet. Grandfather claimed he extracted more fun out of living during one twenty-four hour day than most people did in a year, some in a lifetime. Grandfather promised that when it was the right time for him to die, he would, and he'd get just as much fun out of that, too.

"I'll go in my own time," he said, "when I'm damned good

and ready, and not when some tooth-clucking doctor thinks I'm ready. I've already buried three doctors, haven't I? And I'll get this new young squirt, too. You'll see." Apparently Grandfather hadn't been ready for years and years. I don't know how old he was really. His hair was silver white, but his eyes were young, bright and as blue as Mille Lac Lake.

Several horse owners led by Mr. Raffodil who had lost a bundle on Grandfather in last year's County Fair Stakes, tried to get Grandfather barred from driving in harness races because of his advanced age and general poor health. For his own good and safety, they said, and for the good of racing. Naturally.

Grandfather did have a weak heart. He also had a weak stomach, delicate lungs, and a stiff arthritic back. Once he had a pretty bad heart attack and the whole house was in an uproar. His pulse was flickering and the doctor was fussing over him something fierce. Grandfather gave his chest a thump and yelled, "Beat!!"

His heart seemed to straighten right out after that and got steady again. Grandfather told the doctor to take another listen. He did, and, to nobody's surprise who knew Grandfather, the doctor folded up his stethoscope, put it back in his bag, and went home, muttering to himself, and shaking his head.

When the doctor came back that night, Grandfather was down at the barn feeding the horses.

Grandfather took all his illnesses and accidents in stride. When I told Grandmother how proud I was of Grandfather, and that he was a real stoic person, she said, "Stuff it!"

I was shocked, until she told me the inside story of Grandfather's fluttering heart attack. "What your stoic grandfather did not tell the doctor," she pointed out, "was that he had eaten three fried pork chops and two helpings of home-fried potatoes for lunch all smothered in ketchup."

I was even more shocked. "You shouldn't feed anybody

with a bad liver, a bad stomach, and a bad heart that kind of food, Grandmother!"

"I didn't," she said serenely. "He cooked them for himself. I warned him. I offered him the white meat chicken I had prepared, but your grandfather said he required something with a little more bite and vitality. Your grandfather could have lighted Green Valley for two days from the gas on his stomach."

"Really?"

"Well, maybe only one day," she said, with a chuckle very much like Grandfather's.

"Does Grandfather really have a bad heart, and liver, and stomach?"

"Among other things such as arthritis, neuritis and bursitis. The only good part of your Grandfather's anatomy is his own natural teeth, and he's been digging his grave with those for over seventy years."

"Couldn't you reason with him? Get him not to eat that way?"

"Have you ever tried to reason with your grandfather?"

"There is that," I admitted.

"Indian wrestle me for the seven furlongs, Sam."

Anyway, to make a short story long, which is usually the case when you're trying to explain anything about Grandfather, it was pretty hard to convince the people in the grandstand that Grandfather shouldn't be driving in harness races any longer because of his age. He'd won the trotting championship five years in a row, including last year by seven lengths.

"Beat the old man just once on the track before you complain," the people suggested to those who queried about Grandfather's age.

"He skins the young ones alive!" people said.

"If you ask me," said Frank Hartman, Grandfather's chief rival each year, "that old bugger is like wine. The older he gets, the better he gets."

"He should make way for younger men," Mr. Raffodil insisted.

Now that Grandfather would not withdraw, Mr. Raffodil played his next card. He tried to get Grandfather disqualified on the matter of age and health.

Sam Raffodil Senior was a new, persistent and deadly threat to Grandfather's future in racing. Mr. Raffodil was prepared to spend all the money it took to get rid of Grandfather, either by defeating him on the track, or disbarring him medically. Preferably both. In either case Mr. Raffodil kept insisting that Grandfather was too old.

Grandfather was perfectly agreeable to step aside for youth, he said.

"I'll do it, but only out of charity, not necessity. It's not my advanced age that worries Sam Raffodil, it's my advanced position on the track. Everybody except Frank here is just plain tired of looking at my backside speeding down the homestretch ahead of them."

It wasn't worth the big laugh Grandfather gave it.

Now, once again, Sam Raffodil Senior had successfully influenced the stewards to bring in a heart specialist in order to declare Grandfather incompetent and unfit to drive in this year's Stakes race.

"For the safety of the other drivers, of course," Mr. Raffodil pointed out. "This old fool is way over the hill, but he stubbornly refuses to retire. After all, we *do* have a responsibility here."

Grandfather refused to submit to the medical examination unless Sam Raffodil would submit to similar psychological tests to see if the doctors could find Sam's natural "mean-streak" and what caused it.

"My motor seems to be running pretty good," Grandfather explained to the doctor later, during the examination. Grandfather took the doctor's stethoscope from his own chest, and placed it against the doctor's and listened carefully. He clucked his teeth.

"*You* sound a mite dickery in there yourself, Doc."

The doctor laughed and retrieved his instrument.

"Actually," Grandfather explained, "I'm not over the hill, I'm only over a small mountain range. But I'm climbing up the other side a mile a minute toward the highest peak beyond. So, you tell Sam Raffodil here to stand clear if he doesn't want to get crushed in the old man's avalanche."

"I'll do that."

"Youth is not only a time of life," Grandfather declared, "but also a quality of the human spirit. On that basis, compared to Sam Raffodil, I'm a nursing child."

The doctor was inclined to agree.

The specialist not only collected his fee from Mr. Raffodil, but he cleared Grandfather for one more big race.

"On a youngster," Doc McGovern declared after his careful examination, "these heart rhythms might be suspect, but on a seventy-five year old tiger, they're not all that bad."

The doctor also reminded Mr. Raffodil that he had won five hundred dollars from him by betting on Grandfather in last year's race. That's what really burned Mr. Raffodil's biscuit.

"He's a sick, crippled old has-been," Mr. Raffodil insisted, but he was outvoted. Mostly because the doctor and Mr. Hartman were there as eyewitnesses, so the other two stewards, Gerard Stevens and Mr. Fletcher Potter, knuckled under. Mr. Raffodil was livid, but in spite of his objections, like it or not, Grandfather was cleared.

"What does that quack know about it?" Mr. Raffodil grumbled.

"He's *your* quack, Sam," Grandfather pointed out.

Grandfather walked over to the table by the wall. He sat down, rolled up his right sleeve, and placed his elbow on the table. He held up his right arm. "C'mon, Sam. I'll Indian wrestle you for it. You beat this sick old crippled has-been, and you call the shots. If you lose, it's a seven furlong race for this year's County Fair Stakes."

Mr. Raffodil refused. Grandfather knew he would.

"You'd probably prefer a foot race to wrist wrestling, Sam," Grandfather said, limping back to his chair.

"Don't go too far, old man," Mr. Raffodil threatened.

"Not more than seven furlongs if I can help it. That's about as far as my county fair horse can go, Sam. He's a pure sprinter. But he's the best."

"*That,*" said Mr. Raffodil, quite pleased with himself, "is what we're going to discuss at our next meeting."

"What are you and your New York champion afraid of? If you can't beat us at seven furlongs, you can't do it at all."

Having failed to disqualify Grandfather on medical grounds, Mr. Raffodil fell back on his main plan. "The matter of the distance of the race will be settled next week by the official stewards."

Grandfather looked at their solemn faces. From one to the other, Raffodil, Potter, Stevens.

Conspirators all.

Grandfather sighed. "I know I won't like the verdict."

The smile on Mr. Raffodil's face was both smug and superior.

"Chapter and Verse: A mile and a half!"

49.

From the moment Grandfather walked into the county fair steward's office the next week, he knew something special was up. When Mr. Raffodil said, "The distance of the County Fair Stakes has all been settled," Grandfather *knew* it.

"I received your letter summoning me here," Grandfather told the stewards, letting the oil of their welcome run off his back. Grandfather couldn't backslap since he was leaning on his cane, but he did playfully push Sam Raffodil in the jacket pocket with the rubber end. Unfortunately, he broke Mr. Raffodil's glasses which were in that pocket.

"Am I to understand then that you have refused my suggestion for a seven furlong race?"

"You may."

"If everything was already settled before Frank Hartman and I arrived, without consultation, or participation, we might as well have saved the trip."

Mr. Raffodil smiled coldly as he dug the broken pieces of eyeglass lens out of his pocket.

"There is," he said, "one other little thing about this year's race."

"I thought there might be."

"For the good of the fair, of course."

"Naturally."

Sam Raffodil Senior gave a meaningful glance toward Mr. Fletcher Potter, indicating that he was to recite his piece. Mr. Fletcher Potter coughed nervously.

"We...the stewards, that is...Mr. Raffodil, Mr. Stevens and myself, felt that it might be exciting and novel for the spectators to have something a little...you might say quite different this year. More stimulating."

"Such as?"

"Well, for example, we thought of emulating and following the example of some of the feature races at a number of the large harness tracks in the East."

Both Grandfather and Frank Hartman looked at each other, raised their eyebrows, but didn't say anything. They waited for Mr. Fletcher Potter to cough again and go on. Mr. Fletcher Potter coughed a lot in between words. That was his way of talking as though he had to dredge up the ideas one at a time. Mr. Potter was manager of the bank that Mr. Raffodil owned. People said that Mr. Fletcher Potter had to check in each morning to find out what to *think* for that day. Nobody ever called Mr. Fletcher Potter plain "Fletcher" or "Fletch" or even "Potter." It was always Mr. Fletcher Potter, even when you were joking about him. He was a sad weazened crab apple. Mr. Raffodil had squeezed out all the good juice long ago.

Mr. Fletcher Potter coughed again.

"Get on with it," Mayor Sam Raffodil prompted.

"Instead of the usual two one mile heats with the best three horses from each heat meeting in a one mile final, this year we...the stewards, that is Mr. Raffodil, Mr.—"

"We *know* who they are," Raffodil said, annoyed.

"Yes. Well, we all agreed...cough...unanimously, of course...cough...that it would be refreshing to have something a little different this year."

"You said that," Grandfather reminded him.

Mr. Fletcher Potter swallowed hard and finally spat it out: "This year we are going to have a mile and a half race with no heats at all. It's all settled. There will be no review. That's it. The final word."

"A mile and a half?"

"Twelve furlongs!" Mr. Raffodil said, pounding his fist on the desk in delight.

Grandfather slumped in his chair. He was a thunderstruck, beaten old man in shock. Grandfather told me later that he should have been nominated as "collapsing horse trainer of the year."

"Even my crestfallen was crestfallen," he bragged.

After a long pause, Grandfather looked over at Frank Hartman. Silently, they both rose from their chairs and started to leave. Sam Raffodil came quickly around the desk, cutting off their retreat.

"You don't like it?"

Mr. Hartman smiled at him frostily. "What county fair horse is bred or trained to run a mile and a half, Sam?"

"They do it in Europe and New Zealand and Australia all the time. And now in New York."

"This isn't New York," Mr. Hartman said. "If you want to run your horse In a long race, why don't you take him to New York?"

"Well, of course," Mr. Raffodil said, interrupting another cough by Mr. Fletcher Potter, "if you'd prefer to withdraw, that's up to you." He looked at Grandfather with a flash of triumph. "You'll have to renounce your driving championship, of course."

"Obviously, the length of the race is already officially settled," Grandfather said. "You didn't invite Frank and myself here to consult about it or to ask our opinion. You had us come so you could tell us. Right?"

"That's right. Chapter and verse. It's a mile and a half race, take it or leave it."

Mr. Fletcher Potter intervened, diplomatically. "It was all voted proper and legal like, of course, by the official stewards. After all, you and Mr. Hartman are not on the board. Unanimously, the racing stewards, Mr. Raffodil, Mr.—"

"Shove it!" Frank Hartman told him.

Grandfather looked over at Gerard Stevens who hadn't said a single word during the entire interview. Mr. Stevens was manager of the Feed and Fertilizer Company, the *S. Raffodil* Feed and Fertilizer Company.

"Unanimously?" Grandfather asked Mr. Stevens.

Sam Raffodil tilted his cigar up at a belligerent angle. Mr. Stevens didn't look at Grandfather. He stared down at his shoes and nodded.

"An old harness driver like yourself, at these local fairs, voted for a mile and a half race, Gerard?"

"Exactly!" Raffodil snarled, answering for him.

Grandfather turned away again and started for the door. Mr. Raffodil followed him.

"You're too old for the racing game anyway," he said, "but we wanted you to have this last chance to back down, knowing you didn't have a decent horse to enter this year. Are you in or out?"

Grandfather shrugged, helplessly. "What can I say?"

"So you're out?"

"No, I'm in."

"Good!" Mr. Raffodil was surprised, but pleased.

A defeat on the track was far superior to a withdrawal. Frank Hartman looked over at Grandfather who gave him a "thumbs up" sign which said, "Let's go for it."

Mr. Hartman said, "I'll give it a whirl, too. What can I lose?"

Mr. Raffodil gave them both a cat-and-cream grin.

"You wouldn't like to wager a little something on the side?"

Hartman refused. "That big a fool," he said, "I'm not. We all know that Thunderbolt has won big at a mile and a half in the East."

"How about you, Methusaleh?" Raffodil taunted, turning to Grandfather.

Methusaleh nodded, with a mischievous grin.

"I might be tempted, Sam. I've got a fine sitting-down black stallion named Ebony, and another bumper crop of winter hay coming up. I might wager them even up against your famous New York horse, if you'll throw in to boot that roan-grey back-up saddle pony of Minnie's."

Mr. Raffodil forgot all about the steward's conference. His face turned from a radish to a plum, then became white with rage as the red and purple tide flowed out.

*"Everybody knows my word is good, Sam,
but put yours in writing."*

50.

Grandfather turned to follow Mr. Hartman out. Mayor Raffodil knocked Grandfather's hand off the doorknob, put his back against the door and shoved Grandfather back into the room. Grandfather was about ready to "fungo" Sam Raffodil into left field with his cane. His restraint was saintly. It was not like Grandfather.

"Listen to me, Methusaleth," Raffodil seethed, "that first morning when you pushed me into the watering trough, I warned you that this town would never be big enough to hold the two of us. One of us has to go."

"You shouldn't have let that fester all these years, Sam. I tried to patch it up several times. You know that. Besides, Sam, you were asking to be dunked that day. You were arrogant and impossible."

"Let our two horses settle everything once and for all," Mr. Raffodil suggested. "Everything I own in this town against everything you own."

"It wouldn't be fair to you, Sam. I'm only a small potatoes financier. My assets—"

"I'm not talking assets! I'm talking about your packing up and getting out of this town. Forever! That's worth anything to me. One goes, the other stays."

Grandfather laughed. "You mean like two people fighting a duel at dawn? Winner take all?"

"Exactly!" Mr. Raffodil snapped. "Only this time it's not with swords and pistols, it's with horses. For all we own."

"No thanks, Sam," Grandfather replied.

Mr. Raffodil turned to Mr. Fletcher Potter who handled all his affairs at the bank. "What am I worth locally, Potter? Total resources?"

Mr. Fletcher Potter was flustered like any sensible banker when somebody starts talking about money like it was yard goods. Especially about taking all they own out of the bank.

Mr. Fletcher Potter said "I don't think I could even guess—"

"Approximately!" Mr. Raffodil thundered.

Fletcher Potter scribbled on some paper and came up with an answer. "It's only an approximation—"

"We *know* that!"

"And, of course, this is just Green Valley. It doesn't touch your major assets in Duluth."

"How much? Here. Locally."

"About four hundred thousand dollars."

Mr. Raffodil turned to Grandfather. "How much of that can you raise, old man?"

Grandfather really laughed this time. He whipped out his wallet and peered inside. He figured this would end the idiotic subject once and for all.

"Well, Sam," he said, "you can put me down for fifteen dollars, a pocket full of small change, and two three cent stamps."

"Done!" Mr. Raffodil bellowed, banging the desk.

Grandfather tried to get him to back off.

"You're in a rage, Sam. When you cool off, you'll realize how ridiculous this is!"

"It's the best chance you'll ever get in this world, old man. Grab it!"

"All I have are my animals, my barns, and my house and lot."

"Done!" shouted Mr. Raffodil.

"Against four hundred thousand dollars? That's crazy, Sam."

Mr. Raffodil pounded the top of his desk, and repeated his words, "Done! Done!"

Mr. Fletcher Potter was becoming frantic, almost in a panic.

Grandfather still thought it was only a joke. It had to be. Still, the mischief-maker in him wondered how far Mr. Raffodil was prepared to go while he was caught up in this strange frenzy of hatred.

Grandfather said, trying to end the madness and make it all seem like a foolish gesture soon forgotten, "Of course, you'll have to throw in Chief Little Fork's farm and Einar Olsen's place."

"Done!"

"And the properties of all my friends you foreclosed on."

"Done!"

Grandfather was really enjoying himself now. He was sure it was all a lark on Sam's part and that he'd eventually return to sanity, so Grandfather gouged him, for laughs.

"On top of that, you'll have to return Chief Little Fork's Livery Stable. I don't like the idea of you having anything to do with animals, Sam."

Mr. Raffodil slammed the table with both his open palms. Once, twice, three times, accompanying each slam with the word, "Done!"

Mr. Fletcher Potter finally tried to restrain him. "Four hundred thousand dollars, the Little Fork and Olsen properties, and all those others, against the pitiful collateral he offers! It's madness, Mr. Raffodil."

"Not to *me* it isn't. I've got to be rid of this poisonous barnacle under my skin."

"Try leeches, Sam," Grandfather suggested, slyly.

Mr. Raffodil was enraged. He yelled at Mr. Fletcher Potter:

"You fool! It's not four hundred thousand dollars and cash properties against his assets, it's his solemn promise to leave not only this town and county, but this state! Forever! That's worth a million to me!"

"You can't be serious about this, Sam?" Grandfather suggested.

"I'm deadly serious."

"Done!" Grandfather said, banging his cane on Mr. Raffodil's desk, and sweeping Thunderbolt's framed picture into the waste basket.

Mr. Raffodil raised a threatening finger. It was trembling. Grandfather said later that he'd never believed that people really turned purple with anger until that moment.

"I'll pick your bones so clean, old man, that you won't have an ounce of flesh left."

"You're the vulture who can do it, Sam."

Mr. Raffodil turned to Mr. Fletcher Potter and Gerard Stevens.

"You heard him say 'Done!' That's binding. His word is good with me."

"Everybody knows *my* word is good, Sam," Grandfather assured him, "but put *yours* down in writing."

51.

It nearly started another fight.

Mr. Raffodil was about to leap over the top of his desk. Gerard Stevens and Mr. Fletcher Potter restrained him.

Fuming with fury, Mr. Raffodil threatened Grandfather.

"You'll have my signature on the papers by noon tomorrow with an official attorney's stamp and seal. It will mean the end of you in this town, old man. You can take my word for it. No horse of yours will ever beat Thunderbolt."

"Thunderbolts can kill you dead, Sam, if you're not careful. Fortunately for me, I have a lightning rod by the name of Hiawatha."

"Don't count on it, old man. You haven't heard the worst yet."

"There's more, Sam?"

"Plenty!"

Mr. Raffodil was gloating. "Now that you've given your word, I can promise you that you'll *grovel* before this year's county fair is over!"

"Groveling is not my strong suit, Sam. What news could be worse for me than a mile and a half race? And being suckered into a madman's wager?"

"Try this. I'm not only entering the finest horseflesh money can buy, but I'm bring in the finest harness racing driver in the whole country to handle him. Buckshot Agate!"

That did cause an unpleasant stir in the pit of Grandfather's stomach. He was delighted about tricking Mr. Raffodil into a twelve furlong race, but he hadn't counted on facing Buckshot Agate. Besides, Grandfather knew he'd have to find some way out of that ridiculous wager. He was not a betting man.

But, Buckshot Agate!

He was one of the biggest names in harness racing. Everybody interested in standard bred horses knew about Buckshot Agate. Even if Hiawatha and Thunderbolt were even, Buckshot Agate could easily make the difference. He could lose Grandfather his shirt, not to mention Grandmother's house and garden.

Buckshot Agate was not only the winner of last year's Hambletonian. He was at the very top of the money list as the national grand champion harness driver. Perhaps the best of all time. Buckshot Agate had been on the cover of a dozen magazines. He had been featured in nearly everybody's Sunday newspaper magazine supplement. He certainly didn't belong on a county fair track driving against local talent. Especially those foolish enough to have staked their entire future on the race.

"That's a pretty rich mixture for a small county fair track, isn't it, Sam?"

"The stewards have voted it all legal and proper."

Grandfather could tell by their faces that the other stewards hadn't heard a thing about Buckshot Agate until that very moment.

"Aren't you overdoing it a bit, Sam?"

"Not if it nails you to the cross."

Grandfather turned and walked toward the door with mixed emotions. Jubilation and triumph at the mile and a half race, depression and disgust at his insane wager made in a moment of weakness and anger. He didn't let Mr. Raffodil see any of this, of course.

"Why don't we call the foolish wager off, Sam?"

"Aha! Buckshot Agate put the fear of God into you, did he? Good! I should think so."

"It's not Buckshot Agate or your horse Thunderbolt I'm worried about, Sam. It's the foolishness of the bet. A horse could break stride. Mine *or* yours. A dozen things could happen. Mostly bad. You stand to lose a fortune, Sam."

"Not as much as you, old man. Better break the news to your wife, and order the moving van. You're finished in this town."

Mr. Raffodil came around the desk and jabbed a trembling finger into Grandfather's chest pushing him backwards. "By God, old man!" he vowed, "I'll delight in nailing your hide to the wall this time."

"Be sure to bring along enough nails, Sam," Grandfather suggested cheerfully, regaining his balance.

"I'll bring *horseshoe nails!*" Mr. Raffodil promised. "On the feet of a two-two trotter named Thunderbolt!"

The Fifth Furlong!

"You did what!!?"

Grandfather hobbled down the bank stairs, shrunk up inside his clothes, a man obviously depressed by his own reckless foolhardiness. He crossed the sidewalk and jay-walked to the buggy where Beauty, Prince, and I were waiting for him. We were eager and impatient to hear all the news. It appeared that the news was mostly bad.

Mayor Sam Raffodil was watching us through his office window. Grandfather could see him out of the corner of his eye as he limped across toward the buggy. He pulled himself slowly and painfully up into the buggy, looking for all the world like a whipped puppy with his tail between his legs.

"What went wrong, Grandfather? You look terrible."

Grandfather slumped over the reins, made no effort to start the horses. I was worried. He mumbled under his breath. "I can't talk right now."

"Why not?"

"Trust your tricky old grandfather," my tricky old grandfather said.

It wasn't until we passed the Dow Lumber Company, and were out of sight of Mr. Raffodil's bank, that Grandfather cut loose.

He blew up to about twice his normal size. He exhaled fire and brimstone. He cackled like a mad rooster. He seized my kneecap, a favorite target during his spasms of ecstasy. I nearly jumped out of the buggy the wrong way and up onto Beauty's back.

"Geronimo!" Grandfather hollered.

"The way you looked coming down those outside stairs," I said, "I thought they had talked you out of the mile-and-a-half race."

"Quite the opposite," he chuckled. "They insisted on it. Unanimously! Over my every objection. It was the seven furlongs they threw out. Thanks to our secret morning workout."

Grandfather told me the whole story from start to finish.

"We've got that old skinflint," he said, gleefully, "right where we want him."

"Where's that, Grandfather?"

"By the shores of Gitchee-Gumee, and a mile-and-a-half from the finish line, with his crooked corkscrew head sinking slowly but remorsefully beneath the shining big sea waters!"

"That's wonderful news, Grandfather. Wonderful!"

I was delighted. Grandfather, too, was hilariously happy. This time when he grabbed my kneecap, I tried to jump right out of the buggy, but couldn't. Grandfather outdid himself. He seized my kneecap like it was the handshift on my Uncle Cliff's Ford touring car, and made believe he was driving.

He shifted my kneecap in his iron grasp: "Low! Second! High! Reverse!" he shouted, then shook my kneecap back and forth. "Neutral!"

I yelled and screamed throughout. It tickled like fury. I flew out of the side of the moving buggy. Grandfather pulled up, waited, and helped me back in.

"That chestnut colt of ours," he promised me, "will make Raffodil's big black horse eat Indian corn in the homestretch, or Hiawatha never paddled a canoe for Minnie Ha! Ha! Ha! Ha!"

Grandfather was so overjoyed that he kept right on shouting that for half a block: "Ha! Ha! Ha! Ha! Ha!"

We both sang two choruses of "Wait 'Till the Sun Shines,

Nellie." We sang so loud that Joe Mercer's poodle came running out of his yard and barked at us and chased us all the way down the street. Grandfather leaned down from the buggy and barked back at him, frightening the dog out of his wits.

In spite of Grandfather's seemingly good spirits, his voice sounded a little hollow, and I could tell that he was not too happy inside. He was overdoing his joy, and I sensed something was wrong.

Grandfather admitted it. He said he hadn't told me the entire truth about what had happened in the steward's office. Grandfather kept getting more and more nervous as we approached the turn for Maple Street and home. He was a bit sheepish. Finally he pulled up the buggy and said, "We'd better talk before we drive in."

"What about?"

Grandfather finally confessed, "We did suffer a mite of a setback with Sam Raffodil."

"What kind of a setback, Grandfather?"

"Don't tell your Grandmother about it, it might upset her."

"Okey, I won't."

"You know how green and fractious your Grandmother can run out of the gate when she gets startled by mild little surprises."

"Such as?"

"Just don't let it slip out. Hear?"

"I won't!" I told him. "How can I if I don't ever hear what this mild little surprise and setback is?"

So Grandfather told me.

"YOU DID WHAT!!?"

"Number four: You were a mug."

53.

Grandfather was in trouble up to his ears. The good part was the mile and a half race. The bad part was that he'd wagered everything he owned on a horse, and my grandfather had never bet on anything in his whole life. Grandfather always had told me that betting was a mug's game.

"Then why did you do it," I asked him.

"Because in one mad, fiery moment," he said, "I became so livid and angry at Sam Raffodil and what he'd done to my friends, that I lost my head, thinking that perhaps I might get their homes and their property back."

"Is that so bad, Grandfather?"

"Wagering all I own on a horse? A horse I've driven in only two workouts? A horse who has never won a race in his whole life? Who was born almost dead? Who as a yearling, looked like a dachshund in a doberman's skin?"

"But he's Hiawatha, Grandfather."

"I know that."

I was afraid Grandfather had made the disastrous bet mostly on my say-so about that wild Sabbath-Sunday ride. I felt terrible when I heard about the bet. Grandfather told me not to blame myself.

"I was the one who said *'Done!'* to Sam Raffodil's wager. I thought it was only a joke. I thought Sam would back off. I didn't know anybody could hate another person so much he'd risk everything just to drive his enemy out of town. I felt sorry for Sam. I was trying to kid him out of the wager. Now Sam's holding me to it. He had eyewitnesses."

"Hiawatha can do it, Grandfather."

"That's what I keep telling myself, but I've been raising and training horses all my life, and know how many things can go wrong."

Grandfather admitted that subconsciously, in the back of his mind, had flashed three very tempting things.

"What three things, Grandfather?"

Grandfather listed them on his fingers: One. That Hiawatha could run all day. Two. That destiny had intervened and had come up with a mile and a half race. (Destiny being himself.) Three. That victory for Hiawatha would win back the stolen properties of Elinor Olsen, Chief Little Fork and several other good friends of his—all innocent victims of Sam Raffodil's treachery and false promises.

"You left out number four," I told Grandfather.

"What was that?"

"You were a mug."

"Guilty as charged."

"Can't we hatch and plot, Grandfather? And find a way to cancel the bet?"

"Too late."

"What then?"

"To begin with we'll inaugurate a twenty-four hour watch on Hiawatha, and make sure nothing happens to him."

"Right! The fate of our world is now riding on Hiawatha's shoulders."

Grandfather gave me a whisker rub and a grizzly bear hug before saying, "Not to mention your grandmother."

I was so distressed thinking about Grandmother that I forgot to say, "I hate that!" about the whisker rub.

Have you ever been to a county fair? If you haven't, I'm sorry for you. You have missed everything good in life! When you walk down the midway, you need roulette balls for eyes in order to take in all the exciting colorful things that are happening on every side.

Barkers shouting, big prize-wheels spinning and clicking, winners screaming with delight, guns popping in the shooting galleries, bells ringing as the metal ducks and deer targets fall over, people talking and laughing as they pass you by along the crowded midway eating carmel corn and glazed apples on a stick; happy shouts as the white wooden milk bottles are toppled by a hard fast ball; the continuous player-piano sound of the calliope with its musical whistles on both the merry-go-round and the Ferris wheel; the shrill frightened screams of the girls as they go down that first steep roller coaster dip. The sounds and smells along the midway are enough all by themselves to drive a person crazy.

You can't decide what to buy first. Your nose slowly circles around, testing the fragrant scents in the air like a lighthouse searchlight trying to prevent anything from escaping you: hot dogs, hamburgers, popcorn, melting butter, oranges being peeled, fish being deep-fried, taffy being pulled, bacon and eggs sizzling in the pan, onions frying, bread baking, coffee being brewed, and chocolate fudge coming to a boil—it makes you want to fly right out of your skin with happiness. You close a tight fist over the half dollar, quarter, dime and nickel in your pant's pocket so you can't squander them too soon.

Wherever you look, you see brilliant colored pennants and flags fluttering in the warm summer breeze. Black, gold, green, red, blue and white crepe paper streamers twist in the air, decorating the booths, stands, stalls and show places.

It's a magic fairyland. *Aesop's Fables* come true, along with every childhood story, *Farmer Brown, Bre'r Rabbit, The Gingerbread Man,* and *The Wizard of Oz* all rolled into one. And it's all yours!

Ducks and geese and chickens and turkeys are quacking, honking, cackling and gobbling. From the animal-judging sheds, you can hear the livestock all nervous, and still not settled down on this the first day at the fair. Pigs oink, calves bawl, cows moo, steers bellow, goats bleat, sheep baaa, horses neigh, mules and donkeys hee-haw. And you wouldn't have it any other way.

The stable area is delicately perfumed with the pungent smell of manure, mingled with the fragrant aroma of fresh-cut hay, clover and alfalfa, plus the always present smell of liniment for those minor wounds suffered on the trips from farm to fair, and from crowding, pushing and trampling in the sheds.

Every face is radiant, shining, happy, and eager.

The opening day of the county fair is heaven-on-earth. Everyone has been waiting patiently and looking forward enthusiastically to this very moment. Everything is just as wonderful and exciting as everyone remembered it from last year. And this year it's even better. Fabulous is the word! And it lasts for six whole days!

The Fitzhugh County Fair may not be as grand as the State Fair at Minneapolis, or the World's Fair, but for a county fair it can't be beat. Anyone in Fitzhugh County will tell you that.

Everybody knows everybody, and for the duration of the county fair, everybody *likes* everybody. Or makes believe they do. All local feuds are called off for six days. It's an unwritten law.

It's all smiles, handshakes and cease-fire everywhere in Fitzhugh County, and especially in our town of Green Valley, the county seat. Nobody holds a grudge. Except for maybe a few out-of-county fanatics like Sam Raffodil Senior and Junior and Minnie Raffodil. Angela Raffodil, of course, is something different.

Wow! Is she ever something! I asked Grandfather how a family could come up with such a marvelous person as Angela Raffodil in the midst of all those sour prickly pears. He said it was like breeding race horses. You can come up with a world-beater in the midst of a lot of throw-backs from the same bloodlines. Only time will tell which are good and which are ordinary.

"The sooner they throw Sam Junior back, the better," I told him. "Ordinary my foot!"

Grandfather shook a warning finger at me.

"It's county fair time."

"You're right, Grandfather," I apologized, "and that's the last bad thought I'll have about the Raffodil's until the fair is over and we've won the big race."

Fortunately, I had my fingers crossed behind my back when I made that wild and insane statement.

One of the most important highlights of the opening day of the county fair comes at eleven o'clock in the morning. That's when the Green Valley Marching Band, in their new green and gold uniforms, high-steps all the way from the bandstand in the center of town down to the fairgrounds. People line the streets all the way from downtown right to the grandstand in the fairgrounds. They cluster around the entrance gate and pack the grandstand on the racetrack where the opening-day demonstration finally reaches its climax.

I followed the band along the midway and out onto the dirt track where soon Hiawatha would make mincemeat out of that highly touted champion from Goshen, New York; Thunderbolt Raffodil.

The band paraded through the gate and out onto the dirt track, marching in precision drill: turning, wheeling, reversing, and coming back through their own ranks, never touching. It was a perfect square! Alive with motion, yet they seemed to be standing in one place. It was absolutely marvelous!

It brought down the house. The applause was spontaneous. I was cheering myself without even knowing when I started.

That's what the county fair does to you. You get so darned excited, you applaud and cheer even when the cook throws a pancake high in the air and catches it perfectly on his griddle when it come down. There's something infectious in the air.

Some wise guy hollered: "Author! Author!" when the marching band executed their precision drills.

The drum major was the star of the show with his high hat, and his uniform glistening with braid and gold buttons that caught the sun and flashed into the audience's eyes as he moved. He bent stiffly forwards and backwards at alarming angles. His legs went high in the air like a dancer who can kick over his head.

The drum major was backed by eight drum majorettes in their brief green and gold skirts. They recklessly threw gold batons in the air, and caught them gracefully without one miss. The batons whirled up and spun down into their deft hands and became gold and green windmills, or like airplane propellers whirling around eight abreast. Only silent.

Until the grandstand burst into loud cheers and thunderous applause of appreciation.

Suddenly, the drum major raised his baton, held it aloft to gain the attention of every member of the band, and then brought it down with a jerk. The entire band struck up the loud brassy arrangement of *Under the Double Eagle*, John Phillip Sousa at his best.

I was glad I hadn't been born too late to miss all of this. I felt sorry for those poor souls who would never see or experience a county fair. I followed the band up the track toward the grandstand where they would hold the official morning concert. I did my own dance step behind them strutting up the track as the trumpets and trombones blared, and the big bass drum boomed out the rhythm.

It made you stiffen up your backbone, and in your imaginary dream, you marched proudly up to the front of the judges' stand to receive your medal of honor from the President of the United States of America.

And it was only the first morning of the first day of the county fair!

55.

Just four days before the big race, a flash fire broke out in the stable area.

In less than ten minutes, the whole county fairgrounds was in a panic. One spark is all it takes to ignite a blaze amongst all that hay and wood that can snuff out the lives of every horse before help can reach them.

Fire is the most dreaded scourge among horse barns and stables anywhere in the world. At a fairgrounds it affects hundreds and hundreds of other fair animals besides the race horses, as all are stabled in the nearby barns and sheds. They could all be wiped out or gravely endangered.

Racing people and animal people all live in dread of that one horrifying word:

"Fire!"

Our county fair was no exception.

Everything had been so quiet for the past few days, that Grandfather had invited me to dinner in the fairgrounds main dining room. It was a special treat for me. We left Uncle Cliff to watch over things at Hiawatha's stable.

A three-piece orchestra of piano, drums and saxophone was playing "Rock Me in a Mississippi Cradle" when we came into the dining room. I felt real important.

"As a part owner of a famous racing stable," Grandfather reminded me, "you should feel important."

The orchestra played the latest new hit songs all through our dinner. A violin and a bass came in later and made it an even classier five-piece orchestra. They played some of the old songs, too. Many of Grandfather's favorites. "Dardenella," "The Wabash Blues," "Back Home in Indiana," "My Wild Irish Rose," and great stuff like that.

We had a table all of our own. Waiters and waitresses came to take our order and bring our food. I began to feel that I really *was* a part owner of a famous racing stable. I guess it went to my head.

"Don't blow up and burst," Grandfather cautioned me. "You're about to pop the buttons off your jacket."

Mr. and Mrs. Raffodil came in and sat down at the next table but even that didn't spoil my dinner. We were out of their sight behind some fake palm trees, but I could see them through the branches when I peeked, which wasn't often, as I wanted to enjoy my food.

"What's wrong with Mr. Raffodil, Grandfather?"

"What do you mean?"

"He keeps looking at his watch and staring at the door."

Grandfather was too busy talking with the other drivers who had joined us at our table. They were talking over old times and old races and about the great trotters and pacers they had known personally.

Somebody stuck his head in the door and beckoned to Mr. Raffodil. It was Dan Pickett. Mr. Raffodil got up and left his wife at the table.

"Something funny's going on, Grandfather," I whispered to him, pulling on his arm.

"Not now, son."

He was telling his friends about the time there was a five horse dead heat finish at the first County Fair Stakes. I knew that would take a long time, so I punched him lightly in the ribs.

"Can I be excused?"

Grandfather nodded without interrupting his story.

By the time I was outside, Mr. Raffodil and Dan Pickett were gone. I hurried down to Hiawatha's stall. He was safe, and everything was all right, so I went down the midway to live it up for an hour or so before bedtime. Grandfather had tonight's watch. This was my chance to see the fair at its best, by night. Going up in the Ferris wheel you could see all the lights of Green Valley for miles away, as well as all the brightly lighted booths and sideshows below. I was wishing Angela Raffodil was up there with me, or even a second-best, Margie Kelly.

I glanced over toward the lighted stable area. I saw billows of smoke coming out of one of the stalls in the barn where both Hiawatha and Thunderbolt were stabled. I couldn't tell which stall it was.

From way up at the top of the Ferris wheel I began yelling for the operator to bring me down, fast, and stop the wheel. There was so much laughing and yelling going on, that he never heard me. When I came down the ark to the ground I was screaming bloody murder and pointing to the stables.

"Fire!" I yelled. "Fire in the stables!"

The operator stopped the Ferris wheel, but by that time everybody knew the horrible truth. Fire sirens were screaming and people were pouring out of every building. I could see and hear the bright red fire truck roaring through the front gate. I could hear the clanging of their bells, and I watched the hook and ladder come reeling in close behind.

It was too terrible to wait, so I leaped out of my chair while the Ferris wheel was still moving. I was off that seat and out of that section of the fairgrounds in a shot, bouncing off people on the midway as I raced for Hiawatha's stall.

By the time I reached the stable area, I had to fight my way through a crowd of spectators. I kept shouting, "Let me through! I own one of the horses!"

Nobody believed me, and kept pushing me aside. The hook-and-ladder truck arrived at almost the same time as I did. I swung behind the big machine and followed it into the barn area.

I saw Grandfather limping without his cane toward Hiawatha's stall and opening the door from under which the heaviest smoke was pouring out. He rushed inside. I cried out to him and tried to join him. A fairgrounds police guard caught me by the wrist and held me back.

"You can't go in there," he warned. "Everybody, back!"

"My horse is in there! He needs me!" I yelled, but he held me tight.

As soon as Grandfather opened the door to Hiawatha's stall, huge clouds of smoke came billowing out. There were no flames yet, but the smoke was blinding. I knew Grandfather couldn't stay in there long and survive.

My eyes were smarting, and most of the people around me had begun to cough and rub their eyes. We were right in the path of the prevailing wind.

I broke free, and raced to the stable door, followed by two guards. Grandfather came out just as I reached it. He was carrying a large pail in each hand. He threw them out onto the grassy area.

"Smoke bombs!" he cried. He looked at the firemen rushing up carrying big hoses toward the door.

"There's no fire," he shouted at them, "It's a hoax!"

"Prank, my eye. This is a crime!"

Smoke was still billowing out of the two pails Grandfather had brought out. Grandfather went back inside to open the windows and the two guards went with him. They came out with two more smoking pails each. A few more were found in the adjoining stalls.

"That's the lot," they finally said.

When Grandfather came out this time, I ran and hugged him, and handed him his cane which someone had brought.

"You all right?" I asked.

"Just fine."

"Is Hiawatha all right?"

"They say he is. He was taken to safety with Thunderbolt and Wildfire before the smoke started."

"Where is he?"

"In the big yard at the end of the barns, they say."

"Hip, hip, hurray!" I cheered.

I couldn't tell from the top of the Ferris wheel where the fire was, but it looked like it was in Hiawatha's stable, and I had been terrified!

Bert Phillips, the volunteer fire chief, was pretty upset. All the firemen were. Fortunately, most of volunteer company no. 3 had been enjoying themselves at the fair with their families when the alarm sounded. For once, the volunteer firemen beat the truck and the hook-and-ladder to the scene, but they weren't too happy about having their fun interrupted for a prank like smoke bombs.

"Prank, my eye!" Chief Phillips cried out. "This is a felony. A crime. It could have started a panic among all the animals. I want the wise guy who did this, and I want him bad."

Chief Phillips glared at the crowd, hoping he might surprise a guilty face, I guess. He added: "And I want him fast."

Grandfather agreed with the chief. "All lovers of horseflesh agree with you there, Chief. If this is somebody's idea of a practical joke, we're dealing with a warped mind."

"Any idea who it might be?" the chief asked.

"Not one," Grandfather answered, "Noboby I know could be guilty of such a cruel hoax."

"I've got plenty of ideas," I told Chief Phillips.

Grandfather gripped my arm and squeezed tightly. I started to object, but Grandfather clamped a hand over my mouth, and squeezed my biceps until all the circulation stopped in my whole arm. It hurt so I gave up and went limp.

Chief Phillips broke up the crowd.

"Terrifying and threatening the lives of horses is no joke," Grandfather angrily pointed out when the chief came back. "You can be sure that all the drivers and trainers will get to the bottom of this. Fortunately, most of the stalls in this wing of the stable are empty. Perhaps someone knew that Thunderbolt, Hiawatha, and Wildfire were the only three horses stabled in this particular wing."

"Maybe," Chief Phillips said. "Perhaps the so-called prankster was creating a diversion, so some other crime could be commited more safely in another part of the fairgrounds. We'll have to check immediately."

The hackles went up on the back of my neck, and the back of Grandfather's neck at the same time. We turned, and hurried toward the open yard where they were supposed to be holding the race horses. Grandfather flew so fast with his cane that I could hardly keep up.

Thunderbolt was there , tied to tree. So was Mr. Hartman's horse, Wildfire. But no big red horse, anywhere. We searched every corner of the fairgrounds, over and over.

Hiawatha was gone!

The Sixth Furlong!

"A feeling in my bones."

57.

"Somebody's stolen Hiawatha," I shouted.

Grandfather quieted me down. "Maybe not," he said. "Let's look around. Maybe Uncle Cliff took Hiawatha to another yard, or put him in an empty stall somewhere."

We combed the entire fairgrounds. There were horses everywhere, jumping horses, show horses, Clydesdales, Percherons, other work horses, as well as mules, donkeys and small ponies. But no Hiawatha and no Uncle Cliff.

"Somebody stole Hiawatha," I insisted, "and I know just who it was."

"Now, son. Let's not get carried away. Let's wait until we hear from your Uncle Cliff."

We hurried back to Hiawatha's stall to see if there was any word from Uncle Cliff. Not a word. It's not easy to talk when you're unconscious.

We both heard the moaning sound at the same time, the minute we entered the stall. A sort of a low cry. We looked over at Hiawatha's stall. The mound of hay piled up in the corner began to move.

We rushed over, pulled the hay aside, and there was Uncle Cliff. He was tied hand and foot with clothes rope. There was a gag in his mouth and he smelled of chloroform. We untied him, but Uncle Cliff was still too groggy to tell us anything. He kept rubbing his head. There was a big lump there.

When Uncle Cliff was able to talk, he didn't have much to

say. He didn't know what happened. Something hit him on the back of his head, and the next thing Uncle Cliff knew, he was looking up at us.

Grandfather told him how lucky he was to be flat on the floor or he might have been smothered to death from the smoke. Uncle Cliff was coughing some, but outside of the egg on his head and a sore throat from smoke he was all right.

Uncle Cliff sat up and looked over at the empty stall. "Where's Hiawatha?" he asked.

"That," Grandfather told him, "is the million dollar question."

We searched every stall at the fairgrounds just in case Hiawatha might have been hidden there. People working at the main gate to the fairgrounds swore that Hiawatha had not been taken out that way. They were positive.

We were about to give up for the night when Mr. Raffodil drove up in his buggy with Sam Junior sitting beside him. They both looked very smug, I thought, and told Grandfather so. He said I was overly suspicious, repeating that Sam Raffodil Senior had nothing to gain by engineering the disappearance of Hiawatha. He had to win the match race between Hiawatha and Thunderbolt to win the bet.

"Hear you had a little trouble over here," Mr. Raffodil said, sympathetically.

"How *long* ago did you hear that, Sam?" Grandfather asked.

"Everything's fine over at our stall next door. Thunderbolt's back in and everything's fine. Dan Pickett was walking him around in the yard at the time of the so-called fire and tied him up safely to a tree in the yard."

"How fortunate."

"Wasn't it?" Mr. Raffodil lit his big black cigar. "Tell me," he said, "how's that big red horse, Hiawatha?"

"Somebody stole Hiawatha, and we think we know who," I snapped. Grandfather laid a restraining hand on my shoulder.

"Good!" Mr. Raffodil said. "Go right out and arrest him. I'm sure Town Marshall Anderson will move quickly on any good evidence."

Mr. Raffodil announced to the gathering crowd that he was prepared to organize and supervise a search party that would cover the entire fairgrounds.

"We've already done that," Grandfather told him, knowing that Mr. Raffodil knew it, too. "Three times."

"And found nothing? Pity. But how could they smuggle such a huge horse out of the fairgrounds?"

"We'll find out. If they have."

"Just vanished into thin air, you say."

"Not thin air," Grandfather replied, eyeing Mr. Raffodil with frosty eyes. "Into somebody's horse trailer more likely."

"Have you asked at the front entrance gate?"

"We have. It's being guarded," Grandfather replied, a warning in his words.

"There's no other way a horse trailer could leave the grounds without everybody knowing."

"We know."

Mr. Raffodil shook his head. "Very mystifying," he said, pleased. Sam Raffodil was quite delighted with the cat-and-mouse game. "I checked myself." Mr. Raffodil added, "and the fairgrounds special police guards assure me that there hasn't been a single horse trailer to leave the fairgrounds all evening. Not one single large caravan or vehicle, or motor van or house trailer, that could hold such a large horse."

"Then Hiawatha must still be hidden somewhere on the fairgrounds," one of the fair security police declared.

"Let's get up another search party," Mr. Raffodil suggested, "and try a fourth time. We'll comb every inch." Mr. Raffodil had his big mayor's victory smile on his face. His lips were as warm as the summer, but his eyes were as cold as winter. "In fact, I'll bear all the expenses of a special complete search myself, out of my own pocket. And post a special reward. Call in the National Guard if necessary. We'll search the entire county if we have to.

Money is no object. All of us want to see that big red horse run against my national champion trotter, Thunderbolt. It won't do him any good, but fair is fair."

The people around us were very touched by Mr. Raffodil's generosity. They told him so. They were especially impressed in view of the feud that existed between Mr. Raffodil and Grandfather. They knew how both parties felt. But to see Mr. Raffodil uphold the spirit of the county fair, and come to the aid of a recognized opponent who had been victimized by thieves, brought a sprinkling of applause from the crowd. Mostly from the people from out-of-town.

Grandfather remained silent. But I was after Mr. Raffodil like a hawk after a plump hen. When he said, "Money is no object," I knew for certain that he had stolen Hiawatha. When it came to cold cash, Mr. Raffodil was tighter than the lug-nuts on a 1914 Ford car.

I whispered the truth to Grandfather. "He *knows* we can't find Hiawatha. He's got him in some secret hiding place. I'm sure of it. I've got a feeling in my bones." My voice was beginning to rise. Grandfather quieted me down with his usual painful tactics. But I could tell that he himself was more than suspicious.

Mr. Raffodil rubbed it in. "It would take a genius, or a master-criminal, to spirit a horse away from this closely guarded fairgrounds in front of thousands of people," he said. "Without a trace. A *real* genius." Everybody nodded in agreement.

"We know exactly where to find the dirty crook," I told Mr. Raffodil angrily. "Don't we Grandfather?!"

What Mr. Raffodil said next convinced us both that His Honor, the Mayor, Sam Raffodil Senior, was in the theft of Hiawatha up to his thick red neck. His astonishing words also let us know that if we didn't find Hiawatha, Grandfather would be down the drain. Everything would be lost.

Mr. Raffodil was the "real genius" at the bottom of it all.

58.

"Naturally, I'm sorry about your losing your horse," Mr. Raffodil continued, "but you understand, of course, that this tragedy doesn't let you off the hook as far as our bet is concerned."

"What do you mean?" Grandfather asked, surprised.

"It's a dirty shame about Hiawatha, but you still have to win the County Fair Stakes, or you lose the bet."

"I can't even race Thunderbolt, if I don't find Hiawatha," Grandfather replied. "So all bets will be off."

"Oh, no," Mr. Raffodil said, cheerfully. "You still have two other race horses, Dakar and Tropical. I know one is a trotter and one a pacer, but after all, this race is a free-for-all. Both horses are perfectly eligible and acceptable."

"To *you* maybe," Grandfather snapped, "but not to me. It's Hiawatha against Thunderbolt, a match race, or it's nothing. That was our bet."

"You may have thought that was the bet, but what it comes down to is winning the County Fair Stakes. Nothing else. The names of the horses running, were never mentioned."

"Everybody knew what the agreement was, Sam. Especially you and I. Thunderbolt against Hiawatha."

"You made me put it in writing, old man, and you signed it yourself. I think if you'll read it over carefully, especially the fine print at the bottom, you'll find I'm right. After all, it was *you* who insisted that I put it in writing."

"There was no small print in our agreement," Grandfather

objected. "Not the one I signed in your office. Ask the other stewards, Fletcher Potter and Gerard Stevens."

"No need." Mr. Raffodil threw a copy of the agreement at Grandfather. "Read it again, my friend."

You could tell by the way he said, "my friend," that he meant "my enemy." I think I heard him mumble, "Read it and weep." Mr. Raffodil sat there in his buggy with that big election-day victory smile.

I lost my temper and picked up the shovel by the stable door. "Can I hit him with the manure shovel, Grandfather? Just once? It's the shovel we used to kill that copperhead snake last summer."

Grandfather restrained me. He never said a word. He knew that Mr. Raffodil was enjoying tremendously what he thought was his moment of victory.

"Naturally," Mr. Raffodil smiled, "it *is* a pity that your chestnut horse Hiawatha is out of the running. But you wanted an agreement in writing. You've got it! Now live with it."

"Hiawatha is not out of the running yet," Grandfather warned him.

"Good!" Mr. Raffodil said, genially.

"Besides, both you and I know that you added that small print after I signed that document in your office and left."

"Prove it!"

"I intend to. We'll see what the courts say."

Mr. Raffodil laughed. He took up the reins to drive off, and waved to the crowd. To Grandfather he said: "If it will make you feel more comfortable, phone Potter and Stevens, but you should know that they've already given their depositions that the document you hold in your hand is the exact document you signed. With all the rules clearly described."

I raised the manure shovel again. "Now can I, Grandfather?"

"I've just learned from private sources," Mr. Raffodil told Grandfather, "that your red horse ran all the way out to

Anderson's farm on the Sunday your grandson wrecked my new car. Maybe you can look for the lost chestnut out there. Or perhaps down by the river. He might have felt in need of another urgent treatment of leeches."

Mr. Raffodil laughed cheerfully as he said all these insulting things in that smarmy solicitous voice of his. I like it better when the person who is mad at you, has a mean look on his face and yells right back at you so you can tell he is furious. That's the way Mr. Raffodil usually does it. This time he was too smooth and pleased with himself. I don't like smilers who quietly stick their knife in your ribs while they're cheerfully offering condolences.

"Do they still hang horse thieves, Grandfather?" I asked.

Sam Raffodil Junior jumped down from the buggy and moved menacingly toward me. "You take that back!"

"Make me!"

He tried, but I put on an award winning show of ducking every swing Sam threw. I held the manure shovel up in front of me and Sam Raffodil slammed his fist into it. I could tell it hurt by the soul-warming cry of pain that came out of him. There was murder in his eyes when Grandfather and Mr. Raffodil broke it up.

Grandfather held us apart, and Mr. Raffodil ordered Sam back into the buggy. He went reluctantly. Sam leaned out of the buggy and held up his claxon horn and blew it.

"Ahooouuuaaah!"

"I won't be needing this now," he said. "Now that your race horse was smuggled out of the fairgrounds so cleverly by a *real genius.*" Sam smiled at his father. "Your Hiawatha," he said, "is a goner. Permanently."

Mr. Raffodil gave Sam a hard cuff on the neck. But not hard enough to keep him from making two blasts on the horn and they drove away.

"Ahoooouuuuaaah! Ahoooouuuaaah!"

59.

"Mr. Raffodil was laughing at us, Grandfather," I said, angrily. "He made a fool out of us. He knows exactly where Hiawatha is. *He's* the real genius. Sam all but said so, didn't he? And now he knows how far and how fast Hiawatha can run, too. That's why he kidnapped him. He's afraid he can best Thunderbolt."

Grandfather nodded.

"And it's why he put in the 'small print.' I should have been smart enough to look for his cunning tricks. Now, it's up to us to figure out *how* he smuggled Hiawatha out of the fairgrounds. If he could do that, certainly we should be smart enough to figure out how he did it."

Grandfather pointed to the bottom of the agreement. "Sam added the fine print after I left. After I signed the document. It says that any horse can run in the race for either of us. Sam used the notary public seal on top of my signature. Plus another big stamp from the bank. They perforated the wording so it was hard to read if you didn't look at it closely."

"Isn't that illegal?"

"Not only illegal, but criminal. I'll have our lawyers all over Sam in the morning. Unfortunately, I don't have a copy to show what the document said originally."

"That's not like you at all, Grandfather. Especially when you knew you were dealing with a viper."

"Over-confidence is a terrible thing," Grandfather admitted. "I was so pleased about tricking them into a mile and a half race, that I let Sam outwit me."

"He's a master criminal, isn't he, Grandfather? A regular Rudolph Rassendale, or Dr. Fu Manchu, or Professor Moriarity, or worse, isn't he, Grandfather?"

"Sam Raffodil is peanuts compared to those illustrious villains," Grandfather assured me. "But we're not through yet, Grandson. We are going to make Mr. Raffodil cry, 'Foiled! Curses!'"

"How?"

"Somehow."

We drove silently home from the fairgrounds to Grandfather's barn. The hooves of Beauty and Prince on the dirt road echoed all the way home. We unhitched and bedded down the horses, and Grandfather went quietly over to the oats box and sat down.

I joined him. "If only you'd have let me keep GOG in the stable with Hiawatha as a watchdog, we might have scared them off."

Grandfather grunted. "You're already teary-eyed over the horse. If you'd have lost your pet goose, too, you'd be absolutely no use to me at all."

"Then *how* are we going to make Mr. Raffodil holler, 'Foiled' and 'Curses!,' Grandfather?" I asked him.

"Hatch and plot," he said. "There's nothing else *to* do. Hatch and plot."

We were both still in a state of shock over Mr. Raffodil's trickery and dishonesty in avoiding the match race. There was no way for us to win without Hiawatha. He knew that. And so did we.

We "hatched" and "plotted" trying to think how they could have possibly smuggled Hiawatha out of the fairgrounds. Neither of us "hatched" anything, or came up with even a halfway decent "plot" to rescue Hiawatha. There was no way to save that big red horse until we knew where they had hidden him, and how they had spirited Hiawatha out of the big fairgrounds entrance gate without a trace.

Grandfather finally blew out the lanterns, and we walked up the path to the house.

"Tomorrow," he said. "At dawn."

"Yes, sir. I'll be here. But I won't sleep a wink tonight."

Before crawling into bed at home, I decided that this was one night I wouldn't forget my prayers. Not the short made-up ones like "Thanks, God, for today, have a nice night Yourself."

This was crisis time, and required the official memorized church prayers. All of them. I even used a Protestant prayer I'd learned from Jimmy Middleman, and a short Jewish chant Jake Lefcoe had taught me the summer I lost my baseball bat.

I was using all the ammunition I had. I was going for broke religiously. I'd sit up worrying all night, then at dawn I'd begin to search for Hiawatha. Everywhere.

Grandfather said Muhammad taught the believers to pray five times a day, but told them never to forget their daily work. "Trust in God, but tie your camel," he said. I didn't have a camel to tie, but I'd sure open a lot of doors and windows tomorrow.

I knew this was no time for drowsy mumbling-under-the-covers type of praying. This was a get right down on your bare knees on the cold hard floor and talk turkey to God job. I wanted God to realize exactly how big this crisis was. I'd been pretty easy on Him all summer, and had hardly asked for anything. Just small petty stuff. This time I really needed His help. This was the big one. No nonsense. Grandfather needed His help, and so did Hiawatha. All of us did.

I figured God must appreciate someone as nice as Grandfather who was always doing "good works," and that He would look down upon Grandfather with a charitable and sin-covering eye if I put in a good word for him.

As soon as I finished my prayers, I hopped back into bed. GOG flew up on the woodshed roof. He was knocking on windowpane with his beak to get in. I flipped the covers off, opened the window so GOG could join me before father began his "The goose goes!" routine.

I slipped a rubber band, which I kept handy on the bedstead for just such emergency purposes, over GOG's bill to hold down the "honking." I motioned to him for absolute silence.

While I was up, I quickly knelt down by the bed again for another emergency prayer. "And please, God, don't forget Grandmother. That poor lady is in a peck of trouble, and doesn't even know about it yet. Let her sleep peacefully. It may be her last night. Amen!"

"Oh, yes. P.S. God," I added when I was back under the covers. "Please keep Mrs. Casey, and especially Glad Tidings, totally ignorant about Grandfather's dumb mug's wager. If you could give them both a bad case of the flu so they'd lose their voices until the fair was over, I wouldn't mind. If it isn't too ungodly. Thank you again. William Sears, Junior."

I pulled the covers up around my neck, and quoted my very own father out loud, "Where will it all end?" I lay awake for a long, long time, thinking. GOG kept waddling back and forth across the footboard at the bottom of my bed. Apparently he couldn't see any way out either.

Finally, I went downstairs and fixed myself two peanut-butter sandwiches, a red apple, a piece of cheese and a big glass of milk.

"Where are you, Hiawatha?" I asked as I propped up my pillows to sit up all night. I ate my snack and fell asleep immediately.

It was barely dawn when I woke up, ashamed and embarrassed that I had been too exhausted to "hatch and plot" by myself. I shot down to Grandfather's barn, and was already sitting on the oats box when he arrived.

60.

Grandfather and I didn't have any luck all day. Grandfather searched the town and the county accompanied by two deputy sheriffs. I covered even more ground, all inside the city limits including the Raffodil's Livery Stable.

When I left Grandfather's barn early that morning, I went home for breakfast. I didn't want to lose the friendship of my family by disappearing all the time. I opened the woodshed door, and there leaning against the wall was a shiny new bicycle with a big wire basket and a large brown paper sack sitting inside. A note was pinned to it. It was from Father.

"Sorry I missed you at breakfast. I rented this bike for today. All day. You can cover more ground on wheels. The brown paper sack is your lunch. You'll find two dollar bills inside. Good luck on your search for Hiawatha, Love, Dad."

I had a lump in my throat. I said to myself, "I have lost a horse, but I have found a father."

Even with the help of Father and the bicycle, there was no sign of Hiawatha anywhere. I returned the rented bike and walked home very discouraged. Little did I know that while I had "tied my camel," I hadn't "trusted in God." The Big Fellow was about to break the whole case wide open. I could have saved my tears.

Our telephone rang at midnight!

Mother said, "I wonder who that could be calling at this unearthly hour?"

Father grumbled, "There's a marvelous way to find out."

"Hello?"

"This is Secret Agent Nine. Could I speak to the Chief of all Agents, please. It's urgent."

"I'm afraid William is asleep." Annoyed. "It's almost morning."

"Then wake him up. It's an emergency. A real emergency."

"It always is."

"Tell him to meet me in ten minutes at the usual place."

"I'll do nothing of the kind. I'm afraid I can't disturb him."

"You'd better disturb him. It's about his missing horse."

Secret Agent Nine hung up.

"What was that all about?" Father asked.

I was looking down through the air vent in my bedroom and heard perfectly, and knew exactly what it meant.

Mother explained it carefully for Father, "That," she said, "was Secret Agent Nine seeking immediate consultation with the Chief of all Agents at the usual place in ten minutes."

"Oh," said Father, and went back to reading the *St. Paul Daily Dispatch.*

I came shooting down the stairs. "That call was personal and private, and was for me." No one answered me, so I said, "I have to get dressed and go out."

That received immediate attention. Father pointed to the stairs.

"Up! Up!" he said. "You go to bed immediately!"

Mother agreed. So I went upstairs.

I dressed myself quickly and went out the window, along the woodshed roof, and shinnied down the maple tree. I fell the last five feet when I missed a branch. I hurried along to the usual secret meeting place, the haymow in my Grandfather's barn. I climbed the ladder beside the bay mare Beauty's stall, and shoved my head up into the haymow.

"Hello!" I called.

Nobody answered. I raised my voice, "Is anybody here?"

"Quiet you fool!" someone whispered in the dark. I recognized Margie Kelly's voice. "Don't raise your voice. I may have been followed."

"By whom?"

"I don't know. But I had to come and tell you about Hiawatha."

"What about Hiawatha?"

"Maybe it doesn't mean anything."

"Let me decide that."

"It's something my brother Midge said. He said it was very important."

"So?"

"He was practicing with his bow and arrow while helping Short-Stuff Farley as one of your secret agents watching whoever went in and out of the fairgrounds' gate in case they had smuggled Hiawatha out that way."

"I *know* all that! Don't waste my time."

"Yes, but do you know that my brother Midge shot a practice arrow into the side of a huge loaded hayrack that was waiting to go out the fairgrounds gate?"

I didn't.

"Well," she said snippily, "Midge says the arrow only went a few inches into the bale of hay. It was stuck solidly there. Midge could hardly pull the arrow out. Midge said it was stuck in wood, not hay. He thinks that the whole hayrack was a fake."

"Really?"

"Midge walked all around the entire hayrack while it was waiting to leave. Wherever Midge jabbed his arrow into the hay by hand, the arrowhead stuck in wood. Just a few inches in."

"Why didn't Midge come and tell me this himself? Right away?"

"Because he thought it was smarter to follow the hayrack. It went all the way to the old gypsy campground. Midge thought maybe Hiawatha was inside that fake hayrack and that's how they smuggled your horse out of the grounds."

"Where is Midge now?"

"I don't know. He hasn't come home yet."

"There's no way for me to go out there. I turned in my rented bike."

"You can take my bicycle. And my flashlight."

"Great! I'll ride you home on the handlebars."

"Be careful," she said. "I wouldn't be caught dead in that old spooky gypsy camp at night."

"It's only a freight junction now. There haven't been any gypsies there for years."

"And don't let anything happen to my bicycle."

"I won't."

If either of us had known that her bicycle would wind up in the hands of the law, broken and twisted while I was riding it, I think we both would probably have turned around and gone home to bed.

Right then.

61.

I rode Margie home on the back seat, then set off for the old gypsy railroad junction. Since Grandfather and I were partners, I decided I'd better telephone and let him know where I was going and why.

I called him from Mendocina's Drugstore, the only one open that late. I had to borrow a nickel from Mr. Mendocina. I told him it was a life and death emergency.

"In that case," he said, "take two nickels."

When Grandfather answered, I yelled excitedly in his ear. "Great news!"

"Don't shout in my ear. Do you know what time it is?"

"One of my secret agents has uncovered an exciting clue about Hiawatha's kidnapping. I think we know how they smuggled Hiawatha out of the fairgrounds!"

"I don't want to hear about your secret agents. I've had them up to here. Everytime I turn around I step on one."

"You told me to go ahead and use them if it could help us find Hiawatha."

"Not at this time of night."

"This is very important, Grandfather. It's about a hayrack going *out* of the fairgrounds, not in! Isn't that suspicious? *Out!* Not *in!* And it went straight to the old gypsy camp outside of town where they're holding all those horses for that dog food company. My secret agents and I think that hayrack is how they smuggled Hiawatha out of the fairgrounds!"

There was no response from Grandfather. I hurried on. "Hiawatha might just have been inside that hayrack!"

"Don't shout in my ear."

"It just so happens that they could have sneaked Hiawatha out that way. Right under our very noses."

"Hardly."

"Why not?"

Grandfather exploded my mysterious hayrack theory. "It just so happens," he said, imitating my style, "that the sheriff and I know all about the loads of hay going out to the Soo Line Junction. It's surplus hay from the fairgrounds being shipped out to the old gypsy camp for the Jax Dog Food people to feed the horses out there. A contract."

I was horrified. "You mean they're going to kill all those horses and feed them to the dogs?"

"That's not the point."

"To me, it is. I'm just going out there right now myself and check on it. I've borrowed Margie Kelly's bicycle, and I can be out there in only a few—"

Grandfather hit the roof. "You stay home and leave the dangerous stuff up to your grandfather. That's an order. Don't move a foot toward that old gypsy camp."

"*Somebody* should go out there!"

"Somebody is. At dawn's first light."

I wanted immediate action. "Why not now? This very minute? If there's any chance of Hiawatha being there? Before they hide him again."

"Because," Grandfather said, "I want the law with me. We're going to pin this one on Sam Raffodil. No loop holes."

"But the town marshall is a crook! He's in Mayor Raffodil's pocket. You *said* so!"

"I know. That's why we have to wait for the sheriff's department from the county seat with a few of his special deputies to back us up. I'm sure the dog food people are not involved. But there may be a rotten apple or two in the crew."

"You haven't heard my most exciting clue of all yet, Grandfather. Just let me tell you about the hayrack. You may want to go out there right now. This very minute."

"Go home."

"I don't want to go home."

There was a long pause.

"Can't I even tell you about my famous clue of the hayrack?"

"Go home. No back talk."

"Don't hang up," I pleaded. I was disgusted. I said, "When *is* the dawn's first light tomorrow?"

"We leave the barn in a body at five a.m."

"I'll be there."

"You stay at home. There may be trouble."

"Good! I'll bring my hockey stick."

"You'll have to sit in the car," Grandfather warned.

"If I see Hiawatha, I'm going to come shooting out of that car like a Roman candle and blast everybody in sight!"

"That's why you're staying at home. That's an order."

"Okey! I'll sit in the car," I agreed.

"Quietly?"

"Quietly."

"All right. You can come. But return that bicycle to Margie Kelly. Then go home as soon as you hang up the phone. And stay there. I don't want you going anywhere near that old gypsy campground tonight. Hear?"

"Of course I hear."

"But will you do it?"

"You know me, Grandfather."

"I *do* know you! That's why I say, *Go Home!!*"

"Can't I tell you about the most exciting clue of all, Grandfather?"

"Sleep on it. Tomorrow will be soon enough. Right now I'm in conference with the sheriff. We're waiting for his deputies."

"I'm on my way," I told him.

I didn't say where I was on my way to, and I had my fingers crossed when I said goodnight to Grandfather and hung up the phone. So, it wasn't really dishonest and deceitful. Was it?*

Don't you hate it in the movies when people won't listen to the most important clue of all? Even from their friends, the good guys?

---

* The same to you!

The Tamarack Road in the midnight moonlight.

62.

To myself, on the way out of town, I said: "In a pig's eye I would have sat in that car quietly. One glimpse of Hiawatha, and *Zoom!* I'll run 'em down with Margie Kelly's bike. And knock them in the head with the handlebars! All flags flying!"

As I pumped the bicycle along the Tamarack Road in the moonlight, I kept saying to myself: "This is dumb, real dumb. I shouldn't do it. I should go back and tell Grandfather where I'm going even if I *am* peeved with him. I should make him listen about the arrow and the hayrack. I should tell Grandfather that I just can't wait, but I'll be waiting for him when he and the sheriff and all those deputies arrive at dawn's early light.

Maybe I'll even have a chestnut horse waiting for them; Hiawatha!

I knew in my heart that I wasn't going to call Grandfather again, but I kept telling myself over and over that it was dumb not to call him.

Okey, I admit I was wrong, and I really do hate it in the movies when somebody goes off half-cocked into danger like I was doing without telling anybody about it. The whole darned movie house knows it's wrong and stupid. Everybody except the blockhead who's doing it. Especially when there's a person who really should know all about it, and could probably help rescue Hiawatha, like my Grandfather.

"It's dumb. Real dumb."

But I pedaled right on out to the old gypsy camp. Just like

those idiots in the movies. Until that night, I never knew why those dumbbells did such stupid things.

Now, I knew.

They didn't want to look like a fool. That's why they did such dumb things. They always waited until it was too late to tell anybody, and then they proved to be exactly what everybody watching the movie knew they were, fatheaded, dumb, ignorant fools! Who should have told somebody in the first place, but who were such "dumbbells" they figured they could bring it off alone without help.

Maybe those movie lunkheads loved somebody as much as I loved Hiawatha, and that's what pushed them so far into danger that they finally went over the precipice. Love can make you do real queer things like that.

By the time I realized for sure that I should have returned for "backup" after reporting to Grandfather, I was already riding down the slope right into the heart of the old gypsy camp. It was too late.

I was on my own!

The Hayrack!

63.

A dog was howling as I approached the abandoned Soo Line Junction where the old gypsy camp was located. A solitary lamp was flickering in one of the canvas covered wagons.

I hid Margie Kelly's bicycle in the woods, leaned it against a big pine tree, and stole quietly down through the Tamarack trees. I was searching for the place they might be holding Hiawatha.

Five men where playing cards in a lighted wagon. I could hear the mumble of their voices. Somebody was snoring up a cyclone in the next nearby wagon. There were three automobiles, a van, and a pickup truck. I saw two lanterns moving down by the freight cars. I slunk quietly up toward them, keeping in the shadows and out of the moonlight.

Two men were leading horses up a ramp from a small corral into an empty cattle car.

I couldn't see Hiawatha anywhere. I knew if Hiawatha was already inside one of those freight cars, I'd have a hard time rescuing him without making a lot of noise. But I'd have to do it before that freight train took off for Duluth and the Jax Dog Food factory.

"That's the last one for tonight," the one in charge said.

"What about the grey?"

"Nothing doing. He stays in the hayrack until we get the rest of our money. I don't trust that smiling old windbag."

I knew he must be talking about Mr. Raffodil.

"Maybe we could hold the grey horse out, and sell him ourselves, on the side, for a lot more money than for horse-meat."

"A bargain's a bargain. Besides, I think that's what the old geezer himself has in mind. He said keep the grey to one side because he might want to collect him personally later. Just disguise him, he said."

They both laughed heartily.

"Well," the second man said, "we've certainly done that!"

"And keep your mouth shut around the boss and the rest of the men, unless you want a smaller split."

I hid behind a tree, until their voices faded away. Then I slipped carefully along from tree to tree looking for the hayrack. I found it, parked beneath the overspreading branches of a giant oak.

I walked around the hayrack carefully. I wanted to be sure this was the hayrack that went out of the fairground and was now Hiawatha's prison, and not just another load of alfalfa for the poor horses they had penned up in the corral by the empty cattle cars. There were a couple of loose bales of hay on top of the load, and three bales on the ground with a pitchfork stuck in one of them. That made me think it was not a fake hayrack.

But, on the other hand, maybe it was supposed to do just that. Grandfather always said that when you were dealing with horses not to trust anyone. Not even your own mother, and to keep a careful eye on yourself. Whoever had stolen Hiawatha was very clever. I had to be smarter.

I glanced up into the oak tree. Two huge eyes were staring at me. A lookout! I nearly dropped the flashlight. Before I could throw myself out of sight beneath the hayrack, an old owl hooted: "Whooo! Whooo! Whooo!"

My heart was beating so hard it hurt. When I stopped trembling, I shook my fist at the owl, and continued my search. Slowly, I walked all the way around the hayrack.

It was loaded solid with bales of hay, top to bottom. It certainly looked like the real thing, a big normal load of hay. Remembering what Midge had said about the arrow he shot into the side of the hayrack, I picked up the pitchfork and began poking it into the side of the stacked bales. Probing for evidence.

The tines went "ping". The points went into the hay only a few inches before striking something solid. I tried a few more experimental stabs all along both sides of the hayrack and against the back end.

Ping! Ping! Ping!

No doubt about it.

The load of hay in front of me was a fake!

Midge was right. The bales of hay had obviously been wired, glued and fastened onto the sides of the hayrack to make it look like a perfect bale of hay—part of a natural looking full load of hay on the hayrack.

It was done with great cunning and skill. It would have fooled anybody if it hadn't been for a lucky accident. Thanks to Midge Kelly, Secret Agent Number Seven, and the bow and arrow he'd been given for his birthday, the one I'd told him to leave home and stop practicing while Hiawatha was still missing. Especially when he had such an important job as watching the front gate of the fairgrounds.

It was a good thing Midge Kelly had disobeyed. If Midge had been there with me at the old gypsy camp, I'd have given him a big hug and a fat kiss on the cheek no matter how revolting it would have been to him.

Grandfather was totally wrong about the secret agents. Thanks to them, we now knew for sure exactly how Mr. Raffodil had spirited Hiawatha away from the fairgrounds.

If you looked the hayrack over very carefully, inch by inch as I now did, you could discover the outline of a huge door at the back. It was hung up at the top with huge hidden hinges like a secret panel in a library wall. The door was beautifully disguised like the rest of the hayrack with fake bales of hay. The hidden door was bolted and padlocked at the bottom under the rack.

The padlock was open, hooked loose over the rasp. Quietly

I lifted the big lock off and slipped the bolt. I waited to see if anyone had heard me, then I swung the big door open just wide enough for me to squeeze inside. The door swung closed behind me. I couldn't see a thing. I turned on Margie Kelly's flashlight.

Hiawatha wasn't there!

Only an ugly old gray mare. Another turn of my flashlight showed me that it was a colt, not a mare. And not old, young. The two men at the corral had talked distainfuly about an old grey horse hidden in the hayrack. They were wrong, too. It was a young horse.

They had laughed about it, so maybe they knew the truth. But sad to say, this grey horse didn't look anything like Hiawatha, so perhaps he hadn't been smuggled out of the fairgrounds in this hayrack.

On the other hand, the grey horse began nuzzling my neck just like Hiawatha used to do. "Hiawatha?" I asked him.

The grey horse answered by lifting off my cap and tossing it onto the floor, a favorite trick of Hiawatha's. I turned the flashlight on his grey face. I was delighted but still couldn't believe it.

"Hiawatha?"

Whinny.

"Can you count to five grey horse?"

The big grey horse pawed the bottom of the hayrack five times. It echoed as loud as a bass drum. I shouldn't have asked that question. I was alarmed and snapped off the flashlight.

"Quiet, Hiawatha!" I warned him. "Don't count so loud! We're in a nest of vipers."

We both listened carefully. No sound. Perhaps they were used to hearing those sounds. In the silence all I heard was Hooty, the owl, asking over and over, "Whooo? Whooo? Whooo?"

I was so happy I couldn't bear it. I answered Hooty, the owl right back, while I was hugging that big grey around the neck. "Hiawatha! That's who! Whooo! Whooo!"

Just to make absolutely sure, I dropped to my knees and

switched Margie Kelly's flashlight back on. I looked at the right front hoof of the big grey horse. It was caked with mud. I spat on my fingers and began to rub the dirt away. Gradually it began to take the shape of a star. More spit. More rubbing.

There before my eagerly focusing eyes was a bright nine-pointed crimson star!

It *was* Hiawatha!

I'd found him at last. Absolutely. Positively. The one and only. And I knew it. There could be no mistake. And I didn't care if he was as grey as my grandmother's hair.

This was my horse!

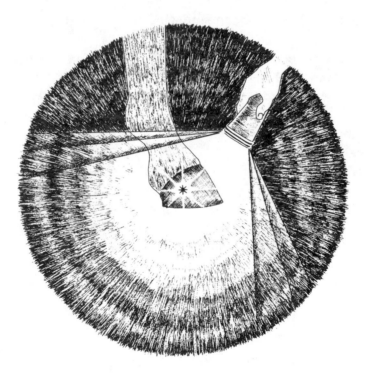

It was Hiawatha!

I hugged Hiawatha's leg like it was the finishing post and he'd just won the big County Fair Stakes. At least, now he had a chance to do it. I was still on my knees, so I said a short prayer of thanksgiving for the miracle rescue. Now, all I had to do was get us both out of there. Quickly and safely.

I realized it wouldn't be easy figuring out how to prop open that big door, put up the ramp, leap on Hiawatha's back, and ride out of the hayrack and the gypsy camp a mile a minute like Paul Revere riding through every Middlesex village and farm, yelling, "On to the fairgrounds! Hiawatha is coming!"

If Sam Raffodil, big or little, or anyone else got in my way this time, I'd run them down, and Hiawatha would stomp on them. The excitement made my scalp creep.

Or was it something else?

Something made my scalp creep.

Maybe the best thing would be to "use my coop."*

Both of us could hide out in the woods and wait until dawn's early light. When Grandfather and the sheriff appeared, we could come barreling out of those tamarack and pine trees and spill the beans. We'd arrest everybody in sight, turn all those innocent horses loose in the corral and empty the freight cars. Hiawatha would be on his way back to the fairgrounds where

---

* My uncle Earl used that expression. He said that most of the trouble in the world was because people didn't "use their coops."

he'd ride Grandfather's colors to glory.

Hot diggety dog! It was almost too good to be true. I was so overjoyed, I wanted one last look at that shiny red star on Hiawatha's hoof. I looked, then switched off the flashlight.

I was startled.

A ring of light still covered the red star on Hiawatha's hoof. I looked at my flashlight. It was off. I looked up. That's when I saw a second flashlight. It was shining directly into my eyes!

I scooted between a pair of long legs in Levi's and tried to escape out the door.

"Grab him, Oscar!"

Oscar did it. I was captured. Helpless in his grasp. Now they had two prisoners in the hayrack. Hiawatha and his best friend, me. But at least Hiawatha was found! And we were together! We were willing to take on the world.

"Somebody's going to miss this kid, and the first thing you know the sheriff will be driving out here."

At dawn's early light! I told myself.

"If they find the kid, they'll find the horse."

"No chance. Beside, we've already been tipped off that the sheriff is coming. At dawn. We'll be ready for him."

"Raffodil says to get the grey horse out of the hayrack and disguise him completely. More than just the grey paint job. Stop worrying. They don't hang horse thieves and cattle rustlers any longer."

Pity, I thought.

"They could still put us away for a long, long time if they nail us and check our record."

"They're not going to nail us. Lead the grey out and tie him to the corral fence. I'll do the rest. We don't want the horse inside the hayrack. He might whinny or paw, and give the show away. I'm going to give him another coat of grey wash and a little gypsy costuming. I plan to hitch him to the crazy gypsy wagon. Even his own mother won't recognize him. Nor will anyone else when I'm through fixing him up."

I could hear Oscar laughing uproariously as they led Hiawatha out of the hayrack. The door slammed and I was left alone.

I kept yelling, "Help! Police! and Murder!" and assorted other things. Oscar came back and put a gag in my mouth and tied a dirty cloth over it. I couldn't see it, but it smelled dirty and oily. Just like Oscar. I couldn't speak, but I kept humming "help!" at the top of my hum.

"You're asking for it, kid," Oscar told me, and cuffed me roughly alongside the head. It made my ears ring.

When I wasn't able to yell, I kept pounding on the floor of the hayrack with my feet. It didn't make enough sound to attract any attention. Except Oscar's. He roped my ankles together and to the wall, and left me.

I finally fell asleep, but awoke with a start when I heard cars or trucks drive into the junction yard. I knew it must be dawn's early light. I began yelling inside my gag.

"Grandfather! I'm over here! Help! Police! Murder! Geronimo!"

No one could hear me. But I could hear them.

"That grey gypsy horse hitched to the funny wagon is Hiawatha, Grandfather. Don't let them fool you, Grandfather! He's not grey, he's a chestnut. They painted him just like you said the crooks used to do in New York. Grandfather! Help! Murder! Police!"

A short time later, I heard Grandfather's voice, and what I assumed to be the sheriff and his assorted deputies, walking around the hayrack. They were searching the grounds for Hiawatha. Grandfather had no idea that I was anywhere near. As they approached the hayrack, I yelled at the top of my lungs. I kept trying to shout at Grandfather through the gag and cloth over my mouth.

Oscar and his friend Pete had been very clever. Now I knew why those extra bales of hay were on the roof. I could hear Pete walking around up there. He was pitching hay down onto the buckboard below. Who would ever think the rest of the hayrack wasn't real.

I yelled my head off, "Look inside the hayrack, Grandfather! Inside! It's a fake!" If only he had let me tell him about it on the phone.

I could hear the sheriff's party moving away. The search was over. Unless I could think of something quickly, Hiawatha and I were lost. I finally stopped trying to yell, and moaned as loud as I could, louder than Old Lady Yellowjacket when her arthritis was bad. It sounded agonizing to me.

I heard Grandfather's voice far off say, "What was that?"

I yelled inside. "It's me, Grandfather! Your grandson. Your partner! Come back!"

But Grandfather didn't.

Oscar laughed and said, "Don't mind old Eddie's toothache moans. He's been groaning like that all day. Mostly because he has to go to the dentist tomorrow." Oscar called to the tent where the men had been playing cards. "Right Eddie? You old woman."

"It's *not* Eddie, Grandfather, it's me," I cried. And I mean, cried. Tears ran down into the cloth that was covering my mouth and muzzling my outcries. I could hardly hear Oscar when he deliberately called Grandfather's attention to the grey horse. Oscar bellowed with laughter when he pointed to Hiawatha at the fence.

"I hear you're a horse trader, old man," he said. "What'll you trade me, or how much cash, for that twelve year old grey? I'll even throw in the old straw hat over his ears, and the antique gypsy buggy bells. The works."

"No thanks," Grandfather replied. "Right now, I have other fish to fry. Let's go, Sheriff. We're running out of time."

I tried to will Grandfather to go over and look at the grey horse, close up.

"It's Hiawatha!" I screamed inside that terrible gag. "Look at his teeth, Grandfather. He's not twelve, he's three! And he's yours!"

Grandfather told me later that he nearly did go over. Not because of the grey horse but to inspect that ancient antique gypsy buggy. It must have been fifty years old. An antique. Maybe later when this is all over, Grandfather said to himself. Aloud, to Oscar, Grandfather said as they headed for the automobile, "I didn't know the gypsies came out here any more."

"They don't," Oscar said. "That special rig and horse are entered in the big parade tomorrow morning. For old time's sake, courtesy of Jax Dog Food."

Everybody laughed at the ridiculous sight Hiawatha made in his newly acquired gypsy finery standing beside a brilliantly painted ancient buggy, all green, gold and red. Hiawatha had a floppy straw hat with holes for each ear. He was wearing a very old weather-beaten blanket with bells along the bottom edges. It was draped over his reluctant back.

The sheriff nudged Grandfather to cut it short. "We still have to search Raffodil's Livery Stable before sun-up," he reminded everyone in the search party. "That red horse has to be somewhere, and I mean to find him."

I could tell they were leaving. I became frantic.

"Go closer to the horse, Grandfather. He'll lift your hat off. He'll count to five. Look at his hoof for the crimson star. Please, Grandfather! He's right in front of your eyes! It's Hiawatha! Don't leave him, Grandfather. This may be his last chance to win the big race. Yours, too. Please recognize him."

If only someone would walk close to Hiawatha, so he could lift his hat off, if only someone would make him count to five.

I knew at last how foolish I'd been trying to do everything by myself just to show Grandfather. I should have forced him to listen to me on the telephone when I tried to tell him about the fake hayrack, instead of hanging up and deciding to show Grandfather who the smart one in our family really was.

Now, there wasn't going to be any glory. For anyone. Not for me, for Hiawatha, or for Grandfather. And it was all my fault for being so pigheaded.

At the very last moment I thought of something to catch Grandfather's attention. I had the bright idea of not hollering or moaning, but of humming. As loud as I could. At least some sound would come out. I knew I was far away, but I tried my best, using all the power of my humming lungs.

Grandfather had written a little song for me the summer Sam Raffodil beat me in the grade school track meet. I was second again. It was a trial race to see who would get into the finals the next day and run for Franklin School against Hibbing. I had decided to drop out and let Sam have the race to himself. That's when Grandfather wrote what he called a plucky little backbone ditty:

> *"When everything you do goes wrong,*
> *Don't give up, just sing a song.*
> *Buckle right in with a bit of a grin,*
> *And never say die, and you'll always win."*

I tried humming Grandfather's song now. Nothing. I tried "Wait Till the Sun Shines, Nellie." I hummed my heart out. "Back Home Again in Indiana," "Giddy Up! Horsey Go Like the Wind." I even tried Grandfather's favorite, "When You and I Were Young, Maggie," but the sheriff, his deputies and Grandfather were already pulling out of the campground.

I was left alone. So was Hiawatha.

Later I heard the night train start up in the yards and gradually pull away. The train whistled as it approached Cayuna Crossing. It sounded melancoly and lonesome. I hoped they had not put Hiawatha on the train with those other poor horses heading for a terrible end.

I tried to be brave. After I cried a little.

It's hard to sleep standing up, but I did it. I knew that horses often went to sleep standing up. I hoped that Hiawatha, wherever he was, was getting some rest, too, and saving himself for the great escape miracle and winning the County Fair Stakes. There had to be a miracle of some kind. I was sure God wouldn't let a dirty crook like Mr. Raffodil kill a wonderful horse and cheat him out of his chance to win the big race. I crossed my fingers and said a short prayer that the big red horse was not on that night train to Duluth.

I forgot all about my pain and suffering the next morning. When it was full daylight, Oscar and Pete led Hiawatha back up the ramp to join me in the hayrack. He hadn't gone out on the freight train. We still had a fighting chance. A slim one, but a chance. A long shot, as they call it in horse racing.

Oscar and Pete were cheerful and laughing. They were confident that the danger of being discovered was now over since they had fooled Grandfather and the sheriff at dawn's early light.

They had only one thing to do. Make sure that Hiawatha and I could not escape. They refastened my bonds, tied me with my knees up against my chin, and stuffed me in a corner.

Oscar's friend Pete still had his eye on Hiawatha. "We could make a sweet profit selling this grey nag as a trotter," he said.

"Outside of the state, of course, say in Indiana. They're big for horses that pull those funny carts down there in Hoosierland."

"You received the other half of your pay this morning," Oscar warned him. "That's it. The horse goes on tonight's freight with the others. Old man Raffodil wants no trace left."

"Yeah. But I've been working him out every day over a mile, just to see what he's got. He's worth thousands! I tell you."

"Forget it!"

"Okey! Okey! But what about the kid? Shouldn't one of us stay to guard him?"

Oscar leaned down over me. He could see my blindfold was loose. He jerked it back up into place more violently than was needed. He retied the knot tighter than ever. I strained to see his face before the blindfold was tightened, but it was still too dark.

Oscar patted the blindfold, checked the ropes on my wrists, ankles and knees. "When the race is over, kid," he said, "we'll come back for you, and when the train to Duluth leaves tonight, we'll set you free. But you make any noise at all, even a squeak, or stir up any trouble of any kind in here, this horse may trample you to death. By accident, of course. Or at least it will look that way. So you better stay quiet huddled up in that corner. And keep you mouth shut! Understand?"

I didn't answer right away, so he kicked me in the ribs. "Understand?"

I nodded my head vigorously.

Oscar lighted a kerosene lantern and set it down on a bale of hay in the corner. I knew by listening to Pete's objection. "If that lantern tips over, this place will go up in a blaze! Pffft!"

"Pity," Oscar replied. "But those are the breaks of the game. Besides, that, too, would be an accident. We'll have no trouble with Raffodil. Just leave everything to chance."

"I'm not worried about Raffodil. It's the police I'm worried about. Maybe we should leave a lookout here," Pete suggested. "Just in case!"

"No need. There's nothing can go wrong here. Let's head for

the fair. That's where the action is." Oscar swatted Hiawatha on the rump with his open hand. "This horse is not going to run in any race today."

"Can we be sure?"

"We can. Old man Raffodil said he has lookouts covering every crossroad between here and town. Marshall Anderson himself is supervising the city streets right down to the fairgrounds' gate."

Pete grunted. "I'd be a lot happier if the kid went to Duluth on the train with the horse, and didn't come back until we were far away."

"Let's go. We'll never make safer money than by betting on Thunderbolt. We'll be on 'Easy Street' by sundown."

"I know I'm not worthy, God, but how about it anyway?"

68.

I was alone in the hayrack. I heard the bolt thrust home and the snap of the padlock. Oscar had been right, Hiawatha and I were out of the County Fair Stakes.

I tried every trick I'd ever read about, or seen in the movies, to break loose. I twisted, rolled on my side, and tried to rub off my blindfold a second time against the hay, the floor and the walls. Hopeless. They'd made sure this time. I twisted my wrists, sawed them against a protruding nail until my hands were raw.

Nothing helped.

Soon Grandfather would be hitching up Dakar and the band would be playing, "Oh, say can you see by the dawn's early light."

The "dawn's early light" on race day had been a big bust so far. Besides, I didn't want either myself or Hiawatha to become too rambunctious for fear of knocking the lantern over.

I tried to get Hiawatha to chew on my bonds, but all he did was nuzzle me and push me over backwards so I rolled into the opposite corner. With my knees tied up that way, I either rolled like a tumbleweed, or fell flat on my side.

I said all the prayers I knew and made up some new ones. I told God that if he'd save us and get Hiawatha and me out of that phony hayrack, I'd become a wonderful person. I'd even be His obedient servant. I'd read that somewhere, and I was pulling out all the stops.

"I know I'm not worthy, Lord," I admitted. But to become worthy, I offered to enter the priesthood, or become a monk, or a healing doctor in Africa, or a revival preacher like Billy Sunday, only better.

I promised to save souls by the thousands in every wicked city in the world until they groveled helplessly at my feet. I'd fast for six months every year and pray morning, noon, and night until they made me a saint with a halo so shiny bright that people would turn around to look at me on the street and follow me to my cold tiny cave in the mountains to share my brown bread and goat's cheese. All that stuff. But God would have to get me and Hiawatha out of that rotten hayrack first, otherwise the deal was off. Also we wanted to win the race.

That's what I was doing now inside that hayrack prison. I even offered to forgive Sam Raffodil Senior and Sam Raffodil Junior for their trespasses and the evil way they'd trespassed against us. That will show you how depressed I had become locked up inside that hayrack. I finally did recover enough to tell God to forget that last bit about the Raffodil's.

"I can't lie to you," I told Him. "I wouldn't give up the pleasure of pushing Sam Raffodil's face in the wet mud for all the hay in Fitzhugh County. Sam is going to get it right in the neck with the worst kind of violence."

"If that makes you discouraged with me, God, then it's just too bad!"

I apologized later for that, of course, and told God that I would leave everything in His capable hands, but that any small favors would be gladly received under the circumstances. He had a lot more marbles in the game than I did, and I was counting heavily on him.

Unworthy though I was, of course. But in a hurry. Please, God.

Amen!

According to Grandfather, I was always trying to make a special deal with God and talk Him into some kind of a bargain.

"That's not praying," Grandfather would tell me. "That's begging."

Grandfather told me that what God wanted was for me to live a good decent life. That, he said, was the finest form of prayer there was. "You might try it," Grandfather said. "You can't bargain with God like beating down a merchant on the price of a rug until you feel you've got the best of the deal."

Grandfather made it clear to me when I was still very small that a person's soul needed food just like his body did. "If you never pray, you'll soon suffer from spiritual malnutrition," Grandfather said, "and you'll have a jaundiced view of everything in life."

I'd already had more than enough, but Grandfather couldn't leave well-enough alone.

"To quote a great president, Abraham Lincoln," Grandfather added, 'You can fool some of the people *all* of the time, and all of the people *some* of the time. But you can't fool *Him any of the time!*'"

Grandfather would point up toward heaven, and then go off into gales of laughter.

"Abraham Lincoln never said that!" I objected.

"I may have adjusted the words a little," he admitted. "Besides," he reminded me, "Heaven's not up there. It's not a place like Duluth or Chicago, it's a state or a condition. It's nearness to God."

Sometimes Grandfather could give you too much of a good thing until you wished you were out at the old swimming hole. When I tried to escape, he would hook me with his cane and pull me up close. "You'll enjoy this," he'd tell me, "you being a scholar yourself."

I knew I wouldn't.

Even so, I wished Grandfather were right there with me now inside that old hayrack, to tell me what to do so Hiawatha and I could escape, and still win the big race. He'd know. I would even be grateful for one of his rotten grizzly bear hugs and whisker rubs. That'll show you how desperate I was.

I lost all track of time. I even dozed off once or twice. I don't know for how long. Once Hiawatha stepped on my foot. I knew it wasn't an accident. He'd done it deliberately to try and wake me up so I could go into action.

"Doing *what!*" I grumbled at him.

Hiawatha's whinny made me ashamed. I didn't want him to know how discouraged I was. I had to do something. I didn't even know what time it was. Maybe the big race was already over.

"Don't you dare say that," I hollered at Hiawatha. It came out like a loud hum behind the gag, but Hiawatha whinnied back.

The Seventh Furlong!

"Bedlam!"

If Hiawatha and I had known what was happening at that very moment in our town of Green Valley while we were still prisoners inside that hayrack, we would have been even more miserable. Not knowing about all the excitement we were missing. I didn't hear a word about that wonderful day until the entire county fair was all over. While Hiawatha and I were locked up inside that dismal dark hayrack, one of the most wildly dramatic scenes in the history of our little town of Green Valley was taking place.

A well known attorney, Joseph Hillary, who Mr. Raffodil had hired to draw up the race-wager document between himself and Grandfather, the one with the hidden fine print, had objected violently when Mr. Raffodil had insisted that he cover the new added fine print with his seal as notary public. Mr. Hillary finally became so miffed with Mr. Raffodil that he quit his job.

Mr. Hillary said Mr. Raffodil had made him so ashamed of himself that he'd stopped shaving. He couldn't bear to look at himself in the mirror. Mr. Hillary already had a halfway decent beard when he refused to bend beneath Mr. Raffodil's pressure any longer.

"I've skirted the edges of decency on your behalf," he told Mr. Raffodil, "but this document is underhanded, dishonest and evil." Mr. Hillary tapped the racing document and tossed it across the desk at Mr. Raffodil.

"You'll do as you're told," Mr. Raffodil barked at the lawyer, dismissing his objections with a wave of his hand. "And, what's more, you'll keep your mouth shut."

"No longer," Mr. Hillary told him. "I quit. And I'm going to spread the truth about this document all over town."

"You do that," Mr. Raffodil warned him, "and you'll find yourself right in it up to your neck."

"It doesn't matter what you do to me, it's what you're doing to the people of this town. Both you and I know that the intent of the bet was a face-to-face match race between Thunderbolt and Hiawatha. That old man has not only lost his horse in a very mysterious way, but that document commits him to race any horse he owns. Right now, it's down to Dakar who has no chance. You hid all of that in the fine print beneath my seal."

"Tough luck on the old man, but that's horse racing," Mr. Raffodil laughed. He picked up the document which Mr. Hillary had thrown down on the desk, and tucked the signed and sealed paper inside his coat pocket.

"I cut myself off from any association with you from now on," Mr. Hilary declared, "and I'm tempted to wager fifty dollars on Dakar just to show my utter contempt for you, and my admiration for that grand old man."

"Please do. I'll give you twenty to one. I can use as much sucker money as I can get."

"Do you mean it?"

"Do you want a signed document," Mr. Raffodil said sarcastically. "With a seal?"

"You've got my fifty at twenty to one."

"Good! And you can bring me as many other sucker bets from these local yokels as you can raise. I'll be at my livery stable until five o'clock tomorrow afternoon." Mr. Raffodil was thoroughly enjoying himself. "If they don't have cash, let them bring produce. Anything they own. I'll take it all away from them. I'll bankrupt this entire hick town. They can even set their own market value. I'll cover it. Every penny!"

"Even a fine horse like Thunderbolt could break his stride and lose, you know."

"Are you threatening me?"

"No, just reminding you that if this case ever comes to court,

I'll testify for the other side."

"That will be hard on your terminally ill wife, and your mongoloid son. If you cross me, Hillary. I'll withdraw all funds."

"Please do." Mr. Hillary was adamant. "And I'll remind you, Raffodil, that sometimes fate takes a hand."

"Rubbish! Thunderbolt has never broken stride in any of his races, and I've brought in Buckshot Agate, the best, to make sure he doesn't now."

"You don't know much about small towns, and small town people, do you Mr. Raffodil. These local yokels, as you call them."

"I know their money is as good as anybody else's. If you want to act as an agent on their behalf, hop to it!"

Secret Agent Number Three, Jimmy Middleman, was dozing in the warm sunlight on top of the high water tower in the heart of town watching for any sign of Hiawatha. Or any suspicious actions on the part of Sam Raffodil Senior or Junior. That was his assignment.

Jimmy was the one who, after the race was over, told me all about the weird and strange sights that began to unfold before his eyes on the morning of the big race. Jimmy thought he was still asleep, or dreaming. He couldn't believe his own eyes.

"About noon," Jimmy reported, "I began to see vehicles of all kinds, and long lines of walking people heading for downtown. They were coming from all parts of Green Valley like spokes on a wheel. Even from out in the country. They all wound up in a bunch, a milling crowd, right down below the water tower where I was watching. They were packed in from fence-to-fence inside Mr. Raffodil's big livery stable yard."

"What kind of vehicles?" I asked him.

"All kinds. Even people on foot carrying things on their backs and heads. Couples holding the opposite ends of things."

"What kind of things?"

"Sofas, beds, easy-chairs, end-tables, lamps, bedroom dressers, clothes, blankets, filing-cabinets, desks—coming down from the streets from all directions, as far as the eye could see. Shouting and yelling."

"Shouting and yelling what?"

"And singing."

"And singing what?"

"Singing: 'Grandfather, Yes! Mr. Raffodil, No!'"

"Why?"

"It was bedlam!"

It was bedlam.

"Hurray for Green Valley!"

70.

"I never saw anything like it," Jimmy Middleman yelled. "I became so excited, I climbed down from the water tower to find out what was happening."

"What was?"

"They were all betting on your Grandfather and Dakar in the big horse race. Against Mr. Raffodil and Thunderbolt."

"But Dakar never had a chance to win."

"I know that! But Mr. Raffodil was giving twenty to one. Mr. Hillary spread the news everywhere that Mr. Raffodil was taking all bets. The people could set their own odds and place their own value on their property."

"Even so," I objected, "Dakar couldn't possibly win. No matter how high the odds."

"I *know* that. But I think the people were trying to show Mr. Raffodil how they felt about your grandfather."

"I can't believe it."

"You'd better. I saw it all with my own eyes."

"I didn't think Grandfather was that popular."

"Of course a lot of them wanted a piece of those twenty-to-one odds against a stiff like Dakar."

I objected quite violently this time. "Dakar's not a stiff. He won the County Fair Stakes last year!"

"Yeah, but against Thunderbolt, we both know Dakar's a stiff. Everybody else—the overwhelming majority—was on your grandfather's side."

"It gives me a lump in the throat to think that all those

people stuck up for Grandfather. When they knew they'd lose. That's really something."

"It gave me a lump on my foot where that huge flock of sheep tromped on me. And that's not even mentioning where I got butted in the rump by Zeke Matthew's goat."

"Zeke wagered his pet goat?"

"Both the nanny and her kid."

This time I did have tears in my eyes. I knew how much Zeke loved that ugly old goat.

"And people brought sheep? And goats?"

"Flocks of them. The whole town was dusty from their hoofs. And steers and horses and ponies."

Jimmy waxed poetic.

"You should have seen what it was like from up there on that water tower. I thought either I was hypnotized, having a sunstroke, or the whole town had gone nuts. I thought maybe it was the end of the world or something. It was a noisy, frightening sight to see for someone who just woke up. Being awake was a worse nightmare than being asleep."

Jimmy was really wonderful. I let him ramble on, not wanting to miss anything because lots of people said this was the day the tide turned against Mr. Raffodil and changed his luck.

"Everywhere I looked," Jimmy told me, "people were streaming toward town. They came on foot, on horseback, on mules, on donkeys, wagons, buckboards, hayracks, buggies— single and double. They even came pushing baby buggies and coaster wagons, driving cars, trucks, panel vans. People carrying things on their shoulders. Men, women and children. Amy Ellison's little sister was hauling her brother's coaster wagon full of broken dolls, old ice skates and a dried out Christmas tree."

"One of the weirdest sights of all was the big flatbed truck hauling the honky-tonk piano. I heard the music coming up Main Street. 'That's a piano!' I yelled. And it was! Mickey Burns was playing it for all he was worth. The piano was from Sandy Murphie's Pool Hall, on the way to be wagered against Mr. Raffodil."

" 'On the nose for Grandfather,' Sandy hollered out to the crowd. When the piano pulled into the livery stable yard, Mickey Burns was pounding out, 'Giddy Up, Giddy Up, My Pony Boy!' "

"Everybody began to sing it. At the end, again they hollered, 'Grandfather Yes!, Raffodil No!' "

"It was wonderful!" Jimmy yelled, doing a jig in front of me.

"Green Valley," Jimmy said, "looked like a huge anthill that someone had kicked, turning loose every ant in town, and they were all heading for Raffodil's Livery Stable."

Jimmy thumped his chest proudly. "And I had the best seat in town."

I hugged him. "Hurray!" I said, "For Green Valley!"

And to think Hiawatha and I had missed all of this, locked up in the hayrack. Hiawatha had already lifted my cap off my head, counted to five a number of times, and kept pawing at the floor of the hayrack.

"Cut it out, stupid!" I said.

Hiawatha could only hear my mumble inside the gag, so he counted to five again. Hiawatha had no idea how tired and exhausted I was. I had to get some sleep, but didn't know if I had a minute to spare. Hiawatha whinnied, as though he were annoyed with me for being so helpless. It burned my biscuit. I yelled at him, but forgave him when he licked my cheek.

I decided in that moment that Hiawatha and I were going to escape. As soon as I woke up from a long nap, I'd think of something. I could still hear Hiawatha whinny as I dozed off.

Two Giants: Midge Kelly and Short-Stuff Farley.

71.

It must have been a long time later when I woke up from my nap. I heard strange noises. They sounded like distant owl hoots.

I knew that the live owl in the hickory tree should be sound asleep in the day time. Or had I slept around the clock? And the race was already over? Terrified at the thought, I was wide awake at once.

I could tell it was someone imitating an owl, so then I really came alive. That was the signal of the secret agents in our bureau. We used it for secret identification. I tried to "hoot" back, but couldn't get the sound past the gag in my mouth.

The "hoots" were coming closer and closer. Finally I heard a human voice say: "Bill? Bill? You in there?"

What a sweet and wonderful sound that was! I recognized it immediately as the voice of Short-Stuff Farley, Secret Agent Number Six. What a marvelous, melodious voice he had. Midge Kelly, Secret Agent Seven, joined in. "You in there, Bill?"

No answer. Short Stuff Farley said, "Maybe your sister Margie's wrong, and they've already killed him dead."

I rolled over to one of the peep holes, and looked out. I could see them both. Short-Stuff Farley was riding Midge Kelly on the handlebars.

Midge jumped off. They leaned the bike against a tree and came cautiously back down toward the hayrack.

"Maybe he's not in here at all." Short-Stuff said.

"He must be," replied Midge Kelly.

"Unless, like you say, they've hung him or burned him at the stake."

"Will you shut up with that!" Farley snapped.

"Or whatever desperate criminals do."

I rolled over to the wall and kicked my feet against the door as loudly as I could. I thumped. *Once, twice, three times.*

I heard Short-Stuff and Midge cry out together: "What was that?!" They were ready to fly home at the first danger.

I repeated the knocks.

"Bill?" Short-Stuff was nervous.

It was hard to kick the door with my feet trussed up against my knees that way. I kept falling over on my back. It was hard to right myself. I found it easier to roll over to the door with my back to it and thump my head on the door.

"He's inside all those bales of hay!" Short-Stuff cried out. "How can he do that?"

Midge scoffed. "I told you this hayrack was a fake when I shot my arrow into it. Hiawatha's probably in there with him!"

"Why doesn't he *say* something?"

"Maybe he can't. Maybe he's gagged."

"Are you gagged?"

Hiawatha whinnied.

"He's a horse!" Short-Stuff hollered.

"Maybe it's Hiawatha making those noises, and not Bill at all."

I thumped the wall once again with my head. Hard. It hurt. I pivoted and kicked the door. Twice. What I really wanted to do was to kick Short-Stuff Farley *three* times, and Midge Kelly *four* times into the middle of next week.

I couldn't get any strength or power into my feet, so I banged my head on the door again. I drummed on it like a tattoo.

"No horse can do that," Short-Stuff cried. "That's Bill! Let's get him out of there."

"How?"

Short-Stuff and Midge found the locked backdoor with its padlock. They tried to pry it open, but couldn't budge it.

"It's no use," Short-Stuff called out to me. "We'll have to go back to town for help."

There was no time for that. If the race wasn't already over, it would be before help came from town. There wasn't a minute to spare.

Midge and Short-Stuff were wheeling the bike toward the road when I backed into the door and pounded on it with the back of my head as hard as I could without seeing stars. In fact, I saw a few.

They heard me, and came back to the hayrack. "Don't you want us to go for help?"

I knocked twice.

"No?"

I knocked once.

"Yes, we shouldn't go? Or no, we shouldn't stay?"

I knocked once again.

Short-Stuff shouted out, "I've got it. Just like in the movie we all saw, *The Death Dealing Rustlers of Rattlesnakes Gulch!* When the victim's tongue was cut out, and he's the only one who knows where the gold is buried. Remember? He blinked his eyes. One blink for *yes*, and two blinks for *no*."

Midge yelled, "Is that right?"

I pounded my head on the door once for "Yes!"

I knew if this conversation went on much longer, I wouldn't have any brains left to drive Hiawatha back to the fairgrounds.

"Is there a way to get you out?"

Knock.

"The door?"

Two knocks.

"How then?"

"What was that again?" Short-Stuff asked.

I rolled and slid on my side to the door, put my back to it, and tried to batter at the door with my fists which were tied up behind me. I knocked one, two, three, four, five, six and seven times. I could hear Midge counting with me.

"One! Two! Three! Four! Five! Six! Seven!"

He was thrilled. "He means *me*. Secret Agent Number Seven! Right?"

I knocked once.

"Hurray!"

"You want Midge to do something?"

Knock.

"Look for another door?"

Knock.

"Underneath the hayrack?"

Knock. Knock.

"On top?"

KNOCK!

"This is exciting!" Short-Stuff shouted at Midge. "Get up there. You're small enough to squeeze through anything. Is that it, Bill?"

I banged my head once on the door, and fell back on the floor seeing shooting stars.

Midge and Short-Stuff both shinnied up the big oak tree, and dropped down on top of the hayrack. I rolled to the air hole at the front of the hayrack and crossed my fingers. I could *do* that without pain.

Tiny pieces of hay began falling down from the airshaft. The next thing I knew, I was looking up at Midge Kelly's head. He was staring down at me. He hollered to Short-Stuff.

"He's here! Bill's in there! All tied up alongside a strange horse!"

"Maybe it's Hiawatha!"

"No chance. This horse is grey."

Midge was trying to wriggle through the small opening. I loved him for being such a runt. In fact, I owed Midge Kelly about three years worth of apologies for all the times I'd called him PeeWee, Squirt, Tadpole, Little-bit, and Weine. *Runt* was the best, I told myself, as Midge came hurtling down into the hayrack yelling angrily back at Farley.

"Don't shove! I'm going! Whoops!"

Down he came on top of me.

Midge hollered back up at Short-Stuff, "I've saved his life. He's alive!"

I kept yelling silently inside my gag. "Take the gag out of my mouth, you idiot." Finally he did. It was heaven!

"As soon as you untie me," I told Midge, "I'm going to give you the biggest grizzly bear hug, whisker rub, and kiss that you've ever had since the day you were born!"

Midge drew back, horrified. "You kiss me," he said, "and I'm going up that hole and leave you tied up down here to die."

Midge hollered up at Short-Stuff again. "I think being in here has scrambled his brains."

When I was untied, Midge and I compromised on a hand-shake. Midge had no idea how happy I was to be getting out of there.

"I'll never care how small you are, Midge. Ever again. To me, you are a giant!"

Midge was more convinced than ever that I was addled. He was also distressed.

"It was crazy for me to come down in here," he said "Now

there are *two* of us trapped, what good will that do?"

"Plenty," I assured him. "I can talk now, and I'll tell Short-Stuff how to get us out of here. That's what's good about it."

I went over to the kerosene lantern on the bale of hay and blew it out. Midge's eyes were popped out. "That's crazy. Having a lantern in here. You could have been burned alive!"

"I think that was the idea."

I told Short-Stuff Farley where to find the toolshed, and sent him for a crowbar and any other useful breaking-out tools he could find. In no time he was back and working on the padlock. I explained exactly where Short-Stuff should place the crowbar.

"Work on the hinges!" I hollered.

I knew it was kidstuff, but under my breath I also kept whispering, "Open Sesame! Open Sesame! Hurry!"

"It's coming!" Short-Stuff yelled.

"Holler when it's ready to give," I instructed him. "We'll both push on this side too."

"Count to five!" Short-Stuff cried out, "then let'er buck!"

When Hiawatha heard "Count to five!" he began counting, banging his right foot down against the hayrack floor. The way it worked out, all three of us inside were counting to five at the same time. We knew our escape might depend upon it.

Midge Kelly, Hiawatha and William Sears counted, "One, two, three, four, five!"

On *four* Midge and I took a running start, leaped into the air and rammed our feet against the inside of the door. On *five* we shoved outward with all our might, just as Short-Stuff gave the final pull on the crowbar.

The door flew open!

Midge and I came flying through, bumped into Short-Stuff, and all three of us went down together in one heap on the ground. No one was hurt, but we couldn't stop laughing.

"Hallelujah!" I hollered. "We've escaped!"

Hiawatha whinnied.

Quickly we lowered the ramp, and Hiawatha came flying down to join us.

73.

"What time is it?" I asked Midge and Short-Stuff, urgently.

"Search me," Midge said.

"I haven't got a clue," Short-Stuff echoed.

Midge looked up at the sun, shaded his eyes, and guessed that maybe it might be somewhere between three and five. Short-stuff nodded, "Or even later."

"It *can't* be!" I cried. "The big race starts at four-thirty, and Hiawatha has to be there on time. He *has* to be!"

Short-Stuff looked around. "Where *is* Hiawatha?"

I pointed to the grey horse chewing on my sweater. "That," I told them, "is Hiawatha."

Midge looked at Short-Stuff, alarmed. "I *told* you his brains were scrambled."

Hiawatha began pawing the earth, anxious to be away. "You stop that," I warned him. "Now that we're free, save those legs for running in the County Fair Stakes."

Both Short-Stuff and Midge could see that the horse was grey, so Short-Stuff nodded at Midge.

"You're right," he said. "He must have been hitting his head against the door too long."

"It's not his *head* that's bad," Midge corrected, eyeing the grey horse. "It's his eyes."

"*This* horse," I insisted, "is Hiawatha."

Short-Stuff scoffed. "That is an old grey mare, not a beautiful chestnut colt."

"It's not a mare," Midge said. "I can see that, but it sure is grey."

I led Hiawatha over to the watering trough, dipped a pail into the water, splashed Hiawatha's right front leg, and began rubbing it with my gag cloth. When they saw the grey color paint begin to wash off, they both found some rags and joined in. The excitement had become intense. Especially when Hiawatha's hoof was clean, and I pointed to the bright crimson star on Hiawatha's hoof.

"I," said Short-Stuff Farley, "am a son-of-a-gun!"

"Hurry," I said. "Help me hitch him up to this old buggy."

"Aren't you going to clean him off?"

"No time. Besides, Hiawatha has enemies waiting all along the road. I overhead their plans to stop Hiawatha at all costs. I'm hoping they won't recognize him. The two who can recognize him are at the fairgrounds."

While we backed Hiawatha into the traces and started hitching him up, Midge Kelly told me about the trouble brewing at my house because I hadn't been home all night. Midge said that my mother had been frantic this morning when she found my bed empty. Especially when she found I hadn't slept at the fairgrounds either.

"There's a sheriff's posse out looking for you everywhere!" Short-stuff said.

"Great," I said, "just great."

I slipped the bit between Hiawatha's teeth and pulled the bridle on. Then we all finished hooking him up to the old antique gypsy buggy. I tugged the silly old straw hat down over Hiawatha's head and pulled his ears through the holes. It made us all laugh. Even Hiawatha.

I draped the multi-colored gypsy blanket, with all the bells ringing, over Hiawatha's back and fastened it in place with straps under his belly. "Are you going to drive Hiawatha into town wearing that crazy outfit?" Short-Stuff asked.

"I told you! I have to. I can't take a chance on anybody recognizing Hiawatha before I get there," I said. "Mr. Raffodil has his spies out everywhere."

"Maybe they'll think it's just a gypsy horse coming late to

the fair for the parade," Short-Stuff suggested.

"The parade was this morning," Midge reminded us.

"Can you think of a better way to get safely into the fair-grounds?" I asked. They couldn't.

Except Midge. He said, "Even if they don't recognize Hiawatha, they'll recognize you. Then they'll know it's Hiawatha in disguise."

Short-Stuff agreed. "You've got to be in disguise, too."

I took off my shirt and started to plaster mud all over my shoulders and undershirt. Midge and Short-Stuff helped. I took off my shoes and socks and went barefoot. We covered my legs and feet with mud. I threw the shoes and socks into the woods. They were the new brown shoes father had bought me for the fair, but I could search for them later. I borrowed Short-Stuff Farley's baseball cap and twisted it around backwards, rubbed mud and dirt on my face, and crawled up into the buggy.

"You both look awful," Midge Kelly yelled happily.

"Good! That's the ticket!"

"C'mon Midge," Short-Stuff said, "these two mud-caked bums need a secret agent's escort. Let's climb up into the back of the buggy and ride shotgun."

"Forget it," I told them. "What I need is a real shotgun."

"You're out of luck there," Midge said, "but I have this whole pocketful of firecrackers and a box of matches." Midge handed me a bunch of tiny ladyfingers.

"I was saving them for under the seats at the band concert tonight."

"For gosh sakes," I grumbled, "what good are these dinky things?"

"Blow up the enemy," Midge suggested. "Or make them think so."

Midge rubbed his rump. "I sure don't care about riding all the way back into town on the handlebars."

"You won't have to," I said, and showed him where I'd hidden his sister's bicycle.

I gave Hiawatha's rump a slap with the harness reins, and he began to gallop up the hill. I never felt better. Ragged clothes, drying mud, dirty face and all. Hiawatha seemed to feel the same. We were two birds released from a cage.

I shouted for the whole world to hear: "C'mon, Hiawatha! This one is for Grandmother's sweet peas and Grandfather's skin. Move it! You ugly old gypsy stallion. Let's gobble up that big black horse!"

Hiawatha whinnied and I laughed out loud. The rickety old gypsy buggy creaked and groaned as we swung up out of the campground toward the road for home.

"Look out, fairgrounds! Here we come!"

The Eighth Furlong!

74.

We wove in and out of the tamarack trees and up onto the gravel path that led to the main road to town. Short-Stuff and Midge were already out of sight, hurrying to spread the news that the country's fastest trotting horse was on his way to the fairgrounds to take his rightful place in the world.

Hiawatha knew he was heading for home, and holding him in check became very difficult. It was harder than on that famous Sunday morning ride down Main Street when we went whizzing away over the Mississippi River Bridge and all the way out to Joe Hartman's farm before I had been able to slow Hiawatha down.

Hiawatha hadn't worked out for three days and he was eager, full of run. That's what Grandfather calls it. I call it "full of beans!"

I knew that Oscar had "worked" Hiawatha those three days, for a mile each. But what did he know about horses? He might have done more harm than good.

Hiawatha was even more anxious to get to the fairgrounds than I was.

"Steady boy," I warned him, pulling back hard on the reins. "Steady! There's a big race still ahead of us if we're lucky enough to get there in time." But Hiawatha ignored me, and leaned into that harness for all he was worth.

"Whoa!" I yelled.

Hiawatha paid no attention.

I tried to explain the facts of life to him as we shot up a long hill. "You've got to be 'scored' exactly right, Hiawatha. Not too much, not too little, and not too soon. You've got to arrive at the fairgrounds absolutely ready, if you hope to run down that old Thunderbolt. You hear me? You have to be in perfect shape just as we go through that entrance gate and out onto the track. That's an order!"

That dumb chestnut horse couldn't understand English, so I tried something else. "Whoa! Hiawatha! Whoa! You hear me? Whoa! You dumb horse!"

He didn't. My arms and shoulders were aching already, and we were barely away from the old gypsy camp.

"You've been out of training for three days, Hiawatha. You're out of shape, and it will take a miracle to win. We'll never do it if you don't obey me. I'm your last chance, horse. When I say, 'Whoa!' You whoa!! You hear me?!"

Hiawatha was more than I could handle. Grandfather had always told me that. Now I knew what he meant. I tried talking turkey to Hiawatha through the reins, the way Grandfather had shown me. I couldn't let Hiawatha leave his race out here on the old Tamarack Road.

"Easy, Hiawatha! Slow it down, boy. Easy does it. All the way to town. No use us getting there to that starting line on time if we've nothing left to win the race."

Hiawatha whinned and showed his teeth, sort of a horse laugh.

"This is Grandfather talking!" I yelled, but Hiawatha knew it wasn't.

"Steady, boy. Pretty please with sugar on it."

Hiawatha slowed a bit, but continued to nearly snap my neck off as he jerked that old rattletrap buggy along Tamarack Road, in and out of pot holes, up and down inclines. The old gypsy buggy screamed and hollered, squeaking for needed grease. It was taking too much out of Hiawatha, but that big red horse didn't care. His rippling muscles told me, "Fairgrounds or bust!"

It was a constant pitched battle between us. Hiawatha wanted to get there immediately at whatever the cost. I wanted him to get there in one piece, still full of fury and fight.

The way he moved along the Tamarack Road, it was all I could do to keep from standing up in the buggy and yelling right out loud, in pure joy!

"Go! You big red horse!"

So I did yell. And frightened Hiawatha into another dramatic spurt forward. The two of us had to start our deadly duel against speed all over again.

My heart was singing with joy as we approached the big horseshoe bend by the old flour mill. The mill wheel was turning, making little waterfalls into Ripple River. Smoke was coming out of the chimney and going straight up into the air. It was a peaceful poster scene of beauty until we swung around the horseshoe bend and straightened out for Green Valley.

The road was clear. Suddenly a big hayrack pulled across the road, and a buckboard, followed by two lumber wagons which shut off both shoulders of the road. There were drivers and helpers in each wagon with whips. Worse. With guns. They had pistols, rifles, and one with a shotgun which he fired off with a loud blast. Straight up into the air.

Both Hiawatha and I jumped. I was scared stiff. We were barely out of the old gypsy camp, and already Hiawatha and I faced disaster ahead.

A roadblock!

It was too late to turn back. In the very first moments of our escape they had us trapped. It was my fault for dreaming of the countryside when I should have remembered Oscar's voice warning me that Mr. Raffodil had every entrance into town covered.

This was the first crossroads between Hill City and Green Valley. I whispered to Hiawatha, "Look like a broken down gypsy horse, or we're in real trouble."

I drew back on the reins and pulled Hiawatha up. I could see they were puzzled by our strange appearance. It wasn't what they expected, so I hollered at them in what I hoped was a halfway decent gypsy accent.

"Clear the road! Gangway! This old gypsy horse is on his way to the big parade at the fairgrounds! Open up a path!"

I nearly fainted with relief when they did.

They moved their hayrack just enough to let me through. Hiawatha zipped into that tiny gap knowing that in a few dozen strides we'd be free!

One of the men hollered at me. "Hey, kid, wasn't that parade this morning?"

I let Hiawatha out a few notches and we whisked between the wagons, grazing the side of the hayrack and locking wheels. I stopped the buggy, and urged Hiawatha to back up so we could get loose.

"Hurry, Hiawatha!" I cried out.

The man nearest me on the hayrack shouted, "He called

that horse Hiawatha! After him! Or kiss your hundred bucks goodbye if he gets to the fairgrounds!"

They all started after me at once. The hayrack in front, with the buckboard and lumber wagon shooting up out of the ditch on the shoulder in hot pursuit.

"That was stupid," I told Hiawatha. "I should have called you Buck or Betsy. Not Hiawatha. Now we're in for it!"

I knew I couldn't let Hiawatha break away and leave them in the dust. Grandfather had told me too many times about horses who left their race in the stable by overtraining and working too hard. But what could I do? Just our luck the Tamarack Road widened out after the horseshoe bend, and when I looked over my shoulder, all of them were coming at me, three abreast, right on my tail.

The one in the hayrack was threatening me with the shotgun. I was pretty sure he wouldn't shoot a child, but he might shoot a horse. In that exact moment, I remembered Midge Kelly's gift when he couldn't ride shotgun himself. I snatched two packets of ladyfinger firecrackers out of my pocket. Nervously I tried to light them from the box of safety matches, but couldn't scratch the side. I was too nervous and the road was too bumpy. Hearing the buckboard coming up on my right side helped. I used the match flame to ignite as many of the long fuses as possible. I heaved the first batch into the buckboard, the second over the top of the buggy at the hayrack. I kept lighting and throwing until I was out of firecrackers.

Midge Kelly had ridden shotgun with a vengeance. Unfortunately, I didn't see it all, but I did see the hayrack and the team of matched bays go off the road up the ditch and into the woods. I even heard the double-barreled sawed-off shotgun blast into the air as the driver was caught across the neck by an overhanging branch, and lifted out of the driver's seat and left hanging in the air, kicking and screaming. The hayrack itself made a loud noise as it cracked and shattered against the trees.

I don't know what happened to the big lumber wagon, except I saw it on its back in the middle of the road with all four wheels spinning, and all four horses running down the road the other way.

Unfortunately, the buckboard was still in pursuit. The driver had tossed the rifle in the air when the firecrackers first went off in the wagon behind him. He had spun the gun around to fire in defense. The driver was furious. He lashed the horses and began to pull up on my right side again. Just then the road narrowed down for the one way Ripple River bridge. I went over the bridge, but the buckboard and team went over the embankment into the deepest part of Ripple River.

No one was hurt, except for feelings, waving fists and shouting dirty words. Hiawatha kept trotting on as though he were entirely unaware of the dreadful encounter.

If Midge Kelly had been there on the buggy seat with me, I would have kissed him no matter how revolting it would have been to him. Hiawatha and I had thrown off the pursuers. At least for the time being.

I would now be alert until I looked into Grandfather's eyes on the track.

"Look at that clock, Hiawatha.
We've still got a fighting chance."

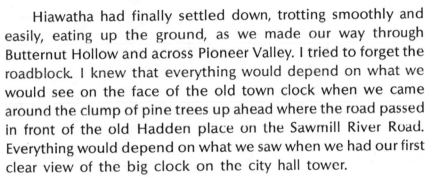

Hiawatha had finally settled down, trotting smoothly and easily, eating up the ground, as we made our way through Butternut Hollow and across Pioneer Valley. I tried to forget the roadblock. I knew that everything would depend on what we would see on the face of the old town clock when we came around the clump of pine trees up ahead where the road passed in front of the old Hadden place on the Sawmill River Road. Everything would depend on what we saw when we had our first clear view of the big clock on the city hall tower.

If only we weren't too late!

"Don't let us be too late, God," I whispered to myself. "I meant what I promised in that dark old hayrack. Every word. I'll straighten out my whole life if only you'll give Hiawatha his chance. I don't want anything for myself. I'm yours, hook, line and sinker, if that old town clock is still on our side."

Hiawatha whinnied, began to speed up, and our tug-of-war began again in earnest yet another time.

There wasn't a sound in all the countryside but us. The clippety-clop, clippety-clop of Hiawatha's hoofs, and rickety-rickety noise of the ramshackle gypsy buggy wheels as they bumped in and out of deeper and more frequent potholes on the Tamarack Road. Every now and then, I said a side prayer for those pitiful buggy wheels for we had not come out of the roadblock unscathed. Our wheels were wobbling like a drunken duck. And above it all, I could hear the jingling and jangling of Hiawatha's blanket bells. It kept my mind off those weak wheels.

Relentlessly Hiawatha swallowed up the ground between us and the fairgrounds. He might have looked silly in that big floppy hat and that moth-eaten multicolored bell-jangling blanket, but I didn't care a whoop. Neither did Hiawatha.

The way he whipped that old buggy down that county road was a thrill to behold. Hiawatha sailed along as though he were pulling a feather.

He was still far too eager. He pulled on the reins, determined to go faster and faster. I had his head turned to one side, tugging on the leather. Hiawatha was snorting and making those repeated throat noises like trotters and pacers do when they're warming up for a big race and are being held in check.

My arm and shoulder muscles were now hurting like a bad toothache just from the strain of trying to hold back that marvelous red horse. But because I loved Hiawatha, I loved every agonizing shooting pain. When the pain became unbearable, I began to sing at the top of my voice like Grandfather: "Wait 'till the sun shines, Nellie, and the clouds go drifting by."

I sang in rhythm to Hiawatha's trot to take my mind off my suffering. The louder I sang, the faster Hiawatha ran and the harder I pulled.

The merry blanket bells were ringing up a storm, the huge straw hat was flopping, Hiawatha's ears would bend back and forth, and I was singing at the top of my voice the way Grandfather did sometimes when things went wrong. I was sure the old man would have been proud of both of us.

I thought Hiawatha was going to pull my arms right out of their shoulder sockets, but I knew I had to keep him from working too hard, too soon. The veins in my neck were sticking out like long pink noodles.

Suddenly, all my pain was forgotten!

We passed Hadden's white farmhouse with the green

shutters and swung around the big curve toward town. My eyes were glued in the direction of the old town clock. We came barreling around that bend like we were entering the homestretch at the fairgrounds.

At last!

There in front of my eyes was the clock!

I let out a yell of joy as we swerved around the bend and headed down the long straight road toward town. All down hill! The clock hands were shouting out to us: *Twenty minutes after three!*

We still had over an hour to go!

I steered Hiawatha over to the side of the road, and let him trot easily for quite a stretch, then slowed him to a walk.

"Look at that clock, Hiawatha. The race will soon be starting. This is my last chance to ease up on you and 'score' you like Grandfather would."

"Look at that clock, Hiawatha!"

78.

By the noisy sound, I could tell the moment we left Tamarack Road and reached the city limits of Green Valley. The city street was packed down hard and solid with gravel.

Bells may be fine for dashing through the snow in a one-horse open sleigh, but for trotting down Main Street on County Fair Stakes day, they attracted altogether too much attention. The loud clop of Hiawatha's hoofs on the hard-packed gravel added to the clamor.

I was tempted to pull over, jump out, and whip off that sloppy straw hat and the jingling blanket now that Hiawatha was warmed up and almost in sight of the fairgrounds. But I knew I still couldn't take the chance. Every second counted and there were probably more enemies everywhere. The men at the gypsy camp had said that Mr. Raffodil was covering every entrance into town.

Merchants and customers who were not at the fairgrounds came out to see what all the racket was about. They had a good laugh when they saw Hiawatha. Some came out onto the sidewalk, others peeked out of windows, but all were pointing and laughing at the odd sight Hiawatha and I made.

"It's not much for style," Mr. Sweetman hollered at me from his ice cream parlor, "but he's all horse. I'd know him anywhere."

Some of the others recognized Hiawatha, too, in spite of his disguise, and shouted out their encouragement. They were hoping that Hiawatha would foreclose on Mr. Raffodil for a change. They yelled, whistled, and applauded as Hiawatha came rattling down Main Street toward the fairgrounds.

"Go, you ragamuffin!" Elmer Bulling hollered.

Elmer was standing in the barber shop door, a towel around his neck, and lather all over his face, but I knew him by his foghorn voice.

If I could have seen into the fairgrounds at that moment, I would have had a fit. Grandfather was just driving Dakar out onto the track. He was followed by Wildfire and Mr. Hartman; and finally Buckshot Agate and the big black horse, Thunderbolt, bringing up the rear. They were beginning their final warmups.

Buckshot Agate touched Thunderbolt on the tail with the end of his whip, and that black horse shot past Wildfire and Dakar so fast, it looked as though they were backing up. I know that's an old expression, but Grandfather said this time it really looked like that. The crowd roared out their appreciation of the mighty, murderous stride of that big black horse. Although Grandfather was the sentimental favorite, it didn't leave much doubt in the minds of the crowd about the inevitable outcome of the big race soon to start.

I don't think many of the townspeople were too hopeful about Hiawatha's chances when they saw him trotting down Main Street in that ridiculous gypsy outfit. Those who recognized him. I knew Hiawatha looked silly with all those trappings, but I was afraid to take them off before we were safely at our final destination inside the fairgrounds.

How right I was!

The town marshall, Carl Anderson, following Mr. Raffodil's instructions, was laying for us.

"They must never reach the fairgrounds!" Raffodil warned,

threatening the marshall. "That's an order! If I go down you go down with me!"

Just to be safe, I turned Hiawatha onto a side street, Oak Avenue, where he would attract less attention.

Even with that precaution, the town marshall was not fooled. Suddenly he jumped out from between two parked cars and seized Hiawatha by the bridle. Hiawatha dragged Marshall Anderson on his cowboy boots for quite a distance, sparks flying up from the nails, but the marshall hung on and kept jerking savagely down on Hiawatha's bridle, cutting into his mouth. Hiawatha came to a reluctant stop.

"You let go of that horse," I hollered. "We're on our way to the fair!"

"Not today, Sonny," the marshall said with a pleased grin.

Short-Stuff Farley and Midge Kelly came riding up on their bikes. Short-Stuff was delighted. "We told the town marshall all about the kidnapping," he yelled. "He's here to protect you."

"Yeah," Midge bragged. "We told him you'd probably try to sneak in on Oak Street, so we brought you a police escort to take you to the fairgrounds."

"You dumb idiots," I bellowed. "He's not our friend! He's the enemy. He works for Mr. Raffodil!"

"Just come along quietly with me," the marshall suggested, "and we'll see that justice is done. After all, you're driving stolen property, and I'm confiscating it."

"He's not stolen!" I objected. "This is my horse, Hiawatha! You've got no right!"

The marshall smiled but hung on tightly to Hiawatha's bridle. "If it turns out you're right, kid, you can make a claim later. I'll back you up myself."

"I can't do it later!" I screamed. "Hiawatha has to be at the fairgrounds in time for the big race. Right now!"

"I'm sure this motled grey horse can't be your chestnut, Hiawatha."

"He is!"

All three of us, Midge, Short-Stuff and myself kept yelling, "He is! It's Hiawatha!"

"This grey gypsy horse," the marshall said, "is impounded."

"Am I arrested?"

"Just detained."

"That's *arrested!*"

79.

The town marshall led Hiawatha into Mr. Raffodil's livery stable.

"This is not the jail," I objected. "This is old man Raffodil's livery stable!"

As we were going through the door, I turned on Short-Stuff and Midge and forgot all about the firecrackers as I hollered at them angrily.

"Some police escort! You were supposed to tell my Grandfather, not a crook. You two are the dumbest, most ignorant secret agents in the whole world!"

Short-Stuff was miffed. "I thought you were awed with wonder at our brilliance."

"That was before Hiawatha was totally ruined by your stupidity," I snapped. "You've spoiled everything. Hiawatha has lost the race. Thanks to you. We're all ruined."

I was almost in tears. Short-Stuff and Midge took off on their bikes. Marshall Anderson led Hiawatha deeper into the dark livery stable and our dream of glory ended.

I was still protesting angrily, but Marshall Anderson ignored everything I said.

"If this gypsy horse turns out to be Hiawatha," he chuckled with a sly smile, "I promise you we'll release him. Until then, this horse is my prisoner."

"When?"

"When what?"

"When will you release him?"

"In time. Whenever somebody reliable comes back from the fairgrounds who can identify him."

"That'll be too late. *I* can identify him. He's my horse! You *know* he's Hiawatha."

"I know nothing of the kind."

"You're a liar, and a crooked cop."

It rolled off his back.

"You're a minor, under legal age. We'll have to have some responsible adult to identify this horse."

"By then it will be too late," I wailed. "Hiawatha deserves a chance to run in the big race. Now!"

"We can't release stolen property willy-nilly on the say so of some young snot of a kid." Marshall Anderson made believe he sympathized, clucking in his teeth at my bad luck. "We'll just lead this gypsy horse into this stall where he'll be safe from thieves, and tie him up until later."

"He's *not* a gypsy horse! You know he's not!"

Marshall Anderson was now taunting me. "He certainly looks like a gypsy horse to me, and nothing like a race horse."

"He was kidnapped. He's a stolen race horse by the name of Hiawatha, the Champion of the World."

Marshall Anderson knew he was infuriating me. He was very pleased with himself. He knew that Mr. Raffodil would be pleased with his day's work, too. It meant money in his pocket. Lots of money. Every minute was precious.

Marshall Anderson could tell that I was on the point of doing something desperate. He reached out and took hold of the front wheel of the buggy, then held up his hand to help me down. "Climb down out of that buggy and hand me the reins."

I leaned forward.

"The reins," he said. "Not the buggy whip."

I was thinking of lashing him with the buggy whip and knocking him galley-west. I knew I had to do something. Quick. I started to crawl down the other side, away from the marshall.

"*This* side," the marshall snarled. "Slowly, very slowly. This red race horse is going nowhere."

"I thought you said he was a grey horse. And a gypsy horse. Not a race horse. You're a liar by your own words."

"It doesn't matter now, kid." The marshall looked at his watch. "He's out of it."

"You're a crook and you're not fit to be marshall of our town. Any town!!"

"Close your mouth, kid." He closed it for me with the back of his hand. I could taste the blood.

He'd hurt Hiawatha and me in the mouth. We were both bleeding, and we wanted to make him pay for it.

But there wasn't any way.

I heard the town clock strike four!

The Ninth Furlong!

"Listen to the whale talking to the minnow."

80.

The town band was completing their drill maneuvers on the main track in front of the grandstand. To the rousing strains of "Semper Fidelis" they marched back to their seats amidst a generous appreciative applause.

The crowd had enjoyed more than enough of the preliminaries. They were now anxious and ready for the main event, the famous County Fair Stakes.

All three horses were out on the half-mile track circling the oval warming up for the start of the race. Soon the track marshall would call for the trotters and the big race would begin. With or without Hiawatha. The stewards under Mr. Fletcher Potter had made it plain that they would not permit any further delays.

Buckshot Agate behind the big black five year old, Thunderbolt, would make mincemeat of both Dakar and Mr. Hartman's filly, Wildfire. Everybody knew that. Especially Mr. Sam Raffodil Senior who was striding back and forth across the front of his private box, strutting really, with a big winner's smile already on his face. He bowed expansively to his neighbors, knocking cigar ashes over the rail onto the track.

Grandfather sat straight and proud in his sulky dressed in his finest shiny silks, orange, black, and white. Dakar strutted handsomely behind Thunderbolt and Buckshot Agate in red on white, with Wildfire and Mr. Hartman hurrying up to become third in line, flashing their royal blue.

There were only three horses entered in this year's race for three year olds and up. Thunderbolt had frightened everyone else off. Still, it was a beautiful breath-taking sight to behold the three high-stepping trotters pass the grandstand in the pre-race parade. The band was playing "The Washington Post March," and the air was alive with excitement.

Mr. Raffodil cupped his hands and hollered at Grandfather as he passed by.

"Found that Indian horse of yours yet, old man? The one you cured with leeches?"

The guests in Mr. Raffodil's box laughed politely, led by the boisterous Mr. Raffodil.

Grandfather ignored the jibes, the happy beatific look on his face annoyed Mr. Raffodil. He wanted to see Grandfather grovel a little, and suffer, or at least look worried.

Mr. Raffodil had no idea what it cost Grandfather to appear so unruffled and calm, so sure of himself. Only I knew that when things were going against him, and the worse he felt inside, the happier and more confident Grandfather appeared.

More than almost anything else, Grandfather hated to lose a horse race. Especially one he knew he had a chance to win. Most of all, he despised losing to Mr. Raffodil.

When the county fair was all over, Grandfather described all these preliminary events to me in minute detail. Every moment of that historic Saturday afternoon. I made him repeat it for me three times. Especially the part when he drove Dakar in front of the grandstand the first time while Hiawatha and I were still being held captive by Marshall Anderson.

The three trotting horses wheeled their sulkies and walked slowly by the stands for the second time, in the opposite direction, so all of the spectators would be able to have a close-up view of the entries.

Grandfather came within a few yards of Mayor Sam Raffodil's private box. His Honor treated Dakar and Grandfather to a running commentary of insults, from "miracle leeches" to "kidnapped horses." Mr. Raffodil even patted his open mouth with the palm of his hand and gave his version of an Indian chant, "Ki yi! Ki yi! Ki yi!" Some of his close henchmen in his box joined in. Most did not.

Mr. Raffodil wasn't alive as far as Grandfather was concerned as he sat proudly on his sulky. Grandfather's savoir-faire angered Mr. Raffodil. He pointed his big cigar at Grandfather as he and Dakar passed by for the last time.

Mr. Raffodil yelled, "You'll die in a pauper's grave before I'm through with you, old man! And in some far-off place!"

Grandfather turned around and grinned wickediy.

"I still have a few tricks up my sleeve, Sam, he called back. "I wouldn't put any more money on this race if I were you."

Mr. Raffodil was worried immediately. Ile bit down on his big cigar and spoke out of the corner of his mouth to his wife, Minnie.

"I wonder what that old devil is up to."

"Now, Sam," Minnie comforted him.

"I don't like that smug, confident smile of his. He's tricky."

Minnie laughed, "Listen to the whale talking to the minnow."

81.

Marshall Anderson jerked savagely on Hiawatha's bridle. He swung the horse's head around, and pulled Hiawatha into the stall. Hiawatha's mouth was bleeding. The marshall knew he'd won and that it was all over. He was about to unhitch Hiawatha from the buggy when the huge double doors at the far end of the livery stable were thrown wide open, letting in the bright sunlight.

In the halo's glare behind them, I didn't recognize Short-Stuff Farley and Midge Kelly. They were mounted on two bicycles, jangling their bicycle bells, riding no-hand monies, and pumping their way into the center of the livery stable, waving their arms and yelling "Geronimo!" at the top of their lungs, and throwing popping and snapping live ladyfinger firecrackers everywhere.

The horses in the stable began to go wild, stomping, pawing, squealing and making other frightened-horse noises. It failed to disturb Marshall Anderson. He took it all in stride, but it *did* scare the dickens out of Hiawatha who already had had a rather full day.

Hiawatha jerked his head up violently. With a powerful thrust of that big red neck, Hiawatha tossed the lawman Carl Anderson galley-west! Hiawatha knocked him into a corner of the stall. Marshall Anderson was stunned.

Everybody was yelling directions at the same time.

The marshall pulled himself up against the side of the stall. I had leaped into the buggy and backed Hiawatha out.

Marshall Anderson came to enough to stagger toward me. He reached for Hiawatha's bridle with one hand, and stretched his other arm out toward me. I grabbed the whip and tried to lash him, but he caught the end and jerked it.

His pull sent me flying out over the front of the buggy and onto Hiawatha's back. I crawled up and grabbed Hiawatha's bridle, and began to ride him like a jockey. Kicking him with my bare feet, I hollered:

"Go, Hiawatha, Go!"

He needed no encouragement. We headed for that patch of bright sunlight at the far end of the livery stable. Marshall Anderson lost his grip on Hiawatha's bridle, but held onto the back of the buggy as we pulled away.

I was hanging on to Hiawatha for dear life. We came out of that building like a stone from a slingshot. Marshall Anderson was still hanging on to the rear end of the buggy. He was hollering at us.

"Stop this buggy! Come back here! You're under arrest!"

"In a pig's eye!" I shouted.

I caught a glimpse of Emil Khusrow, the manager of the livery stable, through the big office window. He was talking frantically into a telephone. Alerting the enemy ahead, I told myself.

"Hurry, Hiawatha!"

Marshall Anderson was now trying to climb up into the back of the buggy. Short-Stuff Farley accidentally shoved Margie Kelly's bicycle into the marshall's legs, tangling up his feet in the wheels and sprockets.

It wasn't the best thing that ever happened to Margie Kelly's bicycle, but it was a wonderful thing that happened to Marshall Anderson. He fell over the bike, lost his grip on the buggy, and tumbled sideways, plunging into the stacked up bales of hay by the doorway.

It was taps for Margie Kelly's bike. One wheel was still spinning merrily as the swaying, leaning stacked bales of hay came tumbling down and covered both Margie Kelly's bicycle and the angrily screaming town marshall Carl Anderson.

He was out of the ball game!

Short-Stuff Farley told me later that Marshall Anderson threatened to send them both to the prison farm.

"As soon as I crawl out from under these bales of hay," he threatened.

But so much hay had toppled down on top of Marshall Anderson that it was obvious that his threat couldn't be carried out for some time. Short-Stuff took off with Midge on the handlebars of the other bike. They headed toward the fairgrounds with Marshall Anderson shouting bloody murder behind them from beneath all those bales of hay. He was shaking one big fist which had poked its way out of the stack.

"I'll get you for this!" the marshall yelled. "I know both your names!"

"Your name is mud!" Midge yelled back as Short-Stuff pumped the bike for all he was worth toward the fairgrounds.

I looked back in time to see Short-Stuff Farley cross-body block Marshall Anderson with Margie Kelly's bike, ripping him away from the buggy and into those bales of hay again. I shouted back at both of them. "I take it all back. You are two of the finest, most outstanding secret agents it has ever been my—"

Midge Kelly, who had a lot of his sister Margie Kelly in him, hollered, "Is there any cash money in it?"

Short-Stuff Farley, whose head was screwed on right—sometimes—yelled at me, "Forget It! Just win the horse race!"

I slid down from Hiawatha's neck and made my way back up into the driver's seat of the buggy again. All in one scuttling motion. Hiawatha and I zipped around the Soo Line Depot lickety-split and headed toward the railroad crossing in front of the fairgrounds.

As we neared the Soo Line tracks, I was upset to hear the town band in the distance. They were playing "The Star Spangled Banner." That meant the County Fair Stakes was about to begin and my time was becoming perilously short.

In my mind, I could hear the foghorn voice of the starter shouting through his megaphone, "The trotters are coming back out onto the track!" and the thought terrified me. "C'mon, Hiawatha," I cried. "Move it, baby. This is it!"

I knew that right this very moment, Grandfather and Dakar would be finishing their final warm-up, and would now be moving slowly around the backstretch and heading toward the starting line. Grandfather had no idea that Hiawatha and I were only minutes away. Almost within eyesight. If Grandfather could have looked through the grandstand, he'd have seen the two of us coming around the Soo Line Depot lickety split.

As we approached the railroad crossing in front of the fairgrounds, a switch-engine backed a line of empty iron ore cars across our path. Hiawatha stopped abruptly to avoid a crash. He danced nervously in his tracks and backed the buggy into a ditch. Hiawatha threshed about, anxious to be off, and jerked the buggy back up onto the railroad crossing.

The train poked along, inching its way slowly forward. I glanced over my shoulder at the town clock. Four twenty! Ten minutes to go!

"Hurry, Mr. Engineer!" I hollered. "Please hurry!"

With a loud squeal of metal the train began to back up instead of go forward. With a loud hiss of steam, the big engine came to a dead stop right in front of us, closing off the crossing.

We were trapped. Blockaded!

I didn't like to do it, but there was no other way. I turned Hiawatha's head to the right and slowly started him walking along the railroad bed, paralleling the engine and the motionless iron ore cars. We were headed toward the front of the engine so we could cross over the tracks. Carefully we bumped our way over the railroad ties.

"Easy, Hiawatha," I warned him, "watch out for those million dollar legs. The footing is dangerous."

The gravel shoulder of the roadbed suddenly widened out by the crossing and Hiawatha began to move forward into a faster walk. When we neared the front of the engine, it started up again. It moved slowly forward, alongside us, just fast enough so we could not pass.

The fireman stuck his head out of the cab alongside the engineer. They both laughed at Hiawatha's straw hat flopping down over his eyes. You could hear the blanket-bells jingling and clanging over the sound of the puffing engine.

"Go, boy!" the fireman shouted, encouragingly, "You can beat this slow old train. Run! Run!"

That's when I knew they were deliberately blocking our way. When Hiawatha increased his speed, so did the train, accompanied by the loud hissing sound of steam, which frightened Hiawatha, and the scornful laughter of the fireman and the engineer.

"You shut up!" I yelled at them. "You're just trying to get this horse hurt. He's a champion race horse. Now get out of our path. We're on our way to win the County Fair Stakes!"

"*Sure* you are!" the fireman roared mockingly. He called to the engineer. "Hey, Jake! Look at this dumb ugly gypsy horse. He's going to try and outrace our train."

I knew they were egging Hiawatha on to try it.

That's when I saw a third person in the cab. I recognized him immediately as one of Mr. Raffodil's men. He was telling the other two exactly what to do. Emil Khusrow had obviously telephoned ahead. The word was out, "Stop that Hiawatha horse! At all costs!"

There was probably a big reward. No wonder the train was deliberately shutting off our path. It was all part of Mr. Raffodil's plan. He dare not let Hiawatha appear. He couldn't afford to take any chances that he might lose the race.

This was the worst thing that had happened to us, by far. All day. I could see the fairgrounds entrance gate, but we couldn't get across.

Whenever Hiawatha began to pick up speed, the train engine puffed vigorously ahead, spinning its wheels and rumbling forward to shut us off. They refused to let us pass and were delighted by our helpless frustration. They shot white steam out at Hiawatha, time and again. He was afraid of it. Twice they frightened Hiawatha off the shoulder, and laughed and applauded from the cab of the engine when he nearly stumbled.

I looked back at the town clock. Eight minutes to go! I had to do something. Something desperate. I jumped out of the buggy, ran down the tracks to the front of the engine, and laid my body across the rails.

"Run over me! See if I care!" I desperately yelled.

The engineer hollered angrily at me. He screeched the huge metal monster to a grinding halt with the steel wheels locked and with me partly under the front of cow-catcher. The men came scrambling down from the cab, led by Mr. Raffodil's stooge.

"Run over me. See if I care!"

As soon as they were out of the engine, I leaped up and raced to the buggy, carrying a handful of gravel in my right hand. Hiawatha was already halfway across the tracks. I snapped the reins against Hiawatha's rump, but he needed no encouragement. We bumped across the tracks in front of the engine, and headed toward the fairgrounds' gate.

Mr. Raffodil's man reached out for Hiawatha's harness, but I drew back my handful of gravel and flung it at him head on. He cried out, dropped his grip on Hiawatha's leather harness. In a flash, Hiawatha and I were free!

We bumped along the railroad tracks racing for the fairgrounds entrance. A weak buggy wheel was about to collapse. It bent in and out and groaned in agony as we whipped along the frontage road. We were headed straight for the wide open gate hoping to be safe inside the fairgrounds at long last!

The Tenth Furlong!

Four minutes to go!

Nothing ever looked sweeter. There was still time! And this was the fairgrounds! I hollered "Geronimo!" again, but it didn't seem anywhere near good enough for what Hiawatha and I had done together this day. I pointed Hiawatha toward that open gate, and he responded by sailing along those last few final yards. On the dead run.

That's when we saw them. All three of them.

Sam Raffodil, Emery Pickett and his brother Wallace Pickett. They had their shoulders against the big solid wooden fairgrounds gate and were swinging it shut.

It was going to be close.

I tried to scoot Hiawatha through. I knew there would never be enough time for us to go all the way around the fairgrounds to the back gate.

Never.

Hiawatha would lose his chance, and Grandfather would lose everything he owned. Including his pride.

The gate swung shut in our faces. I could hear the big four-by-four slam down into its huge steel brackets. Hiawatha was moving so fast he nearly climbed the front of the gate before stopping. I could also hear the insulting sound of Sam Raffodil Junior's claxon horn on the other side:

"Aaaaaoooooooaaahhh!" "Aaaoooaaahhh!!"

Hiawatha and I were beaten.

For the third time that day I was crying. Blubbering like a baby. Not for myself; for Hiawatha. I kept thinking of that old worn out phrase, "So close, and yet so far." I even said, "Damn you to hell, Sam Raffodil!" and didn't feel ashamed of swearing at all.

Jimmy Middleman's father drove up beside me with his huge yellow and green lumber company truck. He had seen the whole thing. He had witnessed our misfortune and my humiliation.

He was livid. Mr. Middleman hollered out the window of his truck at me.

"Pull your horse over to one side, William, and give me some room. Then follow my truck through. Got it?"

"I've got it!" I shouted, wild with hope.

I pulled Hiawatha to one side, and swung him around behind Mr. Middleman's truck.

I've never heard a more glorious sound than the bash that big truck made as it battered its way through the huge fairgrounds gate. It made a gigantic hole for Hiawatha, flapping both sides of the gate wide open.

"Clear the track!" I bellowed. "Hiawatha's coming through!"

We went shooting through that opening in the gate in the wake of Mr. Middleman's truck, like water coming out of the end of a fire hose.

The clock and the fairgrounds tower showed:

Four minutes to go!

Zero Hour.

85.

Hiawatha and I attracted considerable attention as we trotted down the midway on what I hoped would be the final leg of our victorious journey. I didn't have a horn to clear a path for us through the crowded midway, so I kept shouting out loud like the Minneapolis Express bus:

"Beep! Beep! Beep!"

No one recognized Hiawatha in his crazy gypsy outfit, so instead of getting the cheers we deserved, all we received were raspberries, boos, hoots, catcalls and insults all along the midway. Including some trash such as empty soft drink cups and cans thrown at us.

We couldn't have cared less. We were practically home free. What was more, Hiawatha was all warmed up for the race of his life. At least that's what I told myself, confident that I'd done a first-class job, outside of the disasters, and both of us being pretty well emotionally exhausted.

Hiawatha and I made a two wheel turn around the central midway fountain. I pretended it was the homestretch turn as the old buggy careened dangerously, righted itself, and headed for harness racing heaven.

Margie Kelly darted out in front of the buggy waving her pink parasol. Hiawatha went up on his hind legs and nearly crushed her. I went head first over the front of the buggy onto his rump. I had already spent far too much time there, and right at that moment, I didn't have a second to spare. As I fell to the ground, I shrieked at Margie Kelly.

"That was dumb!!"

"Hurry, William!" she shouted at me, "or you'll be too late!"

"I *know* that," I told her, as I crawled back up into the buggy. "Thanks a lot! You certainly didn't help any with your sabotage."

"I had to warn you," she shouted. "Don't go past Dan Pickett's orange stand. Sam and his cronies are waiting for you there. I heard Sam say it was their last line of defense."

"Just great! There *is* no other way. I have to go past Dan Pickett's orange stand, or I will be too late. And thanks to you, I've already lost another precious minute. Out of my way!"

"You'll be sorry, William. They'll gang up on you."

"I've been sorry all day," I shouted at her, "and I'm glad for what happened to your bicycle."

Margie was surprised. "What happened to my bicycle?"

"You'll find out. And put that parasol away."

Hiawatha had reared up again as she opened it. He landed and took off. In two jumps Hiawatha and I were in front of Pickett's orange stand.

All three of them were waiting. Sam, Dan and his brother Wallace. All three began pelting Hiawatha and me with oranges and grapefruit as soon as we drew within range.

Dan and Wallace Pickett each stuck an iron bar into the spokes of the two back buggy wheels. The bars snapped the wooden spokes like matchsticks, and the buggy plopped down on its back axles. What was left of the two back wheels, the rims, flopped over on their side, spinning.

Sam Raffodil hollered at the Picketts. "Remember, my father promised a hundred dollars to anyone who helps keep this horse off the track!"

I was hanging on with one hand to keep from going over backwards. I couldn't prevent it. I flew off the buggy on the left side, hanging on for dear life. Desperately. Someone unhooked Hiawatha's harness so he could be led away and hidden in one of the nearby barns. Dan Pickett grabbed Hiawatha's bridle.

I slapped Hiawatha's rump with the reins, and he pulled free. The two of us went headlong down the rest of the midway heading for the entrance to the track.

I could hear all three of the trotters coming down the homestretch on their final warm-ups. It was zero hour!

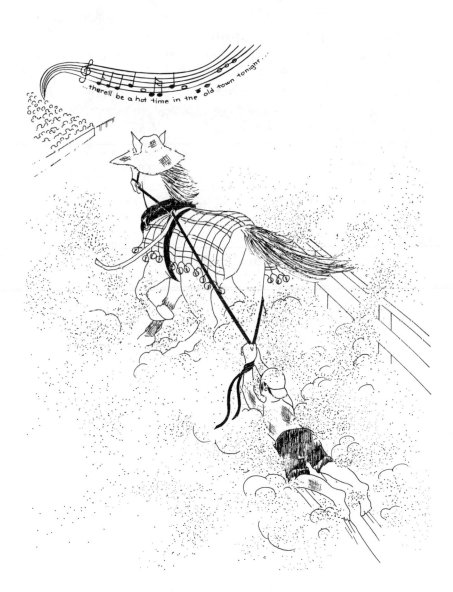

"Whoa! Whoa!"

Word of what had happened was spreading all over the midway like wildfire. "That's no gypsy horse," the people hollered, "that's Hiawatha! He's come back to win the big race!"

There was a rush toward the main race track entrance. Hundreds of people abandoned their lunch, their games and their work. They were flooding down the midway, racing for the entrance gate to follow us out onto the track.

Their hometown horse Hiawatha had made it back. They knew that Hiawatha would need some help to delay the start of the race. If the mob rushing out onto the track from the midway had their way, Hiawatha would get his chance. Even if they had to block the entire track at the foot of the homestretch for the rest of the afternoon.

Carrying banners, balloons, ice cream cones, hot dogs and soft drinks, they headed pell-mell through the racetrack entrance. I could hear them roaring behind me as I went spinning out onto the track with a gypsy horse, and myself being dragged along behind him with the reins wrapped around my wrists and hanging on for dear life and hollering, "Whoa! Whoa!"

The Eleventh Furlong!

"Too late!"

Whoosh! Whoosh! Whoosh!

Thunderbolt, Wildfire and Dakar went flashing past in front of me.

My heart leaped up into my throat which was already filled with track dust. For one horrible moment I thought that Hiawatha and I were too late and that the big race itself was already underway. Officially.

I was crushed and heartbroken.

When I realized that the horses were "scoring" for their final turn, I cried out loud for the umpteenth time. This time for joy.

Hiawatha and I started up the middle of the track toward the judge's stand in front of the grandstand. Rather, Hiawatha started up the track, and I went along for the ride. Hiawatha was still doing unpleasant things to both me and to the track. Hiawatha was galloping full blast with me hanging on to the reins and whirling around in the dirt. I tried to dig my bare heels and toes into the soft dirt to slow Hiawatha down a little.

Impossible!

When the crowd caught sight of Hiawatha in that hat and blanket, hauling a barefooted, mud-covered boy down the middle of the track, like a pike fisherman trolling with spinning live bait, they roared with laughter and thought it was all part of a pre-race comedy act being staged by the county fair for the entertainment of the crowd.

The crowd applauded, laughed, and cheered as Hiawatha

and I approached the front of the grandstand. Then, as we came to a stop in front of the stewards, Hiawatha arched his beautiful neck and pawed at the ground.

I hollered at the top of my voice:

"We're here, Grandfather! We're here!"

Hiawatha didn't count to five this time, he just kept pawing and dancing and prancing like a high school horse. Hiawatha was letting them see that no matter how grotesque he might be dressed, he was all race horse. Gradually, little by little, the crowd began to recognize that funny-looking incredible animal.

Someone shouted out, "That old grey mare is Hiawatha! Someone's painted him to look foolish."

A tremendous cheer went up from the stands. It began slowly, but built in volume until it rose to a deafening tumult. Hiawatha was the hometown favorite, not Thunderbolt. And he was on the track!

I waited impatiently for Grandfather to come around the far turn and start down the homestretch for the first half of his final "score." I leaped to my feet, handed the reins to a track worker, and began waving my arms at Grandfather and Dakar to flag them down.

Grandfather didn't recognize either one of us. Me or Hiawatha. He slowed down and went past me. He could go no farther. The track was filled from rail to grandstand with cheering people from the midway. They were still crowding their way through the entrance and out on to the track. They had it blocked off completely. Grandfather turned, came back, and gave me his cold and fishy eyeballs as he drew near.

"It's me, Grandfather!" I hollered at him. "It's me and Hiawatha!"

Grandfather pulled Dakar up, wheeled, and slowly walked the sorrel back toward us. I began talking my head off.

"I know we're not much to look at Grandfather, but it really *is* Hiawatha. He's here. On time! And he's all right. Now you can run the Raffodils right up the shores of Gitchee Gumee and into the shining big sea waters!"

Grandfather still couldn't believe it, but the roaring chant of the crowd finally convinced him that this hayseed horse was his.

"Hiawatha! Hiawatha! Hiawatha!"

The crowd roared it out.

Grandfather stepped down from his sulky. He hugged me, patted Hiawatha, but shook his head and said, "It's too late."

"He's ready, Grandfather."

"No use kidding ourselves, Hiawatha's been away from the track too long. Besides, Dakar's all warmed up."

"So is Hiawatha."

"Not for this race," Grandfather said. "It's too late. We're under starter's orders."

"Please Grandfather, give Hiawatha his chance.
He's earned it!"

"Hiawatha *is* warmed up!" I insisted. "I 'scored' him myself, Grandfather, slowly and steadily. All the way here from the gypsy camp. He behaved perfectly."

Okey, so I lied a little. It was for Hiawatha. Besides, it wasn't my fault we had all that trouble.

"He wouldn't stand a chance," Grandfather told me. "He's been idle too long. We don't want to humiliate this great horse, son. We love him too much. Get him off the track. There'll be another day."

"Please, Grandfather," I entreated. "I did 'score' Hiawatha myself, just the way you taught me. He's ready as he'll ever be in this world."

Grandfather tousled my hair, but shook his head again.

"I know he *looks* terrible, Grandfather, but that's not Hiawatha's fault. Besides, I *had* to disguise him to keep Mr. Raffodil from having him kidnapped again. That mean old man had booby-traps to stop Hiawatha all the way to this fairgrounds. But he *didn't* stop him. We got here. And even if he loses, he deserves a chance to run. Please, Grandfather, give Hiawatha his chance. He's earned it. And he's a lot more horse than he looks."

Mr. Raffodil kept yelling for the stewards to start the race. "Get that gypsy nag off the track and get on with the race!" he demanded. "These horses are under starter's orders and can't be changed."

"Please, Grandfather. Give Hiawatha his chance. He won't disgrace you."

The crowd, and especially the officials, were getting restless. The crowd kept cheering for Hiawatha.

"Please, Grandfather. You don't know what wonderful things Hiawatha has done just to get here. You're going to lose with Dakar anyway. Maybe Hiawatha can win. At least he deserves a chance. What have you got to lose?"

Grandfather walked around Hiawatha. He shuddered at the old floppy hat. He whipped it off Hiawatha's head and sailed it over the rail into the infield. Somebody caught it and sailed it back to me.

When Grandfather put his hand on Hiawatha's neck, both of Hiawatha's ears flattened way back. He knew who it was.

"Please, Grandfather," I implored.

"You've said that."

"I know we both look dirty and terrible, Grandfather, but Mr. Raffodil had Hiawatha painted grey to hide him from us. Beneath that ragged old blanket with the bells, is the most wonderful big red horse in all the world. I love him." I put my arm around Hiawatha's neck. I pointed at the crowd. "All these people love him, too, Grandfather. Listen to them. They're cheering for our horse. Not Thunderbolt. Hiawatha can beat any horse in the world. You have my word on it."

Hiawatha lifted Grandfather's racing cap off, and when Grandfather bent over to pick it up, Hiawatha pushed his backside with his nose, just like he used to do.

I took up the chant with the crowd as I threw my arms around Hiawatha's neck again and hugged him harder than ever.

"Hiawatha! Hiawatha! Hiawatha!"

I yelled it in rhythm with the crowd. Hiawatha was trying to shake me loose, but I told Grandfather, "I won't let go until you promise to give Hiawatha his chance."

Grandfather dusted himself off, and took another long look at Hiawatha. He felt his legs, one by one, and looked deep into

Hiawatha's eyes. Grandfather limped all the way around the horse, scrutinizing every inch of him very carefully. Grandfather refused to be stampeded by the angry shouts of Sam Raffodil Senior and the chief steward, Mr. Fletcher Potter.

"Get on with the race. Now!" Mr. Raffodil shouted. "It's all been settled. You're driving Dakar, no other horse. They're under starter's orders! So get on with it!"

Hiawatha pawed the earth, danced up and down to show how fit he was. Grandfather still hadn't made up his mind, so Hiawatha reached over and lifted Grandfather's orange, white and black racing cap off his head a second time and sailed it over the fence and into the infield and whinnied. Somebody sailed the cap back onto the track, and Hiawatha stepped on it. Grandfather stroked Hiawatha's leg and gently lifted his hoof from the cap.

An electric spark shot up my back. I could tell by the flash in Grandfather's eyes when he raised up, that he had changed his mind. Grandfather was going to give the big red horse his chance!

"Winner take all, and damn the consequences!" I heard him mutter.

Grandfather turned to me. "C'mon, he said.

All three of us started toward the judges' stand.

"Stomp on 'em, Hiawatha!"

The stewards, led by Mr. Fletcher Potter put up a fierce resistance. They refused to let Grandfather switch horses.

"Too late," they argued. "The horses are already under starter's orders."

Grandfather was fiercely adamant.

"This race," he said, "was billed as a match race between Hiawatha and Thunderbolt with Wildfire along for the ride. Hiawatha is here now, in time to run, and you can't deny him his chance."

"We can, and we will," Mr. Fletcher Potter insisted, egged on by Mr. Raffodil. "I'm sure the other stewards and judges will back me up. It's too late to change now."

Grandfather angrily snatched the program out of the hands of Mr. Fletcher Potter. He opened it to the center fold.

"Read that!" he said.

Grandfather pointed to Thunderbolt's picture on one side of the page and to Hiawatha's on the other. Printed below in big black print were the words, "The Big Race. Thunderbolt vs. Hiawatha! For this year's *County Fair Stakes!*"

"See that?" Grandfather snapped. "Can you read English? Hiawatha's name and picture are featured on the very program you're holding in your hand. That's the race these people came here to see. And that's the race they're going to get."

The judges still hesitated with Mr. Raffodil backing them up.

"Fine!" Grandfather said, "Let's leave it up to the crowd."

Thousands of people were still chanting, louder than ever:

"Hiawatha! Hiawatha! Hiawatha!"

The stewards gave in. Reluctantly. Over Mr. Fletcher Potter's vehement protests. Not to mention Mayor Raffodil's. They had to give in. The crowd which had followed us in from the midway were still blocking every foot of the track from side to side. Thousands of them. Thousands! They sent representatives to the stewards and judges and told them they would not budge, and there would be no race of any kind today that did not have Hiawatha as one of the starters.

Winner take all!

I could tell that neither the stewards nor the judges cared for the ugly mood of that standing crowd, and their roars of anger, when word reached them that the officials might scratch Hiawatha from the race.

On County Fair Stakes day, the three judges had equal authority with the three stewards. Gradually all six of them capitulated. It was a bitter pill for Mr. Raffodil to swallow.

"Okey," the stewards said. "Go and bring Hiawatha onto the track. We'll have the veterinary surgeon look him over before we make our final decision."

"I don't have to go get him," Grandfather grinned. "*This* is Hiawatha." He pointed to the gypsy-clad horse I was holding by the bridle. "And he's ready to run."

The stewards refused to believe that the grey-streaked strange horse that had come galloping up the track with that gypsy hat and all his weird jingle-bells paraphernalia could possibly be Hiawatha.

The head steward, Mr. Fletcher Potter seized his chance and began objecting again. "This grey horse can't run in the County Fair Stakes. He's a clown. A disgrace."

Mr. Raffodil rushed back from his private box to make his presence felt again if there was any chance for a disqualification.

"That's not Hiawatha," he insisted. "That horse is grey, not red. Start the race with Dakar as arranged." He looked at his wristwatch. "We're already fifteen minutes past the official starting time."

"It is so Hiawatha!" I shouted, "and he's partly grey because you had him painted that color. And I can prove you're a horse thief." I looked at Grandfather. "Do they still hang horse thieves? I hope."

Mr. Raffodil ran roughshod over me.

"Are you going to listen to the ravings of a hysterical kid?" He looked at his watch again. "The stewards and judges can't hold up this race while you warm up another entry."

"Fine," Grandfather agreed pleasantly. "I'll race the one right here without a warm-up. Just give me time to get him into a sulky."

The stewards and judges conferred. They instructed Grandfather. "You've got ten minutes to get that horse back out onto the track. If you're not ready, you forfeit your right to race Hiawatha, and the race will be run between Thunderbolt, Wildfire and Dakar. That's final. So leave the sorrel, Dakar, hitched up to his sulky here on the track."

"I don't want to run Hiawatha in my old sulky." Grandfather objected. "I want to use this new one which I bought especially for today's victory." He tapped the golden metal sulky to which Dakar was hitched.

"Your old one was good enough to win last year," the judges pointed out. "Take it or leave it. You've already used up a minute of your time arguing."

"And get that grey horse off this track."

"Gladly," Grandfather said, "and he won't be grey when he comes back. He'll be a beautiful chestnut, a bright shiny copper chestnut. The finest red horse you'll ever see. You're lucky to be alive and here today."

Grandfather and I hurried Hiawatha to the barn. The crowd packed solid along the track to delay the race unless Hiawatha was in it, parted for us magically. Like it was the Red Sea. Many of them still found it hard to believe that the streaked grey horse could be the darling of their hearts, Hiawatha. Still they applauded, danced and whistled as Hiawatha walked proudly between the two sides. The women threw kisses and flowers at him, even their hats, and everybody yelled encouragement.

"Stomp on 'em, Hiawatha!"

"Go big red—or grey! Whatever!"

"We're for you, Hiawatha!"

Stuff like that. Only much better.

Can the old grey mare perform a miracle?

89.

Mr. Raffodil was still violently opposed to this last minute change in horses. He kept yelling that the race was now officially between Dakar and Thunderbolt, since they were under starter's orders. That was the law.

Most of the crowd, however, was on Grandfather's side. They held up their programs and pointed to the picture of Hiawatha and Thunderbolt on the inside. They gave Mr. Raffodil the "raspberry" accompanied by boos and hisses. They had paid good money to see a match race between Thunderbolt and Hiawatha, and didn't take kindly to anyone who might try to prevent it.

Mr. Raffodil finally threw up his hands in disgust and went back to his box in the grandstand. He had gone as far as he could. Besides, he said to himself, taking comfort in the thought, how could any horse who'd been out of training for three days, and who had gone through what Hiawatha had been through ever hope to beat a fresh New York champion horse like Thunderbolt.

"Impossible!" he said.

He took comfort in it.

Grandfather explained all of this psychology to me on the way back to the stables. Now that Mr. Raffodil had seen Hiawatha out on the track in his gypsy costume, looking so dreadful and without a chance to warm up properly, he felt more confident than ever that Thunderbolt would win the race easily. That's why Mr. Raffodil was still so cocky. According to all racehorse training, he was right.

"But Hiawatha *is* warmed up and ready," I insisted. "I told you! I 'scored' Hiawatha myself just like you showed me."

Grandfather ruffled my hair. "I know," he said, but I could tell that even he wasn't sure. Can you blame him?

As we led Hiawatha off the track toward the stable area, one of the trumpet players in the town band began to play a wise-cracking, snarling, snotty version of "The Old Grey Mare, She Ain't What She Used to Be," and by the time we reached the exit, the whole band had joined in, and most of the people were shouting aloud the lyrics. They weren't being insulting to Hiawatha, they were only having fun, enjoying the excitement of a new surprise and unexpected twist to the afternoon.

This marvelous "match race" had almost been snatched away from them, Hiawatha against Thunderbolt! Now Hiawatha was back!

The overwhelming number of racing fans were hoping that "the old grey mare" would come back out onto the track a transformed mighty red racing warrior so they could all holler their heads off:

"Here comes the big red machine!"

It was what I hoped for, too.

"Hiawatha! Hiawatha! Hiawatha!"

"We performed miracle after miracle."

I followed Grandfather into what had once been Hiawatha's stable area. Grandfather had been instructed by the stewards to leave Dakar hitched up out on the track and ready to go, if for any reason Hiawatha had to forfeit, or the veterinary physician had to disqualify him after all he'd been through.

Grandfather threw Hiawatha's famous blanket with the bells into a corner and they rang and banged triumphantly off the wall. While we were both laughing and sponging Hiawatha down, Grandfather asked me how I'd managed to get there.

"It wasn't easy."

"Nothing worthwhile ever is."

"This was the worst ever, Grandfather. That's why I *know* Hiawatha is going to win."

"Don't get your hopes up too high."

"We performed miracle after miracle, magic, wizard stuff, from the moment we escaped from that fake hayrack, all the way from that gypsy camp to the fairgrounds. It was wonderful!"

Grandfather accidentally sponged my shoulder down instead of Hiawatha's. "Oh," he said, "Sorry. I was just overcome with your humility."

"Okey, so I'm not Mr. Humble, but I sure was lucky. *You* played a big part in it, too, Grandfather."

"I did?"

"You did. No matter how depressed I became, I remembered everything you ever told me."

"Everything?"

"Well, the important disaster things."

"Such as?"

"To have fortitude in bearing suffering and adversity. Courage and the stamina to face and overcome hardship. To show pluck when bravely facing every danger, and always to laugh in the face of terrible odds."

Grandfather accidentally squeezed another spongeful of water down my other shoulder and gave me his icy eyeballs.

"Tell me about it," he said, as he prepared Hiawatha for the race. He meant I should tell him about our surprise appearance on the track just in the nick of time, as the big race was about to begin, and to leave out the romance novel. Grandfather had already said that to me a lot of times before.

I almost told Grandfather the entire story, episode by episode, knowing how proud he'd be of Hiawatha. I was about to list all of our miracle escapades:

> Bound and gagged in a fake hayrack
> Escape by my wits and Hiawatha's hoofs
> Roadblock
> Gunfight at the O.K. Corral with ladyfinger firecrackers
> Captured by Marshall Anderson
> The train blockade
> My tender body on the railroad tracks under the
>   cowcatcher
> Going through the big hole blasted in the fairgrounds
>   gate by Mr. Middleman's truck
> The parasol rearup
> The great orange and grapefruit onslaught
> The overturned buggy
> The painful bellyflop
> Spinning down the track like a yellow-bellied grey-
>   hackle while holding onto the reins of a mad gypsy
>   horse with one hand, and digging up acres of flying
>   dirt with my heels.

I was about to open my mouth and reveal it all, when Hiawatha at that exact moment deliberately stepped on my foot.

I mean it—it was deliberate! It hurt.

In a flash I knew that if Grandfather had heard about all those terrible things happening to Hiawatha, he'd scratch the chestnut from the race immediately, and go with Dakar. Fairness to animals always came first with Grandfather. It was a clear-cut never-to-be-changed principle.

I also knew that Grandfather would talk to me later about horse abuse. He'd never give a thought to child abuse by horses. I might even undergo some minor horse whip body bruises in the barn myself. No matter how innocent I might be, and no matter how badly both Hiawatha and I wanted to win the County Fair Stakes for an old man who was way in over his head financially, and whom we both loved very much. Even so, being kind to animals always came first with Grandfather. It was one of the nice things about Grandfather, if it didn't actually turn your stomach as it did mine under the present trying conditions.

It was true, what I said about Hiawatha. I was just about to blow our cover when Hiawatha stepped on my foot. I cried out and Hiawatha whinnied loudly in return.

Of course, it might have been an accident and nothing more than a weird fantastic coincidence. But, you can't tell me that Hiawatha didn't do it deliberately, and that he wasn't saying to me, "Keep your big mouth shut you dummy, or we'll lose our chance! That tender-hearted old man will scratch me from the race."

What a horse! How could he lose?

No one would ever believe it. I know you don't. Thanks to Hiawatha, I decided not to tell Grandfather anything. Absolutely nothing. Hiawatha had saved our skin, again.

Besides, after summarizing all those dramatic disasters we'd been through together, I was beginning to have grave doubts myself that Hiawatha could ever win against a fresh, full of beans, black horse like Thunderbolt. Hiawatha might be lucky to get second, with Wildfire also rested and eager.

"We're the good guys."

91.

So, when Grandfather said, "Tell me about it in detail," I shrugged my shoulders, smiled, and said: "A run-of-the-mill, easygoing, everyday warm-up score by your two best friends, Hiawatha and me."

Grandfather looked at me suspiciously as his sponge slipped and doused me again. This time I knew it was deliberate.

"Cut that out!" I warned him.

"Did you try to work your confidence game on God when you were locked up in that hayrack? Or during all those ordinary, run-of-the-mill, wizard miracles on your way to the fairgrounds?" Grandfather asked.

I was shocked.

"You know me, Grandfather."

"You bet I do. That's why I'm asking."

"We're the *good* guys, Grandfather. God had to be on our side otherwise we'd never have reached the fairgrounds, right? I'm sure He'll help Hiawatha win."

"If you haven't worn out God's patience!"

By this time Grandfather and I had Hiawatha scrubbed and dried. He shone like a newly minted penny.

I scrubbed myself up, too, and before you knew it, Hiawatha and I were both as good-looking as ever. He was so beautiful compared to how he looked inside that hayrack, that it hurt my throat to look at him glistening there in the sunlight, all chestnut-red and glorious.

The veterinarian surgeon came in, took one look at

Hiawatha's coat, grinned at Grandfather, and said, "Good luck, Grandfather. I'm going to wager me a few bucks on this broken-down, bedraggled gypsy horse myself. Sorry to be late, but Sam Raffodil had another veterinarian on his way over here to disqualify Hiawatha. I had to do something about it."

"He never gives up, does he?"

"No, but his veterinarian surgeons do. Especially if someone shoves them down, doubled-up into a rain barrel, headfirst."

He left with a big grin, "Good luck, you three."

As he left Pete Devlin shoved his head in the door. "The stewards say if you're not on the track in three minutes, you forfeit the race."

Grandfather glanced at Pete Devlin, then reached over for a pitchfork. Pete Devlin vanished like magic.

We were ready at last.

"We'll show 'em, won't we, Grandfather?"

"We'll give it a try but if you know any first-class prayers," he replied, "this is the time to say them."

"For gosh sakes, I've *been* praying for three days! Non-stop."

Grandfather caressed Hiawatha's neck. "It's up to the big red horse now, not us."

Grandfather gave me a grizzly bear hug and a whisker rub for luck as I helped him up into last year's sulky. "Well, son," he said. "This is it."

I nodded, tears in my eyes. Everything depended on the next few minutes. I was holding Hiawatha's bridle and rubbing his nose. Grandfather clucked his teeth for "Giddap!" I released Hiawatha and patted his withers as he passed me by.

"All right, Hiawatha," Grandfather said, as he guided the beautiful chestnut colt up the slope toward the entrance gate to the track.

"Let's eat 'em up!"

The Twelfth Furlong!

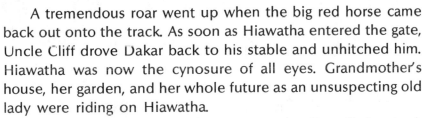

A tremendous roar went up when the big red horse came back out onto the track. As soon as Hiawatha entered the gate, Uncle Cliff drove Dakar back to his stable and unhitched him. Hiawatha was now the cynosure of all eyes. Grandmother's house, her garden, and her whole future as an unsuspecting old lady were riding on Hiawatha.

Hiawatha wasn't allowed a warm-up, so Grandfather took him to the starting line around the track the back way outwitting the stewards that tiny bit. At least it was a small "score." I kept hollering at Grandfather, "He doesn't need it!"

All three horses were swinging into line for the start when I reached my place in the grandstand. Wildfire had drawn the rail, Thunderbolt was in the middle, and Hiawatha on the outside. With only three horses in the race, there was no advantage.

Grandfather was having his hands full holding Hiawatha down. In spite of the Tamarack Road, Hiawatha still hadn't used up all his "beans."

"C'mon, Hiawatha!" I shouted. "Give 'em the old Gitchee Gumee!"

Hiawatha turned his head and looked my way. I swear it! He let out one of his big whinnies and began dancing. He moved over on Thunderbolt, and Buckshot Agate hollered at Grandfather. "Keep your distance, old man," he warned, then added, "You'd better put the horse in the driver's seat and pull the sulky yourself. You'll have just as much chance to win."

Grandfather was too busy getting Hiawatha settled down to

argue. The man standing beside me on the rail at the front of the grandstand said, "Do you know that red horse, kid?"

"I sure do," I told him. "He's a very good friend of mine. We've suffered plenty together. His name is Hiawatha."

"His name is mud in this race," the man laughed.

"Just you wait and see," I warned him.

"Who's the old man of the mountains sitting up behind him?"

"That," I said proudly, "is my grandfather."

"Oh, sorry."

"You'll be sorrier when the race is over. He's the champion driver in this county."

The man pretended to be shocked. "In this whole great big county." Then he guffawed and slapped me enthusiastically on the back. "I'm sorry for you, kid but that's Buckshot Agate out there handling the big black. He just happens to be the grand champion driver of all harness racing in this entire country, not some tiny hick county. Agate is the best there is."

"Until today," I snapped back.

"Don't hold your breath. That old coot with the chestnut is old enough to be Abraham Lincoln's nephew."

The lady on the other side of me said to her husband, "Who do you like, Arthur?"

"I like the old man of the mountains," he chuckled, "Who else?"

"But Thunderbolt is a New York horse. He won the Hambletonian. And Buckshot Agate is the grand champion professional driver."

"Those are the kind of odds that old man eats up. They're going back to New York empty-handed tonight. All of them."

"Do you really think so?"

"Wait and see. You have to get up pretty early in the morning to beat that old begger on his own home ground. I've watched him win here for five straight years, and every year they kept saying he was too old to do it. They tried to get him disqualified. He's made a believer out of me. I don't care if he *is*

Abraham Lincoln's nephew, or even Lincoln's father, my moneys on him."

The man on the other side of me said, "Would you like to have a little side bet of twenty dollars? I'll give you three to one."

"You're taking the black?"

"What else?"

"You're on!"

The man whipped out his wallet, peeled off three twenties and gave them to Arthur's wife. Her husband covered it with a twenty. "Winner take all. Fair enough?"

Arthur's wife said, "I'll hold the money if I can have five dollars worth of that bet myself."

"You've got it," the New Yorker said, and added three more fives. He was delighted with his good luck, and laughed good-naturedly. He told Arthur and his wife, "Why that old man can hardly walk. He had to be helped up into the sulky."

Arthur nodded. "You have to put a bullet into a rifle barrel, too. I wouldn't bet against that old rascal if they wheeled him out to his sulky in an oxygen tent. Now pipe down and watch the race. You may learn something about New York horses and their drivers when they come to the country."

Those words made me feel like a million. I only hoped that Arthur was right.

93.

Hiawatha was still acting up badly. The starter threatened to disqualify him if Grandfather didn't get him under control.

Hiawatha hadn't battled his way from that old gypsy camp in those dreadful clothes to act calm and serene about it now. The big red horse was acting bloody mad about the whole day's humiliating experience, and he was showing it. I didn't blame him. Hiawatha reared up again, putting Grandfather's shoulders almost down on the track.

"Whoa, boy!" Grandfather said soothingly. "Save the dramatics for the homestretch. Steady boy!"

Hiawatha came back down, pumping his front legs like he was riding a bicycle. He hustled along the track toward the starting line to join the other two horses. He was still about a length or two back. Grandfather hurried Hiawatha forward. He knew he'd get no favors from the stewards or from Mr. Raffodil's hand-picked starter. Back then there was no automobile with a moving starting gate. It was a judgement call by the official starter.

The horses had almost reached the starting line. They were now on their own.

Hiawatha had slowly drawn almost even. They would hit the starting post three abreast. They were trotting up a storm. All three of them.

The starter waved his flag and shouted, "Go!"

The County Fair Stakes were on!

With only three horses in the race, post positions weren't as significant as they would have been with eight or more horses entered.

Buckshot Agate, the pro from New York, knew all there was to know about getting a horse away fast. Agate was good, no doubt about it.

When the starter, Gary Stevens, waved his green flag and shouted, "Go!" and the track marshall, Mr. Fletcher Potter rang the starter's bell to confirm an official start, Thunderbolt shot immediately to the front. In no time he took the rail away from Wildfire and had it all to himself.

Hiawatha came up alongside the big black, while Frank Hartman's Wildfire fell behind into third as expected.

The crowd was yelling so loud you couldn't hear the thundering hoofbeats, or the drivers shouting encouragement to their chargers. It was all lost in a continuous ever-increasing roar, a pandemonium. I was yelling myself, and didn't even know I was shouting.

As Grandfather cut over toward the rail to save ground, Buckshot Agate made believe he was whipping Thunderbolt to improve his position up front. Actually, Buckshot Agate snapped his whip sideways, striking Hiawatha's head just as the big red horse moved up strongly on Thunderbolt's right.

Agate's whip caught Hiawatha across the nose. Hiawatha jerked his head back and broke stride. Grandfather had to pull him over to the right according to the racing rules, and Wildfire came shooting by into second place.

Grandfather knew that with Mr. Fletcher Potter as marshall, and with Sam Raffodil Senior having at least half of the judges in his pocket, there wasn't much use yelling "Foul!" this early in the race about something that could have been an accident. Grandfather knew better. He also knew he'd have to go out and win it the hard way. He fought down his anger, planning to save it for the end of the race.

Thunderbolt was well out on the lead before Grandfather coaxed Hiawatha back into his ground-eating stride. Hiawatha never liked being behind.

"Get it back a little at a time," Grandfather warned him, "not all in one big gulp."

I knew there was a good chance that Hiawatha could run down the other two horses before the finish, so I tried not to be too worried. I knew firsthand from the way Hiawatha had zoomed across the Mississippi River Bridge on that famous Sabbath Sunday workout that he could run all the way to Minneapolis on the dead run. And back.*

I hadn't been able to tell Grandfather the exact truth about how far and how fast Hiawatha had run that Sunday morning because on certain rare occasions Grandfather went to the whip himself. Especially if it had anything to do with the bad treatment of animals. But I told you all that before.

I was the only one in the entire grandstand who really knew how much better Hiawatha would get the farther he ran. The gypsy camp run he'd already made, was only a tune-up for Hiawatha. Or was I merely comforting myself because I wanted Hiawatha to win so badly, and was still disturbed by that long list of miracle escapes I hadn't recited to Grandfather? I only hoped that Hiawatha wouldn't be too far behind when the time came for him to put in his scorching finish.

---

* Well, maybe that's a touch of hyperbole.

I was also counting heavily on the natural mean streak in Sam Raffodil Junior. If I understood anything about human nature, Sam Raffodil Junior would show up at the head of the homestretch on the final stretch run, and would make one last attempt to frighten Hiawatha off stride with his claxon "Ahooouuuaaah" horn. Only I knew it would make Hiawatha run faster, and the horn's sound was my secret weapon.

Turning for the backstretch for the first time, Thunderbolt was still leading. Hiawatha was catching up to the back of Wildfire's sulky, moving strongly, steadily. Grandfather was talking to Hiawatha all the time. He kept the chestnut running by the tone of his conversation. Grandfather kept reminding him of the facts of life with an occasional light tickle on the tail with his whip, accompanied by Grandfather's calming horse racing love-talk.

The band was playing "There'll be a Hot Time in the Old Town Tonight" as the horses raced along the backstretch.

Hiawatha had passed Wildfire, and had cut Thunderbolt's lead to one length. Wildfire was one length farther back in third. All three horses were moving extremely well.

When the band stopped playing, the even more exciting sound of drumming hoofbeats could be heard above the murmuring crowd. No one had started to yell in earnest yet. The race was just settling down. There were still over two and a half laps to go.

All three of the beautiful horses seemed to be sailing along without legs or wheels, floating magically in the air toward the far turn.

It was the kind of day and moment that you hoped you'd remember all your life, exactly the way it was, smells and all.

Buckshot Agate went to the whip again, hoping to catch Hiawatha accidently on purpose across the nose one more time with his back swing.

Grandfather was waiting for Agate's tactics this time. He kept Hiawatha just beyond a whip-length away. Buckshot couldn't reach out and whip Hiawatha without showing the whole crowd that it was a deliberate foul. He scowled, leaned sideways for a moment, then decided to forget it, and get back to the business of winning races.

Both Thunderbolt and Hiawatha lost precious ground during this brief encounter. Buckshot Agate by not paying attention to business, Grandfather by going wide to avoid the whip. This enabled Wildfire to draw up until, for a while, it looked like a three horse race once again, and the crowd roared its approval.

Most of the crowd had missed the inside track feud going on between Buckshot Agate and Grandfather, but they were getting all the thrills they expected.

"This is more like it!" the roar of the crowd declared.

Sam Raffodil Senior was worried but confident. He still had tricks up his sleeve. He just smiled and chewed a bit faster on the end of his big black cigar. I didn't even know Mr. Raffodil was standing beside me at the rail until I heard him speak.

"Don't worry about your money," he told his guest. "Agate is toying with the country folks. I told Buckshot to make it look good, and to let the other two stay in the race until the end. When they go around one more time, and start the final lap, then you'll see the men separated from the boys."

Mr. Raffodil looked down at me patronizingly, and patted my head. I knew he was showing off for his friends, so I knocked his hand away.

"If you'd been watching Hiawatha and me on that Sunday morning your car crashed," I said angrily, "you'd know who's going to get separated from the boys."

"It's the old coot's grandson," Mr. Raffodil laughed, as he explained to his guest from out-of-town who I was. To me he said, "I'm afraid nothing's going to help your horse today, sonny." He turned away. "Come on, Daniels, let's go back up to the box and watch the finish. I have a lot of bets to collect."

"All right by me," Daniels said.

I recognized his voice from those dark hours in the fake hayrack.

"I know your voice," I hollered after him. "I'd like you to meet a friend of mine, the county sheriff, right after the race is over!" I yelled, emphasizing his name plainly, *"OSCAR!"*

He turned, whispered something to Mr. Raffodil, and started back after me. Mr. Raffodil grabbed his arm, whirled Oscar around, and they both disappeared into the crowd.

Don't teach your grandmother to suck eggs.

There wasn't any dirt track trick that Buckshot Agate didn't know or try on my grandfather. He kept just wide enough from the rail to force Hiawatha and Wildfire out into the middle of the track, but never wide enough to permit either of them to slip past inside up against the rail.

Thunderbolt and Hiawatha went the first half mile in one minute and one second. That is a sizzling pace for the half mile track in our town. Good anywhere! A two-two mile. In Green Valley, it broke all records for a half-mile.

Hiawatha was still running Thunderbolt to half a length with Wildfire in third by two. I could see that Wildfire was already beginning to tire because of the blistering pace. The horses passed the stand the first time as they rounded the stable area turn and circled the end by the sawmill, leading to the backstretch for the second time.

Frank Hartman put the whip to Wildfire and tried to bring him up close beside Hiawatha who was having such a good time he was beginning to loaf. This gave Buckshot Agate and Frank Hartman a chance to try and maneuver Grandfather into a pocket and hold him there.

Hartman already knew that his horse, Wildfire, couldn't win against Thunderbolt at a mile-and-a-half, and would be lucky even to finish the race. Wildfire wasn't bred for long distance. He was a pure sprinter. But if Hartman could help Buckshot Agate beat Grandfather, it would please him no end. Even though he didn't care at all about Buckshot Agate and his tactics.

For five straight years Grandfather had out-trotted, out-paced and out-foxed Mr. Hartman and humiliated him and his horses, so almost any kind of revenge would be welcome and sweet. As long as it was honest, for strangely enough he and Grandfather were still the best of friends off the track.

Thunderbolt was sailing smoothly down the backstretch in front, looking like a million dollars. Grandfather was holding second against Wildfire who was making a strong move on the outside.

The three trotters were staggered like a stairway at the start of the backstretch. Thunderbolt was on the rail, Hiawatha just outside of Buckshot Agate's right wheel, and Wildfire outside of Grandfather.

Buckshot Agate opened up some daylight with a fast move along the rail. Then he made believe that Thunderbolt was drifting out toward the center of the track. This left a very tempting opening hole on the rail.

Grandfather began to chuckle. He knew that he was supposed to snap at the bait and shoot Hiawatha up inside toward that beckoning enticing opening. The moment he did, Buckshot Agate would close the hole on the rail and Wildfire would shoot quickly up on the outside, boxing Grandfather and trapping him in the pocket. The only escape would be to pull up and come out around them both, or to wait it out patiently and trust to luck. Either way could be too costly at this stage of the race.

Racing luck has decided more races, both flat and harness, than strategy and natural speed, according to Grandfather. No driver can afford to be foolish, or throw caution to the winds, as they say. Buckshot Agate obviously didn't know what kind of hairpin my Grandfather was, I could see that.

Grandfather told me later that he laughed right out loud when Agate and Hartman dusted off that old snare. Especially so early in the race. Grandfather immediately explained the facts of life to Hiawatha, telling him to look sharp.

"Steady, boy!" Grandfather whispered through the reins.

"They're dragging an old friend out of the mothballs!"

Thunderbolt began to drift out leaving that very appealing opening near the rail. Grandfather admitted that it *was* tempting. An inexperienced driver would have been hoodwinked.

The next series of moves were executed by Hiawatha and Thunderbolt, like two skaters on the ice. Buckshot Agate swung out a little further, offering an even greater temptation, one almost too appetizing for Grandfather to resist.

Buckshot swung the big black out, then, with a zooming curve, swept Thunderbolt right back in against the rail to close the trap. He expected to find Grandfather and Hiawatha on the rail right behind him.

Grandfather had matched Thunderbolt's moves with perfect precision. As Thunderbolt cut out, Hiawatha cut in. When Thunderbolt curved quickly back into the rail, Hiawatha zoomed just as quickly back out to the right and shot up level with Thunderbolt's head. Frank Hartman and Wildfire never had a chance to bolt the door. In fact, Wildfire broke stride badly and was left behind on the backstretch in deep trouble.

Grandfather thumbed his nose at Buckshot Agate and hollered with a mocking laugh:

"Don't teach your grandmother to suck eggs!!"

97.

Grandfather had been dead right about Sam Raffodil Senior. He *was* tricky. The mayor was taking no chances. He had other arrows in his quiver. All poisonous. Mr. Raffodil couldn't afford to rely entirely on Thunderbolt and Buckshot Agate winning the race by themselves. Not now when there was so much money, property and prestige at stake. It had to be a sure thing.

"Sure things," Grandfather told me, "are only manipulated off the race track."

Sam Raffodil Senior couldn't put all of his trust in Thunderbolt, even against Dakar. Suppose Thunderbolt "broke"? It could happen to the best of horses in any harness race. Mr. Raffodil was taking no chances at all on "racing luck!" This race was not a matter of sportsmanship to him, it was a matter of winning at whatever the cost.

His Dishonor, the mayor (*I* said that, Grandfather didn't) had planned for every contingency, even for the almost impossible chance of Hiawatha making it back to the fairgrounds.

He'd already lost that one.

Mr. Raffodil had arranged a few special surprises for either Dakar or Hiawatha, whichever one might oppose Thunderbolt. He had hired Dan Pickett and his two sons, Emery and Wallace, to mingle with the crowd that lined the infield rail along the top of the homestretch on that far-off final turn for home.

Their assignment was simple. Make sure that Hiawatha or Dakar, whichever horse Grandfather was driving, went off stride each time he rounded that fatal bend and never finished the race.

They were to station themselves where their actions wouldn't be noticed, in the midst of the crowd, up against the rail. They had armed themselves with long metal pea-shooters. Instead of peas, they were using number two shotgun shell beebees for ammunition to be fired down the sleeves of their topcoats which they carried loose over their arms at the ready.

The Picketts were arranged about twenty feet apart one after the other along the big turn for home. They knew that both Dakar and Hiawatha had a tendency to go wide into the stretch, and their assignment was to make sure they went all the way out against the far rail. They planned to sting Grandfather's horse on the rump, several times each, one after the other as he passed by.

Hiawatha would come around that bend into the home-stretch three times, so among them, they would have nine chances at him. If they could make Hiawatha break stride only once, it should put him out of the race entirely. He would never be able to make up the distance. Failing that they were to startle Hiawatha into swerving so far wide that he would still never catch up and get back into the race. Hiawatha would lose either way and Mr. Raffodil would go out a winner.

A horse can go off gait only so often and still hope to have any chance to win. It's the worst thing that can happen to a horse in a harness race. Mostly, one break is more than enough, unless you're mighty lucky and are quickly back into stride, or have very poor opposition. Even then, it all depends on racing luck.

Buckshot Agate had already made Hiawatha break once at the start with his whip. Mr. Raffodil knew that if he could get Grandfather's horse to break stride one more time, or hopefully twice, the race would be in the bag.

It was all part of his arsenal of dirty tricks.

"Pull away! Pull away!"

Hiawatha swung gallantly around the far turn for the first time. I was proud of him. He had closed Thunderbolt's lead to a length and a half. I could tell by the way Grandfather was restraining Hiawatha that the chestnut was still under wraps, and wasn't being allowed to do his best. It was far too soon. At least I hoped that was the case. That disaster list continued to haunt me.

Grandfather was hugging the rail as close as he could to save ground. Hiawatha was breathing right down the back of Buckshot Agate's neck. Hiawatha's powerful legs were beating rhythmically against the soft dirt of the track. His arched neck was almost arrogant. Whatever else he might be doing, Hiawatha was letting the grandstand know that he was not out of this race by a long shot.

Thunderbolt and Hiawatha were two of the most beautiful animals you'd ever want to see.

As they straightened out for home that first time, Dan Pickett leaned forward. Covering his actions by an outstretched arm, Pickett raised his metal tube and fired the first of the bee-bee pellets.

"Ping!"

Hiawatha leaped, broke, but swung back immediately into stride, so quickly in fact, that it hardly slowed him up. Thunderbolt shot ahead all right, but only by another half length, no more.

Then Emery Pickett let fly. "Ping! Ping!"

Then Wallace Pickett fired. "Ping! Ping! Ping!"

Hiawatha must have thought it was Grandfather after his hide. He didn't break stride at all on the last two multiple "ping-shots." Instead, like any sensible person who's being stung by a swarm of flying bumblebees on his hind end, Hiawatha got out of the neighborhood as fast as he could.

Another of Mr. Raffodil's schemes had backfired on him.

Stung with the sudden pain of the bee-bees, Hiawatha raced up and closed the gap on Thunderbolt as they pounded past the grandstand. He was less than a half a length behind now and rapidly closing.

The two horses went by the finish line the first time neck and neck ending the first half-mile.

For a fellow who had promised himself to sit nonchalantly up in the grandstand, what was I doing down there on the rail at the finish line beating on the fence with both my fists and yelling my head off, "Pull away! Pull away!"

Hiawatha and Thunderbolt were both making that dramatic snorting noise in perfect rhythm to their trotting. Dirt was flying behind each hoof. They were like two ballet dancers keeping perfect step.

I could hear Grandfather's voice talking gently to Hiawatha as they pounded past. Even Buckshot Agate was keeping up a running chatter with Thunderbolt.

Both horses seemed to understand.

"If this isn't heaven, I don't want to die!"

99.

What great fun it is to go to a horse race at the county fair! Hot diggety dog! The winning alone means nothing. Except in this race, of course, where Grandfather had put everybody in the soup with his mug's wager.

But on any given day at the county fair harness races, it's the beauty, the excitement, and the thrill of watching those evenly matched trotters and pacers pounding around the turns neck and neck that makes a person feel alive.

For people who like dancing, pageantry, music and color—this was the only place to be! There's nothing in all the world to match it for excitement and drama. The drumbeat of the horses hoofs act as a stimulant. It's like hearing the rhythm of jungle drums beating over and over again, louder and louder, closer and closer, when something threatening is about to happen.

That's the way it is every year at the county fair, but this year topped them all.

The flashing black, orange and white silks of Grandfather ranging up beside the bright red and white of the Raffodil's, and the royal blue of Mr. Hartman. Saddle cloths shining in the bright afternoon sun. Colorful fuzzy nose bands on Thunderbolt and Hiawatha, one orange, one red. Tails braided in stable colors, as black and chestnut muscles went rippling by the stands inciting thunderous applause and roars of approval.

At this stage of the race no one cared who was ahead, they were only thankful to be there themselves and be a part of it. They would cheer for all three horses equally until the showdown came when the horses went by the grandstand for the final lap with half a mile to go, and the fate of the world riding on it. Grandfather's world, Grandmother's world, and Mr. Raffodil's as well. My tiny world, too.

Thousands of people laughing and shouting and having the time of their lives, dressed in every color imaginable, wearing every shade of blue, red, yellow, green, white, orange, grey, crimson, black, and purple. Rainbow colors everywhere! All waving and shouting for their favorites, arm in arm, holding hands, and bursting with delight at their good luck just at being there and being alive to enjoy the county fair so thoroughly. I didn't know how my own body would survive. My heart was up in my throat during the whole time, and the race still had a mile to go!

The brown dirt track circled an infield now filled to capacity with harness fans and picnic fans. Whole families surrounded by blankets stretched out on the grass and picnic baskets ladened with food, were having the time of their lives. Some were watching the race; some were busy with food, some were chatting with friends and neighbors, some with family members who had come from afar to attend this great social occasion, The County Fair, and catch up on a whole year's gossip. Some were chasing tiny children.

The entire half-mile track, grandstand and infield, was cut off from the outside world by high green hedges backed by tall slender pine trees. The people at the fair were all alone, by themselves, in the midst of their wonder, their roars, their applause, and the distant musical sounds of the merry-go-round and the Ferris wheel.

For one day they were living in a world apart.

A bright yellow sun, a blue sky, and soft floating white cotton clouds all looked down on the big race and blessed it with perfect weather.

There was magic everywhere!

The Green Valley Town Band, and the visiting drum and

bugle corps from the Hill City National Guard took turns entertaining the crowd. The green and gold band with their instruments flashing in the sun, played a stirring arrangement of "The Washington Post March" while the khaki uniforms of the bugle corps marched back and forth in a small square of the infield, impervious to the greatest race ever held in our town track. They beat their drums. They blasted their bugles.

But it was Thunderbolt, Hiawatha and Wildfire who were center stage. Almost every eye was on their every move. We knew we would talk about it for years to come.

If that's not heaven, I don't want to die!

Buckshot Agate waved, "Goodbye, Horsie!"

100.

Frank Hartman's horse, Wildfire, was out of the race. He had pulled up lame. Unfortunately, they were both still on the track, although Mr. Hartman was trying his best to get Wildfire over against the outside fence on the way back to the stable.

It was too late!

Thunderbolt and Hiawatha were sweeping around the bend into the backstretch like a matched pair, sailing around the turn stride for stride. It was anybody's race.

Until the dreadful moment they came unexpectedly upon Wildfire, Mr. Hartman, and his sulky.

There wasn't room for two horses to slip inside of Wildfire. Thunderbolt was on the rail, Hiawatha just outside him on a collision course with Wildfire. Unless Grandfather did something brilliant immediately, there was going to be a terrible accident. Somebody was going to get hurt. It had to be a split second decision.

Grandfather had a rigid code, people first, horses second.

"That's the way it has to be," he once told me. "Sometimes it seems a dirty shame but those are the priorities of life, and we have to be satisfied with them."

Thunderbolt whistled by Mr. Hartman's sulky on the inside, just barely grazing the hub of the sulky wheel. You could hear the "Tick!" as he breezed by, his speed undiminished.

Grandfather, in that same moment, swung Hiawatha to the outside. It looked for certain that he would crash, overturning sulkies, horses, drivers. Grandfather held his breath as he swerved Hiawatha toward the far outside rail.

It was a marvelous piece of horsemanship. Wildfire was still up on his hind legs and Mr. Hartman was holding onto his bridle. They were both standing directly in the path of Hiawatha.

Grandfather grazed Mr. Hartman's right sulky wheel, just barely catching the rubber tire, then bounced free. He had swerved Hiawatha just in time to avoid a fatal crash and keep from running Mr. Hartman and Wildfire down.

A mighty roar went up from the grandstand as Hiawatha went sweeping around Wildfire and Mr. Hartman. All hands safe! Thanks to Grandfather and his big red horse.

The crowd feared that Grandfather and Hiawatha had probably lost the race because of their heroics. Grandfather never heard the standing ovation and cheers. He was too busy trying to send Hiawatha off in pursuit of Thunderbolt. Luckily the big horse had never broken stride.

"Steady, Hiawatha," Grandfather encouraged him.

Mr. Hartman apparently had a change of heart after Grandfather's heroic horsemanship. Frank Hartman was only five years younger than Grandfather, but still he hollered out, "Win, Grandfather! Win!!"

I joined him, yelling fiercely, "Go get him red horse. You can do it! Catch him, Grandfather. You both deserve to win!"·

Grandfather didn't hear me either. He had his hands full. Nor did he hear Buckshot Agate who turned around and yelled over his shoulder at Grandfather and Hiawatha, his right fist held up in the air as a symbol of victory. Agate grinned happily and waved at them, "Goodbye, horsie!"

Buckshot Agate gave the old horse laugh, turned, and let his black champion out a notch.

Unfortunately, Hiawatha had fallen behind. Grandfather was livid. He hated to lose, but he hadn't given up. Not by a long shot. Never! Especially this race which he felt symbolically belonged to Hiawatha, his instrument of justice. He was a sore loser about all horse races. "I'm not perfect," he told me.

I knew that already. I was familiar with Grandfather's bad side as well as his good side, and I could poke a lot of holes in Grandfather's boat. Of course, I was too polite a grandson to do it.

"I'm a good Samaritan at heart," Grandfather confessed, then added, "Except when it comes to horse racing." Grandfather would tell me that a harness driver takes a lot of understanding especially when he's talking about winning horse races.

"Coming in first, is not only the *sweetest* thing in life," he would say, "but it's the only thing with any real flavor at all." Grandfather often explained his philosophy of winning and losing to me. I knew it by heart.

"However, if unpleasant things happen to your horse or your sulky, and you *do* lose," Grandfather said, "and it's not your fault, be gracious. Act like a gentleman at all times. But *until* you *do* lose, roar like a lion and never let up. Bellow like a winner! Holler so loud from the sulky that the wind will blow down trees in Tennessee!"

That's why I knew Grandfather was still in this fantastic County Fair Stakes race.

It's hard to defeat someone like that. No matter how long the odds. They just keep going and going. When you get a man *and* a horse who both feel that way about it, you're lucky to be at the county fair harness races on the day they're both doing their best.

Grandfather knew it was too soon for Hiawatha to start his big final charge. He always saved that for the top of the stretch, but this time Grandfather had no choice. He had to let the big red horse out a little. Thunderbolt was too far ahead to wait.

It was now or never.

Circumstances had altered Grandfather's race plan.

Grandfather leaned forward in the sulky to explain the facts of life to Hiawatha. He gave that magic touch on the reins, and hollered encouragingly, "Now's the time, Hiawatha! Go get him. Pull up there and spit in his eye!"

Hiawatha took Grandfather at his word when the old man let him out. Hiawatha had been wanting to run for at least the past half mile. It was heaven on earth to see the way Hiawatha began to eat up the distance between himself and Thunderbolt. Thunderbolt, of course, had not yet unleashed his own finishing kick and I knew it was a blustering one, but for the moment Hiawatha had all the best of it. He closed on Thunderbolt with a tremendous burst of speed that brought everyone to their feet screaming.

It was a thundering chant, "Hiawatha! Hiawatha! Hiawatha!"

Both trotters were approaching the turn into the home-stretch for the last time. It was now only a question of time, but time was running out fast, there just weren't too many furlongs left.

It's no use saying what might have happened if the big red horse hadn't had to swing so wide to avoid the accident. But you have to win no matter what the obstacles. That's horse racing.

Sure it's wonderful to have two heros, horse and driver, who sacrificed and saved lives, but if they didn't win, all that's remembered is "Place" or "Show."

Neither was good enough for Grandfather.

"This one is for all the marbles!"

101.

Hiawatha was pulling hard at the reins as they went down the back stretch, trying to catch up and shorten Thunderbolt's lead.

I knew this was about the time when Hiawatha began to feel his oats during his long-distance workouts, the time when he began to run his best. I had been plotting the race right along with Grandfather from the very start, trying to judge the pace, and deciding when to turn Hiawatha loose for his barn-burning finishing kick.

Adjusting for the disaster and bad racing luck, I knew this was the time. Grandfather waited a little longer than I would have. I hoped he was right. My arms and shoulders still ached from the time Hiawatha tried to start his finishing run on the old Sawmill River Road.

"Any minute," I told myself, "Hiawatha's hoofs will be smoking."

But Grandfather still wouldn't let the colt out. Hiawatha didn't like it. He was pulling hard now, no show-boating. This was showtime and Hiawatha wanted action. He had his head turned to the side snorting. Less than six furlongs to go. Every muscle was hollering at Grandfather, "Let me go. Let me run! I can do it!"

"Not yet, boy!" Grandfather told him, "I'll tell you when. Steady, Hiawatha! You'll get your chance. Easy, boy! Trust your wise old Grandfather," my wise old grandfather told him.

Out of the corner of my eye, I saw Sam Raffodil Junior run lickety-split across the track. Sam was carrying his "Ahooouuu-aaah" horn.

"Thank you, Lord," I said, "for helping me stomp on a snake-in-the-grass. And if there's any justice at all, that horn of Sam's is going to be Gabriel opening up the gates of judgment."

Sure I knew it was sacreligious, but I also knew that God Himself had never seen a horserace like this one before either. I was sure He wasn't going to hold it against me.

"Remember what I promised out there in the hayrack, Lord? I was a little carried away, but I'll do it all—every word—if you move that big red horse up to the front!"

"You hear me, up there, God?!" I yelled. "Remember, this one is for all the marbles!"

U

Hiawatha moved away from the rail and powered his way up on the outside of Buckshot Agate and Thunderbolt. It was an astonishing move. The roar of the crowd was deafening. Only I and Grandfather knew what made that sudden rally possible.

While Hiawatha was still close to the rail behind Thunderbolt, he passed within a few feet of Sam Raffodil Junior who was leaning out over the rail and pointing his automobile horn at the big red horse. Over the sound of the thundering hoofbeats, loud and clear, came the raucous cry of the claxon horn:

"Ahooouuuaaah! Ahooouuuaaah! Ahooouuuaaah!"

I yelled with delight.

My secret weapon!

It was my wonderful Sabbath Sunday morning all over again! I was driving Hiawatha down Main Street.

"Ahooouuuaaah! Ahooouuuaaah! Ahooouuuaaah!"

"We're coming down the main drag!" I yelled at Hiawatha.

When Hiawatha heard that old "Ahooouuuaaah!" horn, he knew exactly what to do. When Sam Raffodil blared out the claxon horn a second time, Hiawatha didn't hesitate for a moment. I felt sure that it was that same Sunday morning ride all over again for him, too. Hiawatha just hunkered down those chestnut hind quarters of his, dug in, and swept away from the rail. He pulled up alongside the back end of Thunderbolt's sulky in the middle of the track.

It was becoming a homestretch race. The roar of the crowd let everyone in the fairgrounds know. And for miles around.

Sam Raffodil Junior kept up the good work. "Ahooouuuaaah! Ahooouuuaaah!"

"We're past the Dow Lumber Company!" I cried.

"Ahooouuuaaah! Ahooouuuaaah!"

Hiawatha took off. The lead was down to a quarter of a length.

"We're at the Mississippi River bridge!"

"Ahooouuuaaah!"

A neck.

"Over the bridge and into the country!"

"Ahooouuuaaah!"

A head.

"Ahooouuuaaah! Ahooouuuaaah!"

Old Joe Anderson's farm!

Hiawatha and Thunderbolt were even!

Hiawatha was running for his life and for Grandfather's too. He was made of star-stuff and this was right where he belonged, in a championship race, coming around the far turn in second place. It was "catch up" time and Hiawatha loved it. He was being forced by the most difficult and incredible circumstances to make a second run from behind as Thunderbolt began to move ominously ahead.

"Anybody can win from in front," Grandfather always reminded me, "but it takes a real horse to come from behind."

In answer to Grandfather's urging, Hiawatha pulled against the sulky harness with a tremendous surge, and Thunderbolt was no longer drawing away from him. They were now running even. It was a stand off.

"Don't use all of it, Hiawatha," Grandfather urged the big red horse. "Save a little, boy. The worst is yet to come."

Grandfather's eyes were watery, too. Partly from the dirt and dust being kicked up against his goggles, partly because of the tremendous heroic courage Hiawatha was demonstrating. Grandfather admitted later that at least a part of the moisture was good clean race driver tears at the joy of feeling a true champion-class trotter beneath his reins for the very first time in his long, long life of longing for it. To see it! To feel it! Was heaven!

"Thank you, Hiawatha," Grandfather said. "Win, lose or draw, red horse, my life and dreams are all fulfilled."

Then he hollered out loud, "But I wouldn't mind winning!"

Grandfather knew he was urging on a spectacular running horse whose courage had overcome every insurmountable difficulty and hardship. A horse who even now was whisking Grandfather and his sulky around the far turn into the piece of real estate Grandfather liked best in all the world:

The homestretch!

"Ahooouuuaaah!"

102.

Buckshot Agate saw Hiawatha's head coming up on his right. He hated the sound of those remorseless thundering hoofs tracking him down again. What kind of a horse was he up against? Who didn't know when he was beaten!

Grandfather was now on level terms with Agate. Eye to eye.

Buckshot hated those black, white and orange colors. He went to the whip and began to lash Thunderbolt for all he was worth. He knew he had to hold off Hiawatha's homestretch run. If he had one left.

The two magnificent animals were now running neck and neck. Slowly Thunderbolt edged ahead. Was Hiawatha tiring? He had every right to.

The crowd was in a frenzy.

Would there still be time enough? That was the only question. Could Hiawatha come back again? Would the big red horse run out of room and steam before he ran down the big black champion from New York for a third time?

Sam Raffodil Junior had leaped over the fence and was running down the homestretch behind the horses blowing his claxon horn for all he was worth.

"Ahooouuuaah! Ahooouuuaah!"

There was still half a furlong to go and Hiawatha was trailing Thunderbolt by a long neck, but was moving up on him remorselessly.

There are horses who can do that, Grandfather had told me, and they are the ones who write their names forever in the record books. They are game and keep coming back. It disheartens most opponents. But not Thunderbolt. He, too, was among the finest of champions.

Everyone watching that race knew they would never see another one like it in our town ever again. Most likely never again in their lifetime. Anywhere!

The excitement was almost unbearable. The victory hung in the balance—only seconds away. No person in that screaming grandstand could tell what the final outcome would be.

The entire brass band had stopped playing. The musicians were waving their instruments about wildly, hitting each other and not even knowing it. They were shouting so frantically they were numbed by the clamor. The crowd continued their chant as Hiawatha cut down Thunderbolt's precarious lead, inch by inch. The grandstand was an utter bedlam. Everyone was bellowing at the top of their lungs. Even the ladies had become unlady-like. They tore off their hats and sailed them at the track, yelling: "Go Red Horse!!"

The overwhelming majority of the grandstand was rooting for Hiawatha. They tried to push him in front by the sheer volume and force of their voices.

The air was electric as those beautiful, evenly matched trotters stormed toward the finish line, shoulder to shoulder, running an almost perfect dead heat from the sixteenth pole with Thunderbolt barely shading Hiawatha's nose. So close you couldn't call it!

"Boom! Boom! Boom! Boom!"

The crowd came alive with an uninterrupted continuous roar. The roar became a thunderous ovation for both horses. Finally a deafening, ear-splitting tumult.

It had taken "fortitude, backbone, grit, sand, pluck, and guts" to do what Hiawatha had done. He had demonstrated every one of Grandfather's favorite virtues. In huge proportions.

The crowd loved it. They were yelling along with me, but not half as loud.

"Hiawatha! Hiawatha! Hiawatha!"

The excitement was so great and out-of-control and I myself had been shouting so loud and so long, that my chest ached. How I loved that big red horse. I joined in again at the top of my voice as a large part of the grandstand took up their favorite chant once again.

"Hiawatha! Hiawatha! Hiawatha!"

At the sixteenth pole, Hiawatha had eaten his way up to almost even yet another time. Grandfather was putting in a blazing run in the center of the track out of the range of Buckshot Agate's whip. If Thunderbolt wanted to win now, he'd have to outrun Hiawatha. There was no other way. All tricks were over.

It was a horserace!! One on one!!

"Here comes the big red horse!"

103.

I leaped over the rail and started down the middle of the homestretch after Hiawatha and Thunderbolt. I was heading for the finish line myself. I passed young Sam Raffodil like the wind. For the moment, I was Hiawatha closing on Thunderbolt and I was still hollering as loud as I could:

"Hiawatha! Hiawatha! Hiawatha!"

I was coming down the homestretch in third place. I passed Lois LeSarde on the rail. She was shrieking, "C'mon Thunderbolt!" Beside her, pounding the top of the rail with her tiny fists, was Margie Kelly. She was shrilling out with wild delight, "Hiawatha! Hiawatha! Hiawatha! Don't you dare lose, or I'll never speak to you again as long as I live."

Those near the finish line could see Hiawatha edging his way up on Thunderbolt.

"Here comes the big red horse!" they bellowed.

The two beautiful heads were dead even again. The finish line was already in sight. It was going to be terrifyingly close.

Thunderbolt, a real champion, as game as they come, was bravely holding off Hiawatha's late charge. The black horse had a stout spirit himself. He had pulled ahead and was clinging desperately to his slim lead. Now by less than a long nose. Thunderbolt was holding his precious lead by inches. He was doing it on sheer heart.

I was worried that Hiawatha might have used up too much of his final kick catching up in the backstretch after the accident. He'd been forced to open up with his big run far too soon.

Grandfather had tried to save something, I knew that.

I was the only one on that track who realized that it wasn't the trouble in the backstretch that had tired Hiawatha. It was the hayrack, the blockade, Marshall Anderson, the freight engine, the fairgrounds gate, Pickett's Orange Juice Stand: all of it together. The entire disaster list. It would be no disgrace to lose after such a gallant comeback.

Even if he lost, I would love that big red horse with all my heart until the day I died. I would gladly go into exile, a pauper, with my grandfather and grandmother.

But it sure would be tragic. I hated the very thought. There was no time to ask God for any more special help now. I knew I'd worn out my welcome with my constant begging, so I just shook my fist up at the sky and hollered:

"You know what we need down here. Let's see a little of it!"

Photo Finish!

104.

Hiawatha was holding his own as that finish line hurtled towards him. There didn't seem to be any way he could cut down the last tiny lead held by the New York champion. Thunderbolt still had him by that short long nose.

Grandfather was urging Hiawatha along, giving him a touch of the whip to eke out every last bit of Hiawatha's strength and speed. Buckshot Agate had gone to the whip earlier, and was shouting at Thunderbolt and lashing him furiously, protecting his slim, gradually diminishing, margin of victory.

Both drivers were gallantly trying to get their horses across that finish line first by sheer lung power alone, then by lunging forward trying to carry the weight of the sulky over the finish line themselves.

Slowly and painfully Hiawatha had won back precious ground, inch by inch. The long nose became a short nose. The finish line was flying toward them alarmingly fast. No one could hear their pounding hoofbeats over the deafening noise of the screaming crowd.

Together, as though they were traveling in double-harness, Thunderbolt and Hiawatha roared headlong through those final feet toward the finish.

Grandfather was extracting the last ounce of effort from the big red horse, but still Thunderbolt managed to keep the tip of that black nose in front. Barely. Grandfather was talking to Hiawatha with his hands.

"Get him, boy!" he cried. "You can do it! C'mon Hiawatha!

Just a few strides more for the old man!"

Hiawatha, with his big heart ready to burst, did just that.

He must have known that he was running for his dead mother, Mignonette, for Einar Olson, Chief Little Fork, and everyone else from whom Mr. Raffodil had squeezed the juices of life. Hiawatha drove forward against the harness with his last ounce of effort on behalf of every citizen of Green Valley who had bet their shirts on him, but especially for the old man of the mountains, and his very best friend, me.

Hiawatha made that one last spurt and put his magnificent chestnut head right up alongside the black one.

They were even!

Dead even.

They were racing together now in a dead heat, head for head, nose for nose.

First one would inch his head to the front, and then the other. It was still anybody's race! It depended on whose nose hit the finish line first.

Thunderbolt, Hiawatha, Hiawatha, Thunderbolt.

The black, the red. The red, the black.

The *RED!!*

"My public is calling."

105.

Buckshot Agate thought he had won. He turned Thunderbolt around, came back to the judges' stand, doffed his cap, and drove Thunderbolt into the winner's circle. He believed that all the applause was for him. He had a grin a mile wide, and was waving to the crowd when Mr. Raffodil came storming over.

Sam Raffodil Senior knew that Hiawatha had beaten him. He had been standing at the finish line. He wiped Buckshot's grin away with a snarl. The calamity had struck, and Mr. Raffodil began to take it out on Buckshot Agate.

"Get the hell out of there, you damned fool!" he barked. "You lost to that hayseed horse!"

Buckshot Agate still didn't believe it. Before he could reply to Mr. Raffodil, the official announcement came from the judges' stand, loud and clear for all to hear: "Ladies and gentlemen! The winner by the shortest nose possible—"

The rest was drowned out in a thunderous roar. The crowd didn't need to hear, they saw Grandfather's number three being placed up on the scoreboard in the winner's box. They rocked the county fairgrounds with a deafening roar as the orange, black and white colors of Grandfather's winning silks were run up the flagpole.

The wave of sound was so loud that it drowned out the calliope music from both the merry-go-round and Ferris wheel, including the town band, and every other sound in the entire fairgrounds.

It was bedlam! Tumultuous! Chaos!

The judges tried to make the announcement once again. This time they were successful.

"Ladies and gentlemen! The winner by the shortest nose possible, driven by that sturdy old warrior and still champion—

The crowd cut loose again, and the judges hopelessly gave up. Everybody in our town of Green Valley knew that the only sturdy old warrior and still champion had to be my Grandfather, the old man of the mountains, Abraham Lincoln's nephew, and his hick horse, Hiawatha!

The crowd booed Buckshot Agate out of the winner's circle to make room for Grandfather and Hiawatha, the real champions. The mob swarmed around the circle to pay their adulation to the big red horse, the finest trotting machine that any of them had ever seen.

"That ever *lived*, you mean."

I said that last part when I overheard them.

I was hugging and kissing Hiawatha. I was crying at the same time, standing in the middle of the track with tears running down my cheeks. I cried more that one county fair week than I ever had before, or ever have since. There are times when you're entitled, even if you are grownup and a man.

Hiawatha nuzzled me as if to thank me for my part in his great escape from the gypsy camp. I was sure he was telling me how happy he was, too. In turn, he lifted off my cap, then Grandfather's and tossed them both, one at a time into the infield.

The crowd roared approval, laughing, applauding, and crying out the name of the star of the show:

"Hiawatha! Hiawatha!"

Hiawatha whinnied, shook his mane, and nuzzled my neck again. He whinnied in my ear. He had to be saying: "I did it, didn't I. I made them eat Indian corn all the way up to the Minnie Ha Ha Falls."

I rubbed his nose. "You sure did. You gave the Raffodils the old Gitchee Gumee because you're a real Hiawatha!"

Grandfather gave me the honor of leading Hiawatha into the winner's circle.

"After all," he said, "you're not only a part owner in this famous racing stable, but you rescued him from disaster, and saved all our skins."

I brushed Lois LeSarde and Margie Kelly aside, and took Hiawatha's bridle. To the girls, I said, blowing on my nails, "You'll have to excuse me, ladies, but my public is calling for me."

"You'll have to excuse me, ladies, but my public is calling for me."

"It would be a dull old world without you, Sam."

Half an hour later after we'd cooled Hiawatha off properly, and returned him to his stall, I looked out over the top of the stable door and saw Sam Raffodil wheeling his bicycle. As he rode by, I stuck the handle of the pitchfork in the front wheel. Sam Junior tumbled over the handlebars onto the ground.

"I learned that from your crooked friends, the Picketts," I told him.

"You've ruined my bike!"

"Just a few dents in the spokes. Besides, it's not your bike, it's *my* bike now."

Sam was fighting mad when he got up from the ground. He started for me, but when I turned the pitchfork around, tines first, he hesitated.

"You taught me to do that," I told him. "Remember? Besides you lost the bet. I'll thank you for my bicycle."

"Try and get it."

I did.

Sam tried to snatch the handlebars away from me, but Mr. Raffodil stuck his head out of the stable door and hollered at him.

"Pay your debts, you bungler! If it hadn't been for your big mouth they'd never have found that red horse. It serves you right. You can walk for the rest of the summer. Without any money in your pocket. Now, get in here!"

Mr. Raffodil went back into the stable to continue his harangue against Buckshot Agate. Sam Junior followed him, scowling at me over his shoulder, then slamming the stable door.

I wheeled the bicycle over to Midge Kelly and made him a present of it. I don't know what came over me. I wanted that bike and longed to keep it. I'd never owned a bike of my own, but I was caught up in the spirit of Grandfather's rotten integrity again. I *did* owe it to Margie Kelly. It was her bike that had saved the race for Hiawatha.

"It's for Margie," I told Midge. "To replace the bike she lost at the livery stable."

Midge was overwhelmed. "I was wondering how to break the news to her."

"I already told her," I said.

When I offered to embrace Midge for the shotgun fire-crackers, and to kiss him on the cheek, he took off like a shot. I think Midge hollered, "Thanks!" as he wheeled dangerously around the sheep-shearing sheds, but it might have been "Gangway!"

Grandfather came out to join me when he heard Mr. Raffodil leaving the stable next door. He called to the mayor.

"I believe we have a small wager to settle ourselves, Sam," he said.

"I'll send you a check in the morning."

"No need to do that. I don't want your money, Sam," he said. "Never did."

"You mean all bets are off?"

"No, I'm not that naive. But all you have to do is return the properties to Einar Olson, Chief Little Fork, and all the rest of my friends you foreclosed on, unnecessarily, then I'll tear up the written agreement. You can keep your four hundred thousand dollars, Sam. You'll need it to pay off the town's people."

"Done!"

"You wouldn't like to sell that big black horse, Thunder-bolt?"

"I've already sold him. To Buckshot Agate."

"Pity. I doubt if you could find a better horse for next year's race. We were lucky today."

"In a pig's eye," I whispered under my breath.

Mr. Raffodil dismissed my Grandfather's kindness with a wave of his hand. "I'm out of racing. I'll find some other way to nail your hide to the fence, old man. This is not the end of it. Not by a long shot."

"Well, Sam, you can keep your money, but I'm not so sure about your peace of mind. You *did* admit to kidnapping Hiawatha. In front of witnesses. You may have to pay the law for that if they catch your friend, Oscar."

"I'm sure the town marshall, Carl Anderson, will look upon the entire thing as one of those harmless little horse racing pranks."

"I doubt it. Carl Anderson is already in jail for being part of the conspiracy. Among other things he's being charged with child abuse and attempted kidnapping himself."

Mr. Raffodil snarled, "If anybody did any abusing, it was that snot of a kid right there." Mr. Raffodil pointed at me. "If it weren't for him, me and my friends would be riding high."

"You have no friends, Sam. That's why I'm letting you keep the four hundred thousand dollars. You may need it. For attorney's fees. As for myself, I had so much fun out there on the track today, that I don't harbor any grudges. I won't make any trouble for you about it, Sam. The slate's wiped clean."

"Not for me it isn't, so don't soft-soap me, old man."

Grandfather held out his hand to Mr. Raffodil. "Suppose we try to make a new start, Sam. Let's forgive and forget the past. Begin again as neighbors, in a spirit of friendliness and goodwill."

Mr. Raffodil knocked Grandfather's hand aside, and walked angrily to his buggy. He took Sam Junior along with him, by the ear. He scooped up the reins, and began turning the buggy around. Mr. Raffodil scowled angrily at Grandfather.

"I'll nail you, old man, be sure. Sooner or later. Keep looking over your shoulder every deal you make because I'll be there somewhere. This is not the end but only the beginning. Our vendetta will go on until the end of time."

Grandfather laughed and accepted his fate. "It would be a dull old world without you, Sam."

Mr. Raffodil turned the axle so sharply it ground against the side of the buggy. As he came past us, Grandfather called to him.

"Now that you're out of racing, Sam, how would you and Minnie like to buy a matched pair of young dapple greys? For riding out in the country and to church on Sundays? However, I must warn you about one thing—"

Mr. Raffodil was gone in a flash. I couldn't tell for sure whether it was the cramped buggy wheels or his teeth that made that grinding sound.

His face was a wonderful mask of fury.

"Grandmothers are a lot smarter than you think."

107.

I saw Grandmother coming into the stable area with two of her close friends, Mrs. Higgins and Mrs. Carmichael. They were all smiling and laughing, and apparently they had come to congratulate us on winning the race.

I whispered to Grandfather, "Good thing Grandmother doesn't know how close she came to being a pauper."

Grandfather nodded. "Mum's the word."

"Congratulations, boys," Grandmother said, smiling happily. "That was the most exciting horse race I've ever seen. Everybody said that. I'm still hoarse from cheering."

"Thank you, Grandmother," I said. "Do you want to go in and congratulate Hiawatha, too?"

"No," she said. "You do that for me. He looked marvelous in the sunlight from the grandstand, but I think I'll still maintain my aloof distance from the barn and the stables."

She patted Grandfather on the back, kissed his cheek, then said goodbye, and started to walk away. She stopped, and turned back to look at Grandfather.

"And you might thank Hiawatha for saving my garden, my sweet peas, my bank account and my house," she said. "I'd have hated living in some strange town and starting all over again at seventy. Broke and without my personal things. The barns, of course, I can always do without."

Grandmother left us with a cheerful wave, trailing a laugh behind her.

Grandfather hurried to the stable door and called out, "Bess!

Do you mean to tell me you've known about my dumb bet all along?"

She nodded. "You were a mug," she said. "Using your own evaluation."

"Don't I know it. How long have you known?"

"From the moment you began to act so innocent," she said. "That's when I started to send out feelers."

"I'm sorry," Grandfather apologized. "It couldn't have been worse for you."

"Oh, yes, it could," Grandmother said, airily. "I could have lost my mother's Georgian silver, and my favorite Royal Dalton china. That *would* have annoyed me."

Grandfather was bowled over. "You bet your precious things on a horse race?"

"No," she replied. "I bet on a sick unto death little foal." She was quoting Grandfather. She added, "Trained and driven by a hayseed hick country doctor." Now she was quoting Mr. Raffodil.

"When Sam Raffodil said that to me in front of Sweetman's Ice Cream Parlor, I said to him, 'Put your money where your mouth is, you big oaf!' "

Grandfather was still in shock. "How did you know where to lay your bet?"

"I just followed the crowd. I peeked out the parlor curtains one morning and saw a parade of wagons, buggies, trucks, baby buggies, coaster wagons, a flock of sheep going by, and dozens of people carrying things on their shoulders. I thought there was a forest fire and the town was being evacuated."

"I heard about the big excitement," Grandfather said.

"I was about to go out and ask what the trouble was when the phone rang."

"So?"

"It was Mabel, Mrs. Higgins. She said the entire Monday Club was getting together and hiring a school bus to take their best antiques down to Raffodil's Livery Stable so they could bet against that old crook and put him in his place."

"You might have lost everything," Grandfather said, shaken by the thought. "All of you."

"We didn't care," Grandmother said blithely. "That's the way it is when you're young and in love."

She laughed, waved goodbye again, and said, "Don't be late for dinner." Grandmother blew a kiss to the old man of the mountains and was gone.

"Grandmothers," I said, "Can be a lot smarter than you think."

"Can't they though."

Grandfather and I didn't find out until that night at dinner that Mrs. Higgins had bet her Duncan Phyfe table, and Mrs. Carmichael had put up half of the town's greatest treasure—her Gainsborough paintings. Mrs. Carmichael had wheeled one of her two original paintings down to Mr. Raffodil's livery stable in her great-granddaughter's baby buggy when she missed the bus. All because she loathed Mr. Raffodil so thoroughly.

Both ladies had been with Grandmother when Mr. Raffodil told my grandmother to put up or shut up. Mrs. Carmichael said, "I nearly hit him over the head with my oil painting. I couldn't stand that oily, unctuous smile of his."

Grandmother was shocked. "That would have cost you a fortune."

"Not really," Mrs. Carmichael said. "That painting was a copy. I kept the real one at home."

"But I heard you tell Mr. Raffodil it was an original."

"It *was* an original. It was the first time my grandson ever painted a copy of 'Blue Boy.'"

You know something, it was Grandfather who had tears in his eyes when we were packing up our things and putting the last of them into the buggy. That tough old bird denied it, of course. He claimed it was the hay dust, but I knew better. My own head had been leaking tears of joy ever since Hiawatha won the big race. I couldn't stop bawling and I didn't care who knew it or saw it.

"How come two tough stable owners like us have been blubbering like this all day, Grandfather?"

"I don't know about you," Grandfather said, "but I'm allergic to haydust."

"How about being allergic to lying?" I asked Grandfather slyly, as I bent over to pick up Hiawatha's saddle cloth which he had dropped. It was an unhappy choice of words because Grandfather swatted me across my bent over buttocks with the broad end of the manure shovel. Quite gently though. After all, it was a day of victory. Besides it wasn't nearly as painful as his whisker rubs. Also, I deserved it.

We both began to laugh at the same time. Like you do sometimes when nothing's really that funny, but life is sweet. We quickly finished up the work we had to do before going home, putting away blankets, harness, bandages, liniment, all the things and smells I loved about Grandfather's barn, both at home or on the road.

Grandfather was singing, "Wait 'till the Sun Shines Nellie." He reminded me how ridiculous and forlorn Hiawatha had looked standing in front of the stewards and judges with that silly straw hat over his ears, and that bell-ringing blanket covering his body all splotched with grey. I began to sing, "The Old Grey Mare, she's more than she used to be, more than she used to be..."

Then I thought about that wonderful black horse, Thunderbolt, whose heart we had to break in order to win. I liked Thunderbolt very much. Hiawatha whinnied as though he agreed with me.

That's when I discovered I was allergic to haydust myself.

The tunnel of love is a Ferris wheel.

108.

Grandfather and I were still talking a mile a minute, and running the big race all over again. At least a dozen times.

I made Grandfather take me around every bend right from the starter's "Go!" Listening to Grandfather was nearly as exciting as watching the real race.

We were right in the middle of our third re-run when Margie Kelly burst into the stall. She ran over and kissed Hiawatha on the nose. He didn't like it much.

Grandfather reached in his wallet and pulled out a greenback. He said, very loudly, so that Margie Kelly couldn't miss it, and would know she was now dealing with a very important person:

"This is your share of the winner's purse, Son."

"Thank you, Grandfather!"

"It's only fair," he said, "and it's only a part payment for all your help."

That's when I noticed it was a twenty dollar bill.

I said, "Wow!" I slipped the money into my pants pocket fast before Margie Kelly got a look at President Andrew Jackson, and those four big 20's in the corners.

"Besides," Grandfather said, laying it on with a trowel, knowing the uphill battle I'd had with Margie Kelly and Sam Raffodil, "You're entitled. After all, it was you who first discovered that Hiawatha had stamina and was bred for distance. It was you who helped me trick the stewards into a mile-and-a-half race. You were the first one to race Hiawatha through the town streets on a Sunday morning. It was you who made a daredevil's rescue of Hiawatha from the kidnappers and drove him through enemy lines in time for Hiawatha to win the big race today. It's only fair."

I knew Grandfather was stretching it plenty, but I swaggered around that big horse, patting his neck, opening his mouth and looking at his teeth.

"Remember," Grandfather added, "it was you who helped Hiawatha down the homestretch drive by outsmarting young Sam Raffodil."

"Ahooouuuaah!" I yelled. "Ahooouuuaah!"

Grandfather laughed.

"That was our secret weapon, all right."

He gave me a grizzly bear hug and a whisker rub. He gave Margie Kelly one, too.

We both yelled at the same time: "I hate that!"

"You and Margie be back here in two hours," Grandfather advised, "then we'll all head for home together. Maybe we can get there in time to watch the big fireworks display and listen to the band concert. Meanwhile, you two enjoy what's left of the fair before sunset. That's when they start tearing everything down for another year."

Margie and I were off like a shot. Time was precious.

Grandfather stuck his head out of the barn door and hollered, "If you run out of money, there's plenty more where that came from! The sky's the limit today. Everything's on Hiawatha!"

I could hear Grandfather laughing as he went back into Hiawatha's stall. He began singing "Wait 'till the Sun Shines, Nellie."

Hiawatha joined in with a baritone whinny. Neither one of them had much of a voice.

We peanuted and popcorned ourselves, took in the bobs,

the merry-go-round, the bumper-cars, the tunnel of—if you'll pardon the expression—love (hot diggety dog!), and three successive rides on the Ferris wheel.

Directly below us on the Ferris wheel was the half-mile race track, where Hiawatha had triumphed over Thunderbolt. Just to be alive and to be at the county fair was enough, but to be a part owner of a champion trotting horse who'd just won the biggest race of the year, plus walking around the midway with the prettiest girl in Green Valley, eating glazed apples on a stick, and everything else in sight; sitting high up in the sky holding hands and trying to get them apart, but not being able because of the sticky glazed apples—it made us laugh a lot.

I could have died right there and still have lived a full rich life!

The manager finally threw Margie and me off the Ferris wheel. We were the last two customers and had been up all by ourselves long enough, he said. The fair was over. He had to close down until next summer. We were welcome to come back next year, he said, and have the first ride free.

I'm not saying anything about what went on up there in the sky, or whether I kissed Margie Kelly or not, two or three times, because there are some things a fellow doesn't brag about. But I came down with carmel corn stuck on my lips from something— I *can* tell you that much.

In fact, I went up there a boy and came down a man.

109.

Margie Kelly and I walked along the midway hand in hand. It wasn't a midway any longer, it was a disaster area. We watched the workmen tearing down the exhibits one after another and throwing the lumber alongside the road. Almost all the people had left the fairgrounds by the time we came down from the Ferris wheel.

It was becoming a ghost town. Many of the exhibitions were nothing but skeletons of two-by-fours with no skin. The colored canvas was folded into neat piles. Most of the tents and booths were already down. The colored streamers and bright banners that had seemed so happy and free were now strewn about everywhere, lying loose on the ground and blowing in the wind. Colored balloons were lying broken and scraggly on the ground. Some were still caught in the corners of the building by their strings. The band had left and there was no music.

The happiness and fun of the fair seemed to have vanished from everything. The excitement was gone for another year.

In spite of how good I felt myself, there was something melancholy in the air. The faint smell of burning September leaves added to the sweet sadness. When such a good thing is over, it makes you wonder if you'll ever feel that same wonderful way again, ever in all your life.

We hitched up Beauty and Prince to the buggy and tied

Hiawatha on behind. Beauty and Prince were frisky from having been in the barn all day; and enjoying such a lazy time at the fair. Plenty of hay, oats and leisure. They snorted and high-stepped their way out of the main fairgrounds gate anxious to show off.

We drove on through the main entrance. The big gate was still lying on the ground with a huge hole in it where Mr. Middleman had bashed it in with his truck so Hiawatha and I could go flying through. We approached the railroad crossing where I'd lain my body across the railroad tracks for Hiawatha.

When a nearby approaching freight train whistled, puffed, and shot out steam, Hiawatha whinnied loudly. I hollered back at him.

"You and me both, Buster! Once was enough!"

In all of our county, I'm sure there wasn't a happier boy than William Sears. Make that the whole state, or maybe even the country! How lucky can you get? It was almost too much!

Grandfather had saved the old homestead, Margie Kelly had gone up in the Ferris wheel with me, and I'd kissed her into going to the school picnic with me, not Sam Raffodil; and best of all, Hiawatha had turned out to be a real world-beater of a champion who had "Gitchee-Gumee'd" both the Raffodils.

If I'd read all this in a book, I'd never have believed it. It was a happier ending than *Sleeping Beauty, Rapunzel,* and *Cinderella* all rolled into one. You're probably saying to yourself, "It *couldn't* have happened that way. That's not the way life is."

That's all you know, my friend. My grandfather says, maybe that's not the way life is, but that's the way life *should* be. And every once in a while, bingo! You can have it all!

Most of the time, the only thing that keeps a person from having a happy ending is himself. According to Grandfather, *Job* said it best: "Man was born to trouble as the sparks fly upward."

It's those same people who start the sparks flying upward in every direction who make life so miserable for themselves and for all of the rest of us around them. There's nothing wrong with man that can't be corrected, Grandfather says, if everybody would stand up on their two hind legs and start bellowing for justice and maybe stomping on a few of the rotten eggs, and putting a stop to their shenanigans.

"That's not in the Bible," Grandfather said, "but it's in the cards!"

The whole county fair week had been like an old-fashioned melodrama at the Bijou Theatre where everybody was going over the waterfalls in a rowboat. There was no way they could be saved. It was utterly hopeless. Until the giant eagle, who our hero had once befriended when it fell with an arrow in its wing, suddenly swooped down out of the sky, caught hold of the end of the rope and pulled that boat back to safety when half of it was already sticking way out over the waterfalls.

That rescue was nothing compared to our buggy full of county fair week miracles: Mr. Raffodil was foiled. Oscar and the Picketts were all in custody. The town marshall was locked up in his own jail. And the fake hayrack had been confiscated for evidence.

Grandfather said the sheriff and his deputies had had themselves a very busy day, and there might even be a little reward money in it for me and my secret agents.

"That's great!" I told him.

"Why not?" Grandfather said. "We're the good guys!"

Sweet summer's end.

110.

Grandfather cackled with delight and laughed so uproariously at his "good guys" joke he shook the buggy. He gave me a
whisker rub and gave one to Margie Kelly too, as we both
climbed in.

She didn't like this one either.

"I *hate* that!" she said. "I already told you!"

I didn't mind the whisker rub too much this time. I'd
already promised myself I'd never complain about another
single thing as long as I lived. Even whisker rubs and grizzly bear
hugs. Nobody in the whole world deserved to be as happy as I
was, and I didn't want to rock the boat.

Just when I felt I couldn't stand another ounce of
happiness, I looked up into the twilight sky and saw GOG
circling the buggy and "honking" his head off.

Grandfather saw GOG too and said, "I think GOG wants to
get in on the family fun."

"We're going to have to do something about that cheeky
goose. He shouldn't be allowed to fly off wherever he pleases."

"Why not?"

"We love him, and we'll lose him. You'll have to clip his
wings."

"We want GOG to stay with us because he loves us, and not
because he's a prisoner."

"Clip his wings."

"You do that, and you've already lost him."

"Stuff it!" I yelled, and grabbed GOG from off the roof of the buggy by one leg and held him tightly in my arms. "He's mine! And I love him!"

GOG reached up, and first he beak-bit my nose, and then my right ear, hollering "Honk!" and flying off in a frenzy.

We all laughed at that. Especially when GOG flew back to Hiawatha's head and began to tell him all about it.

The fireworks display was already underway. We could see it all when the buggy came out from under the covered bridge. The darkening twilight sky was brilliant with the far-off sounds and bright colors of County Fair Week: exploding skyrockets, bombs bursting in air, and the glorious hues of shooting stars. Appreciative "Ooohs!" and "Ahhhs!" arose from the huge throng watching. Margie Kelly and I joined them with our own outcries of delight. And from time to time, Grandfather. When it was dramatic enough.

The warm night air was delicious, and still full of wonderful leftover summer smells. My nose swung from left to right trying to identify as many of them as possible.

I was so filled with gratitude I could hardly sing along with Grandfather and Margie Kelly as the horses started trotting up Hickory Street. This was the scene of my great Sabbath Sunday Adventure, the one which had started me off as a great harness driver.

To myself, I whispered quietly, "Maple Street, Elm Street! Washington! Hickory! Home!"

Grandfather overhead my whisper, nodded, and said: "Suicide Sunday!"

Quickly, I joined the singing, forming a three-part harmony:
> "There'll be pie in the sky when we die,
> When we die, there'll be pie in the sky;
> So live every day 'till you die,
> And you'll still have your pie in the sky."

Hiawatha, trotting behind, whinnied. And so did Beauty and Prince. Even GOG joined in on our happy party. He was walking up and down Hiawatha's back, one of his favorite places. No doubt he was congratulating his chestnut friend on his great winning race, against *such incredible odds.* GOG waddled up between Hiawatha's ears, and hollered out for the whole world to hear just how he felt about his good friend Hiawatha:

"Honk!"

Grandfather laughed and said, "You can say that again!"

GOG did.

"Honk! Honk!"

The deep, rich red sun was sinking rapidly between the high uprights of the distant Mississippi River Bridge. The river itself, winding through the valley, no longer reflected the bright changing colors of the end of the day, but melted into the shadows.

I pointed it out to Grandfather.

"Look at that!" I told him. "God just kicked a three point field goal. He booted that old sun right between the uprights, and over the crossbar of the bridge itself. How lucky we are! It probably means that Hiawatha will never lose a race!"

"Simmer down!" Grandfather said.

How could I? Would there be such an utterly magnificent and joyful day again? In the lives of three very satisfied people, three happy horses, and one fat jubilant goose? I wouldn't trade this last County Fair Day for all the days in the rest of the year put together.

This sweet summer's end was by far the best day of my entire life.

Beauty and Prince caught sight of Grandfather's barn and began trotting up a storm. By that time, all of us in the buggy were sound asleep.

The End.